Angela Thirkell

Angela Thirkell, granddaughter of Edward Burne-Jones, was born in London in 1890. At the age of twenty-eight she moved to Melbourne, Australia where she became involved in broadcasting and was a frequent contributor to British periodicals. Mrs. Thirkell did not begin writing novels until her return to Britain in 1930; then, for the rest of her life, she produced a new book almost every year. Her stylish prose and deft portrayal of the human comedy in the imaginary county of Barsetshire have amused readers for decades. She died in 1961, just before her seventy-first birthday.

"This book's greatest delight is in its wise or amusing observations on life tucked in as thick as raisins in a rich cake."

—*Chicago Sunday Tribune*

"[Angela Thirkell's] sense of the ludicrous is enchanting. Perhaps, above all, it is her basic human kindness and her remarkable insight into the delicate relationship between parents and adolescent and grown children that endear her books to so many people."

—*The New York Times*

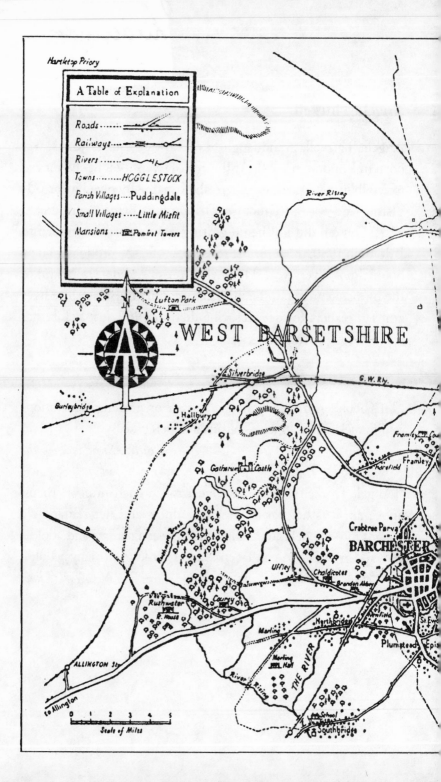

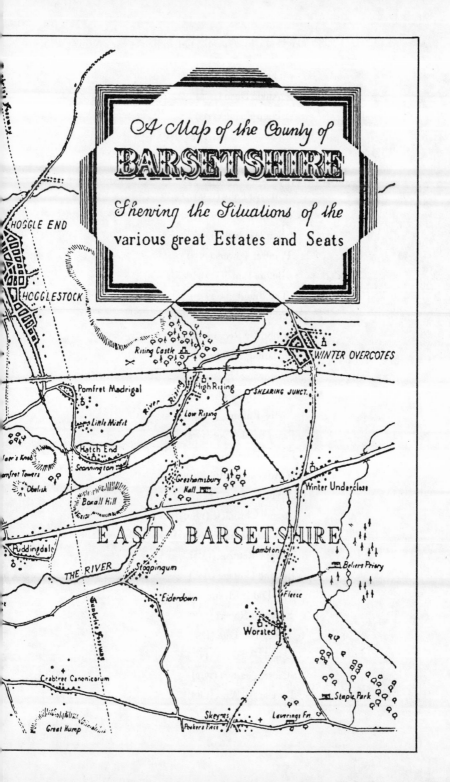

Other books by Angela Thirkell

Three Houses (1931)

Ankle Deep (1933)

High Rising (1933)

Demon in the House, The (1934)

Wild Strawberries (1934)

O, These Men, These Men (1935)

August Folly (1936)

Coronation Summer (1937)

Summer Half (1937)

Pomfret Towers (1938)

Before Lunch (1939)

The Brandons (1939))

Cheerfulness Breaks In (1940)

Northbridge Rectory (1941)

Marling Hall (1942)

Growing Up (1943)

Headmistress, The (1944)

Miss Bunting (1945)

Peace Breaks Out (1946)

Private Enterprise (1947)

Love Among the Ruins (1948)

Old Bank House, The (1949)

County Chronicle (1950)

Duke's Daughter, The (1951)

Happy Returns (1952)

Jutland Cottage (1953)

What Did It Mean? (1954)

Enter Sir Robert (1955)

Never Too Late (1956)

Double Affair, A (1957)

Close Quarters (1958)

Love at All Ages (1959)

THE DUKE'S DAUGHTER

A Novel by

Angela Thirkell

MOYER BELL

Wakefield, Rhode Island & London

Published by Moyer Bell
This Edition 1998

**LIBRARY OF CONGRESS
CATALOGING-IN-PUBLICATION DATA**

Thirkell, Angela Mackail, 1890–1961.
   The Duke's daughter : a novel by
Angela Thirkell. — 1st ed.
     p. cm.
ISBN 1-55921-214-4
I. Title.
   1. Barsetshire (England : Imaginary
place)—Fiction. 2. Country life—England—
Fiction. 3. Gentry—England—Fiction.
I. Title.
PR6039.H43D85   1998
823'.912—dc21   97-40648
                           CIP

Cover illustration:
Detail from *Mariana* by Dante Gabriel Rossetti
Chapter illustrations from *The Boardgame Book* by RC Bell

Printed in the United States of America
Distributed in North America by Publishers Group West, P.O. Box 8843,
Emeryville CA 94662, 800-788-3123 (in California 510-658-3453).

THE DUKE'S DAUGHTER

L es gens du monde se représentent volontiers les
livres comme une espèce de cube dont une face est
enlevée, si bien que l'auteur se dépêche de "faire
entrer" dedans les personnes qu'il rencontre.

MARCEL PROUST

Society people often think of books as a kind of cube
with a side missing, so that the author is in a hurry to
"push inside" any person that he just encountered.

MARCEL PROUST

CHAPTER I

Deep as had been the county's interest in the marriage of Mr. Adams the wealthy ironmaster and Lucy Marling, daughter of old Squire Marling, even deeper was its curiosity about their future. Some felt that though such a marriage was condoned, nay fully justified, by Mr. Adams's renunciation of his own political party and his generous support of the Barchester Conservative Association, it should perhaps stop at that point. Old Lady Norton, known to the whole county as the Dreadful Dowager, had spoken her mind very freely upon the subject at dinner, saying that it was one thing to marry for money but there were limits, and though in her young days one did not discuss such things one could not help thinking about them and wishing that people would marry in their own station.

Her son, the present Lord Norton, remarkable for nothing but being dull and pompous and chairman of several committees where under a good secretary he could not do much harm, said was not our aristocracy largely drawn from good yeoman stock.

"Quite irrelevant, Norton," said his mother, who had always addressed her husband in this way since his Lloyd-George peerage and found it less trouble to continue it with her son. "As far as I know, and you or Eleanor will correct me if I am wrong, Mr. Adams's people were not yeomen."

"Of course they weren't, Moggs," said young Lady Norton,

who lived in a state of highly armed neutrality with her mother-in-law and lost no opportunity of calling her by a familiar name (for pet name we cannot say of Victoria, Lady Norton) which she knew that lady disliked. "But Lucy's all right and anyway Mr. Adams has oodles of money and their children will be yeomen all right, only no one says yeoman now."

"Children?" said Old Lady Norton, "I had not heard of them."

"Nor had I," said her daughter-in-law. "But of course you can't help thinking," at which point both ladies began to do a kind of five-finger exercise on the table and came simultaneously to the conclusion that they ought to call on Mrs. Adams.

"Which reminds me," said the Dreadful Dowager, "that when Mr. Adams took the Old Bank House from Miss Sowerby she moved the Palafox Borealis from the long border and I would like to know where it is," for she was a zealous gardener and had compiled a horrid little anthology about gardens called *Herbs of Grace*. To this statement young Lady Norton did not make any reply, for she and her mother-in-law disagreed on many subjects but on none more whole-heartedly than on herbaceous borders. Lord Norton looked anxiously at them, feeling strongly his vulnerability as a small neutral state between two Great Powers.

"I believe Mrs. Adams has some Speckled Tootings," said young Lady Norton thoughtfully. "If I could get a setting from her—What about Friday, Moggs?"

Old Lady Norton considered Friday favourably and on a mild early autumn afternoon Lord Norton drove his mother and his wife over to Edgewood, where Mr. and Mrs. Sam Adams were settled in the beautiful eighteenth-century house once the property of the old Barsetshire family of Sowerby. When they stopped outside the Old Bank House his Lordship's courage failed him and he said he must go on to Barchester and have a few words with his solicitor Mr. Robert Keith, who was Mrs. Noel Merton's elder brother. His wife and his mother, who though on terms of armed truce were apt to unite against their respective husband and son, exchanging looks of mingled contempt for his cowardice and self-gratulation on his absence, got out of the car and Lord Norton went on his way to Barchester with orders to fetch them again in about an hour.

It was one of those days that are like Keats's *Ode to Autumn*, so golden, so still that one almost fears to break the magic peacefulness by a step or a word. Even the Dreadful Dowager and her daughter-in-law felt something of its circling charm, but one cannot stand in a village street considering eternity for ever, so young Lady Norton very sensibly rang the bell. The door was opened by Miss Hoggett, Mr. Adams's housekeeper from Hogglestock, who had taken care of him in his bachelor days, stayed on after his marriage to oblige, and become the ally and slave of her new mistress, recognizing in her the authority under which her own family had lived, probably since the Heptarchy. The Dreadful Dowager had fully intended to do the talking herself, but as her *face-à-main* chose that moment to entangle itself in the feather boa which she wore all through the summer, her daughter-in-law got in first and asked if Mrs. Adams was at home.

"I rang up this morning to say we were coming," said young Lady Norton.

"Yes, my lady," said Miss Hoggett, her face expressing complete lack of interest in a high degree. "Mrs. Adams is in the garden if you will please to come this way," and she led the two visitors into the wide hall with it small, beautifully proportioned square staircase, through the garden door to the terrace and down a few stone steps into the garden. Here Mrs. Adams and a spare elderly woman were sitting on the lawn in the warmth of the Indian summer.

"Hullo, Lady Norton," said Mrs. Adams, getting up to receive her guests. "Hullo, Eleanor," for the two younger ladies had met over various county jobs during and since the war. "Miss Sowerby's having tea with me to look at the Rhus Sowerbyana," and she pointed towards the far end of the lawn where a kind of Burning Bush in clouds of fleecy purple-pink cobweb was glowing under the late September sun. "She invented it," said Mrs. Adams, looking proudly at her elderly guest.

"I suppose you want a cutting, Victoria," said Miss Sowerby. "You can have one in February. How are you, Eleanor? And how are your girls?"

Young Lady Norton, whose two girls at boarding-school were so dull that one hardly knew they were there, said Vicky had to have a gold band on her front teeth and Ellie had had her tonsils and adenoids out.

"Did they bleed a lot?" said Mrs. Adams with unfeigned interest, to which young Lady Norton replied she didn't know, but Dr. Morgan had been thoroughly satisfied with the operation.

"Is that the one that was at Harefield in the war?" said Mrs. Adams, much interested. "Heather!" she called at the top of a very powerful voice.

A tall good-looking young woman who had been working at the far end of the herbaceous border straightened herself and came towards them, striding easily in brown canvas gardening trousers.

"It's Heather," said Lucy Adams. "She's really my step-daughter only it's too silly. She married Ted Pilward, you know, his father owns Pilward's Entire and those brewery vans with the big grey horses. She's giving me a hand with the garden because I'm not supposed to do too much, but that's all rot. I say, Heather!— Oh, this is Lady Norton, Heather—that ghastly Dr. Morgan has been giving Eleanor Norton's girls tonsils and adenoids."

"There's nothing wrong with her, is there?" said young Lady Norton, nervous for her dull daughters.

"Not a bit," said Heather kindly. "I fell into the lake at Harefield when I was at school and she tried a spot of psycho-analysis on me, that's all. She didn't try again."

Old Lady Norton said she had had some very remarkable experiences with Healers.

We think that Miss Lucy Marling would have stigmatized Healers as Rot. But Mrs. Adams said her father had a man on his estate who could cure animals of anything and she thought he had magic hands.

"He talks to them too," she said. "I mean *sensibly*; not like Dr. Morgan. And he knows the right herbs. It's because he's an Idiot," which to Miss Sowerby and Lucy seemed perfectly reasonable, as indeed it is, for the country halfwit has often more mother wit than his fellows and it is a remarkable fact that the village idiot (who in spite of Them still exists, we are glad to say) is as a rule unusually good at directing traffic, even on market day.

"Dr. Morgan talked too," said Heather, "when I fell into the lake. I never heard so much nonsense in my life. Is tea ready, Lucy?"

Even as she spoke the bell of St. Michael and All Angels softly boomed the half-hour and Miss Hoggett appearing on the terrace rang a silvery bell. Lucy got up and marshalled her guests towards the house where, in the long white drawing-room with its exquisite curtains and its lovely Chinese Chippendale sofa, tea was laid with an elegance that made the older guests feel a butler and at least one footman were hovering in ghostly attendance. Lucy seemed rather vague and disinclined to say much, though zealous in looking after her guests, nor did Heather contribute more than polite small talk, but Miss Sowerby had apparently decided to outshine everyone, especially the Nortons, and gave a brilliant sketch of life at the Old Bank House as it was in her father's time when Barsetshire drove anything up to twenty-five miles to the balls at Gatherum Castle and the status of the nobility and gentry was practically decided by the amount of waste in the kitchen and the servants' quarters.

"I remember my father telling me," said Miss Sowerby, "that when Lord Hartletop—that was the Hartletop whose mother was the *belle amie* of the Old Duke of Omnium—came of age, there were two carcases of beef, forty brace of pheasants, six barrels of beer and all the spoons in the second-best silver dinner-service unaccounted for," at which old Lady Norton, who was renowned for her stinginess, said she counted the silver herself before and after the parties when she used to entertain in her husband's lifetime.

"And the food too, Victoria," said Miss Sowerby. "It was your husband who counted the bottles. He could get more out of a bottle of sherry than any man I have ever known," at which old Lady Norton looked gratified and young Lady Norton did not.

A light tap was heard on the door and in came a neat young woman in white.

"Excuse me, Mrs. Pilward," she said, "but it's time for baby's feed."

"I never knew when it wasn't," said Heather resignedly. "This is Miss Hoggett's niece, Grace Hoggett, Lady Norton. She's wasted here, but she adores baby. So do I. I must say good-bye," which she did to the two guests with a self-possession that confounded even that arch-snob old Lady Norton. Faint yells as of a perfectly healthy baby pretending it was dying of starvation were heard, echoed by Heather's voice as she hurried upstairs. Grace Hoggett followed, shutting the door behind her.

"By the way, Hilda," said old Lady Norton, "what happened to your Palafox Borealis? I meant to get some seeds out of you."

"Which was more than I meant, Victoria," said Miss Sowerby. "You had better ask Mrs. Grantly's delightful servants. They are geniuses with exotic plants. Probably because they are children of nature," at which words her hostess nearly had the giggles, for the Rectory servants Edna and Doris Thatcher had between them five children of shame, all healthy, beautiful, and able to deal with life.

"Mrs. Grantly said she would come to tea or as soon as she could," said Lucy. "Do wait a bit and you can ask her." And very shortly Mrs. Grantly the Rector's wife did come, for in Edgewood the pleasant country habit of doors always on the latch was still kept up and the gentry went in and out of each other's houses pretty freely.

Mrs. Grantly was a handsome mother of four children the eldest of whom, Eleanor, had married Colin Keith, Mrs. Noel Merton's brother. She and her husband had befriended Mr. Adams when he first came to Edgewood and were old friends of his wife's people. She kissed Lucy affectionately, greeted the guests who were all known to her, and said she had had tea.

"You are the woman we want," said Miss Sowerby. "Victoria Norton here wants some seeds of Palafox Borealis. Your nice maids got it to bloom splendidly in the kitchen window."

"Oh dear!" said Mrs. Grantly, "this is *dreadful*. You know you told Doris and Edna it wouldn't flower till 1955."

"I did," said Miss Sowerby. "And I was wrong. Your nice kitchen facing south was what it wanted and it flowered, if I remember rightly, a year or two ago."

"I suppose someone kept the seeds," said Lady Norton.

"Of course," said Miss Sowerby. "And I advised Sid, who is the very intelligent illegitimate son of Doris Thatcher, to let the Royal Horticultural know about them and keep one for himself. I told him to ask fifty pounds. Did he?"

"He did," said Mrs. Grantly, "and I made his mother put the money into the Post Office Savings Bank and I take care of the book for him. And he has planted his seed and gives it the comic bits on the woyreless—at least that's how he puts it—every day. He says it likes them."

"We don't know yet what the effects of electricity on plants may be," said Miss Sowerby. "So that's that, Victoria. It ought to flower again about 1960 by rights, unless of course Sid's woyreless accelerates its development. On the other hand it may be completely exhausted by this artificial stimulus," and she smiled at old Lady Norton as a well-bred elderly hyena might have done.

"Like *Scenes of Clerical Life*," said Lucy. "I've been reading it and it's jolly good. Of course it's not a bit like clergymen now but that's not George Eliot's fault because she wasn't born then—I mean she was, but if she'd been alive now she'd have altered lots of things."

"Doubtless," said Miss Sowerby. "But which particular scene are you thinking of, Lucy dear? Not the man who turned his wife out of the house in her nightgown?"

"Oh, that one's rot," said Mrs. Adams. "I mean the one about where the clergyman marries the Italian girl who thought she had killed the young man only it was really heart failure and the delicate blossom had been too deeply bruised and she and her baby died. I thought it was *ghastly* rot," said Mrs. Adams with the air of one who had reflected profoundly upon *Mr. Gilfil's Love Story*. "Babies are frightfully tough. Much tougher than calves. Emmy told me—"

"I daresay you are right about Palafox, Lucy dear," said Mrs. Grantly, who felt it was high time to stem Mrs. Samuel Adams's artless reflections on life and literature. "If ours does seed, Lady Norton, I will certainly let you know; unless of course the atom bomb has killed us all."

"More likely to stimulate Palafox," said Miss Sowerby to no one in particular.

"But don't *you* want a seed, Miss Sowerby?" said Lucy. "After all it's your flower."

"In Worthing?" said Miss Sowerby. "Cruelty to plants. Palafox has always had a herbaceous border here with a south aspect and a brick wall—an old brick wall—behind it. Could I expect it to enjoy being in my widowed sister's garden in Cummerbund Road? A cat-run. Pebbles on the paths. Clumps of irises everywhere. A euonymus hedge in front and far too much tamarisk behind. And bedded out snapdragons. Good enough for me but *not* for Palafox. I can put up with it, but Palafox couldn't. Blood does tell you know," after saying which she looked round her defiantly as, so Mrs. Grantly felt, young Miss Hilda Sowerby might have looked at a stiff fence before she put her horse at it. And so had she taken every fence in her long life.

"Antirrhinums!" said Miss Sowerby so suddenly that it made Mrs. Grantly start. "Education! Time I was dead. And now the Old Bank House is in good hands I wouldn't mind if I were. You and your husband are good friends to it, Lucy."

Lucy blushed hotly at this praise and mumbled something about doing her best.

"There is only one thing wanting," said Miss Sowerby, looking at Lucy with peculiar kindness. "And as you are so kindly sending me home, my dear, I think I had better go now. One gets tired, you know. Good-bye, Victoria. I don't suppose either of us will see Palafox flower again, so there needn't be any ill feeling. Good-bye, Lucy. Say good-bye to Heather for me."

"She'll be down in a few minutes," said Lucy. "Oh, Miss Sowerby, we did what you said about the nurseries. The east room is *much* better. Heather loves it."

"And don't you?" said Miss Sowerby, looking piercingly at her hostess. "Never mind. You needn't answer. Not just yet perhaps. But later you will," and she kissed Lucy very kindly.

Lucy took her to the car and as it went away the Rector came down the street.

"Oh, hullo, Mr. Grantly," said Lucy. "Mrs. Grantly's here. Come in. Old Lady Norton's here too and young Lady Norton."

"From the fury of the Nortons, good Lord deliver us," said Mr. Grantly, to which Lucy replied with her usual common sense that they couldn't stay for ever and even if Lord Norton forgot to fetch them something could be done about it when Sam came back, and Mr. Grantly said if he were Lord Norton he would forget them all the time, so that they came into the drawing-room in a very good humour. Heather was back from the nursery, there were questions about Master Edward Belton Pilward, and Lady Norton feeling rather out of it took offence in a marked manner and when a few minutes later Lord Norton did arrive she merely said she hoped he had been enjoying himself and so, in an atmosphere of icy universal disapproval, took her daughter-in-law away.

"Isn't she *ghastly*," said her hostess. "I say, Mrs. Grantly, how is Tom?"

Now the Grantlys' elder son had gone back to Oxford after being demobilized, got a second in Greats, recovered from the dejection into which this had (quite unnecessarily) thrown him and, urged by Lucy Marling, as she still was then, had gone to Rushwater where, under the ferocious and able bullying of Emmy Graham, the kind supervision of Martin Leslie and the invaluable advice of Mr. Macpherson, the Leslies' old agent, he had worked at farming with some success. Mr. Macpherson had even gone so far as to say that where ingans were concerned the lad had the root of the matter in him: and such praise from a man of his experience meant a great deal. But his parents had noticed of late with quiet concern—for it was not their nature to interfere—that he seemed rather moody and restless, as if the terrible malaise that assails so many of our young who have undergone ordeal by battle and found that so far as any settled life is concerned the struggle has naught availed, had taken the savour from living and clogged every effort.

"I really don't know," said Mrs. Grantly, her handsome face suddenly showing its age. "Has he said anything to you?"

"No," said Lucy, "but I'll tell you what. I'm going over to Rushwater this week and I'll have a talk with Emmy," which gave Mrs. Grantly a certain amount of comfort, for it was through Lucy that Tom had gone to Rushwater and Mrs. Grantly felt quite certain that Lucy would see it through to the bitter end. Mrs. Grantly did not press her point for she had complete confidence in Lucy, but her face, as her husband noticed with growing annoyance, did not lose its look of anxiety. Though a very affectionate parent, he would at a pinch have sacrificed all or any of his children if (which he realized to be highly improbable) so unclerical an action could have made her happy; but he also realized that she would on the whole have cut him, very lovingly, into small pieces, watered them with her tears, and put them into the oven for Tom. Not that she loved Tom immeasurably more than her other children, but she knew more or less what the other three were, while with Tom, as with every child who has seen war at close quarters, she was conscious of scars she could not see, of the great gulf fixed for ever, and ever widening, between fighting men and civilians, and could only guess through a glass darkly at what he had seen and heard and felt and what effect active service had had on him. These soldiers, volunteer or conscript, so young and so old, so near to our affection, so infinitely and eternally far from our comprehension: how can we begin to help them? And all these thoughts and questionings were turning in his mind while he talked to Heather Pilward about the proposed widening of Barley Street in Barchester, badly needed, yet entirely to be deprecated.

"The only thing," said Heather, "would be to kill about thirty million people. Then there'd be room for us."

The Rector said he agreed with her, and it was a remarkable thing that after every war in the course of which a very large number of people had been killed, and far more now, owing to flying, than ever before, the net result was the doubling of the population. As no one could contest or really explain this horrible fact Lucy suddenly remembered her duties as a hostess, or rather was incited thereto by Miss Hoggett, who came to take the tea things away and then with a curious mixture of immense self-righteousness and deep disapproval put a tray with glasses and bottles on a table by the sofa.

"I've brought the gin and the orange juice and the lime juice, madam," said Miss Hoggett in a martyred voice, "and the real sherry and the ice cubes. Is that all, madam?"

Lucy thanked Miss Hoggett who then went away leaving such an icy feeling behind her that Mrs. Grantly inquired what was wrong.

"Oh, it's only she's teetotal," said Lucy, "but she's an awfully good servant so she brings in drinks almost non-stop, but she looks so persecuted I often wish she wouldn't. Sam and I have proper wine with meals—he's awfully good at wine and surprised Father dreadfully by giving him some good Montrachet at lunch once—but we don't care for cocktails so we don't have them except when people are here. Please Mr. Grantly will you be butler?"

The Rector provided gin and orange for Heather, gin and lime for his wife, and a large glass of orange juice and ice for Lucy. He was just going to pour some gin for himself when he stopped.

"Real dry Escamillo!" he exclaimed, looking reverently at the sherry bottle. "I never thought to see it again. In fact I didn't know any was being imported."

"I think it's ghastly," said Lucy. "It makes your mouth feel like eating alum inside."

Heather, who was very practical, said you couldn't eat it outside. At least, she added hastily, you *could* if Lucy meant the kind of inside that was being inside a house, not inside yourself. Mr. Grantly said that owing to having read Greats, which included some philosophy, he had seen what she meant, but it took an Oxford man to do it.

"I meant *inside*," said Lucy. "It makes your mouth feel like the natives somewhere who shrink people's heads."

"What Lucy means," said Mrs. Grantly, "is that *inside* it makes you feel horrid and shrivelled."

"And what, may I ask, does it make you feel when you are outside?" said her husband, to which Mrs. Grantly said not to be silly and he knew perfectly well what she meant and it was time they were going. But at that very moment the master of the house came in and put an end to these vain gabblings.

Mrs. Grantly, sitting back and holding her peace as life had taught her to do with her four delightful and difficult children, observed with interest how Mr. Adams's entrance altered the whole scene. She saw how Lucy suddenly took on a new aspect, and the words "in the spring a livelier iris changes on the burnished dove" came to her mind involuntarily. In their quick greeting she saw a softer Lucy, a Mr. Adams almost unknown to her. Heather, on the other hand, greeted her father (though with obvious affection) as a kind of equal; as a woman securely established with a well-to-do husband, an excellent baby, and every prospect of as successful and (to Mrs. Grantly's mind) uninteresting a life as anyone could desire. Daughter am I in my father's house, but Mistress in my own, were the words that best explained it.

"Why on earth can't one think in one's own words and not in quotations?" she asked aloud of the company in general.

"Partly laziness, my dear; partly being brought up among books," said the Rector. "And when I say books I mean real books. Not things called *I Was Hitler's Third Housemaid,* or *Inside Franco's Dustbin.* Some people of course are perfectly resistant to books and they aren't the worst kind," and his wife knew that he was thinking of Mrs. Samuel Adams, whose mighty intellect on the whole scorned literature as coming generally under the heading of rot.

"It would be a good thing if a lot of young fellows now couldn't read," said Mr. Adams unexpectedly. "I got on with my reading when I was a kid, because I liked it. My old mother she taught me the alphabet and D-O-G dog, and there's a lot of reading on the bottles and packages at the grocer's when your mother sends you round for a twopenny bar of soap—and it was soap then and it lathered—and there were advertisements and Dad's Sunday paper. I usually got a look at it while he was sleeping off Saturday night. And one way and another practice makes perfect. I used to read the *Pilgrim's Progress* aloud to my old mother when Dad was late coming home as he usually was. She always sent me up to bed when he came in, in case he was drunk, but a kid hears everything in a jerry-built cottage," and as he finished speaking it was evident that he had for the moment forgotten his hearers and was back in the Hogglestock of his hard childhood. Mrs. Grantly saw Lucy's face, anxious and loving, and to prevent further emotion sprang into the breach.

"But surely, Mr. Adams," she said, "you don't disapprove of education?"

"Now, you can't catch me like that," said Mr. Adams good-humouredly. "And that's a question I can't give an answer to all in a hurry. Free education's come to stay. It's a pity; for the working classes—and mind you I belong to them myself—don't want what they get free. If they paid say twopence a week for schooling, they'd see it was worth having. Give them something for nothing and they won't thank you. There's more young fellows than you'd think, Mrs. Grantly, and girls too, that learnt to read at school and when they get bigger they drop it. And there's no reason why they shouldn't if they don't like it. You see reading's natural to you and your lot; it isn't to our lot. And just as reading was getting what you might call universal along come the movies. Do it all by eye. And now it's television and a nice bit of work that is. You sit in the dark to see some damn silly pictures, excuse me Mrs. Grantly but it's a fack, and you can't even mend the kids' pants or do a bit of carpentering for the house. That's where This Lot have got us. All right, girlie," he said, observing Lucy's look of anxiety. "I've finished. And I'm not going to lose my temper over that or anything else. How's your Tom getting on, Rector?"

"We have been talking about him with Lucy," said Mr. Grantly, his fine face clouding, "and we don't want to bother her again. He is unsettled."

"They all are," said Mr. Adams. "And no wonder. I'll tell you what, Grantly—" but at these words Heather Pilward and Mrs. Grantly couldn't help laughing aloud. After a second of blank astonishment Mr. Adams too laughed, most good-humouredly. Lucy looked bewildered.

"It's all right, girlie," he said, reaching for Lucy's hand. "I spoke out of my turn, that's all. What I was going to say was, these young chaps that have been through the war, we don't know what's happened to them. Nor do they, come to that. A lot of them haven't been wounded, nor shot down, nor sunk, nor blown up by mines. But they've seen it all and they've felt it all, and even the finest steel shows a crack or a flaw if you treat it wrong. I was just too young for the '14 war and in the last war, though I say it as shouldn't, I was doing a good job for the country at the Works. But none of us as haven't seen active service can judge the men that have. There's been a lot of casualties from delayed shock and take it from me there's going to be a lot more. You'll find nice quiet men knocking the wife and kids on the head with a poker and half murdering the police that come to fetch them," Mr. Adams continued very seriously, "and I'm hanged if I'd like to judge them. And then you get these high-up blokes, cabinet ministers and heads of civil service departments that took jolly good care to be too useful at home to be useful abroad, if you take my meaning. And they are the ones that are going to be hard upon the war casualties, and boot them out if they can. Churchill fought for us. Eden fought for us. There's some of This Lot that did and good luck to them and when I hear old Attlee bleating away on the wireless I say to myself: 'Well, you're a something fool, but you've fought and I haven't.' I'm talking too much. Mrs. Belton has told me off again and again about it, but I'm too old a dog to learn new tricks."

There was silence for a few seconds. Then Heather asked if they would like to see the new nurseries and Master Pilward, an offer which Mrs. Grantly accepted with enthusiasm, for any nice woman wants to see other people's houses and quite a number of people like to see babies, even when repellently unidentifiable to anyone but their own besotted parents. So the whole party went up the elegant square staircase and then up a less glorious but highly agreeable flight of stairs to the second floor whence came the sweet idiotic fluting voice of a very young baby talking aloud to itself.

In the large low (but not too low) room, Grace Hoggett was

ironing various garments whose smallness at once made Mrs. Grantly want to cry. From a cot in the corner of the room the fluting burbling noises continued. With an air of proud and competent ownership Heather gently pulled back the coverings and Master Pilward was manifest in all his drowsy splendour, with a fat contented face, divinely finished hands, and eminently pinchable legs.

"I thought he'd be *ghastly*," said his step-grandmother, "like pictures in those books about *How Babies Come to Us* and all that rot. But he isn't. He's quite heavenly and when he's awake he kicks like anything. And he weighs eleven pounds two ounces. He was seven pounds when he was born, so that's jolly good," to which life history of Master Pilward Mrs. Grantly listened with a good deal of interest. Partly because she liked and respected babies, partly because never before had Lucy been known to show the faintest interest in the young of the human race. To her nieces and nephews she had been consistently kind and they all adored Aunt Lucy, the purveyor of farm and garden pleasures, but until they could walk and talk she couldn't, as her sister-in-law Mrs. Bill Marling far too often said, have cared less. Straws showing which way the wind blows?

Meanwhile Mr. Grantly, who knew his county extremely well, had thrown Grace Hoggett into paroxysms of shyness by inquiring into her family and had, to her intense confusion, elicited from her that she was called Grace after old Mr. Crawley's daughter at Hogglestock her as married Major Grantly, leastways that was what Auntie said, but Auntie did say some funny things like her father, old Grandfather Hoggett that was, remembering Hogglestock when it was a village, because it stood to reason it couldn't have been a village. Mr. Grantly asked why not.

"Well, sir," said Grace, who had obviously been well trained by her Aunt Hoggett to speak properly to the gentry, "if it had been a village no one wouldn't have lived there, sir. No cinema,

Auntie said, not even once a week. And no shops, not even a Woolworth."

"I daresay you are right," said the Rector. "Well, baby does you great credit, Grace. He's a fine little fellow."

"Oh, he *is*, sir," said Grace Hoggett and, losing her shyness quite suddenly, she gave a rapturous account of Master Pilward's great mental and bodily gifts, to which the Rector listened with his usual courteous attention.

"Do you know our girls at the Rectory?" he said. "Edna and Doris."

"Oh no, sir," said Grace Hoggett. "Mrs. Goble at the post office says they're ever so nice. But Auntie says it doesn't do to be forward," said Grace wistfully.

The Rector nearly said never mind what Auntie says, but remembering that the young of today were far too apt to pay no attention at all to their elders (which has its good points and certainly its bad) he said: "My younger daughter is called Grace after old Mr. Crawley's daughter too. You must come up to the Rectory one day and bring baby, and Doris and Edna will give you tea in the kitchen. I'll speak to your aunt about it," upon which Grace Hoggett went bright red with confusion and pleasure, and the Rector, having done his duty, came back to the rest of the party.

"A first-class baby, Heather," he said. "I like him," which made the usually stolid and self-possessed Heather almost stammer with pleasure.

"I'll tell you what," said Lucy to Heather. "Why don't you get Mr. Grantly to christen him here? Unless the Pilwards would mind?"

Heather said it was an idea and she would talk to Ted about it. The Rector said he hoped no one thought he was touting for babies, but if everyone else agreed it would give him great pleasure, and they really must go. Downstairs they met Miss Hoggett who was clearing away the drinks, and to her the Rector spoke with a Rectorial condescension combined with the respect due to an old and faithful servant of good village stock, which Miss Hoggett much appreciated.

"By the way, Miss Hoggett," he said. "My maids have heard so much about Grace's little charge. Would you and Mrs. Pilward let her bring him up to the Rectory one day and have tea with them? It would give us all great pleasure."

"Well, sir," said Miss Hoggett, rapidly revising her views on Edna and Doris, "I'm sure it's for Mrs. Pilward to say, sir, but as far as I'm concerned I'm sure Grace would like it very much. I hope you don't think it was a liberty, sir, her being called Grace after old Mrs. Henry Grantly, but my old father, that's Grace's grandfather, sir, was dead set on it."

"It's a good name whoever bears it," said the Rector and so got away and joined his wife and the rest of the party, who were standing on the doorsteps or on the pavement discussing the christening question.

"I'm so glad Heather's baby is to be christened here," said Mrs. Grantly to her husband as they walked home. "After all, Mr. Adams is really one of us now and his grandchildren ought to be christened in Edgewood, not at Hogglestock."

The Rector asked what about the Pilwards, to which Mrs. Grantly replied that Heather's husband was, quite rightly, under her thumb in domestic matters, and of course the old Pilwards would be invited so he need not worry.

Her husband said there was only one thing that made him nervous, which was a feeling that Mr. Adams might want to give them some little gift from the Works to celebrate his grandson's christening, such as knocking them up a complete set of church vessels in best stainless steel which might not act acceptable as a present, in a total wacancy of hoofs. And God bless him, he added.

His wife asked if he meant Mr. Adams.

"Don't be so foolish, my dear," said the Rector. "Of course I do say God bless Mr. Adams, but I was thinking of Mr. Dickens."

"God bless him indeed," said the Rector's wife with fervour. "And I was wondering, Septimus, whether the baby will be christened here or at Marling."

"What *are* you talking about?" said her husband.

"Lucy's baby, of course," said Mrs. Grantly.

"Lucy's baby?" said her husband.

"Of course, you elderly blindworm," said Mrs. Grantly affectionately.

"But how?—I mean did she look?—" said the Rector, rather alarmed at these premonitory thunders of Lucina's chariot.

"My dear Septimus," said Mrs. Grantly, with the affectionate contempt for a mere male that overtakes every nice woman when babies are in question, "do you expect her to look like a roasted Manningtree ox with the pudding in his belly already?"

"Of course not," said the Rector rather crossly. "If she did I wouldn't have asked you. But—I mean did she tell you?"

"Oh, these men, these men," said Mrs. Grantly. "My good man, one doesn't need to be *told*. It's something you see—only it isn't there; it's a feeling; it's a kind of peace; it's—oh WHY are men so silly?"

Realizing his complete inferiority the Rector said humbly that he was sure his wife was right and she herself had never looked more beautiful than before the births of her four children, to which his wife replied that he was a bat and a mole and anyone who had eyes would notice Lucy's looks, by which time they had got home and the Rector went to his study to answer letters. The business letters he could deal with and finished them quickly. But when it came to answering letters from relations abroad (for the Grantly family had far-flung cousins all over the world and in other parts of England), or even brother clerics who were writing on professional subjects, he could not pin his mind to work. The question of Tom and his future was worrying him more than he liked to admit. In vain had he told

himself again and again that Tom was grown up; that he had
seen active service, had gone back to Oxford and taken a very
creditable second; had been working at farming seriously over at
Rushwater. All this was true, but it was in the past and now Tom
was unsettled and talked of giving up farming. For what? Of
that his father had no idea, for Tom had not seen fit to enlighten
him and he like most modern parents knew his place too well to
inquire. Again and again in his study when he ought to have
been writing a sermon, or forgetting for the thirty-sixth time
where the book of Ezra came, or doing a review for the *Guardian*
of such books as Dean Crawley's *A Foreigner in Finland* (in
which, much to his family's relief, Dr. Crawley had finally
purged himself of his recollections of a visit to the Scandinavian
countries in 1938), or the Archdeacon's *Short Survey of the
Religious and Lay Aspects of Glebe Land* (Verger and Puse, 300
pp., price 18/6, which made most people feel it unnecessary to
buy it and as none of the libraries had it, it was a dead loss, which
the Archdeacon could luckily well afford, for Plumstead is still a
very good living and he had private means); or Sister Propria
Persona's *Selectivity in the Church Today*; again and again we
repeat in case our readers have lost their place as completely as
we have, when he thought he was working he had found his
mind pursuing the noiseless tenor of its own way, quite disre-
garding its owner's wishes. And of late it had been to Tom that
his mind had wandered when it should have been otherwise
engaged, to that extent that he had seriously considered praying
about him. But prayer is very difficult, even to a clergyman who
is a good pastor, husband, and father, and Mr. Grantly's difficulty was that he didn't know exactly what he wanted to pray for;
in which he was like most other people. For our real prayer, if we
had the wits or the courage to formulate it, would be a general
plea for everything to be all right for ever. So finally he did what
most of us have to do and made a supplication that Tom should
be looked after in whatever way seemed best, almost apologizing
as he did so for not being able to give more explicit instructions

and for what might possibly be considered a work of supererogation. And having cast his wordless plea before his Creator he found that he could deal better with his varied correspondence, though whether this was cause and effect he hardly liked to inquire. Nor did he inquire what a slight bustle in the hall meant, for bustles were his wife's business and he had every confidence in her.

But when soon afterwards supper said it was ready the bustle was explained by his elder son Tom, who had come over from Rushwater with a piece of pork, a gift from Mr. and Mrs. Martin Leslie, who had just been (by proxy) killing a pig.

His parents were loud in their gratitude and Mrs. Grantly admitted that though she was a farmer's daughter (and if he was a gentleman farmer and rode to hounds regularly who are we to blame him) she had never seen a pig killed. Nor, said Mr. Grantly, had he. When he was a boy, he said, he longed to and was forbidden, and when he was older and his own master he no longer wanted to.

"But Emmy saw it," said Tom with some pride. "She told me all about it and next time she's going to have a shot at it herself."

Mrs. Grantly said she didn't know they shot pigs. She thought they pole-axed them whatever a pole-axe was, only of course that was mad bulls; but she supposed they used a humane killer whatever *that* was.

"My good Mamma," said Tom, "I didn't say Emmy *shot* a pig. I only said—oh well, I see what you mean. She only looked to see how the man did it so that she could do it herself, only she wonders what she ought to practice on. I might learn too, because that kind of thing is useful. But I don't expect I'll be at Rushwater so that's that."

Now it had come. Both his parents felt the sinking of what may be called the heart but feels uncommonly like the stomach so frequently felt about our young. Both tried hard to find something to say and remained dumb.

"It's about farming," said Tom, emboldened by the twilight,

for Ordinary Time had set in just as the weather was mild and warm. "Martin has been awfully kind and so have Sylvia and Mr. Macpherson, but I don't think I can make a do of it."

So that was that. And though his parents felt slightly sick they put a good face on it, knowing all the time that their anxiety would most certainly be increased.

"I met a man called Geoffrey Harvey at the Country Club," said Tom, "who is in the Red Tape and Sealing Wax Department. He says they are taking on some extra men without examination if they have good degrees and a good war record. Of course it's only temporary, but if they like you they take you as permanent after a bit. It's not a bad screw. So I've pretty well decided, only I thought I'd tell you first."

"Thank you, Tom," said his father and then found he had nothing more to say, while his mother frantically ran over in her mind several appropriate comments and decided that all would probably offend her elder son.

"Oh that's all right," said Tom. "I'm going to see the man Harvey next week. He's organizing a branch at Silverbridge because the London office is being decentralized, so I can live at home."

His kind-hearted parents both said how delightful and then his mother, greatly daring, asked what the salary was.

"Oh, only two hundred and fifty to start with," said Tom. "But the man Harvey says it goes up regularly as soon as you're permanent. And I was only getting labourer's wages at Rushwater."

His father, noting with a pang that he already spoke of Rushwater as in the past, was rash enough to remind Tom that he had free board and lodging and the use of one of the estate cars as a rule, besides Mr. Macpherson the agent's teaching for nothing; teaching, he said, that beginners would gladly pay to get, which was ill advised on his part, for Tom considered himself far from a beginner. However, he forgave his parents; parents being notoriously out-of-date and half-witted, if well-meaning; and continued to expatiate upon the advantages of the Red Tape and Sealing Wax Department, while his father and mother did their best to seem delighted.

"I can easily get to Silverbridge from here," he said. "If I have breakfast at half-past seven and get the Barchester bus, I shall be at Silverbridge just before nine. Perhaps a quarter past seven would be safer. And I'll be back by six, so I'll have my evenings free."

Miss Grantly saw what her husband was going to say and could have warned him not to say it, but under Tom's eye it was difficult.

"We can have a pleasant winter cataloguing your grandfather's books, Tom," said the Rector. "I have been meaning to do them for the last ten years and somehow with the war and the peace I have never had time. Most of them aren't of much value, but I ought to go through them and see what I can sell. He inherited a lot of Bishop Grantly's theological books and I haven't even taken them out of their cases. And that ball-cock in the storage tank has gone wrong again."

"And Grace will be going to some small dances this winter and would love you to take her," said Mrs. Grantly, feeling she might as well be hung for a sheep as a lamb, though nothing less like a sheep than her younger daughter could well be imagined.

Mrs. Grantly was perfectly right in her surmise. Her son explained with ostentatious patience that a man who had a job in the Red Tape and Sealing Wax Office could hardly be expected to take his younger sister to small dances. He might have added, but did not, that he was a bad dancer and therefore disliked dances and when inveigled into one was mostly to be found lurking in the garden in summer or pretending to have supper again in the winter.

"Well, I'll be pretty busy I expect," said Tom, adding: "How's Harry?"

This red herring was, as he expected, entirely successful. His mother, who loved all her brood almost equally according to their different natures, could not help having a favourite, though it must in fairness be said that the favourite was hardly ever the same for three days running. Tom as her first-born would always have a special place. Eleanor, now Mrs. Colin Keith, also had a special place as the provider of granny-fodder, though her contribution at present was only one baby of very tender years and living in London at that. Her son Harry, now doing his military service before going to the University, was her beloved younger son, while Grace was her darling youngest.

But for the time being Harry was highest in her love and we think this was not so much because of his intrinsic charm and worth (though he was an agreeable boy with affectionate ways) as because he was hardly ever at home now. And if anyone thinks this is unkind, we appeal to mothers in general to say whether the child at a distance is not often more cherished than the child near at hand, simply because its more odious traits are less obvious than those of the child at home.

By the time Tom had collected news of his brother and his sisters and of his niece in London, it was time for him to go back to Rushwater and his loving parents felt for the nth time how happy the home could be with no resident offspring. As he went off in one of the ramshackle little Rushwater cars a great peace descended on the house. It was almost dark now, alas, but the evening was warm and roses in late September sweetened the warm dead air. In the distance a glow in the sky showed where Barchester and Hogglestock lay. From the kitchen came the sound of the wireless and the cheerful uninhibited voices of Edna and Doris and their various offspring who were being chivvied to bed, while the deeper voices of one or two male admirers mingled their soft Barsetshire with the general happy confusion.

"What are you thinking about, my dear?" said the Rector.

"I was thinking," said Mrs. Grantly, "how nice it is when the children aren't here. I mean I miss them dreadfully but—"

"I know, I know," said her husband.

The only other event of this day worth recording is that while the Nortons were having their evening meal young Lady Norton suddenly said: "Oh Lord, I forgot the Tootings."

"Who are they, dear?" said Lord Norton.

"Those Speckled Tootings," said Young Lady Norton. "How stupid of me."

"I do wish, Norton, that you would think before you speak," said his mother. "You are just like your father."

"Well, mother, I can't very well think if I don't know what you are all talking about," said Lord Norton, justly (as we think) aggrieved.

"Mrs. Samuel. Adams's. Speckled. Tootings," said his mother with awful clarity.

Lord Norton said was it a Dry Fly.

"They are Hens. And very good Layers," said his wife, whose expression of face implied the words "And shut up, you fool," even if her mouth did not utter them.

"I'll ring Mrs. Adams up," said Lord Norton, who was really good-natured, though stupid even beyond what is permissible to the son of a Lloyd-George baron. And he made as if to rise.

"Not now," said his wife. "It might upset Mrs. Adams."

"You cannot be too careful with the First," said old Lady Norton, to which Sibylline words her son replied that he hadn't the faintest idea what she was talking about, upon which his mother and his wife entered into a league against him and talked over, across, round, and through him for the whole of that evening.

"Sam," said Lucy Adams to her husband after dinner while Heather was upstairs with Master Pilward. "Do you think *anything* could be so divine as Heather's baby?"

"Well, my girl, if ours isn't, I'll join the Labour Party again," said Mr. Adams. "You know I'm not much good at saying what I think, girlie, but I'll tell you what—"

"I suppose you're going to tell me your word is as good as your bond?" said his wife.

"So it is," said Mr. Adams stoutly. "But what I do mean is that I'm blest if you aren't better-looking every day, Mrs. Adams. It suits you down to the ground."

"Then we'll have six at least," said Lucy stoutly and she looked at her husband with a love that was already maternal.

CHAPTER 2

We need hardly say that the news of an Adams baby almost ousted in county conversation the misdoings of Them, and there was a kind of silent struggle between the clergymen of West Barsetshire for the privilege of what our formerly lively neighbors the Gauls are pleased to call holding a child over the fonts; though why plural we shall never know, but they must please themselves. Correctly speaking it is perhaps the god-parents who do the holding, but the principle is the same. The Dean as acknowledged leader of the clerical party (for no one even considered the Bishop for a moment) was held to have as it were first pick, but he disappointed his backers by withdrawing almost at once, feeling, we think, that his supreme triumph in christening Mrs. Robin Dale's twin girls could not be surpassed and that he was now *hors concours*. An ill-judged attempt was made by the Rev. Enoch Arden whose chapel of ease Mr. Adams had formerly attended to claim the future baby as one of his flock, but Mr. Adams who had left him on account of his Communist doctrine that Jack was as good as his master, which, said Mr. Adams, didn't make sense seeing that then his master would be as good as Jack when everyone knew he was a sight better or he wouldn't be where he was, refused to see him when he called at the Works and told his secretary Miss Pickthorn to give him a cheque for his League of Christian Soviet Endeavour and make it payable to bearer as he looked half starved poor beggar. Mr. Miller of St. Ewold's said to his wife that indeed, indeed, a christening, if it were not irreverent to say so, was the most beautiful and moving of the Church's rites, but being very modest took no further steps. The Archdeacon at Plumstead said he waived all claim, and as he had no claim at all we think he showed his usual good sense. Father Fewling at Northbridge thought wistfully that a baby had perhaps a better chance with a little incense and then blamed himself severely, because babies bring everything with them and have no real need of anything except the words of acceptance, as properly appointed.

But none of these gentlemen made any public mention of their feelings, nor would it have made the faintest difference if they had; for Mr. Adams like a wise and provident man of business had engaged Mr. Grantly almost before it was decent to do so.

It was on a bright, chill March morning that Miss Adams, very red in the face, rent the air with loud yells, than which no more beautiful sound had ever been heard; or so her parents thought. Her father, finding himself for the first time in his life unable to concentrate, summoned Miss Pickthorn from the Works, who at once took command of the secretarial department and enjoyed herself frantically on the telephone. Mr. Adams had been a little afraid that two such outstanding characters as Miss Pickthorn and Miss Hoggett might clash, but owing to Miss Pickthorn's supreme tact in asking Miss Hoggett's advice about everything and saying how the one thing she really wanted was a nice cup of tea, that grim guardian relaxed her vigilance and went so far as to tell Sister Chiffinch, who was in command upstairs, that Miss Pickthorn reminded her of the late Lady Dumbello's secretary who was an Admiral's daughter and quite the lady.

We need hardly say that Mrs. Marling (who of course had known all along that Lucy would die in giving birth to triplets and she would have to bring them up, which is a well-known nightmare of grandmothers and seldom if ever realized) was on the spot as soon as Ed Pollett the handyman could be got to drive her over in the clanking old car.

"Oh, Miss Hoggett, how *thankful* I am!" she said to that faithful retainer who opened the door. "Can I go up? Or perhaps we'd better ask Sister Chiffinch first. Oh dear! It is all so sudden," which considering that she had known about the baby ever since it was humanly possible to know, was perhaps an overstatement.

"I'm sure you're upset, madam," said Miss Hoggett, playing up violently. "Would you like to see Mr. Adams, madam? He's in the library. And shall I bring in some tea, madam?"

"Oh yes, *do*," said Mrs. Marling.

"And I'll tell Sister Chiffinch," said Miss Hoggett and went upstairs.

Mrs. Marling opened the library door and there, among the books he had lavishly but judiciously bought at various times, aided by such authorities as the Dean, Mr. Carton of Paul's College, and Mrs. Morland the well-known writer of thrillers, sat her son-in-law, creator of the great Hogglestock Iron Works, employer of hundreds of men and women, consulted increasingly in county activities, as wealthy as They will allow one to be, and looking as if he had been up all night (which he had not) and been drunk ever since (which he most certainly had not been).

"Oh! Sam!" said Mrs. Marling.

"Well, it's the first time you've called me that," said Mr. Adams, getting up to meet his mother-in-law. "And may I say I'd as soon do my biggest casting with an air raid on than go through this again," and to Mrs. Marling's surprise—except that by now nothing was surprising—he clasped her in his strong arms and knocked her hat on one side, to which Mrs. Marling responded with equal fervour.

"Dear Sam, we *are* so happy," said Mrs. Marling, beginning to cry. "William is getting up the last of his Uncle Fitzherbert's port and we want you to come and help us to drink it. It is so delightful that it is a girl. Not but what a boy would have been just as nice, but after all Lucy is a girl and—" upon which exceedingly muddled reasoning Mrs. Marling began to cry again from sheer joy, and as her son-in-law was not much better it was a good thing that Miss Hoggett came in with tea, which calming beverage did them a lot of good and before long kind Sister Chiffinch came down.

"Now isn't this a lovely surprise," said Sister Chiffinch. "Who'd have thought of a dear wee mite being born in this really quite antique house though if the truth were known," said Sister Chiffinch archly, as if Mr. Adams and Mrs. Marling were in some way responsible for the baby (as indeed they were), "I daresay many a Happy Event has occurred here in the Olden Times. Such a pet she is, Mrs. Marling. Eight pounds, and as I said to Mrs. Adams when I put her on the scales, for a first it is a very good weight."

"I hope Lucy had a fairly good time, Sister," said Mrs. Marling, straightening her hat and trying to look sane.

"As easy as falling off a tree," said Sister Chiffinch, though the comparison even to Mrs. Marling's slightly dazed wits seemed peculiar. "We just had a wee spot of trouble and then a little stranger began to use her lungs. She ought to be called Melba. And, as I was saying to Miss Hoggett, such a dear considerate little lady. Daddy knew nothing till we were all washed and comfy in the cot and I went in to tell him, luckily in an ever so sweet dressing-gown that Mrs. Admiral Hornby gave me when I was up at Aberdeathly for her third, for Matron at Knight's, where I trained, always made it a great point that a nurse should have a nice appearance in the sick-room. Not of course that it exactly applies in this case because Mrs. Adams is as well as possible so we really cannot call it a sick-room for she has eaten a nice breakfast and is longing to see her Mummy," at which word, never used in the Marling family, Mrs. Marling blenched. "Or Granny I should say," Sister Chiffinch continued, "but really, Mrs. Marling, no one would take you for a grandmother."

"But I am," said Mrs. Marling, who had a strong *snobisme de grand'mère.* "I have four grandchildren in Yorkshire and three in Camberley."

"So our little Poppet makes eight," said Sister Chiffinch brightly. "And now will you come up, Mrs. Marling? Daddy has been up already and when Mrs. Adams has seen you, Mrs. Marling, we must close the curtains and try to have a little nap," and so, having tanked right over her patient's husband and mother, she took Mrs. Marling upstairs.

Lucy looked very handsome, her mother thought, and wrapped in a kind of golden content. Miss Adams had a very cross red face, fingers and toes of exquisite delicacy, and a light fluff on her head. As for her eyes, which Sister Chiffinch and Lucy said were the most beautiful they had ever seen, they were so tightly shut that only the tips of her lashes appeared among the rolls of fat.

"I'm awfully glad she's a girl, Mother," said Lucy. "I mean I'd have been just as glad if she had been a boy but as she's a girl I like it best. Is Father pleased?"

Her mother said he was delighted and getting up some of the last of his port to drink the baby's health and they wanted Mr. Adams to dine with them if Lucy could spare him. For though Mrs. Marling was sincerely attached to her son-in-law, she still found it easier to call him Mr. Adams unless under the strain of great emotion. And really there was no reason why she shouldn't.

"Have you thought of a name for her?" said Mrs. Marling.

"Well, Sam's mother was Hilda and his wife was Rose," said Lucy, and if Mrs. Marling felt any disappointment that her own name was not mentioned, she did not show it.

"That's why Heather's called Heather," said Lucy. "I mean her mother wanted to call her after a flower like herself, so she chose Heather. We didn't like Hilda much and it might sound as if we were calling her after Miss Sowerby, so we thought Rose Amabel, or Amabel Rose. Which do you like?"

If ever humility was rewarded (which it mostly isn't) it was at that moment, for Mrs. Marling had hardly dared to hope that Lucy's child should bear her name.

"I rather thought Amabel Rose," said Lucy. "A.R.A. would be nice initials—wouldn't they, my sweet," she added to her daughter, in a voice that her own mother had never heard and which nearly made her cry all over again.

"Tell Father and Oliver to come and see me soon," said Lucy, "and Emmy. I want to know about the new cowsheds," and even as she spoke she was half asleep. Her mother put a swansdown kiss on Amabel Rose's gossamer-jelly cheek and tiptoed away.

Lucy woke for a drowsy lunch and slept again till four o'clock when Heather Pilward came to call on her step-mother and her new half-sister. As for her father, to whom she was truly devoted, she would have torn him to pieces in a Bacchanalian frenzy sooner than forgo a delightful gossiping talk with Lucy.

"Let's see," said Heather. "Edward Belton is my son and Daddy's grandson and your step-grandson. So I suppose Amabel Rose will be my step-granddaughter. No, that's wrong. Step-grandmother. No. What on earth is she?"

"I've been thinking very hard when I wasn't asleep," said Lucy, "and I think it's—I mean she's your half-sister. If she had a father and mother that weren't your father and mother she'd be your step-sister."

"No she wouldn't. She wouldn't be any relation at all. I'll tell you what. If you had a daughter before you married Daddy, she'd be my step-sister."

"But I couldn't," said Lucy, "because I wouldn't have been married."

"Well, could Edward Belton marry Amabel Rose?" said Heather.

"If it was cows he could but I don't *think* people," said Lucy cautiously. "No of course he couldn't, because he's Sam's grandson and she's his daughter."

"Daddy's *your* husband and *my* father," said Heather, her face as intent as if she were working a problem in higher mathematics. "So Amabel Rose is his daughter and Edward is his grandson. Is there any law against daughters marrying grandsons?"

"Well, I couldn't marry any of Father's grandsons," said Lucy, "because they are at school. And anyway Father only married once. Let's get the prayer-book. It's on the shelf by the window."

"Right," said Heather, sitting down again. "Shall we do A Man mayn't Marry or A Woman mayn't Marry?"

Lucy said as Edward was a man they might start with him and check it with the woman ones.

"Well, he mayn't marry his Grandfather's Wife — that's you," said Heather, "but he wouldn't want to anyway. Let's see, he mayn't marry his Mother's — no that won't do. They don't seem to have thought about it properly."

"Well, look here," said Lucy, slightly flushed. "If I were really Sam's wife — I mean if I were your mother — you would be Amabel Rose's sister. Where does that get us?"

Heather said, almost pettishly for her, nowhere.

"But there was the woman who married seven husbands one after the other," said Lucy, knitting her brows. "Only she didn't have any children. I wonder why," she added thoughtfully.

"Well, listen," said Heather. "Can Daddy's daughter marry his grandson? Because that's what it is."

"Well, it's not there," said Lucy.

And luckily at about this point Sister Chiffinch came in and said Amabel Rose must go to bed, which as she was already in bed and had been there ever since early morning and was likely to remain there for a long time, seemed a work of supererogation. So Heather kissed Lucy and Amabel Rose and went away.

At tea-time Mr. Adams was allowed, nay encouraged, by Sister Chiffinch to have tea with his wife and younger daughter. That kind creature Sister Chiffinch poured out tea for them and made bright conversation, largely about her friends Wardy and Heathy that she shared the flat with and how Wardy had painted the living-room walls a really sweetly pretty shade of pink and Heathy had bought some new lampshades.

"And when I tell you," said Sister Chiffinch, "that they are made of real antique parchment with people's wills or something on them, we really feel we are quite in Ye Olden Times."

Mr. Adams said it sounded very nice and comfortable and if she and her friends smoked he would like to give them a set of stainless steel ash trays, to which Sister Chiffinch replied archly that she must confess to just a whiff now and then, but *never*, of course when on duty because the mere idea of cigarette ash falling on a wee baby was quite unpleasant. Matron at Knight's, she said, had always told the probationers that what they did outside the hospital was their own affair, but inside was inside.

"But she wasn't above turning a deaf eye to things," said Sister Chiffinch. "She really *understood* human nature and if you understand that you understand probationers, because a lot of us used to have a cigarette outside if we had a moment off and some of the young medicals happened to come along occasionally, and Matron came sailing past us one day and believe it or not she looked just straight in front of her as if we weren't there at all. It taught we nurses tact, Mr. Adams. She's retired now and lives at Folkestone with a friend and she's on the Town Council. And now, Mr. Adams, you mustn't think me a spoil-sport but our patient must be quiet. So say Au Revoir but not Good-bye."

We think this was the first time in Mr. Adams's hard-working life that he had been completely taken aback. Obedient, even cowed, he kissed the top of Amabel Rose's head and laid his wife's hand against his cheek and with one last look at her went away.

"A real Sir Lancelot," said Sister Chiffinch, and though the application is obscure we think we know what she meant.

When Mr. Adams got to Marling he found his host in a mild delirium, looking at nursery garden catalogues. At the sight of his son-in-law he got up slowly (for in the winter when he could not get out much he was always stiffer in the joints) and came towards him with both hands out. "Well, my boy," he said, "I don't know when I have been happier. Didn't quite take to you at first you know, but it was Lucy's affair and she's got a good head on her shoulders."

"That's all right, Squire," said Mr. Adams, who knew Mr. Marling liked this pleasant outmoded manner of address. "And Lucy's all right and so is the baby. She sent you her love and wants to know when you are coming over to see her," upon which Mr. Marling suddenly became a doddering centenerian and said he didn't suppose he'd ever get over to Edgewood again.

"I'm gettin' stiff in my old age and I don't like these long drives," he said. "I'll have to get Ed Pollett to drive me over. The car's fallin' to pieces but it will last my time, I daresay. Time I was dead and buried."

"Nonsense, Squire," said Mr. Adams.

"All very well for a young man like you to say nonsense," said Mr. Marling, "but I know what I'm talkin' about. Three-score years and ten it says, and that's good enough for me. I ought to have been dead years ago if I'd paid attention to the Bible," to which Mr. Adams replied that doubtless his father-in-law was right, but he mustn't think of dying till he had seen Lucy and the baby.

"I'm glad it's a girl," said Mr. Marling. "There's not much chance for boys now. Schools are damn expensive and then you get another war and when they come back they're unsettled and the stay-at-homes have got the jobs. War isn't what it was in my young days, Adams. I was in the Boer War myself; volunteered with the Barsetshire Yeomanry, and look at me now. But these modern wars, they're killing our boys. Better for some of them if they were killed outright than come back with their nerves all to bits and walk the streets looking for a job. There's that feller Harvey. He and his sister were in the village one winter. Fine handsome woman she was and a damned bore—thought she'd caught Oliver at the time. Harvey went to France in 1939 with the Red Cross," said Mr. Marling in a voice of intense scorn though not directed against that noble body, "and by the beginning of '40 he was back in his government job, wax candles or something. Indispensable!" And he made a noise of deep contempt.

"That's right, Squire," said Mr. Adams cheerfully. "I'm a bit of a shrirker myself. But if I'd left the Works God knows what those damned fools would have done. Half of them didn't know pig iron from chromium steel. Let's forget it. And if I can ever help a good returned man to a job, well I will, and everyone knows Sam Adams's word—" and here his voice died away. But his father-in-law had not noticed, being like the elderly, and indeed like most of us, more interested in his own thoughts. Then Mrs. Marling came in with Oliver, just back from London, and they sat down to dinner, which was a good deal interrupted by telephone calls from the county to ask about Lucy and congratulate her parents.

"Oh, not *again*," said Oliver when for the eighth time a summons came. "I'll go, mother," at which his father remarked with a slightly senile leer at his son's departing back that Oliver thought it might be little Jessica, and when they talked about Miss Amabel Rose and how beautiful, accomplished, and sweetly mannered she was and how extraordinary was her likeness to Mrs. Marling's father and Mr. Marling's mother and Bill Marling when he was at Eton and Mr. Adams's own mother. And as Mr. Adams had never known the late Lord Nutfield nor the late Mrs. Marling nor known Bill at Eton, and his host had never seen the late Mrs. Adams, dead these thirty-odd years, they agreed unanimously.

"Well, my boy, how's little Jessica?" said his father when Oliver came back.

Oliver said, with ostentatious forbearance, that he had not seen her lately, and as his father, enlivened by claret, was obviously going to ask Who's your Lady Friend, though perhaps not quite in those words, he prevented (in the Biblical sense)

such goings on by saying it was Isabel Silverbridge to congratulate Mr. and Mrs. Marling and send her love.

"Dear Isabel, how nice of her," said Mrs. Marling, for during
the preceding year she had become very fond of the wife of the
Duke of Omnium's heir and only surviving son. And we may say
at this juncture that owing to a reprehensible laxness on the part
of Mr. Trollope, the official historian of the Omnium family,
we are in some doubt as to whether the eldest son of the family
was a Marquess (or Marquis), or a mere Earl. If the College of
Heralds can offer a definite ruling in this subject we shall be
grateful, failing which we shall treat Lord and Lady Silverbridge
as Earl and Countess, Lest all, as the poet Cowper remarks,
Should think that we were proud.

Presently the port was put upon the table and Mr. Marling
terrified everyone by insisting on filling the glasses himself in a
rather tottery way. A large drop fell on the white tablecloth near
Oliver who at once put salt on it, which made his father look at
him ferociously and mutter something about Old Maids.

"Not a bit, Squire," said Mr. Adams. "My old mother was in
good service at Hartletop Priory before she married my old Dad,
and if Dad spilt his beer, as he was apt to do when he'd had a
glass too many at the pub and then another glass at home, she
always said the third footman at the Priory told her salt on port
stopped it iron-moulding. She was walking out with him till
Dad came along, which was the worst day's work she ever did in
her life, poor soul," to which Mrs. Marling very prettily replied
that it was the best day's work in the world for Lucy, and then
Miss Amabel Rose's health was drunk and even Oliver felt
slightly affected.

"I hope you don't mind, mother," he said, "but Geoffrey
Harvey is coming in after supper. We are doing some work for
him at the office and he wanted to see me," and of course his
mother said she would be delighted.

"Poisonous feller," said Mr. Marling. "Sister looks like an
educated rocking-horse," which was so near the truth that no

one could keep from laughing. Then Mrs. Marling went away, wishing she had a daughter or even a secretary to keep her company, for she had become very fond of the present Lady Silverbridge when she was Isabel Dale and had lived with her for a time. But most of us, especially as the world is now, will have to learn to be lonely and never perhaps was there a time when so many people, in spite of overcrowding everywhere, felt such loneliness of the spirit; and more in the winter than in the summer when you live in the country. Nor was her loneliness diminished by the arrival of Geoffrey Harvey. She did not in the least wish to entertain him, but it would obviously have been cruel to inflict him upon the men downstairs who were having a peaceful family talk, so she called over the banisters to Mrs. Pardon the gardener's wife who was obliging and asked for coffee upstairs.

"And tell Mr. Marling, will you, Mrs. Pardon," she added.

"*He* won't come, madam," said Mrs. Pardon. "If you'll pardon my mentioning it he's telling the other gentleman about the Bor Wor," which Mrs. Marling rightly interpreted as her husband's very dull reminiscences of the Boer War, during which he had been in charge of remounts most of the time and heartily bored. Though not so much as he had bored other people about his exploits afterwards, she lovingly thought.

"Black or white for you, Mr. Harvey?" said Mrs. Marling when the coffee had come.

"Black if I may, because I *know* how good your coffee must be," said Mr. Harvey. "Most people's is absolute Mud. And pray not Mr. Harvey, considering how long we have known each other. You know, I always think of you as Amabel. Such a delightful name. The Heir of Redclyffe."

"And Miss Lee," said Mrs. Marling, rather crossly.

Mr. Harvey looked perplexed.

"Ah! the literary touch!" he said, with a sympathetic smile for which his hostess could willingly have put the poker down his throat.

"And sugar, Mr. Harvey?" said Mrs. Marling, so firmly that Mr. Harvey said no more about Christian names, and inquired tenderly after the little grandson.

"My little granddaughter is doing very nicely," said Mrs. Marling. "My son-in-law is here and they will be up in a few moments. How is your sister?"

"Riding the whirlwind and directing the storm as usual," said Mr. Harvey. "She is Head of E. and P. at the Ministry of General Interference, you know, at the special branch at Gatherum."

Mrs. Marling, hardly able, though kind and courteous by nature, to repress her boredom, asked what E. and P. was.

"Department of Efficiency and Purging," said Mr. Harvey. "You see there are bound to be misfits in every government department and Frances has to conduct a kind of Secret Service through the G.I.P.S.S."

"The what?" said Mrs. Marling.

"Forgive me, dear lady," said Mr. Harvey with a diplomatic laugh, which sounded to Mrs. Marling like a nasty spiteful giggle. "We poor civil servants get into the shocking habit of initials. The General Interference Personnel Secret Seeding. Rather like Wimbledon shall we say? Only on a different plane of course. To squeeze out the Undesirables. Sometimes we have no valid, I should say no apparently valid reason for getting rid of one of the personnel, and then we fall back on the G.I.P.S.S. In my own case, of course, on the R.T. and S.W.S.S., and that of course is the Red Tape and Sealing Wax Secret Seeding. It works marvellously. No one can appeal against it and no one of us is personally implicated. The undesirable clerk, or secretary, or whatever he may be is quietly jettisoned."

"*Spurlos versenkt*," said Mrs. Marling, trying to keep her feelings out of her voice.

"Exactly, dear lady," said Mr. Harvey, with such complacence that Mrs. Marling nearly said what she felt. But luckily the men came up and though Mr. Marling and Mr. Adams were not particularly pleased to see Mr. Harvey he was Oliver's guest and must be treated accordingly. Presently Oliver took him away to discuss whatever it was they were going to discuss, for what it was we neither know nor care, nor are we going to put ourselves out to invent it. Mr. Marling went to sleep sitting bolt upright and looking very distinguished, while Mrs. Marling and her son-in-law had perhaps the most intimate talk they had ever had, founded on their common dislike of Geoffrey Harvey, their deep love of Lucy, and their besotted admiration of Miss Amabel Rose. And before he left he said that if she didn't think it would annoy her husband, he would send his car over tomorrow afternoon to fetch him, and after tea with Lucy the car should take him back, for which Mrs. Marling was deeply thankful, as their own little clanking car in the cold spring weather did her husband no good at all.

This chapter cannot be properly finished unless we give Miss Amabel Rose the space she deserves. For a baby who does nothing but eat and sleep and occasionally opens wide-set blue eyes, smiles a secret smile which as Sister Chiffinch indignantly said was NOT wind, and goes headlong into sleep again besides, as her mother said, smelling of heaven, deserves every attention.

On the following day her grandfather came to see her, though it was really more to see Lucy, for whose well-being he had been deeply and silently concerned. To do honour to the occasion he had dressed for the part, looking rather like something out of Bracebridge Hall, including a kind of flat-topped grey bowler still affected by himself and Lord Stoke. When his son-in-law's car had come to fetch him he insisted on sitting beside the chauffeur and giving him odds and ends of agricultural information such as: "Nice bit of corn land that used to be. All council houses now," or: "All that was under grass when I was a boy and now it's beet," or again: "All this talk of Siberian wheat. Barsetshire wheat was good enough for us and bread was bread then; not husks and alum." To all of which the chauffeur, who was a born mechanic and was never happy except when driving, or preferably taking a car down with loving, greasy fingers, made no reply but "Yes, sir." For Mr. Adams, having been well brought up by his mother in the old tradition, quite rightly insisted on good professional manners from anyone he employed professionally.

We do not quite know whom Mr. Marling expected to find on his arrival, but whatever his preconceived ideas they were rudely though not unpleasantly shattered by Sister Chiffinch who, summoned by Miss Hoggett's underling, came crackling and rustling down to meet him and wafted him upstairs.

In the bedroom, lit by the cold afterglow of the March sunset and the whispering flames of a good coal fire, he found his daughter sitting up in bed and in her arms Miss Amabel Rose grossly replete with her second tea (or her first supper, we cannot be positive which) in a kind of warm abandoned swoon; to whom he immediately and for ever lost his heart.

"Hullo, Father," said Lucy, reaching to kiss him over the baby's fat comfortable form. "Isn't she divine?"

"Nice young lady," said her father, who was not going to commit himself, though in spirit prostrate at the baby's rose-petal feet. "Glad it's all over, my dear. She's a fine specimen. Wish my old mother could have seen her," which as old Mrs. Marling had died some thirty years previously was hardly reasonable. "Your mother rang up Lettice and Bill so I daresay you'll be hearing from them," said Mr. Marling, alluding to his elder son and his elder daughter who lived at Camberley and in Yorkshire respectively. "Well, I'm not long for this world, but I'm glad I've seen your child, Lucy. Didn't want to see you an old maid. I had an idea you might like that feller Harvey at one time."

"Geoffrey Harvey?" said Lucy. "I'd as soon have married the Bishop. How *could* you, father?" and then she made very businesslike inquiries about various cows and fields that had formerly been under her supervision and was on the whole pleased with her father's reports, till Sister Chiffinch made herself visible and took Mr. Marling downstairs with such archness that he wondered if he ought to pinch her; but most luckily didn't.

While Lucy was still happily in her bedroom—that haven which one so unwillingly leaves for the rough world—her brother Oliver came to see her. It was not his fault that he had not come sooner, for his parents had the first right, Sister Chiffinch had rationed visits to one a day, and he was in London through the week. But on the following Saturday he came down by an early train and took the bus over to Edgewood. Nieces were no novelty to him, for his elder brother and his sister Lettice both had girls, but his feeling for Lucy's baby was a very special one. They were the two unmarried children of the house, loving their home deeply, always with the knowledge that this could not be their abiding place, that when their father died all would be changed. Lucy had loved her brother Oliver partly for himself, partly for his weaknesses, while he had loved her because she was Lucy, without ever seeing her full worth. Now they met again, each with an *arrière pensée*, because Oliver was thinking that Lucy as wife and mother was perhaps not quite so sympathetic as she used to be, while Lucy was wondering if Oliver would ever get over dramatizing and pitying himself; though she did not put it in those words.

"Isn't she divine?" said Lucy. "Say 'Uncle Oliver,' darling," but Miss Amabel Rose was asleep and took no notice.

"Indeed she is," said Oliver and laid his little finger in one tiny hand which even in sleep closed upon it with a grip of iron, so he sat down by the cot and waited patiently for his release while he and Lucy talked about Marling and his work in London and the book he was writing about the seventeenth-century poet Thos. Bohun, Canon of Barchester. As he had been writing it for nearly ten years his friends had either forgotten it or were sick of hearing about it, but Lucy had always listened and never criticized and for this he missed her. Perhaps for other things too, but as he did not speak of them we do not know.

Miss Isabel Dale, staying at Marling as a kind of friend-secretary before Lucy's wedding, had typed it for him in triplicate and given him very sensible advice to try to make it a little longer or it wouldn't be a book at all, only an opuscule, which word had rather comforted Oliver. But now Isabel was Lady Silverbridge and would in time be a duchess and Oliver felt a certain diffidence about approaching her for advice, all of which he poured out to his sister Lucy till Sister Chiffinch came in and said he must say au revoir for the present, upon which he took offence, concealing it so well that Lucy apologized to Sister Chiffinch when she came back and said Oliver was writing a book.

"I thought there must be a Something," said Sister Chiffinch. "When I was nursing Mrs. Adrian Coates with her first it was at her father Mr. George Knox's house at Low Rising, you know, the one that writes books—well he was just writing a book then, really my memory is quite failing for I know Wardy got it from the libery and Heathy and I read it from cover to cover. Well, as I was saying—"

"You weren't," said Lucy rebelliously, but Sister Chiffinch did not hear and tanked on—"when Mr. Knox was writing a book he could be quite savage. But he always apologized afterward and he gave me the sweetest souvenir when I left, a photo of himself and Mrs. Coates and her husband and the baby in a lovely silver frame and signed in his own writing. A gentleman like Mr. Oliver ought to get married."

"We thought he would," said Lucy, who like most of us found the warm comfortable intimacy of her quiet life highly conducive to gossip. "We thought of lots of people like Frances Harvey and Isabel Dale that's Lady Silverbridge now, or Susan Dean, or perhaps Eleanor Grantly, but they all got married to someone else."

Sister Chiffinch said a little bird had told her that young Mr.

Marling was quite an admirer of Jessica Dean and really it was
not to be surprised at, she was so sweetly pretty and such a clever
actress. To which Lucy disloyally replied that Oliver couldn't
help being in love with Jessica but he couldn't possibly have
afforded to marry her even if she hadn't married Aubrey Clover.
Lucy thought of the day of Mr. Adams's housewarming or
rather garden-warming party when Jessica had told Oliver that
she had married Aubrey Clover and she remembered his stricken
face. He had recovered since then and had become *l'ami de la
maison* in the Clovers' flat, but still there was no sign of a wife for
him and his hair was receding rapidly from a rather knobby and
shiny forehead. Lucy in her secure happiness as wife and mother
longed for her dear Oliver to have an equal bliss, but so far no
nymph of suitable age and condition had arisen and if she did,
Lucy felt she would need to be very patient and strong-minded
as well. Presently Sister Chiffinch shut out the chill green
evening sky and the bedroom was given over to domesticity.
And here for the present we may leave Lucy as secure as anyone
can be in such treacherous days. But for the moment all is well
and we feel that it will continue to be well.

At Rushwater the latest news of Lucy and the baby was
brought back by Emmy Graham who had been over to Edgewood, not so much to see the baby as to discuss with Lucy the
merits of a new artificial manure called Growalot, which some
held to surpass Washington's Vimphos and Corbett's Bono-
Vitasang and Holman's Phospho-Manuro; but as they were all
controlled by the same man and that man nominally Mr. Holman though Mr. Adams had bought a working majority of his
shares at his own figure, we do not think there was a penny to
choose between them.

Martin Leslie and his wife Sylvia were sitting in what was still
called the Morning Room at Rushwater because it had been
called that for so many years. But now with its shabby curtains
and worn chair-coverings, with agricultural literature of all

kinds scattered about and a roaring wood fire, it was merely a comfortable meeting-place for its owners who after hard work in the open air were inclined to do nothing in the evening till Martin Leslie roused himself and went off, still limping a little from his war wounds, to the estate office in the stable yard. In the first year or two when they lived there old Mr. Macpherson the agent used to come over to dinner two or three times a week and help Martin in the office, but he now found the evenings too much for him and one of the family visited him nearly every day; sometimes Martin; sometimes his golden wife Sylvia with her two children; sometimes Emmy Graham who lived at Rushwater and was considered to know as much about cows as anyone in West Barsetshire, besides a complete understanding of bulls which put the old cowmen to shame; sometimes Tom Grantly who, as we know, was thinking of leaving Rushwater for the Red Tape and Sealing Wax Office.

This evening old Mr. Macpherson was to come to dinner, because it was his birthday, and then be carefully wrapped up and taken back by one of the party. Tom Grantly had gone to fetch him and Martin and Sylvia were feeling sleepy and comfortably tired.

"I must say Grandpapa was a brick to put down so much wine," said Martin as he poured out sherry. "If I died it would practically pay the death duties."

"Then don't, darling," said Sylvia. "Not till Georgy is old enough to manage the place," for Miss Eleanor Leslie, whom our readers may remember in her perambulator on the occasion of old Lady Emily Leslie's eightieth birthday, now had a brother and quite possibly might be acquiring something else of the sort before long. Martin looked adoringly at his wife whose natural sweetness and good sense and patience charmed him every day anew, and wondered what a fellow like himself with a gammy leg had done to deserve such happiness.

A loud noise then resolved itself into Emmy, just back from her visit to the Old Bank House at Edgewood. She flumped down in a chair where she sat most inelegantly with her knees wide apart and a hole in the knee of her stocking.

"Oh bother!" she said as she caught sight of it. "I *thought* that would happen. It was when I put the car away and there was a roll of barbed wire at the back of the garage. Never mind, they're only old cotton ones. I did have some nylons, but they're no good. You only have to touch them and they run from top to bottom."

"It's an awful nuisance," said Sylvia sympathetically. "It's the turning them inside out when you wash them that's the trouble. There always seems to be something spiky in one's hands. A bit of nail or rough skin or something. It's no good putting grease on your hands at night or wearing gloves in bed or anything, because the minute you begin working it's as bad as ever."

Martin reached across and took his wife's hand, looked at it searchingly, kissed it and restored it to her.

"Darling," he said and Sylvia felt that she was well repaid for everything, with full measure pressed down and running over.

Emmy looked at them with the curiosity of the savage who first sees the palefaces, but made no comment and then Tom Grantly came in with Mr. Macpherson.

The old agent now showed his age far too visibly. His clothes looked as if they were hung on a skeleton, so loosely did they fit; his hands were marked with the brown blotches that come to some of us with advancing years and the veins stood out like mountain ranges on a map. His blue eyes were not so clear as formerly and when he sat, letting himself slowly down into a chair, his knees looked as if they would pierce his trousers. He still did a day's work. That is to say he managed to get about and gave orders to the men, but Martin had to oversee his overseer. It was tiring and difficult work to gather what he let fall, but Martin had accepted it as part of his heritage from a long line of landholders and only wished his leg would let him forget it more often; for the lighthearted Italians whom he was supposed to be liberating at Anzio had damaged the leg past remedy with a machine-gun.

"Many happy returns of the day, Macpherson," said Martin, raising his glass of sherry. "It's eighty-three, isn't it?"

"About that," said Mr. Macpherson cautiously. "And her leddyship would have been the same age. I was a young callant of thirty when I first came here, thinking I knew everything, and her leddyship was— Well, Martin, you mind your grandmother well and what like she was. Eyes like a hawk's that just looked through you and a smile that wrung your heart. Clarissa is the most like her, but there's not one of the family can touch her. Aweel, aweel," and he looked at the fire and fell silent till Deanna, a young lady from the village who unaccountably preferred working at Rushwater to going into an office or a factory, put her head in, said: "It's ready," and went away.

To an outsider the birthday dinner would probably have seemed very dull. A working landowner and his wife; a female cousin with a mop of fair hair and a tanned skin who was practically never seen out of breeches and knew bulls inside out; a young man out of the army learning to farm, and an old estate agent; and splitting one bottle of champagne to drink the old agent's health. But to anyone who knew Barsetshire it was the county in miniature with its tradition of work, its acceptance of the immutable law that practically all those who depended on one were in their different way lazy, incompetent, untruthful, grasping, but none the less their children to be helped while young and allowed when old to go on living at a very low rent or none at all in cottages that could have been let for enormous sums to outsiders. And their lives were devoted to Rushwater, which would use them, as it had used Mr. Macpherson, till their eyes were dim and their clothes hung loosely on the skeletons that lurked in them. And plenty of good looks among them too.

With the dessert (for when the kitchen gardens and fruit trees were leased to Amalgamated Vedge Ltd. Martin had reserved the right of keeping what was wanted for the house) the champagne was broached and Martin, raising his glass, wished health and happiness to Mr. Macpherson and offered the thanks of Rushwater and the Leslies for all he had done for the place.

Mr. Macpherson, moved beyond his wont, made to stand up and speak, but Sylvia gently pulled him down again.

"You're right, Mistress Leslie," he said, going back to his native Doric as he did when moved, in spite of fifty-three years' absence. "I'm no very fit to stand now. Fifty-three years have I worked for Rushwater—and for her leddyship—and the grasshopper is a burden. The zeal of her house hath eaten me up; see Psalms, sixty-nine, the ninth verse. But it was Her house—Her house. I thank the Lord for all His mercies. And I thank you too."

His hearers, all more moved than they liked to admit, found a curious mist before their eyes and Martin thought he had heard the old man say "my bairns" before he had resumed his seat, but only spoke of this afterwards, to his golden Sylvia.

"And now," said the old agent when the ladies (Emmy unwillingly counting as one) had retired and Martin had poured a libation from his grandfather's port, "what have you to say, Tom, about your idea of leaving us? That Red Tape and Sealing Wax Department will be a poor change from Rushwater."

"I daresay it will be," said Tom Grantly, nervous but standing his ground. "But I'm not doing enough here, Mr. Macpherson. I mean I've simply loved it all and I can't say thank you enough for all you've taught me—and Martin and Sylvia and Emmy too—but after all I don't really belong here."

"And where do you belong?" said Mr. Macpherson.

"I—I don't really know," said Tom, looking nervously at the two other men and finding interest, but not the sympathy he wanted. "I mean I do feel I ought to be really *doing* something."

"Well, what have you been doing?" said Martin. "Certainly not nothing and therefore, as sure as two negatives make an affirmative, something. Rushwater will miss you. And we shall miss you."

"It's awfully good of you, Martin," said Tom, digging holes in the tablecloth with a fork as he spoke, "and I do love it, but it isn't going to get me anywhere. I mean it's awfully nice to work with you and Emmy, but——" and his voice trailed away, as uncertain as his thoughts.

The old agent leaned across and took the fork from him, saying as he did so: "It was Her tablecloth. I mind her leddyship showing me the initials on it when first I came here," and raising a corner of the cloth he showed the monogram of H.E.L. "Henry and Emily Leslie," he said. "All embroidered by hand and she had twenty-four of them."

"And this is the last," said Martin and a silence fell, full of memories to Martin and Mr. Macpherson, highly embarrassing to Tom.

"Well, Tom, if you've made up your mind you must do as you feel best," said Martin. "We shall all miss you. And if Red Tape doesn't work, come back. We've plenty of work for you here. Good luck."

He raised his glass, as did Mr. Macpherson, and they drank to Tom.

"Thanks most awfully," said Tom. "I feel a most awful heel, leaving you like this. But I feel I ought to be earning my living. I mean a career with a future in it."

It does the greatest credit to Martin and his agent that neither of them showed any outward feeling at this extremely ill-advised remark. Martin inquired about the prospects of getting a stand-pipe and trough in the Five Corner Field. Mr. Macpherson said it would require consideration.

"Excuse me butting in, sir," said Tom, "but I think we can do it with gravity from Wooden Spring. It would mean a hundred years of piping but we could run it over ground."

"And this callant is leaving us to serve the Mammon of Unrighteousness!" said Mr. Macpherson.

"Come, come, Macpherson, it's not so bad as that," said Martin kindly, as Tom was redfaced and almost in tears.

"Who will the lad be working for?" said Mr. Macpherson. "This Government. And whatna Government is that? Ane Monstrous Regiment. And you will be changing Rushwater for that, you poor misguided lad. Well, may the Lord protect you, for I doubt you'll be needing it."

As Mr. Macpherson was looking like the Major Prophets all rolled into one, Tom kept silent.

"I wonder why it's called Wooden Spring," said Martin. "It never occurred to me before."

Tom, with some diffidence, said perhaps Odin or Woden.

"Prætorium here, Prætorium there," said Mr. Macpherson who found in Scott something applicable to every situation in life, "I mind the naming o't. It used to be called Booker's Spring till your grandfather, Martin, when he came into the place, put a wooden trough below it for the cattle and a kind of wooden arch above it and the name stuck like a flea on the wall."

"And who was Booker?" said Tom, yearning to reinstate himself by a show of intelligence.

"Look at the beechwoods up yonder," said Mr. Macpherson with slight impatience. "Beaconsfield, Buchenwald, Bukovina, you get the name all over Europe. And now, Martin, I shall go and sit with your good leddy for a while and then this lad will take me home," at which words Tom felt he was forgiven, but a sense of guilt, of desertion, remained with him all the same.

In the shabby comfortable morning-room Sylvia and Emmy, by a blazing fire, were having an agreeable relaxation from bulls and cows by discussing the cottages at Hacker's Corner which were let, as they always had been, at a totally uneconomic rent to tenants who took it all as their right and expected their landlord to do all repairs, outside and in, even to the refurnishing of old Cruncher's bedroom when he had deliberately put a lot of straw on the fire to make a nice blaze and the Barchester engines had to be summoned to deal with the result. Talk was on familiar subjects of farm and field and stock. Everyone was comfortably relaxed and Emmy yawned to an extent that threatened dislocation till Mr. Macpherson said he must be going home and was not above leaning on Martin's arm as they walked to the stable yard.

"I'll drive him," said Tom, who had followed them, and Martin thanked him with one of his rare smiles. The old agent hoisted himself stiffly into the car and in a few moments they were at the gate of Mr. Macpherson's delightful little Regency house which had very improbable stucco battlements, a small church porch, an elegant veranda, and was enclosed by an iron fence except where a well-kept lawn was bounded by a ha-ha. Mr. Macpherson thanked Tom and took Tom's young strong hand in his own thin gnarled hand as he wished him well and then went into his house. Tom drove back with mixed feelings of gratitude to the old agent, hopefulness about his own future with the Red Tape and Sealing Wax Department, and a quite unaccountable sick and sinking feeling in his heart; and as everyone had gone upstairs when he got back he had to carry his anxious heart to bed with him.

CHAPTER 3

Among the many friends interested in Miss Amabel Rose Adams was Mrs. Belton over at Harefield. In the dark days of the war, when the Hosiers' Girls' Foundation School occupied Harefield Park, the Beltons had moved to Arcot House in the village of Harefield. To their house Heather Adams, then a boarder at Harefield Park, had been brought frightened and dripping after having fallen through the ice on the lake entirely through her own disobedience. Her father's gratitude to Mrs. Belton (and to her son Freddy, then a Commander in the Royal Navy, who had picked Heather out of the lake and brought her to his parents' house) had been deep and lasting and a sincere friendship had grown between them with excellent results. Mr. Adams had been able to do Mr. Belton a good turn with the War Agricultural Committee who wanted to plough a piece of his grassland for wheat, which land was well known to produce the finest crop of weeds and stones in the county. Mrs. Belton had taken Heather Adams in hand and helped her to become the sensible self-possessed and quite good-looking woman she now was. She had also been consulted by Mr. Adams about the Old Bank House at Edgewood and helped him with her excellent taste and knowledge to give it the curtains and furniture that it needed. And now Mr. Adams had married into the county and had a baby, and Mrs. Belton felt her work for him had not been in vain. That his wife was Lucy, also her own name, rather pleased her, and there was some distant connection between Mrs. Belton's own family the Thornes of Ullathorne and Lucy's maternal grandfather Lord Nutfield, whose pride in his old barony had been alloyed by the arrival in the Lords of a later peer, indistinguishable from him except by one letter.

When the Beltons' elder son Captain Frederick Belton, R.N., he who had pulled Heather Adams out of the lake, married Susan Dean, elder sister of Jessica Dean, the actress, his mother had made a flat in Arcot House for the young couple and their first child (not that there was yet a second, but it seemed improbable that they would stop at one). But life with a baby on an upper floor has its disadvantages and most luckily Dowlah Cottage had fallen vacant through the death of Mrs. Hoare, widow of a former agent of the Pomfret estate, and as Mr. Belton still owned it and several other houses in Harefield he was able to let the Freddy Beltons have it.

During the lifetime of the late tenant it had been almost impossible to see the house at all, so full was it of Jacobean dressers, Cromwellian chairs, Spanish leather screens, Moorish fretwork arches, heavy velvet portières embroidered with sun-flowers under the influence of the æsthetic movement, grand-father clocks, *étagères*, and some very doubtful Dutch Old Masters with at least an eighth of an inch of dirt and varnish on them; all legacies from relations of Mrs. Hoare and her late husband. But when these had been removed to continue their career as lega-cies with new owners, Dowlah Cottage was revealed as a very pleasant two-story dwelling with a wide passage running from the front door right through the house and a nice garden which, like all the gardens on that side of the High Street, had a back door into a lane.

Here Captain Belton and his wife and their gifted and un-usual baby boy who had been christened Frederick but was usually called Baby (to prevent confusion with his father and grandfather though the probability of one being taken for the other seemed so remote as to be negligible) were living in great happiness and we are glad to be able to add comfort, for Susan Belton's father was a wealthy consulting engineer and had dowered all his daughters handsomely, partly from parental affection and sense of duty, partly from a wish to get the better of Them while the going was good. Though how long They will allow parents to leave anything to their children, with or without death duties, we cannot say.

In Dowlah Cottage, on a nasty, chill Monday morning in June, were Mrs. Freddy (as she was usually called in the village), her mother-in-law, and her brother-in-law Charles Belton who was a master at the Priory School over at Lambton and spending the half-term at home. The owner of the Priory, Sir Harry Waring, had died during the past winter and his wife, probably because she had no particular wish to live, had died not long afterwards.

"It's time I was gone," she had said to her niece Leslie Winter, whose husband was owner and headmaster of the very successful Priory School. "Harry always needed me and I am quite sure he is needing me still. And I have always wondered if we should see George again," to which Leslie Winter had no answer, for George Waring had been killed in 1918, just before the Armistice, and one can only guess about a future life, hoping and trying to believe that those responsible for it will make it possible to meet people one has loved, and that the lads who will never be old will be able to recognize the parents and friends whom the years between have aged and changed.

"I think George will be pleased to see us," Lady Waring had said to Leslie, the day before she died. "And if on thinking it over he doesn't want to see too much of us, we shall quite understand, bless him. And I am sure there will be something useful that one can do," and Leslie said afterwards to her husband Philip Winter that heaven would be no heaven for Uncle Harry and Aunt Harriet unless they could do unpaid work for other people. And as these were almost Lady Waring's last words, they may be her epitaph.

And now their nephew was Commander Sir Cecil Waring, because his childless uncle's title was one of those rare Baronetcies which can go sideways and so had come to Cecil Waring, brother of the Headmaster's wife. And what was more he was not so badly off even when They had confiscated everything They could lay hands on, having inherited through his mother a considerable fortune at an early age and invested much of it in good farming land round the Priory.

"Do bring Cecil over next time you come, if he isn't too busy," said Mrs. Belton to her son Charles. "I expect he would like to see Arcot House," for it is well known that anyone who has what is called "a House" likes nothing better than seeing other Houses, and poking into the servants' (if any) bedrooms and comparing notes about converting the old kitchens into a Boys' Club with two ping-pong tables in the old scullery and darts in the game larder.

Charles said he was sure Cecil Waring would love to come, but what he really adored was sailing, and the only thing he had against the Priory (apart from its extreme hideousness and inconvenience) was that there was no water handy and it was a good hour's run and more to the sea.

"What a pity the lake isn't bigger," said Mrs. Belton, hospitably inclined.

"Or deeper," said Charles. "Do you remember when that ghastly Heather Adams crashed through the ice, Mother? Lord! what a sight she must have been when Freddy brought her up to the house. Fancy anyone marrying her," to which his adoring mother replied that anyway no one had seen fit to marry Charles as yet, so he needn't talk.

"Oh, well," said Charles and his mother was pretty sure he was thinking of Lady Graham's second daughter Clarissa, with whom he had what his mother called an understanding. "But Cecil has a couple of collapsible dinghies, Mother, like the one the Mertons have, you know, you can fold them up like a deck chair—"

Here his sister-in-law interrupted to say that she had never yet succeeded in folding a deck chair properly at the first go.

"Nor unfolding them neither," said Charles, with memories of himself as a small boy squashing his fingers (not badly) in a deck chair and then being smacked by Nanny Wheeler for doing it. "But why shouldn't we bring them over and have a punting race on the lake. Upstream, twice round the island and then whoosh! up the straight to the home end. I'd like to see Cecil getting his pole stuck in the mud."

His mother and his sister-in-law thought this an excellent plan and then Dr. Perry the old friend and physician of the Belton family looked in; not professionally, but to satisfy his insatiable curiosity about things in general and hear about the new owner of the Priory; also to talk about himself. Mrs. Belton asked after his wife and the boys.

"I ought to say the distinguished young men," she said, "but I can't help thinking of them all as boys."

"Nor can I," said their father. "But boys or men, one of them has decided to chuck the hospital and go into partnership with me."

"Thank God!" said Mrs. Belton, with a fervour that quite alarmed the family. "I mean we have always been so afraid of what might happen when you retired, Dr. Perry, if you ever did. Suppose we had Dr. Morgan," and she paled almost visibly at the thought.

"*That* female!" said Dr. Perry. "Psychoanalysis for the cottages when what they need—and what's more they expect it—is a good dose of salts. Have you heard the latest about her?"

His hearers hadn't and waited in rapt expectation.

"She's got a job at the Ministry of Nutritional Hygiene," said Dr. Perry, rubbing his hands and chuckling.

"Well, bad luck to her wherever she is," said Charles cheerfully. "Who's she psyching there?"

"I don't know and I don't care," said Dr. Perry, "but her chief is Dr. Mothersill and there'll be wigs on the green."

"And no idea of how to dress, either of them," said Mrs. Freddy Belton, who had not committed herself up till now, not from laziness or shyness, but she was not a consulting engineer's daughter for nothing and liked to study her strains and stresses before hazarding herself.

"I'd give twopence to see their hats," said Mrs. Belton fervently and then fell silent; for the day on which Dr. Morgan had appeared at the Hosiers' Girls' Foundation School breaking-up in a jaunty Robin Hood hat with a feather and a depressed veil and had met Miss Pettinger the unpopular Headmistress of Barchester High School wearing its twin, was just before the day on which Charles, concealing it from his mother till the last moment, had gone back to his regiment after a night's leave and vanished. All was well. Charles had come back safe and sound and (apparently) not emotionally disturbed, but his mother would till her dying day remember his empty room with his clothes strewn on the chairs, the bed and the floor; and her own dumb anguish. Perhaps even beyond her dying day. Who knows?

"I'd give sixpence to see them fight," said Dr. Perry with sad want of *esprit de corps*. "But who do you think is coming into partnership with me? Gus."

Mrs. Belton, who had always found it difficult to remember which of the Perry boys was which, expressed her great delight and satisfaction, and said that was the surgeon, wasn't it.

"No, no. That's Jim," said Dr. Perry. "Gus is skin diseases and he thinks a few years in the country as a G.P. will be very useful to him. Everyone's getting queer with the food They give us. Of course the cottages have always lived on tins and now it's worse than ever. Gus thinks we may get back to leprosy with luck and then he can study it without going to India or wherever they have lepers."

"Well, that is *delightful* news," said Mrs. Belton, alluding we think to the proposed partnership rather than the prospect of lepers with rattles up and down the High Street. "I know now. Gus is the one with the bushy eyebrows. And how is Bob?"

"So fine his old father hardly dares to look in at 208 Harley Street," said Dr. Perry, not attempting to conceal his pride. "Five guineas for a consultation and a secretary and a parlourmaid in grey and white to open the door. Consulting physician, that's the game. He's going to marry soon I think. A nice young woman. She's an Honourable and it's a great help to a consultant. A Lady Clara would put people off, but an Honourable gives tone. It's a funny racket, Mrs. Belton. It'll be ten guineas in a year or two, when he's got a family. But he keeps up his hospital work just the same. He's a good boy," and Mrs. Belton thought there was perhaps a faint tinge of regret in Dr. Perry's voice for a son whose ways were parted from his ways. Of this we cannot judge. "And what does Mrs. Freddy think?" said Dr. Perry, becoming the family doctor again.

"She thinks that she is very glad none of your sons are gynecologists," said Susan stoutly, "because I'd rather have you than all your sons in one," which pleased Dr. Perry greatly.

"Well, I suppose I must go on my rounds," he said. "Oh, my wife wants to know if all or any Beltons will come to tea on Saturday," which invitation was accepted with pleasure by Mrs. Belton while Susan said she would have loved to come, but what with putting Master Belton to bed and getting supper ready for her husband, she was sorry she couldn't. And we may say that she did not look sorry in the least. Charles, suddenly very important, said he had to ring Cecil Waring up about bringing the dinghies over to Harefield and having a regatta and having done so announced his intention of going over to the Priory and clinching matters.

"Well, if you come back too late for tea, come in and have some sherry," said Dr. Perry, who looked upon all young men as more or less his sons. "It's only Empire, but the boys say it's not bad," which invitation Charles accepted very nicely.

Plassey House, where the Perrys lived, was smaller than Arcot

House and its sash windows less elegant, but it had the advantage of a beautifully carved shell-shaped projection over the front door and the largest cedar tree in the county except those in the Palace grounds. As it was half past four on an English day in high June Mrs. Belton found Mrs. Perry in her comfortable and slightly overfurnished drawing-room with French windows on the garden, lighting the fire.

"You know," said Mrs. Belton, "I never come into your room without thinking of our working-parties in the war. What fun they were."

"I enjoyed them immensely myself," said Mrs. Perry. "We all felt so safe when we were knitting for the forces and Mr. Churchill taking care of us all. And really the bread and the cakes were just as nasty then as they are now, and I often wish we were back in the war again. We knew where we were then. Have you heard about Gus?"

Mrs. Belton said she was delighted that Dr. Perry was having a son for a partner and hoped she would see him soon.

"Yes, indeed, he's here this weekend and he will be here for good in September," said Mrs. Perry. "And I asked the Updikes. I'm afraid Ruth has taken offence, but she always does," and then a stop was put to any private conversation by the faithful maid Ruth, who apart from being quite devoted to the Perrys had every defect of sulks, complaining, and tactlessness. As she put the tea-tray down she grudgingly acknowledged Mrs. Belton's pleasant and not in the least condescending greeting and after looking stonily at her employer through her hideous steel-rimmed spectacles went out, hooking the door with her foot as she did so.

"There is a permanent mark where she does that," said Mrs. Perry sadly. "We did think of having a brass door-plate put there. I don't mean the kind that says Physician and Surgeon, but just one of the ones one has on the handle side of the door above and below the handle, only lower down," which sentence was a fine example of how difficult it sometimes is to make a

perfectly plain statement. "I don't think we'll wait for the
Updikes. She has all the family at home for the weekend and I
expect she is rather busy."

"Has she been in trouble lately?" said Mrs. Belton, for Mrs.
Updike was celebrated for pricking, scalding, bruising, cutting,
burning, electrocuting, pinking, and crimping herself in more
ways than seemed humanly possible, all with the gayest good
humour.

"Not since Saturday as far as I know," said Mrs. Perry. "My
husband went over to Mr. Updike's office about some law
business or other and found Mrs. Updike with a lump like an
egg on her forehead because a roller blind had fallen on it."

"I've never known a woman so much the prey of inanimate
objects," said Mrs. Belton. "Do you remember Mr. Carton's
tea-party some time in the war when she was late and your
husband brought her along with a bandaged wrist? She was
trying to pickle walnuts and let the vinegar boil and nearly
blinded herself and then upset the rest over her wrist. Oh dear,
what happy times those were."

"And so say all of us," said Mrs. Perry. "Oh, have you seen
Commander Waring yet? I hear he is perfectly devastating and
hasn't the least use for women, but as I haven't a daughter it
doesn't matter."

Mrs. Belton said she had been hearing a lot about him from
Charles and told Mrs. Perry about the proposed dinghy punting
race for which Mrs. Perry at once entered her son Gus and any
other sons who happened to be about at the moment, and then
the faithful Ruth, exuding offence from every pore, opened the
door to what appeared to be a kind of Noah's Ark procession of
Updikes.

Since we last met her Mrs. Updike had seen all her brood
safely established, if such a thing as safety exists now. Her elder
son after rushing up the military scale to Lieutenant-Colonel
had returned to the law and was, like Gus Perry, going into
partnership with his father. The elder girl had gone from the

WAAF's into several responsible jobs and was now head of the Barchester Public Library. The schoolboy was almost a chartered accountant and the schoolgirl had found herself a very good job in a large travel agency; so the two younger children were seldom at home. But the ex-Colonel and the ex-WAAF lived at home, keeping an indulgent eye on their mother whom they looked upon as an eccentric but lovable child of a larger growth.

"You don't mind my bringing the chicks, do you?" said Mrs. Updike to her hostess. "They aren't often both free on the same afternoon and it seemed a pity to waste them. We would have been here before, but I was oiling the lock of the spare-room door and somehow the key fell out of the window into one of those large rosebushes with millions of those thorns that are so small that you can't even see to take them out with a needle," and having made what evidently appeared to her a perfectly reasonable explanation she smiled and sat down.

Mrs. Perry said she was very sorry and it didn't matter a bit. But how, said Mrs. Belton, had the key managed to fall out of the window when Mrs. Updike was oiling the lock.

"Oh, I suddenly remembered I had read somewhere that the best way to oil a lock, or perhaps it is to housebreak, is with a feather," said Mrs. Updike, her pretty tired face flushing with interest in her narrative. "I knew I hadn't a feather in the house because I did have some ostrich feathers but I gave them all to something or other, so I wondered if there were any feathers in the garden and then I could go down and get one," at which point she paused, evidently seeing the whole incident in her mind's eye.

"Do you often find feathers in the front garden then?" said Mrs. Belton, who wondered if Mrs. Updike hung featherbeds out of her window in the Continental fashion.

"When she forgets to shut the fowls up," said her son.

"Which is mostly," said her daughter, but both spoke very kindly.

7

"So the key was all oily and slipped through my fingers like macaroni—*cooked* macaroni, I mean," said Mrs. Updike, still gazing with her blue eyes into the past. "And I must have turned the key the wrong way before I took it out to oil it, so the door was locked. So I couldn't get out."

"So what *did* you do?" said Mrs. Perry, by now as fascinated as Mrs. Belton.

"Mother screamed," said her son. "A very fine scream," he added with an air of appraising legally his mother's achievements. "And I was upstairs and came rushing down."

"And I was downstairs and came rushing up," said his sister.

"And they rattled the door, poor darlings," said Mrs. Updike, looking at them with pride and gratitude, "so loud that I couldn't explain. So I leant out of the window and screamed till the postman looked up, because he had just brought the afternoon post, and he most obligingly found the key, so I was saved. Oh dear!" she added, as she took off her gloves. "I quite forgot to wash the oil off," at which her children laughed with a kind of proud affection and Mrs. Perry firmly took Mrs. Updike away to be cleaned.

After this they had tea quite peacefully with no more startling interruption than a wasp who evidently looked upon the tea-table as a personal enemy and attacked it with sound and fury till Mrs. Updike's son after stalking it for some time tracked it into a jam jar and with great presence of mind plugged the spoon-hole with a bit of scone which he had been kneading for some time to that end.

Presently Mr. Updike came in, rather tired as he often was but very ready for gossip, and asked Mrs. Belton if she knew about Church Meadow.

"The War Agricultural aren't after it *again*, are they?" said Mrs. Belton, who vividly remembered her husband's agitation when the body had tried to compel her husband to grow wheat on the worst bit of soil in the county. "Besides the Hosiers'

Company bought it. They talked about a school there, but nothing happened. They've been using it as playing fields."

"Well, I happened to run into their solicitor in Barchester," said Mr. Updike, "and he tells me the plans for a big new Hosiers' Girls' Foundation School are approved and they've got the permits. Probably they will be stopped halfway through, or told they can have rooms but mustn't have doors or window frames, but anyway they are hoping to start next spring."

"Will they have a very tall tower?" said Mrs. Belton.

"A tower?" said Mr. Updike. "I couldn't say. I've not seen the plans. Why?"

"You'll think I am foolish," said Mrs. Belton, "but if my husband could *see* anything, I think he would die. He has got used to the school being at Harefield—in fact he rather likes it—and he is quite resigned to their having bought Church Meadow. But if they made the new school *very* high we would see the top of it over the hill and he would go mad."

"I don't think you are at all foolish," said Mr. Updike. "There isn't so much land left unspoilt in England that we can afford to lose it. But I think for you to see anything in Church Meadow from Arcot House, it would have to be at least two hundred feet high. Probably more because there's a good dip to Church Meadow. And now perhaps you can tell *me* something, Mrs. Belton. What will happen to Harefield Park when the school goes?"

"I wish I could," said Mrs. Belton, suddenly looking much older. "We can't possibly afford to live in it, and Freddy and Susan couldn't either. And Charles has his schoolmaster's pay and two hundred pounds that old Aunt Mary left him and possibly enough capital to bring in another hundred when we are dead—and then They would take most of it. Even a lunatic asylum would be better than nothing."

"Perhaps it won't be as bad as that," said Mr. Updike kindly but not, Mrs. Belton felt, with very much assurance. "There are bound to be big concerns looking out for property. For instance,

I happen to know that Amalgamated Vedge Limited are wanting accommodation for their large staff and a nursery garden for trying new seeds," and he paused as if waiting to see the result of his words before he said more, but Mrs. Belton looked so grey and drawn that he said perhaps they might talk about it another time and slipped into the general conversation.

It sometimes happens even under the present government that Nature having begun the day in a thoroughly bad temper is getting over it by tea-time. The wind had fallen, the grey clouds had gone with the wind, and the stone terrace outside the drawing-room was almost basking in the sun. So a move was made and they all went into the garden.

"Not a deck chair for Mother, please," said young Updike. "She is bound to get shut up in it and squash her fingers," but his mother had already taken a cane garden chair. Three of its legs were on the terrace, the fourth was on the very edge of the stone and as she sat down the fourth leg plunged deeply into a flowerbed.

"I think the wooden bench for Mother," said her elder daughter to no one in particular, so Mrs. Updike was installed where (it was hoped) no further accident could pursue her, and for at least five minutes peace reigned till a very loud ringing of a bell broke into the desultory conversation.

"Oh dear; a baby I suppose. Or an abdominal," said Mrs. Perry. "Always just at the wrong time," but instead of a baby or an abdominal it was Ruth, her face more disapproving than ever, followed by a shamefaced Charles.

"I say, I'm most awfully sorry. I only just pulled it out and then I let it go," he was saying to Ruth who, ignoring him, remarked: "It's Mr. Charles and the other gentleman and I suppose I can clear away now or I'll never get my supper laid," with which words she walked straight through Charles—or he afterwards said she had—and was heard clashing china in the drawing-room.

"I say, I'm most awfully sorry, Mrs. Perry," said Charles, "I only just pulled it out and it slipped out of my hand and sounded like the fire engines."

Mrs. Perry said it didn't matter a bit as Ruth could not possibly be crosser than she was and they had offered to have an electric bell but she had said she didn't fancy electricity and if the fellow that came to read the meter gave her any more of his cheek she'd tell him what she thought of him.

Gradually the whole company became aware that the person described by Ruth as the other gentleman, a tall, spare man with rather a hawk's nose and piercingly light blue eyes, was looking on with a quietly amused face.

"I *am* so sorry," said Mrs. Perry, getting up. "Ruth was being so difficult that I quite lost my head for a moment. You came with Charles."

"My name is Waring," said the newcomer. "I think you know my sister, Leslie Winter."

"Yes, indeed," said Mrs. Perry warmly, "especially in the second half of the winter term. You must be Commander Waring."

"I am—as far as one can be humanly certain about anything now," said the newcomer. "May I ask why you know Leslie better at one time than another?"

"Infectious diseases," said Mrs. Perry. "It's the worst time. The boys manage Christmas and overeating splendidly, and January isn't too bad. But in February they all go down with measles and mumps and whooping-cough and things and send for the doctor all day long."

"Just the same with midshipmen," said Commander Waring. "I must apologize for coming in upon you like this, but Charles here insisted."

"Oh, come, Cecil," said Charles Belton. "I didn't insist. It's your car."

"Possibly," said Cecil Waring. "But you were driving it."

"Only because you said I could," said Charles. "She's a beauty,

Mrs. Perry. A 1949 Ocelot. I got eighty out of her easily down the Worsted Hill."

"Then you were an idiot to do it," said Dr. Perry, who with Gus had come across from the surgery while Charles was speaking. "Well, Waring, I'm glad to see you. Haven't seen you since you had influenza at the Priory about thirty years ago. Your uncle and aunt always had Dr. Ford, but he was away. He and I have usually worked in with each other up there. Have you had flu again lately?" but Commander Waring had to disclaim any infectious diseases.

"And where were you last?" Dr. Perry asked, rather unfairly we think nobbling the distinguished visitor for himself, while his wife waited impatiently to make further introductions.

Cecil said out East.

"Oh, I say, sir," said Gus Perry, who had been so obviously bursting with impatience to speak that his mother wondered, dispassionately, if people ever really had apoplexy from suppressed emotion, "did you ever have leprosy?"

"Never," said Cecil.

"I did hope you had," said Gus frowning with sad concentration till his dark bushy eyebrows almost met. "You see skin diseases are my line and I can't get a leper. There were a few cases down by the docks when I was at Knight's, but they were mostly Lascars. You don't ever notice anything, do you, sir, like"—and he gave a scholarly and detailed description of one or two revolting symptoms, any knowledge of which Commander Waring again had to disclaim.

"Never sir?" said Gus, unwilling to believe the worst.

"No, never," said Cecil firmly, at which several of the company couldn't help laughing.

"The worst of Gilbert and Sullivan now," said Mrs. Updike unexpectedly, "is that the audiences are so awful."

Dr. Perry said it was a democratic age, adding as a rider that as far as he was concerned anyone could have it for sixpence.

"Oh, I don't mean *that* kind of awful," said Mrs. Updike,

wrinkling her forehead in an effort to make her own thoughts clear to herself. "I mean clapping everything before it's finished and encoring everything six times. It makes one almost want to *hiss*," at which words her pretty tired face flushed with enthusiasm as she pushed the bench back a little and knocked against a large tub of agapanthus, whose heads disintegrated and showered their blue flowers over her.

After this Mrs. Perry took the meeting in hand and very firmly introduced Commander Sir Cecil Waring all round, who rose gallantly to the occasion, giving a general impression to all the men that they were old messmates and to all the women that he was in love with them. After which he skilfully cut loose, made off on another tack and brought up all standing by Mrs. Belton.

"Charles tells me that you would like to take your collapsible dinghies on the lake," said Mrs. Belton.

"Charles is a delightful fellow," said the Commander, "but not a good Flag-Captain. What I would like, is to be allowed to ask you whether you could consider favourably Charles's suggestion—not mine I may add—to practice punting a collapsible boat on your lake. Probably we shall all fall in."

"We would *love* you to," said Mrs. Belton. "But I must warn you that Charles has an unfair advantage, because the Noel Mertons over at Northbridge have one and he has punted it on the river there, which is much more dangerous than the lake. And you will bring your sister and her husband, I hope. And perhaps a few of the boys? They'd love it. How are you getting on at the Priory?"

"So-so," called Cecil Waring. "It's all rather a muddle at the moment. Leslie and her husband have done so well that they will need bigger quarters; much bigger. How people have enough money to send their boys to prep schools, let alone public schools, I don't know."

"They haven't," said Mrs. Belton. "But they go on doing it, even if they have to live in the stables. It's so difficult for foreigners to understand. The average Englishman will pay *anything* to get his darling children off his hands. But can't they overflow into your part?"

"No," said Cecil. "And if they wanted to, which they don't, I wouldn't let them. Uncle Harry had let everything go about the place, poor old fellow. I want to get it on its feet again. And there are some boys I'm interested in. Sons of warrant officers and ratings who served under me. I should like to turn the School wing into a kind of home for them and try to get one or two reliable men for the estate. Uncle Harry had let the woods go absolutely to pieces. There must be thousands of pounds worth of timber rotting there."

Mrs. Belton said that her husband had a good deal of experience with wood and woodmen on his own estate and perhaps her son-in-law Admiral Hornby who did a good bit of forestry up at Aberdeathly would like to talk to him. And then Gus Perry and Charles Belton with a tray of glasses and sherry, and a tray with a siphon and a cherished half-bottle of whisky to honour their naval visitor, put a stop to their talk for the present. Everyone refused whisky, which touched even Dr. Perry's leathery sardonic heart, for he knew most of them would prefer it and were saying sherry from consideration for his purse. Cecil Waring, rather to the surprise of Mrs. Updike, who had expected him to ask for rum and drink the King's health with one foot on the table, asked if he might have orange and plain water. Mrs. Perry pressed him to change his mind.

"No, thank you," he said. "A sundowner is a good rule and I stick to it even in summertime. And I really like orange and water, though no one but Leslie believes me. I admit that at this time of the year a sundowner is rather a misnomer, but in winter it has its points."

Young Updike said Commander Waring ought to live at the North Pole in the winter and then he could have a sundowner all day for months and months.

"Which reminds me," said Mrs. Updike, getting up so suddenly that the sherry slopped over the rim of the glass onto her dress, "that I left our meat ration in the oven to thaw out and I *know* I forgot to turn the regulator down. It must be quite burnt by now."

"It's all right, Mother," said young Updike. "You had turned the gas right off, so I put it to whatever it says on the thing you ought to put it to and it ought to be cooked in about half an hour." His sister quietly squirted a little soda-water onto her handkerchief and wiped her mother's skirt and then they took their parent away.

"What an enchanting woman," said Cecil, looking after the Updikes. "If ever I married I should like one exactly like her," to which Mrs. Perry replied that if Mrs. Updike were anyone else she would be quite intolerable, but being herself she was some-how perfect.

"I say, Mother," said Charles, who had been fidgeting for some time, "we ought to get back. We've got to unpack the dinghies."

"Won't Commander Waring stay to supper?" said his mother.

"He would love to," said that gallant officer, so after thanking the Perrys for their party they walked up to Arcot House where, in front of the door, was the 1949 Ocelot, a large shapeless bundle covered with a tarpaulin lashed to its back.

"Goody, goody," said Charles. "Let's get them off the car. We can put them in the shed by the lake."

Cecil Waring said he would not like to keep Mrs. Belton waiting and looked at her in a kindly, questioning way.

"Well, that's extremely nice of you," said Mrs. Belton, "and as Wheeler, who was the children's nurse and never forgets it, likes us to be punctual, perhaps it *would* be as well if the boats could wait," at which Charles looked disappointed but said nothing.

"By the way," said Mrs. Belton as they went into the drawing-room, "do you like to be Commander or Sir Cecil if one introduces you? My son-in-law is an Admiral but not a Sir, so I don't quite know. Christopher Hornby is his name."

"Oh, he'll be a Sir before long," said Cecil Waring. "I know all about him. Pray introduce me in any way you like, but may I ask you, considering how long my uncle and aunt knew you, to call me Cecil. It's a ghastly name, but my own."

Warmed by this echo of Touchstone Mrs. Belton said she didn't think it was so very ghastly and why did his people call him it, and even as she spoke the words felt that the late and lamented H. W. Fowler might have criticized her style. But apparently her guest found nothing wrong with it.

"It's a silly story," he said. "My people didn't know if I'd be a boy or a girl—"

Mrs. Belton said that was a thing even doctors didn't know and what on earth was the use of pre-natal treatment if you didn't know whom you were treating. Charles wished he could disown his mother, but Commander Waring, quite unmoved, continued: "—so they chose a name that would do for either. And as it worked, they did the same for my sister Leslie. And thank goodness there wasn't another, as they might have called it Esme," which made them all laugh.

"Well, well, what's the laughing about?" said Mr. Belton, who had been in the little room behind the dining-room, a token representation of the Estate Room at Harefield.

"Nothing, Fred," said his wife. "This is Sir Cecil Waring— Commander Waring—Sir Harry's nephew."

"Your uncle was an old friend of my family," said Mr. Belton, with the grave courtesy that so well became him. "Are you settling at the Priory?"

"I hope so," said Cecil Waring. "It's a question of accommodation. I want the whole Priory for a scheme of my own, and my sister and her husband need bigger premises for their school but can't find them. It all turns on that. Meanwhile we go on as we are."

"I hope you will be able to stay at the Priory," said Mr. Belton. "I've had to turn out of Harefield, you know. Couldn't afford to live there. We like Arcot House, but I was born at Harefield and I would have liked to die there."

"I was born in Kensington, but I wouldn't mind dying at the Priory when the time comes," said Cecil Waring. "The people on the estate expect it, you know," and then talk about family places and one's duties as a landlord went on through dinner and Mrs. Belton had secret pleasure in seeing her husband at his best.

"Then you are out of the Navy now?" she asked presently.

"Not exactly," said Cecil Waring. "I got a bullet—or a bit of shrapnel—no one seems to know exactly what—inside me on D-Day and the Admiralty don't like it. It doesn't hurt, or hardly ever, but it walks about inside me. I don't blame it for trying to get out. I would."

Encouraged by his matter-of-fact way of speaking, Mrs. Belton asked if it was likely to work out of itself.

"None of my medical boards can agree," he said. "It might come out at my big toe if I live long enough, or it may decide to move to a vital spot and kill me. Or it may stay where it is."

"Like a pearl in an oyster, eh?" said Mr. Belton, which was so obviously intended for real sympathy that no one could mind it.

"If we have another war the Admiralty will have to make up their minds," said Cecil Waring. "Meanwhile I call myself a half-pay officer. It sounds nice and eighteenth-century."

Charles, who was too well-mannered to interrupt but broadly speaking considered every extra minute given to his parents a minute less for dealing with the boats, made a reference to them.

"A boat-race, eh?" said Mr. Belton. "When I was at Brasenose I did a bit of rowing. I rowed six in the College second boat. We were bumped on the first day, I remember. There's not much room on the lake you know."

Cecil Waring explained good-humouredly that what he and Charles proposed was to punt the boats, as he had been told the lake was not deep.

"That's right," said Mr. Belton. "If you fall in there's plenty of mud and it's silting up worse and worse every year and I haven't the money or the labour to get it cleaned. I used to have a couple of fellows to cut the rushes every year, but now I can't get the young men and it's too much for old Humble. You do as you like. I'll show you the place before you go."

Charles, who had meant to do the showing himself, felt aggrieved but soon forgot to keep up this attitude in the excitement of driving Cecil's car down to the lake and unloading the boats, which he and Cecil quickly unfolded and put into the water. At that end of the lake were the remains of a building from which water used to be pumped to a small piece of artificial water higher up. It was now mostly in ruins and had formerly been a place of attractive terror to the young Beltons, who against their nurses' reiterated commands had happily climbed among the wheels and beams. A part of it had been turned into a boat-shed and this was in tolerable repair.

"You can keep your boats here, Waring," said Mr. Belton when he had infuriated his son Charles by showing Cecil Waring the pumping-house at great length. "We managed to keep this shed in pretty good state. That's the old boat the rush-cutters used," and there was the flat-bottomed boat, which Commander Waring pronounced to be more or less seaworthy. "And you'll find some punt poles on the wall. I had them all wrapped up in tarpaulin after they were last used, whenever that was."

"By Jove, they aren't in bad condition," said Cecil Waring after examining them. "Shall we have a go, Charles?"

Not unwilling, Charles agreed and the boats were ready for use in a few minutes.

"Sorry, but we'll have to take our shoes off," said Charles. "I don't think these coracle-things will stand them. We'll have to use something with rubber soles for the real races. Come on."

With masterly bends and swoops he sent his coracle flying across the lake followed by Cecil Waring, among the lily pads and halfway round the island, when the thick bed of rushes stopped further progress.

"We'll have to get these cut," Cecil Waring shouted to Charles.

"More likely have to cut them ourselves," Charles shouted back. "Old Humble isn't fit for it. Come on. I'll race you up the straight."

Cecil Waring put his whole body into this peculiar form of punting and in spite of nearly losing his punt pole in a sudden treacherous depth, drew up at the home end with a flourish.

"That's a nasty pot-hole," he said to Charles. "I nearly lost my pole in it."

"Oh that. It's a spring," said Charles. "The water never quite freezes over it. That's where Heather Adams fell in one year. It was all her own fault because we had put up a Danger sign and she was too cross to see it. My brother Freddy got her out and mother put her to bed. That was the day I went back to my guns. I must say the parents were awfully decent about it. I think they really minded a bit," in saying which words, though they may sound inadequate, Charles Belton was showing unusual sympathy for the older generation who can only stand by and wait.

While the two men were on the lake Susan Belton had come down to see the sport, with her husband, Captain Belton, R.N., back from London where he was working at the Admiralty, and no sooner had the adventurers landed than the two naval men fell into shop, making Charles feel rather out of it. But he was a sweet-tempered creature and took it in good part. Mr. Belton had gone home some time ago, for the evenings in that chilly summer were no pleasure at all to anyone and there was an unspoken competition between him and his wife to grab and keep Mrs. Morland's new Madame Koska book which Mrs. Belton had got from the county library.

"She's dedicated it to Lisa Bedale," said Mr. Belton who, taking we think unfair advantage of his wife, had gone up to her bedroom while she was talking to their faithful and tyrannous old maid Wheeler and stolen it from the bedside table. "Never heard of her."

"You have," said his wife, almost sharply. "It's Lady Silverbridge."

"Lady Silverbridge was a Dale," said Mr. Belton, speaking as Messrs. Burke and Debrett rolled into one. "Bedale isn't a Barsetshire name."

"It isn't a name at all," said Mrs. Belton. "She writes under that name. I suppose we'll have to open the grounds for the Barsetshire Archæological in August. We really ought to do something about them. It's our turn. Perhaps Lord Silverbridge would speak. Have you their letter, Fred?"

"Whose?" said her husband, looking up with ostentatious patience from his book.

"The Archæological's, of course," said his wife. "I saw their envelope at breakfast yesterday."

"Yes, my dear. I've got it," said her husband in the abstracted voice of a lotus-eater. And then impelled, though unwillingly, by his innate courtesy, he got up and went to his study, with Mrs. Morland's thriller tucked firmly under his arm.

"Thank you, Fred," said his wife when he came back, pretending not to have noticed his Rape of the Book. "July— August—the Archæological haven't got anything the week after Bank Holiday. The second Saturday in August would be best if it suits you. Charles will be here unless he is going abroad and we might get the rushes cut. And Elsa and the children will be down."

"Well, my dear, you have to arrange it all, not I," said her husband. "Dr. Ford always says a doctor has to let old people kill themselves in their own way and I daresay he's right."

"The second Saturday in August then," said Mrs. Belton, ignoring his ungentlemanly remarks about old people. "Does Orchid, the lovely mannequin, get away from the private asylum?"

"I shan't tell you," said her husband. "But you can take it to bed. I've looked at the end and—"

"No," said Mrs. Belton. "That's cheating. I shall tell Mrs. Morland, with which awful threat she kissed the top of her husband's head and went upstairs.

But long before this the glacial atmosphere of a summer evening had driven the rest of the party back to Dowlah Cottage where Freddy Belton and Cecil Waring were able to continue their delightful conversation about all the places where they might have met each other during the war and didn't, and confided to each other what they thought of Sir Joseph Porter, K.C.M.G. (grandson of the well-known First Lord of the Admiralty), Permanent Secretary of the Red Tape and Sealing Wax Department and celebrated for thwarting, burkeing and generally obstructing any friendly relations between that body and the Admiralty.

"Sorry, gents, but we've only beer," said Captain Belton when his wife had gone to bed. So beer it was and then Cecil Waring and Charles went back to the Priory.

"I must say my part looks a bit gloomy," said Cecil Waring as he looked at his hideous ancestral (for three generations) home with not a light showing on his side and then at the Priory School wing with cheerful clashings and giggles coming from the kitchen and lights in several windows.

"Is that you, Cecil?" said the voice of the Headmaster, Philip Winter.

"It is," said his brother-in-law. "And I've brought your beggarly usher back with me. We're going to have a sporting event at Harefield. Punting collapsible dinghies round a lake with a bottomless pot-hole and entirely blocked by rushes."

"Like Mopsa the Fairy," said Mrs. Philip Winter, she who had been Leslie Waring, and a look of amused understanding passed between her and her sailor brother.

"Too, too Jean Ingelow," said Charles, parodying, we regret to say, his friend Clarissa Graham with whom he had what his mother had called an understanding: which we think describes it very well.

"So long as it doesn't clash with our Parents' Day," said Philip, but as the Harefield Regatta was to be in August all was well.

CHAPTER 4

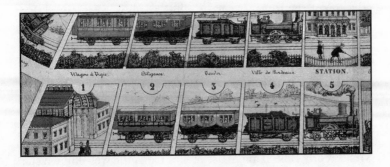

The county did not take so much interest in Cecil Waring's return to his hideous ancestral home as might have been expected. Partly because of petrol being let loose, and even more because of everyone being increasingly busy and harassed; though had the county known its good fortune it might have counted itself lucky beside unfortunate London, the step-sister of cities, all browbeaten, ill fed, and driven to dumb frenzy by (a) hordes of prosperous swarthy aliens who got everything they wanted and (b) food after five years of peace more mercilessly rationed in quality and quantity; not to speak of the hard-working inarticulate masses who could not afford even their wretched portion of controlled butter or controlled meat.

Cecil Waring himself remained entirely unconscious of the county's defection. He had his much loved sister Leslie Winter at hand, he got on very well with her husband, Philip Winter. He also enjoyed the society of Charles Belton, of the senior master who had just got his second pip by the skin of his teeth before peace broke out, of the junior master who like Charles had been a captain, and of a new master, Mr. Swan, formerly celebrated at Southbridge School for what in the army he had learnt to call dumb insolence. And though Cecil Waring was distinctly older than these gentlemen, who were very nearly thirty now, he had the youthfulness of mind which so often accompanies his noble profession and was accepted by the staff as an equal, especially where cricket was concerned, for he had always been as keen a cricketer as the Royal Navy can allow and it was rumoured that he had put up nets and a matting pitch on the deck of the battleship in which he had last served: but this we are not in a position to affirm or deny.

The second half of the summer term was now well on its way and Cecil Waring had watched the young gentlemen at play, bowled to some of them, kindly batted some of their bowling and considerably abated the conceit of young Dean, nephew of Mrs. Freddy Belton and Miss Jessica Dean the well-known star at the Cockspur Theatre.

"The worst of a prep school," said Philip Winter, as he with his staff and his wife and his brother-in-law were having some South African sherry on a Sunday before supper, "is that the boys grow up."

Charles Belton said they grew up at public schools too.

"Not so badly as at prep schools," said Philip, stoutly defending his own grievances. "They come here trailing clouds of glory—few and tattered I admit, but clouds—and they leave us as fledgling devils. At a public school they arrive as devils and gradually become respectable."

"I wasn't respectable," said Mr. Swan indignantly. "I used to look at masters through my spectacles and make them nervous."

"*Touché*," said Philip. "But I was young then and still believed in Russia. I even went so far as to begin learning the language, till I used my brains."

"What on earth did your brains tell you?" said his wife.

"They told me there wasn't any book by any Russian that I wanted to read," said Philip. "And if anyone says *War and Peace* I shall tell them that Stendhal gives you a better impression of war in two pages than Tolstoy in two hundred. And that, in case any of you were thinking of saying it," he added, "is showing off."

"O.K., Colonel," said the senior assistant master. "But to go back to what you were saying, one is going to miss the fledgling devils. Addison and Pickering, for instance. Do you remember the Breaking Up when they and young Dean found a hedgehog strangled in the strawberry nets where they had no business to be and had a funeral?"

"I do," said Philip. "And Pickering fell off his bicycle and skinned his knee and then showed off the yorker he was going to bowl and fell down in the drive and skinned it all over again."

"And Matron put peroxide on Pickering's knee," said Leslie Winter, "and all the little beasts came to watch it fizzle," and the amount of warm affection that Leslie put into the words "little beasts" would have surprised anyone who did not know how much one can love them. She had always liked little boys, partly because they made such excellent nursemaids for Master Noel Winter (called after Noel Merton) and Miss Harriet Winter (called after Leslie's aunt Lady Waring), and when nice Nannie Gale went for her holiday Leslie could always leave the children in charge of one or two of the young gentlemen while she attended to her other duties.

Presently Marigold, the village problem-girl, who performed in an affable and *dégagé* manner the duties of parlourmaid at the Priory School, opened the door, said: "It's ready," and went away leaving the door open. This her employers rightly considered as an announcement of Sunday supper and the party went into the dining-room where Marigold was looking at herself in the mirror over the large old-fashioned sideboard.

"I thought you were going to the Barchester Odeon tonight, Marigold," said Leslie Winter.

"Well, I was, Mrs. Winter," said Marigold, "because it's a lovely film with that new star Pippa Parson, she's got a lovely quoffour with a side parting, it's ever so chick" and as she spoke Marigold raised a rather dirty hand with stumpy fingers and blood-red nails and smoothed a long tress which hung like yellow seaweed over her right eye, thus clearly intimating to her audience that her coiffure was modelled on that of Miss Pippa Parson, "but Geoff Coxon said he wanted to go to the dogs, so

I said if it was the money he grudged I wasn't one to put up with a fellow that was mean. I cried ever so when the words had left my mouth, Mrs. Winter, but Mum said a girl didn't had ought to make herself cheap, so I came back. But I dessay Geoff'll be after me all the same," and with a final caress to the depressing golden lock she went out of the room sideways, turning the full battery of her charms upon Cecil Waring, who took no notice of her at all.

"Dreadful girl," said Philip Winter, but as someone made this remark, or one very like it, at pretty well every meal no one took much notice. "How did you get on with your little boats, Cecil?"

"Very well indeed," said his brother-in-law. "Charles's people were extremely kind, and if we can get the rushes cut we ought to have a very good regatta. There was a young Updike who seemed keen and a son of Dr. Perry's who wanted me to have leprosy."

"How *horrid* of him," said Leslie Winter. "Why?"

"Scientific zeal, I think," said her brother. "I shall have to go over to Silverbridge some time this week, Leslie. Uncle Harry owned some houses there and I shall have to see his lawyers."

"Walker and Winthrop?" said Leslie.

"Well, they're either that, or Winthrop and Walker, or Walker, Walker and Winthrop, or—anyway," said her brother, "it is a Winthrop that I'm going to see. They have had an offer for The Lodge, that old house across the bridge, and as the Red Tape and Sealing Wax people have been after it I would like to get it settled. Once let your house to a Government Office and you might as well have the military quartered in it."

"Or Mixo-Lydian refugees," said Philip. "By the way what happened to those dreadful Brownscu's who were at Southbridge?"

But no one had any news of that odious couple who, we are glad to say, were safely at Bathwater Cold, away in the Cotswolds, running a school for peasant-weaving, folk-dancing, and (incidentally) how to live in Arctic conditions with very nasty food and quarrelling all the time.

After supper and some amicable and ill-informed discussions of world affairs the whole party settled down to talk school shop. Leslie noticed that her brother was rather quiet and asked him afterwards if he was bored. Not a bit, he said. In fact he rather liked being bored.

"Oh dear! You ought to get married," said Leslie, at once offering the happily married woman's panacea for all earthly troubles, to which Cecil Waring replied that much as he liked the idea he had never yet seen the girl, or married woman either for that matter, that he could bear the idea of being shut up in the same house with for more than a weekend; if that, he added.

"There wasn't ever anyone—?" said Leslie hopefully.

"Not a sight nor a smell of one," said her brother, letting down the Royal Navy's reputation for gallantry with a run. "I love them all. But marry them—no! Besides—" and he stopped.

"I know what you were going to say," said Leslie. "Your bullet or whatever it is. But you don't *understand*, Cecil. I'd have married Philip if he had lost all his arms and legs; if he had been going to die next day."

"You're a good girl," said her brother, "and a plucky one. And I may say a lucky one. And Philip is an extremely decent chap. Don't bother about me, old girl. Even if I did fall in love I couldn't very well propose marriage. I've still got an ounce or so of metal wandering about inside me. It wouldn't be fair."

"Do you think women *want* fairness?" said Leslie. "They want what they want, you old idiot. Come and look at the children."

So they went up to the night nursery and saw Master Noel and Miss Harriet lying in a most divine and abandoned way in the arms of Morpheus and then Cecil said he must go home.

The polite way to get from the School to Cecil's part of the Priory was to leave from the front door, walk along a gravel path and go into his quarters by the old back door. But there was a simpler and far more pleasant route through the school kitchen and so by a stone-flagged passage. In the kitchen Selina Hopkins the school cook and her mother Mrs. Allen who had been nurse to the old Warings' boy, killed just before the Armistice in 1918, were having cups of tea.

"You can have some tea, Master Cecil, and Miss Leslie too if she likes," said Nannie Allen, which being equivalent to a royal command, her ex-charges sat down on the clean scrubbed kitchen chairs at the clean scrubbed kitchen table and accepted cups of very strong heavily sugared tea.

"Well now, Master Cecil, what have *you* been up to this last week?" said Nannie Allen.

Cecil, feeling that her unspoken rider was, "and don't do it," gave her a brief résumé of his visit to Harefield with Charles and the plan to have punting races on Mr. Belton's lake.

"Well, Master Cecil, if you get your feet wet and catch a nasty cold, don't say I didn't tell you," said Nannie. "Miss Belton married Admiral Hornby," which remark, though savouring of Mr. F.'s aunt, was well understood by Cecil and Leslie to be a threnody for Elsa Belton who being married to her Admiral could not be free for Nannie's Commander. "Give my regards to Miss Wheeler when you go, Master Cecil. She was Under me once and if you told her to wash anything she *washed* it. Not like the girls now—a lick and a promise. And there's Miss Emmy Graham, Lady Graham's eldest daughter," said Nannie thoughtfully.

"And if it comes to that there is the Duke's daughter," said Cecil rather impatiently, "and I think Lady Lufton has two girls."

"No need to show temper, Master Cecil," said Nannie. "What's the matter, Selina?" for her daughter's lovely eyes were brimming with tears, as indeed they did on every possible occasion, without in the least spoiling her looks.

"It's only poor Lady Lufton," said Selina, her pretty silvery hair seeming to wind itself into yet more elaborate tendrils as she wiped her eyes. "Fancy his Lordship dying and there's the two young ladies and poor Lord Lufton being the Lord now, at his age and all. It seems as if it had to be."

"Had or not, it *is*, Selina," said Nannie. "And if his young Lordship has been properly brought up he'll know that whom the Lord loveth He chasteneth."

"And think of the death-duties," said Selina through her tears. "Millions and millions that Cripps is taking they do say, and poor young Lord Lufton and his mother and the young ladies. And they do say Lord Lufton is a great friend of Margaret's. There was a piece in the paper about it and a photo with—"

"Now my girl," said Nannie, in such a voice of authority that both the Warings felt quite pale inside, "if you mean Her Royal Highness the Princess Margaret, you say so. If your father had heard you talk like that he'd have—well I don't know what he'd have done," at which the Warings nearly had the giggles, for it was well known that the late Mr. Allen, a dashing commercial traveller, had drunk himself and his business into the grave within a couple of years of his marriage, leaving his penniless widow to fend for herself and the little Selina.

At this moment ex-Sergeant Hopkins, Selina's husband who gardened and did a thousand odd jobs for the school, appeared at the kitchen door and was just going to retire from the tearful scene when Nannie Allen saw him and sharply told him to come in and shut the door after him and not keep them all in a draught, which he obediently did.

"Make some more tea, Selina," said Nannie Allen. "I could do with another cup and I daresay Miss Leslie and Master Cecil could too."

Neither of the Warings wanted any more tea, but sooner than face Nannie's displeasure they basely said how nice it would be and by the time the kettle had boiled Marigold came in, her golden hair more over one side of her face than ever, her mouth freshly reddened.

"Ow. Sorry, I'm sure," said Marigold, stopping dead at the sight of the gentry.

"Take that nasty stuff off your mouth, Marigold, and you can have a cup of tea," said Nannie Allen. "Where have you been?"

"Well, I had Words with Geoff and I said I wouldn't go to the Odeon with him," said Marigold, obediently rubbing her mouth with a very dirty handkerchief, "but when I'd said it I cried ever so and then I came back here and then Geoff took his Dad's car and we got to the Odeon in time for the big film. We raced every car on the road, Mrs. Allen and it was a ever so lovely film. It's all about Lord Nelson, a Nadmiral he was like Admiral Hornby, and he met Lady Hamilton at the Isle of Capree and they had a lovely song-and-dance number, 'Meet me in Trafalgar Square.' And there was a lovely newsreel of Margaret at the races in—"

"Now, Marigold, that's not the way to speak," said Selina virtuously. "Her Royal Highness you say, or Princess Margaret. And don't let me hear you talk that way again."

"Nor me neither," said Nannie Allen. "Anyone would think you were old Cripps. And don't slouch over your tea like that."

"Pack-drill; that's what that Marigold wants," said Sergeant Hopkins. "These girls they don't know the King's Regulations. Another cup of tea please, Ma."

"Well, Nannie, we really must—" Leslie began, when Marigold, taking a rather toothless comb from a dirty bag and smoothing her golden lock, said: "Geoff Coxon says Lady Hamilton's legs hadn't got anything on me and he'd meet me in Trafalgar Square any night I liked. He's a lovely boy."

On this Nannie, Selina, and Sergeant Hopkins spoke their minds very strongly, and Marigold was sent to bed.

"And what her room is like, Miss Leslie," said Selina in a hushed voice. "I wouldn't like to tell you."

"No, don't," said Leslie, who felt that the supercharged domestic atmosphere was getting too much for her. "Good-night, Nannie. Good-night, Selina and Hopkins."

Cecil Waring gave Nannie Allen a hug at which she bridled

with pleasure, said good-night to Selina and asked Sergeant Hopkins if he would come over to Harefield one day and help to cut the rushes on the lake.

"Anything you say, sir," said Sergeant Hopkins.

Leslie accompanied her brother down the stone passage. At the door of his part of the Priory she kissed him good-night.

"It is heaven to have you here, Cecil," she said. "But I do wish—"

"No, Leslie, I am *not* going to marry either of those Lufton girls," said her brother. "Nor anybody. Not unless I fall in love."

"And she does," said Leslie, and fled back down the passage.

The Commander went to his sitting-room and began to deal with correspondence about his various philanthropic—or rather, phil-whatever-the-Greek-word-for-boy-is-ic schemes. His sister Leslie Winter saw his light as she went to bed.

"Cecil is very late," she said to her husband.

"And so are you, my love," said Philip. "And do try to remember that Cecil is grown up."

"But *I'm* not," said Mrs. Philip Winter, the highly competent ex-civil servant, the pleasant and well-poised wife of the Headmaster of a preparatory school so flourishing that its proprietor hardly knew what to do with it.

"I know that, my love," said Philip. "And I love it. And you. But do leave Cecil alone. If he wants a wife he'll find one. The luck of the Navy."

Accordingly next day Cecil Waring got into his car and drove to Silverbridge. This town, as most people acquainted with Barsetshire know, is celebrated for its very steep High Street which runs down to the river, there spanned by a handsome eighteenth-century bridge with rather a high hump, which combination of hill and bridge is so dangerous to heavy traffic that the Southbridge United Viator Passenger Company's buses and all motor lorries have to go round by the lower road; which has probably saved the life of the fine old stone and brick houses in the High Street.

Cecil Waring drove straight to the lawyer's office; a good handsome old red brick house in the middle of the town where after the old fashion he did his business on the ground floor and lived above it, which as he was an elderly bachelor worked very well. The two men had corresponded and telephoned but had not met and each, to his interest and pleasure, saw in the other exactly what a lawyer and a Commander ought to look like. Mr. Winthrop was a spare man with keen eyes behind his rather old-fashioned glasses, an equally old-fashioned bow tie with his morning coat and what Cecil afterwards described to the Winters as a post-office mouth exactly like Wemmick.

"Well now, about The Lodge, Sir Cecil," said Mr. Winthrop actually, and to Cecil's intense pleasure, putting his fingertips together. "It was well kept up, as indeed all your late uncle's house-property was, and we shall have no difficulty in letting it. The question is, to whom. As I have wrote to you, the Red Tape and Sealing Wax Department have made an offer for it. They can pay a good rent and your money will be safe. Whether you like to let to a government department it is of course for you to decide."

Cecil said that was exactly what he wanted to consult Mr. Winthrop about, to which Mr. Winthrop replied that he could lay facts and figures before his client but could not attempt to influence his personal feelings.

"Well, I really don't know what they are at the moment," said Cecil. "I don't want the house and I do want a good rent and good tenants. Have you had any other offers?"

"Several," said Mr. Winthrop. "Amalgameted Vedge, the big market-garden combine, have approached me. So have the Holman Fertilizer group—you know they include Vimphos and Bono-Vitasang and Phospho-Manuro and several other chemical fertilizers."

He paused, waiting to hear his client's views.

"I must say they all sound pretty depressing," said Cecil, to which Mr. Winthrop replied that he must decide for himself.

"I had much rather you decided for me," said Cecil, at which the lawyer smiled in courteous deprecation of the whims of a well-to-do naval gentleman.

"I am not busy this morning," said Mr. Winthrop. "Suppose we go down and look at the property. I had arranged to meet a representative of the Red Tape and Sealing Wax Department this morning and show him the establishment. Will you come with me? He need not know that you are the owner, and it may help you to come to a decision."

This seemed to Cecil Waring a sensible arrangement and he agreed.

"I can run you down," he said.

"Would you very much mind walking if you aren't pressed for time," said Mr. Winthrop. "It is one of my greatest pleasures to walk down the High Street and over the bridge. One cannot appreciate them from a car."

Commander Waring was amused by his lawyer's hidden romance and agreed, so the two men went down the steep High Street where fine old houses still stood, though alas too often masked as to their lower stories by shop fronts.

"We haven't got a Gaiters' yet, nor a Sheepskins' nor a Lukes and Huxley," said Mr. Winthrop, naming three of the great combines whose fascias (we believe this to be the correct trade expression) have set the Mark of the Beast (which words we use in an entirely Pickwickian sense) upon so many beautiful country towns, great and small. "People who want them can go to Barchester," and though nothing was further from Mr. Winthrop's mind than to show contempt for the cathedral city, it sounded very much as if he found it on the whole less a flower of cities than his native Silverbridge. So they came to the river and the stone hump-backed bridge. When they were at the middle Mr. Winthrop paused.

"You know," he said, "I have always lived here, but I never get tired of this view," and Cecil Waring, looking at it for the first time since his boyhood, could not but agree.

In former days a good deal of traffic had come into Barsetshire by the river. By the time the river reached Barchester it was not so navigable and Silverbridge had been, from the Great Age of the wool trade onwards, the unloading port for boats and barges. For some two or three hundred yards along the river was a wide stone and cobble-paved wharf with a row of high warehouses on the land side. Cranes and ropes and pulleys to fill their higher stories were everywhere and the great stone bollards along the water front were heavily scored where ships' ropes had moored vessels to the quay. One depressed horse was standing in the shafts of an empty cart, looking as limp and relaxed as Petroushka at the end of the ballet.

"It was quite a busy port in my grandfather's time," said Mr. Winthrop, to which Cecil found no adequate answer, so they pursued their journey down the other side of the hump and fifty yards or so along the road to where a lane forked off to the right. Passing under a low red brick wall with rhododendrons behind it, they came to a wrought-iron gate between two brick pillars. A short drive brought them to a gravel sweep and a red brick house which sat as comfortably and lovingly among lawns and flower-beds as a broody hen among her young. From the house the ground, bounded on its far side by a row of tall, clipped limes, like a fortress wall, fell away towards the river. At the end of the slope was a terrace with a pierced brick wall and a brick summer-house at each end of it, all incredibly peaceful in the sunshine which had obligingly appeared as if to make the scene perfect.

"My grandfather used to tell me that when he was a boy and people still dined in the late afternoon," said Mr. Winthrop, "he was allowed to sit with the gentlemen as they took their wine in one of the summer-houses and fish out of the window with a piece of string and a bent pin. There were plenty of boats up and down the river then. Sir Harry's last tenants were retired Indian Army people, very quiet and orderly, paid regularly and went to church every Sunday," at which announcement Cecil felt vaguely that Mr. Winthrop regarded him as responsible for the orderly and God-fearing behaviour of further tenants. "The church," Mr. Winthrop continued, "is in the grounds, as you see, and a clergyman comes over to take an eleven o'clock service and gives no trouble at all," and then as they walked back Commander Waring saw, embowered in lime trees, a small and agreeable red brick church with a gilded vane on the little tower.

"I expect you would like to look over The Lodge," said Mr. Winthrop and Cecil obediently followed him with a feeling that the house was even now transferring all responsibility for its own safety and happiness from Mr. Winthrop to himself, and that it was of the utmost importance that he should live up to its standards.

Mr. Winthrop took from a pocket a large key and opened the front door. They stepped into a hall, panelled with white wood, running back to a glass door at the further end through which they saw another large lawn and beyond it the wall of a kitchen garden.

"Only deal," said Mr. Winthrop, tapping a panel affectionately, "but they understood good proportions then. The drawing-room is the same," and he stood aside for Cecil Waring to pass into the room, also running from back to front of the house, with elegant carved and painted mantelpieces and, as Cecil's naval eye noted, a wooden floor as well joined as the planks of a ship."

"There are some old curtains and carpets," said Mr. Winthrop, "but they are all stored upstairs. The dining-room is on the other side of the hall," and they went across into a square room, also panelled.

"All the evening sun in here," said Mr. Winthrop. "When people dined at five or six they could sit and enjoy the sunshine. No Summer Time then. And after dinner it must have been very pleasant to walk or sit in the garden. Would you like to see the rest?"

The owner said he wanted to see it very much.

"Service room behind the dining-room and a modern kitchen behind that again," said Mr. Winthrop opening doors. "The old kitchens downstairs are in very good condition and perfectly dry, but I doubt whether anyone will use them again. The stairs go up here. They are not very grand but they are well lighted from the skylight, as you see," and he led his client up a square oak staircase into a wide corridor that ran the length of the house.

"Four good bedrooms," he said, opening and shutting doors. "Two modern bathrooms and two small rooms. The Chinese wallpaper is about a hundred and fifty years old. And there are more bedrooms on the top floor, but I daresay you have seen enough."

Cecil Waring said he would like to see it all while he was there and he thought Mr. Winthrop's post-office mouth relaxed a little. So they went back to the staircase and up another flight to another corridor.

"Two bathrooms, four servants' rooms if you have any, or could be used as nurseries," said Mr. Winthrop. "And one large room in front which would make a good boxroom and general storage place," and he opened a door and stood aside for his client to go in. It was a long, rather low whitewashed room, with five windows overlooking the garden and the river. A good deal of furniture was stored in it and a number of large chests. In one corner a light wooden staircase against the back wall led to a wooden door and ended in a little gallery along the end of the room.

"What a work-room!" said Commander Waring. "One could have everything here—books, tools, work-tables—"

"—and a rope-walk," said Mr. Winthrop gravely, and both men laughed.

"You might like to see what is behind the door," said Mr. Winthrop, and his client ran lightly up the stair, turned the key and opened the door. In front of him was a sight calculated to drive any boy, or adventurous girl, or even a naval officer mad with joy. Behind the parapet along the front of the house was an enchanting prospect of tiled roofs and brick chimney-stacks with lead paths between them and all round the edge. Twenty-five years or so earlier young Cecil Waring would have climbed every roof (to the detriment of the tiles) and attempted to scale the brick chimney-stacks. Commander Waring contented himself by walking round inside the parapet and observing to the south the curve of the river, to the east and north his own grounds and the long line of the downs, to the west and the south again the roofs of Silverbridge, the deserted wharves and the humped bridge. A home to love and to live in. And then as his excellent common sense reasserted itself he considered that this would be no place for the scheme he had in mind. Naval orphans, however worthy of their hire, would not do in so essentially a family house as this. It would not be large enough and it would, if one were truthful, be far too good for them. He came inside, shut the door, and went down the little staircase.

"I must say it is a perfectly delightful property, Winthrop," he said. "I wish I could live in it myself, but I can't. There are all my uncle's old tenants at Beliers—and other reasons."

"Well, if you can't you can't," said Mr. Winthrop reasonably. "You'll find a lot of curtains and things in those chests." He opened one of them and took out a curtain of heavy gold brocade flushed with rose-pink.

"Drawing-room," he remarked. "Two sofas and four large chairs to match. Dining-room curtains the same. Long carpet for drawing-room, real Persian; like a flower-garden," said Mr. Winthrop with a fervour of which his client would not have suspected him. "Two very fine lustres in that crate. I've got the complete catalogues in my office," and he put the curtains away and shut the chest.

"There are some people in the garden," said Cecil Waring, leaning out of the window. "Would it be the Red Tape people?

One of them is a woman. Perhaps we had better go down and see."

"I don't know about any woman," said Mr. Winthrop as they went downstairs. "Mr. Harvey of the Red Tape and Sealing Wax has an excessively annoying sister who is at the Ministry of Interference at Gatherum. It might be she."

Commander Waring opened the front door (his own front door, he reminded himself with a thrill of ownership) and went out into the sunshine. The man and the woman had gone down the lawn and were looking out over the river, but another woman was standing in the sunshine on the gravel sweep. The sun was in Cecil Waring's eyes and he could hardly see her face, though he noted with approval her elegant nylon-clad legs and her sleek dark head.

"Trespassers will be prosecuted," said the stranger.

"Do you mean me?" said Cecil Waring.

"I would know better whether I meant you if I knew who you were," said the stranger. "I really meant myself."

"Cecil Waring at your service," said that gentleman, amused.

"Cora Palliser at yours," said the stranger. "And those are my brother Jeff and his wife. I believe we have no business here at all, but someone said The Lodge was to let so we came to see. They are looking for a house."

"Perhaps I had better explain that it is my house," said Cecil Waring. "It belonged to my uncle, Sir Harry Waring, and I can't live in it because I must look after his place which is a hideous house, but all the people on the estate expect one to."

"The Nelson touch," said the stranger, not unkindly. "Is this house really to let?"

"It is," said Cecil. "And I believe the Red Tape and Sealing Wax people are coming to look at it this morning."

"But my *dear*," said the stranger, "you cannot let this house to an office. It is a *gentleman's* house."

"I had never seen it before, but since going over it I have been thinking much the same myself," said Cecil. "The man from the

Red Tape has an appointment to see it this morning and that's why I'm here with my lawyer," and at that moment Mr. Winthrop joined them.

"Lady Cora," he said, almost bowing over the stranger's hand with a kind of gallant, old-fashioned courtesy. "Have you met Commander Sir Cecil Waring?"

"Only informally," said Lady Cora casting something uncommonly like a wink in Cecil's direction. "Listen, Mr. Winthrop. Silverbridge and Isabel are house-hunting. Is there a chance for them here?"

Mr. Winthrop said that a Mr. Harvey from the Red Tape and Sealing Wax Department was meeting him by appointment to look over it at half past eleven, and pulling out his old-fashioned gold watch he added: "Tut, tut, it is a quarter to twelve already," which greatly impressed his hearers.

By this time the other visitors had joined them.

"How are you, Winthrop?" said Lord Silverbridge. "I don't think you have met my wife?" and while Mr. Winthrop bowed again over Lady Silverbridge's hand as he had over her sister-in-law's, Cecil Waring was able to look at a tall pleasant-faced not-quite-young man and an unusually beautiful woman with the oval face that is so rare, fair hair, and very blue eyes.

"May I be introduced?" he said.

Lady Cora was obviously about to make some kind of introduction when Mr. Winthrop, who had his own ideas of protocol (and we venture to say they were good ideas), formally presented Commander Sir Cecil Waring to Lady Silverbridge.

"We heard," said Lady Silverbridge to Cecil," that The Lodge might be in the market. Might we ask, informally, whether this is so?"

Cecil Waring looked at Mr. Winthrop.

"It is your property, Sir Cecil," said his legal adviser. "Mr. Harvey has duly applied for a permit to view on behalf of the Red Tape and Sealing Wax Department and should be here now. He is in fact," said Mr. Winthrop, again consulting his majestic gold watch, "twenty-five minutes late," and even as he spoke a large and shining car was driven into the sweep and came to a standstill with a great swishing of gravel and out got Mr. Harvey, followed by a rather commanding not-so-young woman and a young man.

"I am afraid we are a little late, Winthrop," said Mr. Harvey. "I was in Conference and when Britannia calls, I must obey. My sister has come to give us the feminine touch," to whom Mr. Winthrop made a small bow which seemed to the lookers on to imply that the feminine touch was exactly what he could well have dispensed with. "And Thomas Grantly, one of our young neophytes," said Mr. Harvey. "You see I am well protected by my bodyguard."

Mr. Winthrop, giving no sign of seeing anything of the sort, said he had exactly half an hour at their disposal and this was the owner, Commander Sir Cecil Waring. He then looked round for the Silverbridges, but they had discreetly removed themselves to the river and were exploring the summer-houses. Lady Cora, who had been looking on with an air of detached amusement, now came forward and spoke to Miss Harvey, who as our readers may not remember was helping the Ministry of General Interference at Gatherum Castle by dismissing the female staff, directing married women and children into their jobs, and putting the children in crèches which were known to her friends and ill-wishers as baby-farms.

"Geoffrey!" said Miss Harvey. Her brother started nervously. "This is Lady Cora Palliser."

"So much more sensible than the old fashion of introducing the gentleman to the lady," said Lady Cora. "I adore looking at houses. Can I come round with you, Sir Cecil? Or do I say Commander Waring? And this is—" and she looked, kindly, at the third member of the visiting party.

"Oh, I'm Tom Grantly," said that young gentleman. "My people live at Edgewood."

"I know all about you," said Lady Cora, "from the Adamses.

I *adore* Mr. Adams. He put a new washer on the stable yard tap for father. And I'd as soon hear Mrs. Adams on pigs as anyone; sooner in fact. I adore them both. And you were farming over at Rushwater, weren't you?"

"Yes, I was," said Tom, who had been at first a little shy of Lady Cora but realized that she was what he inelegantly thought of as a good sort. "But I frightfully wanted to do something *real*, and I'm on approval at the Red Tape and Sealing Wax."

"Well?" said Lady Cora, mocking him a little with her dark eyes. "Does it approve? Do you approve? Is it real?"

"We are licking our young cub into shape," said Mr. Harvey who had overheard, with a laugh, but Lady Cora had turned and was going into the house.

"I am sorry that my time is limited," said Mr. Winthrop. "If you approve, Sir Cecil, I suggest that we should make a quick tour of the house and then if Mr. Harvey has specific points to raise we can discuss them later. Just now the matter in hand is for him to see the accommodation," to which Cecil agreed and for the second time that day Mr. Winthrop opened the rooms.

"The hall would be draughty in winter," said Mr. Harvey, "but we could easily put a partition across the end—"

"Which would black out the light," said his sister.

"—and have strip lighting installed,'" said Mr. Harvey with a swiftness that Lady Cora much admired. "It's a fine drawing-room. We could have at least twenty desks here and block up the fireplaces. Is there central heating, Waring?"

Cecil said he did not know.

"Central heating was installed by the last tenants," said Mr. Winthrop. "I understand that it was not satisfactory. Also the insurance people are raising a question about it."

"Oh, we can settle them easily," said Mr. Harvey. "And the dining-room? That would take at least ten typists. And behind it?"

Mr. Winthrop said a serving-room and a kitchen.

"Of course, Geoffrey, you will want the kitchen in the base-

Very well then: servants' hall for meals and the kitchen next
to it."

"No, Frances," said Mr. Harvey. "I would keep this kitchen
and use it as a dining-room for the senior staff and turn the
serving-room into a kitchen. We could make arrangements for
the junior staff elsewhere. Possibly in the old kitchen; and put in
a service lift from the serving-room, which will then be the kitchen,
to the basement. One kitchen would be enough. Economy is our
catchword—I mean watchword."

Mr. Winthrop, looking rather ostentatiously at his watch,
said unfortunately the basement kitchen was under the other
side of the house and a service lift from the present service room
would come out in the wine cellar.

"Well, we can leave that for the present," said Miss Harvey.
"And now, what about the first floor, which you would be using
for offices, I suppose. Oh dear, is this the *only* staircase, Sir
Cecil?"

Cecil, who was divided between rage and amusement, said
that he had only been over the house for the first time that
morning, but Mr. Winthrop knew all about it. Lady Cora,
catching his eye, adumbrated a wink and then made her face
perfectly blank. Mr. Winthrop with unmoved countenance led
the explorers upstairs, followed reluctantly by Cecil.

"Stop and talk to me," said Lady Cora, pulling Tom Grantly
by the sleeve. "I want to hear *all* about the Adams baby. Never
mind those others. And tell me about yourself. Where were you
in the war? My elder brother, the one you met just now, was in
Italy mostly and my younger brother Gerald was killed on
D-Day and lots of my friends were killed at Arnhem—poor
lambs," she added sadly.

"Well," said Tom. "I was training in England for quite a lot of
the war and when I did get abroad I wasn't even wounded. It
wasn't my fault," he added, anxious to please this elegant goddess who was condescending to inquire into his life.

"Dear boy, I know it wasn't your fault," said Lady Cora. "We can't all be heroes—or heroines either. The number of blitzes I was in and never anything worse than having a pair of gloves pinched in a First Aid Station you wouldn't believe. One just has to bear these things. And then what did you do?"

So Tom told her how he came home and went to Oxford and read Greats and somehow felt dissatisfied and how his father had been jolly decent about it and let him try to get taken on as a 'prentice estate agent and how he couldn't make a do of the book part though he loved the outdoor part, and how he had been working at Rushwater for the Martin Leslies and loved the work but felt he ought to be doing something more real, something with a career and a future in it.

"You may make a career in an office," said Lady Cora, quite kindly, "though if your Mr. Harvey is in any way like his sister, it will be a blighted career. Have you any idea what the prospects are, for a young man?"

Tom, who found Lady Cora's rather imperious manner not at all unpleasing, indeed almost flattering, said he supposed one would get on if one stuck to the job.

"Get on where?" said Lady Cora.

"I really don't know," said Tom, suddenly discovering that to be criticized and laughed at by one's family was one thing, and to submit to the same treatment from a delightful and good-looking woman who was also a Duke's daughter quite another. "One might be the Head of a Department, or even a Permanent Secretary."

"Take it from me," said Lady Cora, "that by the time you are as senior as that, most of the top dogs—top bitches I'd call them if we were alone—will be women. And God help the men. And the other women even more," she added dispassionately.

"Do you really think so?" said Tom.

"As far as anyone really thinks anything now," said Lady Cora, her dark eyes almost dim. "The people one cared for were

killed. England is in the mouth of the lion. But I'm talking
nonsense. You are young still."

"I suppose I'm about your age really," said Tom, suddenly
overcome by courage. "I'm twenty-eight. Not that you *look* as
old as that," he added, his courage deserting him.

"But I am," said Lady Cora, looking away across the lawn.
"I'm even older." Then suddenly turning her dark eyes upon
Tom she said: "I really was showing off myself. I won't do it
again," and she laughed with her low amused laugh.

"Then I'll show off too," said Tom. "I bet you don't know
where the mouth of the lion comes from."

"Of course I do," said Lady Cora. "It's—it's—oh, it's in the
Prayer Book somewhere."

"Psalm Twenty-two," said Tom. "I'm sorry," he added, self-
convicted of spiritual pride. "You see my father's a clergyman
and I read Greats."

"As far as I know neither would make you know your Psalms
unless you really wanted to," said Lady Cora. "Listen, Tom. If
the Red Tape people take this place I'll blow it up. Isabel and Jeff
must have it. Did you hear those awful Harveys blethering about
putting partitions into the rooms and strip lighting. I'd as soon
have soldiers in any house of mine. Sooner."

"They are pretty awful," said Tom, and then suddenly remembering loyalty to one's superior officers he added, without
much conviction, that Geoffrey Harvey wasn't a bad sort.

"Little liar!" said Lady Cora, with a look of conspiratorial
amusement.

"'Each glance of the eye so bright and black, Though I keep
with heart's endeavour—'" said Tom, not looking at her.

"That's Browning," said Lady Cora. "I didn't know anyone
read him now. Gerry adored him. What made you say that?"

"I think I have grown up," said Tom, to which Lady Cora for
once had no answer at all, nor could the discussion well have
continued, for the Harveys came quarrelling down the stairs in a
way to put anyone off his or her stroke. The subject under

consideration appeared to be the top attic where the curtains and carpets were stored; from which the door high up in the wall led to the roof.

"That room is simply made for a dormitory, Geoffrey," said Miss Harvey. "Put in partitions and fixed basins and there you are."

"I do wish, Frances," said her brother crossly, "that you would stop being so partition-minded. It's as bad as the partition of Poland.

"Cheap humour won't get you anywhere, Geoffrey," said his sister. "Still, do as you like. I only came here to give what advice I could—"

"—and *could* you!" said Mr. Harvey in a loud aside.

"—and if it isn't taken that is your affair," said his sister. "What do you think, Sir Cecil?" but Cecil did not at once answer, for he saw Lady Cora and Tom Grantly in what appeared to be intimate converse. There was no reason why they should not be. None at all. But it takes one a moment to come to this reasonable conclusion. Having come to it, or persuaded himself that he had, he said to Miss Harvey that as Mr. Winthrop was acting for him he felt he had better leave any business matters in his hands.

"We will let you know in a few days, Mr. Winthrop," said Miss Harvey. "We must rush now. Such a busy life at the Ministry of General Interference that one has to keep on the go all the time. Come along, Geoffrey."

"Excuse me one moment," said Mr. Winthrop. "You do not wish to proceed with the matter today then, Mr. Harvey?"

"My dear fellow," said Mr. Harvey, at which moment Tom Grantly said afterwards that he had seen the tips of Mr. Winthrop's wing collar vibrate with rage, "my Department cannot move in a hurry. We have to consider."

"Then I take it that no offer has been made," Mr. Winthrop continued.

"Offer?" said Mr. Harvey, who had just caught sight of Tom

Grantly laughing with Lady Cora. "I don't know. I really can't say. We have wasted far too much time here. I will ring you up. Are you coming, Grantly?"

"Certainly, sir," said Tom, getting to his feet almost as promptly as if he were still in the army. "Good-bye, Lady Cora."

"Good-bye," said her ladyship with a friendly look. "We will have another talk. I am going to improve your mind."

"You have already," said Tom, blushing furiously, and he followed his chief and his chief's sister to the waiting car.

Lady Cora, who had come out to watch them go, waved her handkerchief towards the river and almost at once Lord and Lady Silverbridge, emerging from one of the summer-houses, came across the lawn to them.

"Well, have you sold it?" said Lord Silverbridge to Cecil Waring, who looked at his lawyer.

"Not in the least," said Mr. Winthrop. "Mr. Harvey talked a great deal about the changes he might make, but he has not made any offer, good or bad."

"Oh, could we just look at it?" said Lady Silverbridge. "Just in case?"

It is difficult to refuse a very beautiful woman and if she is a Countess as well it is unreasonable. Mr. Winthrop, after again consulting his watch for form's sake, took the Silverbridges upstairs.

"What chance?" said Lady Cora, raising her dark eyes to meet Cecil Waring's blue eyes.

"Of what?" said he.

"Having the house," said Lady Cora. "You can't have those too too dreadful typists and people here. *Do* let Jeff and Isabel have it."

"I expect I shall have to," said Cecil. "Do you wish it?"

"If wishes were horses, Beggars would ride," said Lady Cora, looking away from him out of the window. "We are almost beggars now. I'm sorry. Even if my wish were a horse I *do* wish it."

"Then they'd better have it," said Cecil. "In any case Harvey is intolerable."

"You won't regret it?" said Lady Cora.

"I do not think I could regret anything that gave you pleasure," said Cecil. "I shall speak to Mr. Winthrop. And don't thank me too much, Lady Cora," he continued, as she made as if to speak. "Glad as I am to be able to please you in any way—in *any* way," he added, almost as if he were speaking aloud to himself, "it is an added pleasure to be able to inconvenience both Mr. Harvey and Miss Harvey," at which Lady Cora laughed her own rather husky attractive laugh and said that if he could find anyone nasty enough to marry Miss Harvey she would be deeply obliged, as she was making life for her female underlings at Gatherum a floating hell.

"I'm sorry that nice boy is in the Red Tape gang. Your Mr. Harvey has his knife into him already because the poor lamb was being nice to me while you all looked over the house," said Lady Cora. "Let's look at your garden while they are upstairs." So they went out by the door at the back of the hall, across the lawn and so into the walled kitchen garden, where an old gardener was removing the debris of the first peas. On seeing them he stuck his fork into the ground, leaned on it picturesquely and prepared to humour the gentry. But here he had miscalculated. Cecil Waring he might have tackled and floored, for that officer though brought up as a country boy had been so long at sea that he did not know the country people very well and was still a fairly easy prey. But Lady Cora, who knew nearly as much about her father the Duke of Omnium's remaining tenants as he did, had an unerring eye for impostors and dealt with them kindly but faithfully, so that when the old gardener said: "Nice morning, my lord," she replied that it was after twelve and this was Sir Cecil Waring who owned the house.

"After twelve?" said the old gardener. "Time I was off. I like my beer and if I don't get my beer there's others as gets it."

"And what is your name?" said Lady Cora.

"Grobury's my name," said the old man, "and Growberry's my nature," at which his hearers laughed; Lady Cora because she was amused though not impressed but Cecil, we fear, rather sycophantically.

"My brother and his wife are coming to live here," said Lady Cora. "He's Lord Silverbridge. He adores wall fruit, especially apricots," and she threw Cecil a glance of amused defiance.

"Ar," said the old gardener. "That's talking. When I was a boy there was apricocks in all the gentlemen's gardens. And now there's none. And for why?" and he paused dramatically.

"I don't know," said Cecil, feeding that he was cutting but a poor figure as a landowner.

"Some say dormice," said the old gardener. "Dormice is vermin and my dog he eats 'em. But it's not dormice," and he pulled up a tuft of grass and wiped the times of his fork.

"My turn," said Lady Cora. "What is it then?"

"Ar," said the old gardener. "That's what nobody knows. Not the gentry nor no one. My father's old uncle he was a master baker and he didn't know neither."

The rather valueless conversation might have gone on for much longer, skillfully leading up to a suggestion by the old gardener of great and consuming thirst and the transference of money from the Commander's pocket to Grobury's, had not the wrought-iron gate of the walled garden announced by a harsh grating squeak that visitors were approaching, and Mr. Winthrop with the Silverbridges came down the grass path.

"Well?" said Lady Cora to her sister-in-law.

"I can't tell you how perfect," said Lady Silverbridge. "We could shut up some of the rooms. And of course that top room would be the most *heavenly* nursery. Do you think—?" and she looked towards Cecil Waring, to which question Lady Cora replied that if between them they could not persuade Sir Cecil to do whatever they wanted, her name was stink.

"Oh, Sir Cecil," said Lady Silverbridge.

Cecil turned and his susceptible sailor's heart nearly stood still at the vision before him. Only two well-bred English-women; but so exquisite, so equal in their dark and their golden beauty; in Lady Cora's dark eyes and dark sleek hair and exquisite legs; in Lady Silverbridge's pure oval face, her blue eyes, her fair hair and her Juno-like figure, that he would willingly have fired a salute of a thousand guns for them on the spot.

"Oh, Commander Waring, have we *any* chance?" she said. "Of course the hall and the drawing-room are quite perfect, but it is the big attic. It would be *heaven* for a nursery."

Even Cecil Waring was beginning to put two and two together and all the chivalry of the British Navy rose in him— not unaccompanied by a sincere wish to thwart Mr. Geoffrey Harvey.

"I am in Mr. Winthrop's hands, Lady Silverbridge," he said with a kind of formal courtesy that suited him very well, "but unless he has any legal objections, I should like to have you as my tenants more than I can say. The house would be safe with you," he added.

"Oh, Mr. Winthrop," said Lady Cora, "*don't* have a *caveat* or whatever it is," and she laid her lovely fine-boned hand on the old lawyer's arm.

"The only *caveat* I can see," said Mr. Winthrop, who was enjoying himself immensely, "is *Caveat Emptor*. Which means that you should not buy a pig in a poke. But if your lawyers will get in touch with me, I see no reason at the present moment why you should not become the lessors of The Lodge."

"My *sweet!*" said Lady Cora, to the old lawyer's great amusement and satisfaction. "How soon do you want it, Isabel?"

Lady Silverbridge's lovely oval face assumed a slightly pinker colour as she said it would be very nice if they could get in almost at once, because then they could get the nurseries ready by November.

"Make it 'almost at once,'" said Cecil Waring with an echo of the quarter-deck and he looked at Mr. Winthrop whose post-office mouth spread into a grim smile as he said that he would do his best to satisfy all parties.

The Silverbridges and Lady Cora then went away in her shabby little car and Cecil Waring walked back with his lawyer over the hump-backed bridge.

"When you've lived as long in one place as I and my people before me," said Mr. Winthrop, as they walked up the steep High Street, "you will find almost everything repeats itself—has its roots. That is history, I suppose. Old Grobury's people were bakers here in a very good way of business, a long time ago that was. I was looking through some old papers of the firm's the other day and the Grobury of that time, somewhere in the fifties, was one of the principal creditors of that queer half-mad clergyman Mr. Crawley—the Dean is his grandson, or great-grandson I am not sure which—who was accused of stealing a cheque. It was a mistake and he was completely cleared. His daughter married Major Grantly, and that young Grantly who came over with the Red Tape people is her descendant. Life is very queer when you've seen as much of it as I have. But it all works out in the end. Well, good-bye, Sir Cecil, and we shall do our best for you. Lord Silverbridge is going to stand for Parliament, but I don't know whether it is to be Barchester or Silverbridge. Of course he couldn't have done it without his wife's money. She was a Dale and inherits a good deal of what is left of the Dunstable and Scatcherd fortunes. But you wouldn't know about all that. Good-bye. You will hear from me if there is anything to be signed. It has been a pleasure to meet you."

Commander Waring said the right things and drove homewards, reflecting as he went how impossible it was to know the county unless you had always known it all your life and wondering if he could ever hold his own in it. For though his boyhood had been spent a good deal at the Priory the sea had claimed him from his youth onwards. The Priory really needed a mistress. But who would care to live in so incommodious a house and have naval orphans in one wing. And how could one have naval orphans till Philip and Leslie had found a better home for their school. He almost wished he were safely back in the Mediterranean; perpetually on the alert, in hourly danger from aeroplanes and submarines, but at least feeling the ground firm under his feet.

CHAPTER 5

We do not for a moment wish to delude our readers nor cause them needless anxiety. Mr. Winthrop got to work and was presently able to assure Lord Silverbridge he could take possession of The Lodge almost at once. The Duke and Duchess of Omnium came over to inspect it, were delighted, and offered contributions of pictures, carpets, and furniture from the rooms at Gatherum that would never be used again. As the Duchess and her daughter-in-law were on very friendly terms Lady Silverbridge accepted some of them gratefully and said she simply could not bear others, especially the large malachite table with ormolu and lapis lazuli legs and the recumbent alabaster figure of a stout numph (known as the Gatherum Hebe) whose charms were so thinly veiled as to make her even more repellent than she would otherwise have been.

"You are quite right, my dear," said the Duchess. "We have tried to sell them repeatedly, but no one will buy them. They wouldn't suit The Lodge at all. Gerry painted a beard and moustache on her while he was small and Plantagenet was furious. Luckily it was only his nursery water-colour paint-box and washed off. You would have got on very well with him."

"I am sure I would," said Isabel Silverbridge. "I couldn't help liking any Palliser. Jeff and I want to call the baby Gerald if he is a boy. If he is a girl—" but the Duchess would not hear of such a thing, and then the Duke, who had been gossiping with old

Grobury in the garden, came in to suggest that Isabel should
have some Canalettos for the long drawing-room, to which she
did not say no.

"You *are* so good to me," she said, when the position of the
Canalettos had been settled and plans made for bringing various
nursery furnishings over from Gatherum.

"I think you are good to us, my dear," said the Duke, "and
Silverbridge is a very lucky man."

"I wish Cora could find anyone who would make her
happy," said the Duchess, who in her delight at having a real
daughter-in-law to gossip with treated her almost as her own
generation. "She is seeing a lot of that young Grantly from the
Red Tape and Sealing Wax office. It's quite a good family of
course, but——"

"I wish you wouldn't worry, dear Duchess," said Isabel. "She
is only being kind to him. She can't help being kind. He tells her
about the cows at Rushwater and she finds it very restful," at
which they couldn't help laughing.

"That's a very good arrangement you have," said the Duchess.
"I mean having a serving-room and a kitchen behind the
dining-room. I wish we could have something like that at
Gatherum."

"And that nice cloak-room at the back of the hall," said his
Grace who enjoyed nothing more than poking round the domestic side of other people's houses. "I always think it is such a
good idea to have *two* rooms; one to wash your hands and hang
coats and the other——"

"Yes, Plantagenet," said the Duchess. "But it is a question of
pipes. If the General Interference people will let us use their new
hot-water system we might manage it. But I don't think they will."

"It does seem an extraordinary thing," said the Duke, "that we
have two miles of copper piping in the Castle and can't have hot
water."

Lady Silverbridge asked if Cora couldn't do something.

"She would if she could, I am sure," said the Duke. "She is a

very good girl. But she has so much to do. The Red Cross and
the Conservatives and the gardens—our men are pretty old now
and we can't get new ones and if we did they don't know
anything. I wish we had a man like your old Grobury, Isabel."

"So do I, Duke-Father," said his daughter-in-law, who had
invented his name which rather amused his Grace. "I'd sell him
to you for sixpence if I could, for he is a frightful bully. But I
don't think he could go and live with foreigners at his age," for
the Countess of Silverbridge came of good county stock and
knew that—for the old people at any rate—to move more than
two or three miles from the neighborhood they had been born
and brought up in was like going to Xanadu or the Klondike.
"But I'll have a talk with Cora about the hot water."

"Thank you, my dear," said the Duke, who had an affection
for his daughter-in-law that might have made some daughters
slightly jealous but, as Lady Cora herself said, she couldn't
possibly produce an heir to the dukedom and Isabel not only
could, but was going to: so what. "I wonder sometimes if Cora
wants to marry. She is such a good girl and works so hard for us.
She might feel a sense of duty to us," said his Grace, who had
suffered from that noble failing all his life and sacrificed many of
his own pleasures to it.

"She has brought that young Grantly to Gatherum two or
three times," said the Duchess, dispassionately, as one to whom
Tom Grantly was neither here nor there, except in the eye of the
beholder.

"Darling Duchess, don't be a goose," said her daughter-in-
law, most affectionately. "He is just about Cora's age so she
thinks of him as a schoolboy, and gives him jam-tarts and takes
him to the pantomime."

The Duke said there wouldn't be any pantomime till Boxing
Day and he would like to see a pantomime again, even if it was
only the Barchester one, upon which Isabel said she would take
the whole family and they could all join in the choruses.

"You are so kind," said the Duke. "I never knew anyone with

money—you must not mind my mentioning money—who used it so well and wisely as you do. There was a very good song, I remember, before this last war, about Gorgonzola in the Barchester pantomime. Do you remember it, my dear? There was a very good line about You put it on the shelf And it runs off by itself. Gerry sang so loud that we were nearly turned out."

The Duchess said she remembered it very well. But, she added, would it be WISE for Isabel to think of a pantomime? To which her daughter-in-law replied that as the baby was due in the middle of November she didn't see why they shouldn't go on Boxing Day, and she would take a box.

"A box for Boxing Day. How very appropriate," said her father-in-law, pleased with his own joke, and then the Duke and Duchess went away.

"Beauty. And Brains. And Goodness," said the Duchess when she and her husband were alone. "How lucky we are, Plantagenet," and we do not think there can have been a better tribute from any mother-in-law to any daughter-in-law.

At this time Lady Cora was spending a week at The Lodge to help her sister-in-law to get settled, as Lord Silverbridge went for two days a week to London where he worked in a publisher's office, but was giving it up before Christmas so that he could give more time to his wife and to politics and nurse the constituency of Barchester. For Mr. Adams had announced his intention of not standing again and Lord Silverbridge had unanimously been selected by the Barchester Conservative Association as their candidate. Though we do not wish to be tactless it was only because of his wife's wealth that he could afford to accept the offer. But Isabel loved the country in whose service her first love had fallen and almost wished she were less comfortably off so that her sacrifice might be greater; for which her husband had chidden her, saying that she really must consider her offspring's future, and they had laughed about it.

* * *

"That's that," said Lady Cora when, after her parents had gone, she came down from the nursery-to-be where she had been whitewashing and painting, both of which she did as well as everything else she did, and with no apparent effort.

"It's all looking very nice," she said, flopping elegantly on a sofa in the drawing-room. "What's my face like?"

"There's some pale yellow paint on your eyebrow and a bit of whitewash in your hair," said Isabel.

"They can stay there," said Lady Cora. "Anyone coming to tea?"

Isabel said not so far as she knew.

"Well, it's after five now, so doubtless Tom Grantly will be coming and almost equally doubtless Cecil Waring and thank God doubtless *not* the Harvey man," said Lady Cora. "But not just yet, I hope. I simply *must* relax. I can't think how Michael Angelo ever painted the Vatican or whatever it was. If I've had one blob of whitewash in my eye when I was doing the cornice I've had twenty. But it's a lovely job and the Heir ought to be grateful."

Her sister-in-law thanked her very much and said she wished she wouldn't work herself so hard.

"What else is there to do, my sweet?" said Lady Cora. "I'm not married so I can't have children. Don't mistake me though. I know ALL about sex-psychology and how wonderful it is to have a dear little one even if you don't know who the father was, but somehow it doesn't click. I'm good. It sounds a silly thing to say and it's through no fault of my own. But I am."

"You are an angel," said Isabel, quite truly meaning it.

"Just arrested development," said Lady Cora. "If Froggy hadn't broken both his legs at Arnhem and then been shot . . . Oh, well."

"Cora; darling!" said Isabel.

"Froggy once began to write a Limerick about me," said Lady Cora. "It began:

'There was a young person called Cora
Whose parents got poorer and poorer,'

but it never got any further. I think it was going to end with
someone's heart getting sorer and sorer. Well, that's that. He
was a younger son and hadn't a penny and was in love with every
night-club hostess in London. I expect I shall go and live at
Worthing when I'm old, like Miss Sowerby. Only I haven't even
a widowed sister to go to."

"Then you must look on Jeff and me as your widowed sisters,"
said Isabel with the complete unreasonableness of real affection.
"You can have the old laundry for yourself and clip the heads off
flowers in a mushroom hat."

"And be Poor Aunt Cora, or That Ghastly Aunt Cora," said
that lady, and her spirit which had seemed to Isabel to be far
away behind the gloomy shadow of her dark eyes returned with
a dancing light.

"Oh Lord!" said Lady Cora as the swish of gravel under a too
rapidly applied brake came in from the drive. "Not callers!"

"Only Lady Lufton," said Isabel guiltily. "I had quite forgotten that I met her at the Women's Institute Do in Barchester
and asked her to tea. She looks so *dreadfully* widowed, poor
thing. He died oh, the winter before last I think, and they are
very poor and she is so sweet and so helpless. I think he was one
of the marvellous husbands who did everything for her and all
the county things and everything."

Gloria Fletcher from Silverbridge who was obliging as parlourmaid because she was too frightened to say No to her Auntie
Eva Fletcher who was obliging as cook, was heard clattering on
her very high cheap heels to the front door and after a short
interval the drawing-room door was opened and Gloria's voice
said: "Ow, I'm sorry, but it's Lady Lufton please Lady Silverbridge and the young gentleman," after which social effort
Gloria fled back to the kitchen, where her Auntie Eva said

sharply to get the tea things and goodness knew what girls were coming to. Calling Lord Lufton the young gentleman indeed!

"But he *was*, Auntie Eva," said Gloria. "He was a ever so nice young gentleman, ow, ever so tall. I *did* feel sorry for him."

"It's nothing to the way you'll feel sorry for yourself, Gloria, if you don't do things the way I tell you," said her aunt. "His name is Lord Lufton. Young gentleman indeed! You might as well say Lord Silverbridge was a nice young gentleman. The idea!"

"Ow, he's a *lovely* man," said Gloria, licking a cup and rubbing it with her apron.

"What's that you're doing, Gloria?" said her aunt. "Licking the cup! Anyone'd think you'd been born a refugee."

"There was lipstick on it, Auntie Eva," said Gloria.

"And let me tell you, Gloria, that it's no business of yours what's on the cups," said her aunt. "And if you'd washed those cups properly last time the lipstick wouldn't have been there. Hurry up now. Her Ladyship will be waiting for tea. She's got two to feed now."

"It's four, Auntie," said Gloria. "It's Lady Silverbridge and Lady Cora and Lady Lufton and the young gentleman."

Finally beaten by her niece's entire want of social sense, Miss Fletcher told her to take the tray in and look where she was going, an injunction which Gloria carefully obeyed till she got to the drawing-room door when, realizing the impossibility of knocking at the door (which she had been repeatedly told not to do unless it was a bedroom door) with a heavy tray in both hands, she compromised by putting the tray on the hall floor, banging the door and scuttling back in terror to the service room.

Meanwhile Isabel had welcomed Lady Lufton, who was an anxious-faced woman with a very gentle expression, and a very tall young man who looked as if everything to do with life, from brushing his hair and shaving to putting on his clothes and tying his shoelaces, was a trial and anxiety to him.

"This is Ludovic," said Lady Lufton. "Ludovic this is Lady Silverbridge and this is Lady Cora Palliser."

Young Lord Lufton took the ladies' hands with what Lady Cora afterwards described as moist energy, so damp and nervous was his grip, but appeared to be unable to speak.

"I do think it was nice of you to come," said Isabel to Lady Lufton. "I loved your speech at the W.I. and we are starting a little branch here, so I hope you will give me some good advice."

"They are *such* dears," said Lady Lufton. "I feel quite wormish when I address them. They know *everything* I don't know. Things like insurance stamps and which days the last bus from Barchester is at half past seven instead of half past ten so that you can't go to the cinema and—"

And doubtless her list of the practical knowledge of the W.I. would have been much longer had not Gloria's thump on the door interrupted them.

"I think it is my young maid from Silverbridge," said Isabel. "She is often too shy to come in."

"Can I help?" said Lord Lufton, the first words he had spoken. "I could see what it is if you like," and he got up and opened the door and picked up the tea-tray which he put on the table in front of his hostess. He then shut the door and sat down.

"Tell me what you are doing," said Lady Cora, ready to entertain the young man so that Isabel could talk comfortably with Lady Lufton. "We were so very sorry about your father's death."

"So was I," said Lord Lufton, suddenly thawing, "and it was quite dreadful for Mother. He did everything for her. I'm doing my best, but it isn't much. I got out of the army in '46, and then I sent myself to an agricultural college for a bit and I got Lord Pomfret's agent Roddy Wicklow to take me under him for a bit and I'm doing a bit of farming and I'm thinking of having a bit of a go on the Bench. I ought to. Father always did."

Apart from his obsession with the word bit, and heaven knows our beloved young run every catchword to death even more than we did, Lady Cora thought very well of young Lord Lufton, whose native kindliness and honesty somehow made her forget his rather vague shambling appearance.

"You know," he went on in a confiding way that touched Lady Cora, "we have had to give up Lufton Park altogether. Father sold it during the war. It was my grandfather who gave up the hounds and the place in Scotland. I hoped Mother and the girls could live at Framley, but it's too expensive and it made Mother so unhappy to see the gardens going to ruin."

"I wish to goodness my people could get rid of Gatherum," said Lady Cora with some vigour. "It's a white mastodon. An elephant would be easy in comparison. We are pigging it in the old servants' quarters. So where do you all live really?"

"Oh, it's rather complicated," said Lord Lufton, speaking earnestly through a large slice of Miss Fletcher's very good cake. "We have let half of Framley to the Manager of Amalgamated Vedge. It is quite separate from our bit and he keeps the garden beautifully. We were afraid he might want to turn it into a vegetable garden but he *hates* vegetables. We have the little side garden and enough kitchen-garden for ourselves."

"And what will happen if you get married?" said Lady Cora, deeply interested in his simple story, only one of thousands.

"I'd love to get married," said Lord Lufton, "because it would be so nice to have someone to talk to. I mean Mother and the girls are angels, but a man does feel a bit cramped sometimes."

"You are telling ME," said Lady Cora. "It isn't so bad for a woman, but it must be quite, quite irking for a man."

"It is," said his Lordship, very simply. "And when I do marry, I mean if anyone would have me," he added, "we'd have to do the best we could. Mother and the girls say they'll go to the Old Parsonage. We can get possession at any time and it would be very comfortable. I believe the clergymen used to keep footmen and carriages, but of course that is out of the question now. But it is a very nice house and faces northeast and southwest. I think that's the best aspect, don't you?"

Lady Cora said she hadn't really given her mind to it and as far as she could make out Gatherum was built with the sole purpose of making all the rooms as dark and cold as possible. Luckily, she said, the Ministry of General Interference had the nastiest part.

"Don't you like them?" said Lord Lufton. "I'm so glad. They have someone called Miss Harvey and she was beastly to Mother at some meeting or other."

"In that case," said Lady Cora, "we are friends for life."

"Are we really?" said Lord Lufton, his sad and we must confess rather spotty face suddenly lighting in a very attractive way.

"Word of honour," said Lady Cora, holding out her hand. "And Pal of a Palliser," at which Lord Lufton laughed for the first time and suddenly looked years younger.

"How old are you?" said Lady Cora. "I'm over thirty. It's dreadful."

His Lordship, evidently much flattered by this confidence, said he was twenty-six and would be twenty-seven quite soon.

"Oh, what a child!" said Lady Cora, raising her hands and her dark eyes in dramatic surprise. "And you sit in the Lords too?"

"Yes, but I don't like it at all," said Lord Lufton. "I mean I know it's my duty but London is so expensive, so I usually stay with Mother's old cousin in Buckingham Gate. She has turned her house into a kind of boarding-house for her friends. They are all awfully nice but I don't go as often as I ought. I really can be useful at Framley you know, and if our tenant buys a bit more of our land for Amalgamated Vedge, I could repair some cottages or even build some new ones."

Lady Cora, who had not a very clever American heiress in her family tree for nothing, pricked up her ears at this and asked what Mr. Amalgamated Vedge was like. Lord Lufton said he was really a very nice kind of fellow, to which Lady Cora replied that if he hadn't said "really" she could have believed him better.

"Well, he *is* nice," said Lord Lufton, almost stammering in his anxiety to clear himself before Lady Cora. "I mean he does really like Framley and he did several things for Mother that weren't in the lease and he sends his man with a motor-mower to do our lawns and I think his chauffeur cleans our car, only I'm not supposed to know about it. I really feel most frightfully grateful to him. Mother thinks he wants to marry one of the girls but he doesn't. And I wouldn't if I was him," said Lord Lufton, regardless of grammar.

"Tell me about your sisters," said Lady Cora simulating interest so well that she almost deceived herself—not an easy thing to do.

"Well, Maria breeds cocker spaniels," said Lord Lufton, "and Justinia is doing secretary to the Dean just now. They are both older than I am."

Had Lady Cora followed her first impulse, as she usually did, she would have dismissed the whole affair as a crashing bore. But there was something so disarming about Lord Lufton and his wish to do his duty as a peer and as an impoverished country gentleman, that she put on a look of interest that would not have deceived any of her friends and said what unusual names they had.

"They are family names, I think," said Lord Lufton. "I know Justinia is, like my awful Ludovic. Do you know that the Pomfrets' elder boy is called Ludovic because my mother was his godmother and she wanted it. Poor little devil, what a time he'll have when he goes to school."

"Did *you?*" said Lady Cora, throwing into her eyes and voice a sympathy which would not have deceived any of her friends.

"Oh, no. No one worried about *me* much." said Lord Lufton. "You see I'm a quiet kind of fellow. But I do wish Father hadn't died, though I suppose I oughtn't to say so," at which ingenuous mixture of feelings Lady Cora couldn't help laughing, though very kindly.

"Ludovic," said his mother, "Lady Silverbridge has offered to show us the garden. Perhaps we shall see something that will interest Mr. MacFadyen."

Lord Lufton at once got up, if at once can be applied to the unfolding of his long body and legs, and opened the door for the ladies.

"And who is MacFadyen?" said Lady Cora, who had waited for the married ladies to precede her (though technically, as all educated people should know, a Duke's unmarried daughter precedes an Earl's, and all the more a Baron's wife).

"Oh, he's Amalgamated Vedge," said Lord Lufton. "He's Scotch and he comes from my grandfather's old place in Perthshire. It makes such a difference. And he is a gentleman though he isn't. At least I don't mean that. I mean—" and he stammered, hopelessly entangled in the difficulty of explaining one's thoughts when one doesn't quite understand them oneself.

"I know what you mean," said Lady Cora. "My great-grandmother was Glencora MacCluskie. Her father was the Lord of the Isles and we have a lot of Scotch cousins and we still have a bit of property in Fife and practically every single person on the estate is a gentleman—and the women are gentlemen too," she added, perhaps feeling that the now degraded word lady was not good enough. And at this Lord Lufton's last shyness melted and he began to tell Lady Cora all the things he wanted to do for his tenants and she, suddenly feeling that he was in a way an equal, began to tell him what her father was trying to do for his tenants and without noticing it they followed the two married ladies round the kitchen-garden and then across the big lawn to the river. Chairs had been hopefully left on the terrace, but the grey sky and the chill breeze did not invite them to linger. Lady Silverbridge and Lady Lufton, still deep in Women's Institute talk, walked back towards the house planning to get all the better-known Barsetshire writers (not including Mrs. Rivers whose husband being Shropshire enabled them to discard her as it were) to give talks through the winter; which plans for helping others made them both talk at once and rather loudly.

"I can do most country talk," said Lady Cora, "but not cows. I can't do them at all. Father's bailiff can speak like Prince Giglio for three days and three nights without stopping about short-horns. I really could not care less if I never saw a cow again—but one has to pretend."

"I'm so glad you told me, because I would hate to bore you," said Lord Lufton. "You see I take a great interest in cows," and Lady Cora's opinion of him went up, because he knew his own mind and also considered her. So eagerly were they talking that Cecil Waring and Tom Grantly came upon them almost un-awares just as they reached the house.

"I feel I ought to explain myself, even if I don't apologize," said Cecil Waring, when introductions had been made and they had all thankfully taken refuge in the drawing-room. "I found some old maps in my uncle's estate room, Lady Silverbridge, and I thought you might like the survey of The Lodge and its grounds in 1723. Evidently he got it from the owner when he bought the place. Winthrop had never heard of it."

Lady Silverbridge accepted it with gratitude, opened it the wrong way up and said she thought the river was on the other side.

"So it is," said Cecil Waring, "if you put it the other way round. They were the people who made the terrace and the summer-houses. People called Prettyman. They came down in the world and Winthrop says the last of the family were two old maids who kept a school in Silverbridge."

"My great-grandmother or something was at school there," said Tom Grantly. "The one whose father didn't steal the cheque," which would appear to anyone unacquainted with Barsetshire a decidedly negative qualification. "There was an awful row about it, I believe."

"They always seemed to be having rows then," said Lord Lufton. "One of our parsons at Framley nearly got jailed for cheating about a horse or backing a bill or something. It must have been rather fun."

"Not fun for the poor parson, Ludovic," said his mother. "I always think the clergy are *dreadfully* underpaid and I daresay it would have been worse then because money was worth less. At least it was really worth more only you couldn't buy so much with it—or do I mean it was worth less and you could buy more. Whichever way round you think of money it is *most* confusing. I always ask my lawyers about mine and they know absolutely *nothing*, so then I feel safe, because if they can't understand it they can't expect me to."

Possibly the men were able to plume themselves on a slightly more accurate knowledge of economics, but all the ladies felt that Lady Lufton had put it very well. Lady Cora who had slipped away and got some sherry, having quite rightly no faith at all in Gloria's capabilities, now came back with a tray. This of course made all the guests say they must go, after which they proceeded to not go (or not to go, if you prefer) for another half hour or so.

"You know everything, Lady Cora," said Cecil Waring.

"Do I?" said Lady Cora, breaking off the talk she was having with Tom Grantly and turning to Cecil.

"So far," said Cecil. "It's cows. I'm thinking of starting a few cows at the Priory and I don't quite know how to begin."

"Well, here's the expert," said Lady Cora, turning to Tom.

"Oh no, really I'm not, sir," said Tom. "Emmy knows a million times more than I do. I was at Rushwater for about a year and she taught me an awful lot. But I'm in the Red Tape now."

"It seems a bit of a come-down," said Cecil Waring, but not unkindly. "Could you give me some advice about good milkers? I want to give a couple of cows to my sister and her husband who have the Priory prep school."

"I'm afraid I couldn't really," said Tom. "I mean I could tell you what I think, but I wouldn't like you to trust me. Why not come over to Rushwater, sir? I'm going there next weekend and I can always bring anyone."

Cecil said he would like it of all things if Mr. and Mrs. Martin

Leslie would not object and Tom said they always loved to see anybody.

"I say," said Lord Lufton, who had been listening. "Do you think your friends, or is it your cousins, would let me come too? I would so love to see a prize milking herd in its own home and if there's anything secret I'll swear not to look. I'm always reading about them, but it would be splendid to see the real thing," to which Tom replied that he was sure the Leslies would love it.

"And the remarkable Miss Leslie who knows all about bulls?" said Cecil.

"But there isn't a Miss Leslie," said Tom, "or at least there is but she's only a baby and so is her brother. You mean Emmy Graham. She'd love to show you everything. It's a wonderful place. I'll ring them up and tell them. Oh, I'm sorry, Lady Silverbridge, but I must go or I'll miss the Barchester bus and then I'll miss the connection to Edgewood. Could you come too, Lady Cora?" he added, as they said good-bye. "I do wish you would. I came round this way specially to see you. I brought you a few dead flowers. I picked them at Arnhem. I was up there with my guns and we couldn't do anything while those poor beggars were coming down. It was worse than anything else in the war. I felt most awfully sorry for you, if you don't mind."

"Dear Tom, how very sweet of you," said Lady Cora, her eyes darkening as she spoke. "I shall always think of you as a *real* friend."

"Thank you," said Tom. "I'd love you to have them. But friends the merest, Keep much that I resign," which words he said with an ease and lightness which would much have surprised his parents. Though we must add, on their behalf, that they could have said many things which would have surprised him.

"That's Browning," said Lady Cora, her dark eyes amused through unshed tears. "Bless you. I shan't forget. Damn! I haven't got a bag, and she put the little bunch of dead flowers

down the front of her dress. Tom was now saying good-bye to
his hostess, and Cecil Waring saw what Lady Cora had done
and went away feeling that on the whole all the disagreeable
things poets had said about women were true.

The next weekend was not very warm. On the other hand it
was not so blastingly cold as some and at least there was no wind.
On the terrace on the south side of Rushwater House, outside
the windows of the great dismantled drawing-room, one could
sit in precarious comfort, and here on Sunday after church the
Martin Leslies and Martin's cousin Emmy Graham were waiting for their guests, or rather for Tom's guests. With them was
Mr. Bostock, the Vicar, who mostly lunched with them on
Sundays, partly because it seemed right to them to open their
doors to the Church, partly in remembrance of the interest that
Lady Emily Leslie, whose presence seemed to Martin, her most
beloved grandson, son of her first-born, to be always about the
house and garden, had taken in the Vicar's domestic arrangements.

Mr. Bostock said here they were with yet another summer
drawing to its close, which nobody could deny.

"I have been thinking about the Harvest Festival," said Mr.
Bostock.

"We'll give you the usual fruit and vegetables," said Martin
Leslie, "and a couple of sheaves of barley. We've had quite a
success with it and Macpherson is delighted. I don't know what
you'll do with it though."

Mr. Bostock said he could accept the sheaves as a loan, which
led to an interesting and uninformed discussion as to whether
Harvest Offerings were under a kind of taboo. Martin's wife
Sylvia said after all the fruit and things mostly went to hospitals
and *they* weren't taboo. At least not unless they were Infectious
Diseases or Consumption.

"But what seriously worries me," said Mr. Bostock, who had
been thinking his own thoughts during the taboo talk, "is the
bread. It does not seem to me suitable to offer bread of the really

dreadful colour that They make us have. Nor the way it goes bad so quickly. I would even say that it is not meet nor fitting."

At this point Martin was forcibly reminded of a remark of Mr. Wickham, the Noel Mertons' estate agent, to the effect that he always liked being with parsons because you never knew what they'd say next.

"Let's ask Agnes," he said, alluding to his aunt Lady Graham who was Emmy's mother. "She always has an excellent answer for everything, and the sillier her answer is the more sense you usually find in it," and then their guests began to arrive.

The first to come was Tom Grantly, on his bicycle. He had often been back to Rushwater since his decision to do something really useful in the Red Tape department and though he still hoped that in time some usefulness might come out of what he was doing, he thought of Rushwater a great deal. It is deeply to the credit of Martin and Sylvia Leslie that they never showed any criticism of his choice and were truly pleased to see him whenever he came. Sylvia's generosity was part of her being. So was Martin's, but there was also in him the memory of his past during the war and he knew what the ten-year soldier tells, that for any man, old or young but perhaps even more for the young, who went through our last triumph of experience over hope, there has been such warring in his mind, his soul, and often alas his body, that very few people have the right to judge what he does, or to try him by the old standards, and that the best one can do for him is to stand by.

Him Emmy at once took away to see a very interesting malformation of tail in one of the latest calves. A few minutes later Lady Graham and her daughter Clarissa arrived and the family, as usual, became so entirely sufficient to themselves that even Mr. Bostock felt gently outside.

"Do you know the Luftons, Aunt Agnes?" said Martin.

"Now *do* I?" said her Ladyship. "Yes, I *know* I do, because I was on the Committee with Lady Lufton and I could never remember who she was," which her hearers, who were used to her, rightly took to mean not that Lady Lufton was personally so dull as to be unrecognizable but that Lady Graham could not at the moment remember her maiden name. "Where is she?"

"It's not her, it's her son," said Martin ungrammatically. "He's interested in cows and Tom asked him over. And he's asked Cecil Waring too, the one that owns the Priory at Lambton, and Lady Cora Palliser. It's all cows."

"I know Cecil Waring's cousin," said Lady Graham. "He was Sir Harry Waring's only son and he was killed just before the Armistice. I danced with him at parties when I was a little girl and he was a young officer. I should like to meet this man. He inherited the baronetcy, didn't he?" said her Ladyship, whose memory of names and attributes was almost never at fault. "And dear Cora, I cannot think why she is not married. I think there was someone in the war—but I don't know. Oh dear, it is all too, too sad. I am sometimes almost thankful that darling Mamma is dead. She would have been so unhappy about all the young people who aren't happy."

"She would, bless her," said Martin, who had seen Clarissa quietly slip away while her mother was speaking. "And talking of young people, have you heard Clarissa's results yet?"

"Oh yes. She got a very good second," said Lady Graham. "As it was all about arithmetic and science and things I think she was very clever. And now of course, she doesn't know what to do. None of them know, except the odious pushing ones like that dreadful girl who was staying with the French people who took the vicarage the summer you were seventeen, Martin, but I can't *think* what her name was."

"Nor can I," said Martin, which would have annoyed Mrs. Lionel Harvest, *ci-devant* Miss Stevenson, who now had what she called a salon in Bloomsbury, very much needed.

"She did want to go into Mr. Adams's works," Lady Graham continued, "but now she doesn't. The fact is, Martin, I believe she has come to her senses. You know, the war upset some of the growing-up-age girls almost as much as it upset the people who were doing something. They felt they ought to be uncomfortable."

"What did Uncle Robert say?" Martin asked.

"He always knows," said Lady Graham proudly. "When she wanted to go to college and get a scholarship, Robert said he supposed she had better if she wanted to and the girls were my business. And now he says he hopes she has got it out of her system. He has wonderful judgment," said his wife proudly. "It reminded me of when we got engaged. It was at a ball—"

"Darling Aunt Agnes," said Martin, "I can tell the story backwards in my sleep and you are quite perfect," and raising her hand he kissed it.

"There was a delightful Austrian, a friend of Robert's, who used to kiss one's hand quite charmingly when he came to call," said Agnes.

"And that one too," said Martin, though very affectionately, which did not make the slightest impression on his aunt Agnes and then Cecil Waring arrived in his 1949 Ocelot, almost at the same time as Lady Cora in her useful car and Lord Lufton in a very old rackety two-seater from which he emerged, as Martin afterwards said, exactly like a Pharaoh's serpent; which allusion will mean nothing to those who never knew those long terrifying objects, somehow concomitant to Guy Fawkes's Day.

Sylvia made all the guests welcome and then sat back, as she often did, letting Lady Graham have her head, if we may use so violent an expression about her Ladyship's inspired inanities. It would have taken far more than Lady Graham to disconcert Lady Cora or Cecil Waring, those seasoned adventurers in war and peace; but Lord Lufton while admiring her deeply with all his romantic mind was rather alarmed by her snipe-flights of conversation.

"You are Ludovic, aren't you?" said Lady Graham turning her lovely eyes on him in a way that gave him the impression that she found him the most interesting person present: an impression, we may say, often received even by those who knew her best. "I remember so well the year you were born, because your

mother was at the Hunt Ball, only of course not dancing. That
was before you were born, but one really hardly noticed it, except
that she was not dancing. And now you are *so* tall."

"I wish I wasn't," said Lord Lufton. "One bangs one's head on
things and I can't get ready-made suits."

"Nor can I," said Lady Graham with fervour. "Even if I were
starving I would *have* to go to my own tailor. He was nine
guineas when I first went to him and now he is forty-five, but of
course I go just the same. He *will* make my jackets too tight in
the sleeves but he cuts skirts like an angel. Who is *your* tailor?"

Lord Lufton named a firm, long honoured in the hinterland
of the Royal Academy, which turned out to be also Sir Robert
Graham's tailor and he and Agnes became great friends, and
Lord Lufton's heart which but a week or so previously had been
distinctly affected by Lady Cora now fell down flat at Lady
Graham's feet.

"Mother would awfully like it if you would come to Framley,"
he said, basely using her name as a shield.

"But of course I will. I don't really like driving with all this free
petrol because it is what the government wants us to do, else
why make petrol free?" said her Ladyship, who appeared to
attach to the word free a meaning which in this case it had not
got. "But I should love to see Framley. I haven't been there since
the year James lost his first tooth and the reason I remember it is
that Nurse meant to keep it and show it to me, and the nursery
maid threw it away by mistake and cried for three days. James is
in the Guards now and likes it immensely because he says if
there is another war he is bound to get killed at once and it will
save trouble later on."

It did just occur to Lord Lufton that there was a flaw in this
reasoning, but deeply wounded by the arrow of the blind god he
was in no condition to argue.

Lunch was now announced by the loud beating of the family
gong and they all went in. Sylvia had said earlier in the day that
it was impossible to arrange the seating as six of the lunchers

were family and Mr. Bostock and Tom practically were, and it was agreed that Martin should have his aunt Agnes on one side and on the other side Lady Cora, as the only female outsider present. Agnes called Lord Lufton to sit by her, which he readily did and the rest disposed themselves. On the far side of the large round table was an empty seat. Lord Lufton was between Agnes, who was carrying on a long family talk with Martin, and Sylvia who never had much to say, so he tried to look interested and happy and wondered why there was an empty chair. As they were serving themselves there was a certain amount of coming and going between the table and the sideboard and when Lord Lufton had returned to his seat with a rather greedy helping of asparagus (though there was so much that he did not feel guilty) there was in the chair opposite him a girl he had not seen before; so like Lady Graham that she must be her daughter, but with a finer chiselling of the face, a mouth even more exquisite, and dark eyes gleaming like a falcon's. His heart took so deep a breath at the sight that he was almost unconscious for an instant. Then it resumed its steady beat, his eyes cleared and he knew that all was up with him.

"Hullo Clarissa," said Tom Grantly who was next to her. "I've been looking for you. Where were you?"

"I went to see Gran's sweetbriar in the churchyard," said Clarissa. "You know it had to be cut back last year, but now it is so thick again that those hideous iron railings are quite hidden. So I picked some," and she looked down at a little handful of sweetbriar in her lap. "I really don't know what to call it," she said. "Bouquet is too big. Nosegay is too niminy-piminy. If a sheaf could be small it might be a sheaf. Spray is too elegant. Bunch is too fat."

"Try sprig," said Tom sympathetically, for he knew how Clarissa still missed Lady Emily. More than a child ought to do, thought Tom from the summit of his great age. Lady Graham, smiling a welcome across the table to Clarissa, thought how like she was to the pictures of Lady Emily as a girl and with so many of Lady Emily's gifts and graces. Whether she had in her the perpetual and sometimes slightly indiscriminating, Agnes lovingly said to herself, fountain of love that rose in her grandmother could not yet be told. So far her grandmother had been her greatest love. With Charles Belton, that dear nice boy, she had what they had all agreed to call an understanding, but her mother did not think her heart had ever been touched and sometimes wondered if one of the splinters of the magic mirror had flown into it as it did into the boy's in the story of Kay and Gerda.

"After lunch," said Emmy Graham in an overpowering voice, "I'm going to take Sir Cecil and Lord Lufton round the cowsheds, because that's what they want to see. Anyone else want to come?"

"I'm coming of course," said Tom Grantly.

"Oh, I didn't count you," said Emmy, but this was obviously meant for great friendliness and Tom took it as such and listened with serious interest to Emmy's account of the row she had had with the Milk Marketing Board, from which she had come off as far victorious as one ever can be against organized bureaucracy strong in its own conceit and salaries.

Martin had been quietly talking to Lady Cora, who recognized in him just such another as her father, only younger, devoting his life and his war-marked body to the service of his land and his people, with a wife as devoted as the Duchess and on the smaller scale of Rushwater equally competent, and what was almost as much in Lady Cora's eyes, very beautiful with her golden hair and her deeper golden skin. If she had known that Martin was feeling much the same about herself she would have been surprised, but Martin was not for nothing of the Pomfret stock in which beauty and distinction in its women had always been a boast and took considerable pleasure in the bone structure of her face and her dark eyes, so quick to reflect every change of thought. So between Lady Cora talking to Martin on one side and Clarissa talking to Tom Grantly on the other, Cecil

Waring was left alone. But loneliness in a crowd is not unknown to naval officers and perhaps it becomes a second nature with some: we do not know. At any rate he gave no sign of it and enjoyed the good home-grown lunch.

"And how are you getting on at the Red Tape?" Clarissa asked Tom Grantly, with her little air of superiority which Tom was old enough to find amusing.

"And how did you get in your Schools or whatever you call them?" said Tom.

"I got a second," said Clarissa. "Professor Henbane said I ought to have got a first."

"Well, who was stopping you?" said Tom, with sad lack of chivalry; but during his apprenticeship at Rushwater he had come to look upon and treat Clarissa, a frequent visitor to her cousins, as a sister; a relationship which usually includes a good deal of plain speaking. "And anyway I don't suppose old Henbane knew what he was talking about."

"He's not a he, she's a woman," said Clarissa, "and knows more about the Counter-Irritant of Constant Relations than anyone. And anyway she didn't mean I ought to have got a first only someone gave me a second because they were jealous or anything. She meant I *ought* to have got one."

"Which leave us exactly where we were," said Tom. "I suppose what you mean is that if you had worked harder you would have done better."

"It was Strains and Stresses," said Clarissa. "I ought to have stayed on another year really. But I didn't want to," she added, fingering her sweetbriar. "And the women who did get firsts all wanted careers. I really don't know what I want, Tom. Gran would know, though she had never heard of X and Y in her life."

Tom, who had got to know Clarissa pretty well during the last two years, saw with concern that she was really downhearted about her second class, though it is a class of which no one need be ashamed. It was probably the first time her imperious will

had ever met a check and Tom thought she was taking it hard.
"There was an old man of Sid Sussex," he remarked,

> "Who said that YW plus X
> Just made XYW,
> But the dons said: 'We'll trouble you
> To confine your remarks to Sid Sussex.'"

There was a fraction of a pause and then Clarissa smiled, for
as Tom had noted, she very rarely laughed, and taking a sprig of
sweetbriar from her lap gave it to him.

"Thank you, my dear," she said, with her way of being more
grown up than she really was. "You are quite right. I need to be
laughed at."

"Well, I'll laugh at you as much as you like," said Tom, "and
I'll begin by laughing at you for thinking a second matters. So
like a woman."

"Didn't you mind yours?" said Clarissa.

"Well, I did," said Tom truthfully. "But Father was awfully
decent about it. I'll tell you what you *do* need though. It isn't to
be laughed at."

"What do I need then?" she said, interested as her charming
sex always is in any argument *ad feminam*.

"You need to be needed," said Tom.

Clarissa's falcon dyes were veiled for a moment, even as Lady
Emily's used to be.

"You know too much, my dear," she said, in her most grown-
up way, but Tom felt certain that he was right, and was touched
with a kind of elder brother's compassion for this elegant clever
creature, composed of such warring elements. Clarissa turned to
Cecil Waring and asked him about the Priory, saying she had
often been to the Priory School but never seen the other part of
the house and Cecil suggested a plan for showing her its full
horror when next she visited the Winters. And then a general
move took place.

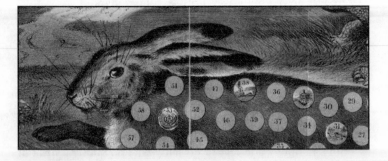

CHAPTER 6

For the next half hour or so the party sat on the terrace, drank coffee, and discussed plans for the afternoon. Agnes, her invariable custom when she revisited Rushwater, was going to see Siddon the old housekeeper and talk over past glories. Emmy had organized a cow-program for Cecil Waring and Lord Lufton, to include a personally conducted tour for hikers among the pastures of Rushwater and a Ramble through the cow-sheds, the whole to be concluded with a Grand Milking Display by Emmy and Herdman the old cowman, with Tom as honorary assistant. Lady Cora, whose quick apprehension had seen that Martin Leslie ought not to do too much, asked if he would show her the kitchen-garden and then Mr. Bostock had to tear himself away to take the Children's Service, to which Clarissa, to his surprise and gratification, proposed to accompany him while Sylvia, seeing gratefully that her husband would be in safe hands, said she would see them all again at tea-time and disappeared in the direction of her nursery.

"You are doing very well here," said Lady Cora to Martin, when the Cow Addicts had started on their Ramble, and the bell was ringing for the Children's Service. "I wish my father could see it. Cobbold, that's his bailiff, is a first-class man on stock in general, but he doesn't really know bulls. Your Rushwater bulls always get first prize at the Barsetshire Agricultural and the

Bath and West. I think Cobbold will blow his brains out next time."

Now whether Lady Cora was speaking in pure good faith, or had realized that Martin's quiet manner concealed ambitions, or was sorry for his limp and wished to distract him, we do not exactly know. But whichever it was it succeeded and as they walked slowly towards the kitchen-garden Martin spoke modestly but confidently on the subject of bulls and conceived a very good opinion of Lady Cora, which opinion was confirmed when she asked if they could sit on a stone seat near a lily pond and observe the beautiful orderliness of the vegetables in their rows.

"War?" she asked, as he sat down with a slight awkwardness.

"Italy," said Martin.

"Blasted Italians," said Lady Cora. "The man my sister-in-law, Silverbridge's wife, was engaged to was killed there. That learns one to liberate people."

Martin, recognizing in Lady Cora a spirit as disillusioned as his own about the feelings of the liberated towards the liberators, said it was the Americans who were learning now in Korea what the ten-year soldier tells, adding Poor Devils.

"Well, they had their warning," said Lady Cora. "Kipling wrote 'Take up the White Man's Burden' for them; and it's now or never."

"God help them," said Martin, but so simply that Lady Cora did not feel uncomfortable. "My father was killed in 1918 and my mother married a very nice American. Their boy is in the American army now. I suppose things go on and on like that for ever."

"I might have married a man who was killed at Arnhem," said Lady Cora. "But there it is. One might as well listen to the wireless as think what might have happened. If only one could help one's friends—oh, well. Tell me about your winter food."

So they sat very comfortably in the sun as long as it was out, talking of this and that, but the sun had the sulks, as so often in that depressed summer, and then the air was chill.

"You did say something about helping one's friends," said Martin presently. "Would you come and see our old agent Mr. Macpherson? He is from Dunbar. He has lived here for fifty years but he loves to speak about Scotland and I know the Duke still has a place in Fife."

"And a bonnie place too," said Lady Cora assuming a very pretty lilt in her voice "I should love to see your Macpherson."

Accordingly they walked through the kitchen-garden to the stable yard and got into the disgraceful rattle-trap old car that Martin used for his estate work and in a few minutes were at the agent's house.

"He won't be in the garden in this weather," said Martin. "Come in," and he opened the front door which in the friendly country fashion was never locked in the daytime and brought Lady Cora into the sitting-room with its long windows on a veranda. Here Mr. Macpherson was sitting in a large armchair with a book and a newspaper on a table beside him, evidently in a Sunday afternoon doze, but he roused himself at once at the sound of voices.

"Don't get up, Macpherson," said Martin. "This is Lady Cora Palliser. The others are all doing the cows, so I brought her to see you."

"I'm glad to meet you, Leddy Cora," said the old agent. "You'll be kin to the Lord of the Isles."

Enchanted to meet someone who knew Families, Lady Cora sat down by Mr. Macpherson and plunged into relationships.

"The Duke still has property in Fifeshire," said Martin.

"No need for you to tell me about the Kingdom of Fife, Martin," said Mr. Macpherson, slightly intoxicated by patriotism and a Duke's daughter. "Many's the time when I was a young callant I have looked over from East Lothian to the Paps of Fife. Dunbar is my home, Leddy Cora, and East Lothian is as good farming land as you will find anywhere north of the Cheviots. It was there I learnt my trade."

Lady Cora at once fell in with his humour and spoke of her

father's property and the people on the estate, putting just enough of the country into her speech to charm the old agent's ear.

"And you're no married, my leddy," he asked, when Lady Cora had described her own family.

"I might have been," said Lady Cora. "But I wasn't."

"And fine I ken why," said Mr. Macpherson. "The Flowers of the Forest—many's the time I've heard her leddyship say those words when she thought of her own son, father to Martin there. Cobbold is his Grace's bailiff, if I'm no mistaken."

Lady Cora said he was.

"I will do more for his Grace because he is a laird in Fife than because he is Duke of Omnium," said Mr. Macpherson. "Tell yon Cobbold to come over and see me, my leddy, and I may be able to set him right on a point or two. He's no a bad lad but it's a pity he was born south of the border, though I must say that Emmy and that young Tom Grantly are no altogether de-feecient in intelligence," which remark Lady Cora quite rightly considered to be a high tribute to the cow-mindedness of the two young people.

"You have a look of Lady Emily, my leddy," he said. "It is the same flash of the eye—those dark eyes of hers—the bones that tell of good stock—the pride and the gentleness. But she was far above all others," and as he ceased speaking he fell into a kind of muse which Martin judged it better not to disturb and quietly took Lady Cora away. When they got outside he saw that she was near crying and indeed he had felt moved himself far beyond what he liked.

"He can't last very long," said Martin, accepting life and death as real country people can more easily do.

"I can't do much for him," said Lady Cora unashamedly drying her tears. "But Cobbold shall come over and see him before the week's out and I'll tell him to let the old man think he is wanting to learn. He isn't *really* of course, but he won't be above listening to what Macpherson says and pretending he thought of it himself. You wouldn't mind?"

"I'd tell a dozen whopping lies a day if it would give him pleasure," said Martin. "Thank you so much, Cora," and whether she noticed his mode of address we cannot say.

Meanwhile the Cow Addicts were having an extremely pleasant afternoon. The ramble through the pasturelands of Rushwater was not only instructive but very beautiful, the green meadows running up to the woods where a great beechen hanger clung to the side of the downs whose austere whalebacks rose to the sky. Wooden Spring was visited and the three men each threw a twig or a stone into it and wished, for Emmy said that was the thing to do.

"What did you wish?" said Emmy.

"But one never tells," said Lord Lufton, outraged. "That's the whole point of wishing wells."

"Well, anyway this isn't a well, it's a spring," said Emmy, which Tom contradicted flatly, saying that the wishing well in the woods above Southbridge was a bubbling spring.

Emmy said she had wished that her hair would curl but it hadn't, which was really a good thing as she would look awful with curls.

"I like your hair just as it is," said Cecil Waring, upon which Tom disliked him at once; but at once liked him again because he was such a decent sort—which is Tom's expression, not ours. "Suppose we all tell what we wished," Cecil continued. "I wished for the Winters to find a bigger place for their school because they need one and I need the school buildings. How long does one have to wait for the wish to happen, Miss Graham?"

There was a silence. Tom hit Emily in a fatherly way.

"Oh, me!" she said. "No one calls me Miss Graham."

"Then I will amend my question," said Cecil Waring. "How long do I have to wait for the wish to happen, Miss Emmy?"

"Well, it's supposed to happen the same day," said Emmy,

accepting Cecil's mode of address with her usual *sang-froid*. "But if it doesn't, you dip a leaf in the water and keep it safe. And when you want the wish you burn the leaf and say: 'By my Knowledge.' Then it either comes true or it doesn't."

"The old woodman at Framley used to eat snails alive," said Lord Lufton, whose shyness had suddenly melted when he found himself on sure ground. "He said they told him when it was time for planting and he always said:

> 'Hick, hock, hackery hail
> Out of his housen comes the snail,
> Joseph's snail upon the Thorn
> Sain the day the Tree is born.
> Into my belly goes the snail
> Hick, hock, hackery hail.'"

"It sounds all right," said Emmy, regarding Lord Lufton with considerable respect. "It's the kind of thing one *would* say. Come on now and see the cow-sheds," and she took Lord Lufton under her wing, imparting a great deal of valuable information to him, so that his diffidence fell away and he talked to her as comfortably as he would to his sisters Justinia and Maria, confiding to her all his ideas about cows.

"I know it sounds silly," he said, "because I do have to be in London for the Lords, which is so dreadful, but of course one must do one's duty. But we get quite a long time when Parliament isn't sitting and I think a milking herd would be a good thing."

"Of course it would," said Emmy. "Have you a good cow-man?"

"I don't know," said Lord Lufton, rather overawed by Emmy's competence. "His name is Pucken, from over Northbridge way."

"If you've got a Pucken, they're all right. They were here long before the Conquest and before anything," said Emmy. "Tell

him to come over and see me. I'm always here unless I'm at
Holdings with Mother for a few days. What's it like being in the
Lords?"

"Oh, it's all right," said Lord Lufton. "It's awfully dull sometimes, but lots of things are dull and one does them. Like
shaving every day," which caused Emmy to laugh immoderately
though most good-humouredly, and to vow to herself that she
would help him as much as she could.

They had now reached the cow-sheds which, owing to our
ignorance, we shall not describe. Suffice it to say that they were
the most modern part of Rushwater and apart from a few trifles
such as a wireless, a Hoover, a radio and television set, an electric
washer, and a refrigerator, were not unlike the new houses that
foreigners get in London while the Londoners live in their
patched ruins. Each spotlessly clean cow had her name embla-
zoned on the wall and looked as if her hoofs were blacked every
morning.

"I say, Herdman," said Emmy, "Tom's come to help today
and this is Commander Waring only he's Sir Cecil, and this is
Lord Lufton."

"Ar," said Herdman who, wearing his white milking-coat and
an old straw hat, looked rather like the gentlemen who used to
paint Ripolin on each other's backs on the hoardings. "So you're
back, Mr. Tom."

"Only for the day," said Tom, with a queer ache at his heart.
"How's Bluebell?"

"She's fine, Mr. Tom," said Herdman, who though solid
Barsetshire had not entirely escaped the influence of the films.
"She had a fine bull-calf last month, but you fine people wouldn't
know about such things."

"I *do* know," said Tom indignantly. "Emmy told me."

"Born with a caul, he was," said Herdman. "I've got her at
home. Got her in one of those big biscuit tins, I have. Sir Robert
Graham's man Goble over at Little Misfit would give five
golden pounds for that caul. But he won't get it, Mr. Tom."

"I should think not," said Tom indignantly. "What are you going to do with it?"

"Ah, that'd be telling," said Herdman. "My father he lived here man and boy for eighty-five years, Mr. Tom, and a gormed old nuisance he was at the end, and he told me what to do with the caul and I know what to do with her. But I can't stand idling here or Lord Lufton will be telling Pucken we're a set of—" but respect for the distinguished guests made him omit the rest of the sentence.

Tom now borrowed a white coat and he and Herdman and Emmy gave a virtuoso exhibition of milking. The sun lay in golden beams athwart the cow-sheds, the soft comfortable noise of cows chewing and occasionally whisking a tail mingled with the steady drumming sound of the milk squirting into the pails under experienced fingers, and a rich, satisfying smell of well-tended cow and fresh straw filled the air. Presently the milk was taken away to have done to it whatever it is one does to milk. Emmy and Tom hung up their white coats and Herdman, as representing the cows, bade a courteous farewell to Cecil Waring and Lord Lufton, receiving a small gratification from each with complete self-possession.

"Now the bulls and then we'll have tea," said Emmy. "Herdman's hopeless with bulls. Come on, Tom."

Just as he did a year ago at Rushwater, Tom escorted Emmy to the stall where Rushwater Churchill, the future World Champion, was standing foursquare in the half-light, thinking so far as we know of nothing at all. Becoming aware of company he whetted his horns against his crib and gave what we can only describe as a token bellow. Tom, under Emmy's watchful eye, slipped into the stall and spoke to the bull who gave him a kind of half-nod as who should say: "Here's that youngster again. I might as well do the civil."

"I'd sooner be in the engine room after an explosion than go into that animal's den," said Cecil Waring. "What does he weigh?"

Tom, over his shoulder, gave a figure that passed the bounds of credibility.

"But that's what he is now," said Emmy. "He wasn't that when you left us. How did you know?"

"I don't know," said Tom, surprised at himself. "I just thought he must be that."

"Oh, Tom," said Emmy. There was admiration in her voice, but also the faintest shade of reproach and Tom felt so small and guilty that he could have allowed Rushwater Churchill to gore him almost with pleasure when he reflected that he had deliberately left the world of bulls for the Red Tape and Sealing Wax Department. But the past cannot so easily be undone.

"Would you like to come in?" said Emmy to Lord Lufton.

Whether his Lordship really wanted to, we cannot say, but if a lady invites one it is difficult to refuse. Almost without hesitation he went into the stall. The bull looked at him with placid contempt and returned to his occupation of horn-whetting.

"Old chump!" said Emmy, hitting the bull affectionately.

While they were thus occupied Clarissa had come into the yard and was standing in the doorway, looking at the bull-worshippers. Lord Lufton could not see her face, for the full afternoon sun was behind her, and perhaps it was as well that he could not, for the surprise and admiration in it might have upset him considerably. As they went back to the house he found himself by Clarissa, who asked him in her detached, grown-up voice, how he knew so much about bulls.

"I don't," said Lord Lufton. "Your sister asked me to come into his box, so I supposed it was all right."

Clarissa did not answer, but she looked up at him for a moment and in that moment he forgot everything else. The moment passed and the Mithra-worshippers went into the house for tea.

Mrs. Siddon the housekeeper, who had a rigid sense of what was correct, had put tea in a corner of the big drawing-room and unsheeted some of the chairs. After the Children's Service, while the Cow Addicts where still on their tour, Clarissa had amused herself by filling the great Chinese vases with branches of beech and the tallest flowers of the garden. Some of the party remembered that Lady Emily had sat there on the last celebration of her birthday, but the thought was not sad. Rather did it make them feel that she was too far from them. Agnes was in her place. She could not be what her mother was, but in her own way she was the focus of the party even as her mother had always been. With the real kindness that underlay her apparent vagueness and even idiocy, she had observed Lord Lufton during lunch and felt a certain compassion for him. So tall, so lanky, his clothes so untidy, so evidently trying hard to fill the place to which his father's too early death had called him, so farouche yet eating confidingly from a hand that he trusted, he touched his mother's heart. Not that she wished for a moment to usurp any of Lady Lufton's rights, but from what she had seen of that lady, anxious and lost in her widowhood, she did not think she could be much support to her tall, burdened son. Someone strong and practical, that was what he needed. Someone like Lucy Adams only of finer clay. Someone like her own Emmy, but not with her dear Emmy's one-track mind. Someone like Mrs. Belton's Elsa only less bullying and not with a husband and three children. It was all very difficult. As she thought of it her thoughts must have reached Lord Lufton, for he looked across the table at her. She smiled and his thin anxious face—too thin, too anxious she thought—lit up with an expression of gratitude that she found very touching.

"I took Cora up to see Macpherson, Aunt Agnes," said Martin who was next to her. "She made a complete conquest of him and I expect he will cut us all out of his will. He wants to see you. Could you go up before you leave? I will run you over in the car."

"Of course I will go, darling Martin," said his aunt. "I feel so sorry for poor Ludovic Lufton. Those sisters of his are so capable and his mother is so incapable and I am sure darling Mamma would have wanted us to do something for him. But what I cannot think."

Martin suggested that if his aunt Agnes asked Ludovic to come and see her at Holdings it would cheer him up like anything and then they talked quietly about the family under cover of a rather noisy tea and Martin said how they missed Tom and wondered if he would make a success of the Red Tape and Sealing Wax job.

"If he is under that quite dreadful Mr. Harvey he will *not*," said Agnes with what was for her considerable energy. "Robert had to deal with him during the war and says he is quite impossible and has a name for breaking his underlings if he doesn't like them. It must be *most* worrying for his mother."

Martin, taking it that his aunt Agnes referred to Tom Grantly's mother rather than Mr. Harvey's, agreed and said he really did not know how Tom was taking it and as Tom at the moment was having a rather dashing flirtation with Lady Cora they felt they need not be troubled for his immediate welfare, and Lady Graham turned to Cecil Waring. Being the two most grown-up people in the room they got on very well and Lady Graham listened with her usual deceptive air of interest to his plans for turning the Priory into a kind of home for naval orphans, if his sister and her husband could find a suitable house for their rapidly growing school.

"It all sounds very delightful, but what will your wife say?" said Lady Graham.

Cecil, being used to responsibility, took this very well and said he hadn't got one, but if he had he was sure she would say the right thing.

"I daresay you know," said Lady Graham, "that Mr. Belton whose wife is a kind of cousin of mine through the Thornes, will probably have the big house at Harefield on his hands again. It might be a possibility," and Cecil was interested and promised to pass on the news to the Winters.

"And do you know," he said, "that Charles Belton has forced me into a kind of regatta on the lake at Harefield. I have got two folding dinghies and there are to be punting races in them and I should think several deaths by drowning or suffocation in the rushes. I am sure Mrs. Belton is asking you. But may I ask you first, and your enchanting Clarissa of course."

Lady Graham said she loved anything to do with boats.

"When I was on my honeymoon," she said, "Robert took me in a gondola in Venice and went to see some charming Americans who lived in a Palazzo whose name I have forgotten. I can't remember their name, but they always stayed at Claridge's when they came to London. And the Fourth of June is so pretty except for the rain and its always being so cold. I suppose they choose a cold day to make the boys hardy," said her Ladyship and her nephew Martin thought, as he had often thought before, that if ever there was an inspired idiot it was his aunt Agnes, bless her. But Lady Graham under her sweet silliness was not unobservant and was quietly considering the case of Lady Cora Palliser. Rushwater and Gatherum had been on friendly calling terms and dined with each other from time to time before the 1939 war, but there had never been any great intimacy. Agnes, always absorbed in her family and her local duties, had hardly seen Lady Cora since 1945 finally brought the Fall of England, and was interested in her, though mostly from the point of view of whom she might marry. Lord Lufton was too young; or to put it better Lady Cora was grown up and so far he was not, though Agnes felt sure that would come with time, for a sense of duty to one's country and county are more than childish tags. Cecil Waring appeared to admire her, but every sailor had a ready-made character for gallantry. Tom Grantly, that nice boy, was obviously at her feet and would obviously get no further. It was a pity that Lord Dumbello was still in the nursery. Oliver Marling was out of the question. And so concentrated was her Ladyship's mind on this important subject that her nephew Martin had to say her name twice to get her attention.

"If we are going to see Macpherson, we had better go now, Aunt Agnes," he said. "You'll be wanting to get home. Are you coming with us, Tom?"

"Rather," said Tom, "I did want to go, but I didn't know if Mr. Macpherson would like me to. I mean—"

"We are all glad to see you, Tom, always," said Martin and his aunt Agnes thought how like darling Martin was to darling Papa in his simple authority, as of a man who knows his own place and will always take it and will use it for the benefit of those less fortunate. "You know the doors of Rushwater are always open," and there was no answer to this, so Tom did not try to make one though his heart was heavy.

For the second time that day, for the how manyeth time since he had succeeded to Rushwater, Martin's shabby little car clanked up the road to Mr. Macpherson's house, where the old agent received Lady Graham almost with tears of joy. She sat by him and held his hand while he spoke of Lady Emily and Mr. Leslie and the family he had loved and served, and praised Emmy and Martin for their loyalty to the Rushwater Tradition; a state of mind so unusual in the old Scotsman that Martin half expected him to die on the spot.

"And what have you to say for yourself, Tom?" said Mr. Macpherson, which is a difficult question to answer at the best of times and was peculiarly difficult for Tom.

"Well, I'm awfully glad to see you, Mr. Macpherson," he said. "Rushwater Churchill is looking wonderful. Do you remember when he chased Herdman around the stall and Emmy had to come in and she whacked him over the nose?"

"That's all very fine," said Mr. Macpherson, "but it's an auld sang. What about yourself, Tom?"

Tom said he was very well.

"I'm no doubting it," said Mr. Macpherson, getting as Tom said afterwards to his parents more like John Knox every moment. Though what grounds he had for comparing Mr. Macpherson and his long life of devotion to others with the quite odious self-expression (to use a foolish modern term) of that divine, not to speak of his unforgivable sin of rudeness to a queen, precluded by her position from answering back, we do not know. Any more than we know why the lay preacher of the present deplorable and monstrous regiment should have been rude to monarchs whom their position and their honour forbid to reply.

The silence which succeeded to this remark was so heavy that even Agnes noticed it, nor was the situation at all improved by Mr. Macpherson remarking: "Awell. Who will to Cupar maun to Cupar," which though not altogether clear to the Sassenach Tom left him in no doubt as to the old agent's views on the Red Tape and Sealing Wax and all the labours of its hands.

"Well, Tom, I must be stepping," said Mr. Macpherson, we think under the confused impression that he was taking leave of Tom rather than Tom of him. "You are a puir misguided creature but you will come home again," with which words he appeared to forget that Tom was in the room. Martin whispered to him to go and wait with the car, which he did, feeling horribly guilty yet conscious that he had not meant to do anything wrong. Martin and Lady Graham were not long in joining him.

"Poor darling Mr. Macpherson," said Agnes. "He thinks I am darling Mamma," at which Tom in the back seat, feeling rather like Jo than everyone was allus a-chivvying on him, said under his breath to himself: "Not so much of your darling" and then was horrified at his own behaviour.

While they were away Sylvia took Lady Cora and Cecil Waring to see the Temple, that peculiar monument halfway up the hill behind the house in and about which so many young Leslies had played, pointing out to them such objects of interest as the place where Martin used to play single-wicket cricket with the boot and knife boy and the sawmill where one of John Leslie's boys had nearly cut off his finger. When they reached the top of the hill Sylvia remembered that she had forgotten the key, but neither of her guests minded, for to have to look at objects of interest owing to the misguided zeal of one's hosts is sometimes more than flesh and blood can bear. An elderly man carrying a bill-hook went past, touched his cap and said good evening in his soft Barsetshire.

"Wait a minute, Higden. I've got a message for you from Mr. Leslie," said Sylvia. "Forgive me," and she left her guests.

In front of Cecil Waring and Lady Cora the hill that they had just climbed by a winding path among the beeches fell steeply away to the west, so that they almost looked down the chimneys of Rushwater in the hollow below. Beyond the house the tower of the church was visible and then pastureland, cornland, and water-meadows stretching in a golden haze to the distant blue hills.

"Dazzle and glare," said Cecil Waring aloud to himself as he shaded his eyes the better to see the prospect.

"I didn't think there was anyone who knew *Parables from Nature*," said Lady Cora. "Poor Twinette. She was swept away by the broom, wasn't she? I think the one I liked best was Purring when you're pleased. Can you purr, Sir Cecil?"

"I have tried to learn, Lady Cora," said the Commander.

"Oh, all right, Cecil then," said Lady Cora. "It is rather sudden, but then look at Romeo and Juliet."

"I do," said Cecil. "And they hadn't known each other any longer than we have."

"On the other hand, we haven't fallen in love at first sight," said Lady Cora coolly.

"No indeed," said Cecil. "Do look at the hills."

And indeed they were worth looking at. A painter, we suppose, sees what he sees. We, whether for good or ill, are apt to see what painters have seen. An undoubted Claude (Lorrain, Gelée, what you will) lay before them, a setting sun descending upon lapis lazuli hills, drawing over them a veil of finest gold-dusted gauze, trees in the level light taking unaccustomed shapes, their shadows lengthening to the east. Here and there in the middle distance a wisp of blue smoke curled self-consciously upwards. The last level rays caught the gilded vane on a spire and from the downs above sounded the peaceful monotonous tone of sheep bells.

"Todger's *can* do it," said Lady Cora. "How lovely the view is," she continued, addressing herself to Sylvia who came back to them, more golden than ever in the golden light. "I am sorry but I really must be going. I can't tell you how much I have enjoyed myself. If you and your husband can get away, Mother would love you to come to Gatherum," and they went talking down the hill. Lady Cora repeated her invitation to Martin.

"We can't offer you much," she said, "but you might like father's bailiff and we've got a rather threadbare maze and there is always Miss Harvey and the General Interference people."

Martin said they would love to come when the Barsetshire Agricultural Show was over.

"I have hardly seen you, Lady Cora," said Tom Grantly, suddenly materializing from behind a hedge, rather dirty. "I've been helping Emmy to clean a drain. I'm most awfully sorry."

"Come to Gatherum," said Lady Cora. "Ring me up early. I've got an extension by my bed. And we'll pull the Horrible Harveys to pieces. My eye is as bright and black as ever— Browning," with which words, not at all unkindly spoken, she got into her car.

"Oh—I'll come down and open the gate for you," said Tom, burning to immolate himself in some way.

"Don't bother," said Cecil Waring. "I'll do it. Good-bye, Mrs. Leslie, and I hope you'll come over to the boat-races," and slipping into his 1949 Ocelot car he twisted neatly around Lady Cora's car, preceded her down the drive and was at the gate with half a minute to spare.

"One moment, Cora," he said as she slowed to pass his car. "Why not come back to the Priory for supper? My sister Leslie Winter and her husband would love to see you. And if you don't like driving back alone—"

"My dear Cecil!" said Lady Cora. "When did anyone last offer to accompany me? Not since Gerry and I and some of his friends were in Piccadilly the night all the glass was broken and Jermyn Street was bombed. But I'd like to come to supper. I simply *adore* little boys. Go ahead and I'll follow."

Accordingly they twisted through the Barsetshire lanes till they came to Lambton and so up the hill to the Priory School. Here on the lawn Philip Winter the Headmistress and Leslie his wife were sitting in deck chairs with three little boys cross-legged on the grass beside them, for it was their custom to have three of the older boys to supper on Sunday and to preface the meal by instructive literature. The literature of the moment was John Buchan's *The Thirty-nine Steps* and Messrs. Dean, Pickering, and Addison (alas! in their last term) were the three. Leslie Winter had just come to the delightful part where Richard Hannay (as yet without a commission, a title, or the wife who in his American friend Mr. Blenkinsop's beautiful words couldn't scare and couldn't soil) is prisoner in the villian's house hidden in a ring of trees on the top of a hill. The boys were rocking backwards and forwards in ecstasy; Pickering and Addison were breathing loudly through their mouths in defiance of hygiene while Dean was following the story with pantomimic gestures, his eyes fixed in vacancy as incident followed incident.

Suddenly Dean's arm was thrust upwards.

"Oh, sir," he said. "It's the Commander come back. *Please* can you not stop reading, sir."

Philip looking up saw his brother-in-law with a tall handsome woman.

"End of reading," he said. "Sorry, but there's a lady and one must be polite. But I'll read you the rest of the chapter when you are in bed."

"Truthernonner, sir?" said Pickering.

"Truth and honour," said Philip and got up to greet his brother-in-law's guest.

"I've brought Lady Cora Palliser back to supper," said Cecil. "Will that be all right, Leslie?"

"Of course," said Leslie and after greeting Lady Cora asked her to sit with them.

"I hope we didn't interrupt the story," said Lady Cora, sitting down in a deck chair with a fine display of her exquisite legs.

Leslie said they always stopped when visitors came and Philip read them the rest in bed.

"I'll tell you a story then," said Lady Cora. "Once upon a time there was a little girl—"

"What was her name?" said Dean.

"It was Cora. And she had two brothers and they all lived in a castle with their father and mother and the castle was so big that there were two miles of hot-water pipes all made of shining copper. And they had an ENORMOUS bath with ten taps."

"What came out of them please?" said Pickering, jiggling up and down violently as he spoke.

"Hot and cold and douche and shower and sitz and needle and wave and plunge and whirl and waste," said Lady Cora all in one breath, which gave the little boys the giggles.

"Did they turn them all on, please?" said Addison.

"They did," said Lady Cora. "And their nurse smacked them."

"Hard?" said Dean, his eyes gleaming.

"Awfully hard," said Lady Cora.

"I bet I could have smacked them harder," said Pickering. "I can hit a cricket ball right up the pitch—"

"And get caught," said Dean, at which witticism the little boys had the most delightful giggles.

"Not so much noise, or Lady Cora can't tell you the story," said Leslie.

"And one summer," said Lady Cora, "it was very hot and they said could they sleep out in the woods in a hut by the little stream, because they had read a story about a shepherd boy called Colin who had a stream beside his cottage. So their mother said they could if Nannie didn't mind."

"I bet she did mind," said Dean. "I bet sixpence."

"You can't, you idiot," said Addison. "Matron's got your money."

"Shut up," said Philip.

"And in the book Colin's father made the stream run right through the cottage," Lady Cora went on, "so what do you think their father did? He told his men to dig a channel right across the floor of the little hut so that the water could run into it. And when they went to the hut in the woods that evening a little stream was dashing and splashing right through the hut, in under one wall and out under the other and they lay in bed and watched it till they went to sleep."

"REALLY?" said Pickering.

"Really and truly," said Lady Cora, which caused the little boys to throw themselves into a Laocoön scuffle of legs and arms to express their pleasure.

"And did they dine off mince and slices of quince?" said Pickering.

"What were her brothers' names?" said Addison.

"One at a time," said Lady Cora. "They did dine off mince, but the quinces weren't ripe yet so they were made into jam. And the brothers were called Jeff and Gerry."

"Where are they?" said Dean.

"Jeff is living at Silverbridge," said Lady Cora, "and he has a wife called Isabel who is as beautiful as a princess."

"I bet my mother's as beautiful as that," said Dean.

"I bet she isn't," said Addison, more as a social repartee than with any animus. "And where is Gerry?"

"I don't know," said Lady Cora. "But he was always happy wherever he was, so I expect he is happy now. And that's the end of the story. Good-night."

Strictly speaking it is not the part of a guest to send her host's pupils to bed, but a Duke's daughter must be allowed a few privileges. The little boys, recognizing authority when they saw

it, said good-night to Lady Cora. Dean, to her charmed surprise, kissed her hand with a kind of clumsy grace.

"Please come and see us in bed," he said.

Lady Cora looked to Philip for sanction. He nodded, so she
promised to come and say good-night before she went home.

"Where's your home?" said Pickering.

"In a castle," said Lady Cora and then their Headmaster sent
them, quite obviously incredulous of the castle, away to the
house.

"What nice boys," she said.

"Dean is the nephew of Jessica Dean the actress," said Leslie.
"She teaches him those delightful manners. They all go on to
Southbridge next term. We shall miss them dreadfully."

Lady Cora felt that the Headmaster's wife might cry at any
moment for the loss of her innocents and turned the conversation to the remarkable hideousness of Beliers Priory, built
c. 1850 by a Waring who had married a City heiress. The result
had been a pile—for we can use no other word—combining
inconvenience and discomfort in the highest form and by now
qualified to rank as a period piece. Cecil Waring said, not
without a touch of pride, that in its way the Priory was even
uglier than Pomfret Towers without being huge enough to
impress by mere shapeless bulk alone.

"You wouldn't care to see it before supper, I suppose?" he said,
to which Lady Cora replied that nothing would give her greater
pleasure and that if anyone was a good judge of hideous houses
she was, having been born and bred at Gatherum which could
have made the Priory its washpot and cast its shoe over it
without troubling to lift a finger.

"There was a real Priory here before the Reformation," said
Cecil Waring as he walked with Lady Cora by the outside and
official route to his own quarters. "It was lower down by the
Dipping Pools and the Board of Works have got the ground
plan in the original stone with grass between; very prettily done
too. They say the Pools were stew ponds for the Prior's table, but

no one really knows. If we walk round the grass plot you can see the Priory better."

They walked round the circular drive and stopped at the point furtherest from the Priory the better to appreciate its beauties.

"Of course Gatherum is bigger," said Lady Cora, appraising the hideous pile with a dispassionate eye, "but I do honestly think the Priory is uglier."

"I shouldn't have liked to say so myself," said Cecil Waring, "but as you have said it first, I agree. In fact I shall have it on my tombstone that I owned the most revolting house in West Barsetshire. We enter by the Baronial Porch. Bolton Abbey in the Olden Time."

The door in country fashion was on the latch. Cecil opened it and stood aside for Lady Cora. In front of her was a short flight of stone steps almost pitch dark.

"Courage," said Cecil. "Excuse me," and he passed her and opened another door with a grill in it. Inside was a square stone-flagged hall with a high dado of fumed oak panelling. Hundreds of hooks for hats and coats were on the side walls and below them two of those interesting benches about six feet long and twelve inches wide, of varnished wood, intended for male servants waiting for their masters, and a large leather-seated chair with a beam beside it and a great pile of weights for anxious sportsmen to find if they needed to sweat another half pound off, or dared to relax to a good dinner.

"They used to sleep here sometimes when the men were playing cards late," said Cecil, "and they must have rolled off onto the floor with a whack sometimes."

"Like Lord Welter's house in St. John's Wood," said Lady Cora.

"You don't read Henry Kingsley?" said Cecil, incredulous and excited.

"Of course I do," said Lady Cora. "What do you take me for? And what's more we've got *all* his books at Gatherum, which is more than anyone else has."

"I do envy you," said Cecil Waring. "I've only got the ones that have been reprinted."

"You will envy me even more," said Lady Cora with a provocative look in her dark eyes, "when I tell you that they are all Mine. Not Father's."

"I do envy you," said Cecil.

"You can come and see them some day," said Lady Cora. "And now," she added, rather as if Cecil were an idle schoolboy who had to be recalled to his lessons, "do show me the rest of your house," which last word seemed to Cecil to be rather a putting of him in his place. But it was not worth while pursuing this thought, so he opened one half of the big double doors that led to the main house. Here, to Lady Cora's quick, amused eye, was exhibited a large high square hall with a central skylight. On one side was a carved stone open fireplace of Hollywood size; opposite it a staircase with a balustrade of heavily carved dark wood went up past a very hideous window of sage green, puce, and gamboge panes. On the first floor was a continuous line of leaded casement windows round the hall and above it stone-coloured walls rising unbroken to the roof.

"How perfectly GHASTLY," said her Ladyship, in deep admiration.

"Isn't it," said Cecil, flattered by her criticism. "I'll just show you the ground floor. It was used for wards and recreation rooms when the Priory was a hospital," and he led her through what we can only call a handsome suite of rooms with furniture stacked and dust-sheeted, all communicating with the hall and each other. Outside the long drawing-room was a terrace overlooking the gardens, the fields beyond, and the woods across the valley.

"That's Golden Valley," said Cecil, "and the woods on the far side are Copshot Bank. Jasper, our old half-gipsy keeper, had a grandmother in Golden Valley who was a witch and used to turn into a black hare. He shot her in 1942. When Leslie and I were little we used to love to watch the men playing cricket down the field there, because one saw them hit the ball and then a few seconds later we heard the smack of the bat on leather. It proved something or other and we were frightfully conceited about it."

"I know," said Lady Cora sympathetically. "Physics—whatever they are. No pursuit for a gentleman."

As this appeared to be more a general reflection than to be directed against himself, Cecil only laughed and took her upstairs—not by the baronial staircase but by a winding stone stair in a kind of turret excrescence—to the first floor where a dark corridor ran round the hall, lighted only by the leaded casements they had seen from below, with bedroom doors on the inner wall.

"This was very good for running races in," said Cecil Waring seriously. "And Leslie and I used to look through the windows when there were house parties and sometimes drop things like nutshells on them."

"And then what happened?" said Lady Cora.

"Nothing," said Cecil. "But next day Uncle Harry beat me and Leslie was sent to bed instead of going to see the beagles. Life was life then," he added nostalgically.

"If ever I marry," said Lady Cora, "my husband will have to beat the boys and I shall send the girls to bed. And when they are grown up they will all boast to their children about it. Anything else to see?"

Cecil said only second-best bedrooms on the top floor, twelve of them; and only two bathrooms in the whole house, he added proudly.

"I live in what were the housekeeper's quarters," he said, "where my uncle and aunt lived when the central part was turned into a hospital, and Leslie's school is in what was the long wing at right angles to the house where the servants lived and all the kitchens and things were. Now I'll take you back by the short way."

He led her down a short flight of steps and into the long stone passage already described, at the end of which they passed the half-open door of the school kitchen.

"Is that you, Master Cecil," said a voice of authority from within.

"It's Aunt Harriet's old Nannie," said Cecil. "When I hear her call me I know exactly what Nelson felt like every time he went to sea."

"Because if it is you're keeping everyone waiting for supper," said the voice. "Come in. I want to see you."

Lady Cora when describing this scene later to her brother and his wife said that Cecil Waring's knees knocked together and his teeth chattered. This we must state, for the good name of the British Navy, was not so, though Cecil certainly felt the Nelson touch of a sinking at the pit of the stomach. But the meteor flag of England sustained him and, opening the door wider, he stood aside to let Lady Cora go in.

As usual, thought the owner of the property, there was an air of Dickensish comfort about the scene that no other part of the house had. Being summer there was a nice fire and Nannie Allen was knitting by it while her daughter Selina gave the finishing touches to the evening meal and her husband ex-Sergeant Hopkins studied the football pools.

"Good-evening, Nannie," said Cecil and making a virtue of necessity he added: "I have brought Lady Cora Palliser to see you."

We did not know ourselves until the very moment of penning (or to speak more correctly pencilling) these lines, that Nannie Allen and Lady Cora Palliser had ever met. But Nannies do not forget their former charges.

"Good evening, my Lady," said Nannie Allen. "You'll excuse my getting up, but my arthritis is a trouble. Does your Ladyship remember me? I was temporary in the nursery once at Gatherum when Lord Gerald's nurse was on holiday. He was the most beautiful baby I've ever seen except of course Mr. David Leslie and my Master George."

"That's Uncle Harry's only boy, who was killed in 1918," said Cecil softly to Lady Cora.

"I do remember you—just," said Lady Cora. "Jeff and I called you Allie and you had a daughter who came to see you in the holidays called Selina."

"Quite right, my Lady," said Nannie, relaxing as a keen examiner may relax when a good examinee is before him. "This is Selina. She lost her first and then she married Hopkins," who on hearing himself cited stood up and saluted.

"Oh dear, my Lady," said Selina, her lovely eyes brimming without any effort or any grimace, "fancy seeing you again. And poor Lord Gerald was killed, my Lady. I saw a piece in the paper about it and I *was* so upset. He had his second tooth, my Lady, when I was there."

"And his Lordship would have had it just the same if you hadn't been there, Selina," said Nannie Allen severely. "And I saw in the paper, my Lady, that Lord Silverbridge had married a nice young lady. You ought to be thinking of getting married yourself one of these days, my Lady," and Lady Cora could see that Nannie was mentally calculating her age.

"Well, when I do I'll send you some wedding-cake, Nannie," said Lady Cora. "I know my mother and father will be glad to hear about you. So will Jeff. He has a very nice wife and they are going to have a baby."

Having done her duty she shook hands with Nannie Allen, smiled to Selina and stood waiting for Cecil Waring who was talking in a low voice to ex-Sergeant Hopkins. Hopkins had saluted and fallen back a step and Lady Cora was turning to go when the ill-starred and unwelcome Marigold burst into the kitchen, with a something black in her hand.

"Ow," said Marigold, and seeing Sir Cecil and Lady Cora she began to back.

"Come here, my girl," said Nannie, "and don't come barging and tow-row-ing in like that when Sir Cecil and Lady Cora Palliser are here. And what's that you've got in your hand?"

"Ow, Mrs. Allen, it's my new black cami-knicks," said Marigold, brandishing a garment of black sateen edged with lace of the revolting colour known in lingerie circles as ecru. "I got them cheap off one of the usherettes at the Barchester Odeon."

"Cheap come and cheap go, and that applies to *you*, my girl," said Nannie. "I really don't know what you girls are coming to. Showing your underwear in the kitchen and her Ladyship and the Commander here. That's the way girls go wrong."

As a rule Marigold was immune to Nannie's snubs, treating them as part of life; but this evening not only to be snubbed but in front of a real Lady too, was too much for her. Tears that any film star might have envied coursed down her cheeks bringing a good deal of cheap make-up with them. Lady Cora, feeling quite certain that Nannie's next words would be a short but trenchant comparison between Marigold and Jezebel or the Whore of Babylon, decided to intervene with ducal powers.

"Now don't be so silly, Marigold," she said. "Stop crying. And if you want cami-knickers you'd better get pink ones. The girls that wear black never get the star parts. Have you got a hand-kerchief?"

From the top of her stocking Marigold reluctantly produced a repulsive and tattered grey rag.

"Well, wipe your eyes and then burn it," said Lady Cora. "Have you got five shillings, Cecil?"

The Commander, fascinated, produced two half-crowns.

"Now do you see these?" said Lady Cora.

"Yes, miss," said Marigold in a tear-impeded whisper.

"Next time you go to Barchester," said Lady Cora, "just forget about the boys for a minute and go straight to Sheepskins' and you will find a lot of very pretty handkerchiefs with flowers on them for one shilling each. Buy five and mind you wash them—properly—every week. Mrs. Hopkins will let you boil them if you are good. And take all that mess off your face. You've got a good skin and you are doing your best to spoil it. Just a little powder and a little lipstick. That's all I wear. And that will give you allure," said Lady Cora, stalking her all on this word of power.

"Say thank you to her Ladyship," said Nannie Allen and Selina almost with one voice.

"And do what Lady Cora tells you," said Cecil, who after a short talk with Sergeant Hopkins had turned his attention to the foregoing scene. "She had her photograph in the *Tatler* last week. Come along, Cora. Selina is waiting to dish up. You've got that all right, Hopkins?"

Hopkins saluted and said Yes sir with what looked almost like a conspirator's wink and the visitors went away.

The evening meal was pleasant and the food good. Lady Cora knew about Charles Belton's people. The two other masters were at once her slaves and the new junior master Mr. Swan had met her younger brother in an O.C.T.U. After supper Lady Cora reminded her hostess that she had promised to say good-night to the three little boys, so Leslie Winter took her up to the dormitory where some twelve or fourteen boys were sitting up in bed chattering like sparrows. At the sight of Lady Cora shrill appeals for a story rent the air.

"Please," said Dean, who appeared to be spokesman for the dormitory, "could you tell us about the house in the wood again because the other chaps don't believe you had a stream running through a cottage. I told them they were silly fools," he added, looking askance at Lady Cora to see how she would take this dashing form of speech.

Nothing loth, Lady Cora sat at the end of Dean's bed and told again how her father had caused a stream to be diverted so that it flowed through the earth floor of a little hut and her audience listened spellbound.

"Please," said Pickering when the story was over, "what were the names of your brothers?"

Lady Cora said Jeff and Gerry.

"And do they go to the hut now?" said Addison.

Lady Cora said the elder brother had a house of his own now and a very beautiful wife, upon which a tumult rose among the little boys about beauty in women; one or two instancing Leslie

Winter (who had the looks of good blood and breeding which can almost take the place of beauty) as the most beautiful person they knew, others (which nearly made Lady Cora cry) stoutly maintaining that their mothers were the most beautiful women in the world.

"And what about me?" said Lady Cora, very seriously.

> "'O dear Lady Cora,
>   She is as sweet as Flora,
>   And I do adore her,'"

chanted Master Dean, upon which all the little boys burst into a riot of pillow-throwing and pommelling and general expressions of enthusiasm and *joie de vivre*, till Charles Belton who was on duty that evening appeared and produced calm.

"I suppose it is time for me to go," said Lady Cora. "I must kiss them good-night," and she went from bed to bed giving a kind of auntly hug and kiss to each of these pleasing anxious beings. Some of the little boys were surprised, a few were shy and darted under the bed-clothes, but her old friends Dean, Addison, and Pickering nearly throttled her with tight hugs from their macaroni arms till she had to beg for mercy. As she was leaving the room, Dean, who was nearest the door, having had his good-night hug said: "Oh, please where is your other brother? You didn't say."

"Oh, Gerry," said Lady Cora, feeling her reputation at stake and hunting desperately for the right thing to say. "Well, I really don't know. He went away but I expect I'll find him some day."

"Where?" said Dean, with a little boy's horrid persistence.

"I don't quite know," said Lady Cora. "He can't come to me, but I expect I shall go to him," and she went away, followed by a cheerful, unmelodious bellowing of Dean's hymn of praise in her honour.

"What a divine set of devils you have," she said to Leslie Winter as they went downstairs. "You will come to Gatherum in the holidays, won't you? And now I must say good-bye to your husband and Cecil and go home."

The two men were standing outside the front door talking. Cora thanked Philip Winter for a delightful visit to his young gentlemen and asked him to bring any of them to Gatherum at any weekend to see the maze and the cottage with a stream running through it.

"And good-bye and thank you for a delightful evening," she said to Cecil Waring.

"I am glad you enjoyed it," said Cecil. "But it isn't good-bye yet. I am taking you home."

"But you can't!" cried Cora and even as she spoke her heart gave a most unexpected thump. "I've got my car if you remember."

"Of course I remember," said Cecil. "I am very good at remembering. I am driving you home and Hopkins will follow with your car. Then when I have landed you at Gatherum I and Hopkins shall drive back together."

"Oh, but—" Lady Cora began and then, suddenly realizing that her life was being arranged for her, she got into Cecil's car, Hopkins following in her car after a short interval. The evening was not very warm; no evenings were very warm, alas, that summer; but there were lovely lights and half-lights in the chill landscape. They talked of the day's events, of the charm of Rushwater, of Lord Lufton's anxious overburdened appearance and Emmy Graham's remarkable gifts with cows.

"The person who really worries me is that nice boy Tom Grantly," said Lady Cora.

"I noticed that you and he were talking very friendlily—if that is a word," said Cecil.

"We both read Browning," said Lady Cora as if that explained everything. "I wonder why on earth he went from Rushwater to that dreadful Red Tape and Sealing Wax Department. The man Harvey is almost as unpleasant as his sister which," said her Ladyship rather sententiously, "is no easy task."

And then Lady Cora, not unversed in the art of pleasing, led him to talk about Beliers Priory and his hopes and plans for his philanthropic (or should we say philopedic) schemes, showing an interest, a grasp of the house and its possibilities, a practical vision of what might be, that quite won his heart: and when we say heart we do not wish to be misunderstood. Or not yet.

When they got to Gatherum Castle they found the Duke and the Duchess hoeing and weeding the drive, for the damp summer had produced as healthy a crop of weeds as one would wish to see.

"Well, my lambs," said Lady Cora. "Everyone at Rushwater sent their love and then I went over to Beliers. I must say the most revoltingly hideous house I have ever seen. It beats Gatherum hand over fist," which artless remark made Cecil Waring rather anxious, for he did not want the Omniums to think that he and Lady Cora had been disparaging Gatherum which was the senior in hideosity by several years. But the Duchess relieved him by saying that she had been to Beliers once or twice in old days and though Gatherum and Pomfret Towers were much bigger she rather thought that Beliers was the ugliest.

"And as I always say to people," said the Duke, who was sitting on the bank pulling some loose threads off the turn-ups of his faded grey flannel trousers, "when you live in a house you don't see the outside of it."

"I wish you wouldn't fidget with your trousers, Plantagenet," said the Duchess, though very kindly. "You know we've had the turn-ups repaired once and Hamp says they won't stand it again. If ever you want a jobbing tailor who *really* understands clothes, Sir Cecil," said her Grace earnestly, "Hamp is excellent. He comes and stays here for a few nights once a year and goes through my husband's clothes. Last year he put the most beautiful leather edges on the cuffs of his shooting-coat and used the little bits he cut away to darn one of the pockets that a ferret had bitten."

"How kind of you, Duchess," said Cecil, "but Hamp is an old

friend at Beliers. He used to make skirts for Aunt Harriet and do odd jobs for my uncle."

"I didn't know he could make skirts," said the Duchess. "I have some Scotch tweed upstairs. Do you think I could trust him? Your aunt, I remember, had a very distinguished figure," and the Duchess looked rather sadly down her own comfortable shape. Cecil, hating to see her depressed, said he felt sure that Hamp would appreciate the honour and make an excellent job and he must be getting home. He looked round for Sergeant Hopkins, but neither Hopkins nor Lady Cora's car were visible and Cecil had a moment's horrid pang, wondering if the old army habit of pinching had made the Sergeant drive Lady Cora's car into Barchester and sell it for a bottle of rum.

"I expect your man is in the stable yard," said Lady Cora.

"I'll take you round, Waring," said the Duke, who dearly loved being useful. "No good shouting because no one hears. And if they do hear they don't come. I'll take you round, my boy," and he led Cecil round the house.

"Of course all this is the old servants' quarters and not *half* so ugly as the main building, I am afraid," said his Grace, for the old Adam dies hard in us, especially in our pride about possessions that have no particular value. Not to be outdone, Cecil said that he was living in the older part of the Priory where there was a stained-glass window, probably Munich *circa* 1850, which he fondly believed was only second to the glass of St. Mungo's in Glasgow.

"You know Scotland then?" said the Duke. "You know we have a place up in Fife?"

Cecil said he only knew the Clyde from war experience and then they turned into the stable yard where Hopkins was talking to an old groom. At the sight of the Duke and the Commander he sprang to attention and saluted.

"I've given her Ladyship's car a bit of a clean, sir," said Hopkins.

"Proper good clean too," said the old groom, who was almost unbelievably chewing a straw. "Not like these youngsters."

Cecil Waring, mindful that a tip given to one's friends' servants greases the wheels of life for the friends even if not to one's own immediate benefit, bestowed largesse on the groom and went back with the Duke and Hopkins to the front of the house, where he said good-bye.

"A lovely afternoon," said Lady Cora. "I adore Leslie's little boys. May I come again? I am simply bursting with ideas about your reformatory."

"Do," said Cecil. "And will you come to the punting races we are going to have at Harefield? I expect several deaths."

"I should love to," said Lady Cora. "I punt extraordinarily well," and Cecil thought he had never seen her look so handsome; a dark Diana; a moon in clouds. "And do keep an eye on the poor boy Tom Grantly if you can, Cecil. So nice and *such* a lamb among wolves."

Not a goddess, Cecil thought. Only a woman. A woman whose beauty, whose poise, whose charm—idle thoughts. Better to concentrate on the future of Beliers and forget her. And he forgot her with such fervour during the drive home that Sergeant Hopkins told his wife it looked as if her Ladyship had turned the Commander down and that he, Hopkins, had never been so frightened since he was running away from old Rommel in North Africa.

CHAPTER 7

Now that petrol was free, which expression merely meant that you could now buy as much as you liked if you could afford it instead of those who could afford it being able to buy as much as they liked, the county began to go visiting again and to renew the many family links that depended on mechanical transport. It is true that Lord Stoke had driven himself, or been driven, all over the county in a dog-cart in summer and his mother's old brougham in winter, and it was said on credible authority that he had in the warm summer of 1949 made a tour of the seats of nobility and gentry in Barsetshire by a system of relays to which his older friends had contributed here an old hunter who had no objection to being driven by so good a whip, there a youngish cart-horse too heavy to bolt with so determined a driver. And it was common property that he had taken Mrs. Morland, the well-known novelist and his old friend, to the Flower Shows and the summer meeting of the Barsetshire Archæological in a pony trap.

This year (as we have just reminded ourselves and found the reference with considerable difficulty) the Barsetshire Archæological was to have its August meeting in Mr. Belton's park at Harefield. Not that there were any remains, Roman, British, Saxon, or otherwise, but the grounds were spacious, Harefield Park itself a handsome Palladian building and the deer popularly supposed to be descended from the deer that Tyrell was aiming at (or not aiming at) when he shot William Rufus. Furthermore at the Annual General Meeting in June Lord Stoke, who being deaf was able to talk for at least an hour never boring himself in the least, brought forward a theory that the spring under the lake at Harefield, locally known as Froggy's Bottom, was formerly dedicated to Frigga the wife of Odin, taking the very reasonable view that if no one else had a different suggestion his had better stand.

Ever since Lord Lufton had told Emmy Graham that his cowman was a Pucken, Emmy had planned a meeting. All was peaceful at Rushwater so she was spending a week at home with her mother at Little Misfit and this seemed to her a good opportunity as it were to vet Pucken, to which end she summoned Lord Lufton, his cowman, and her parents' old friend Lord Stoke on a chill damp Sunday. As the Priory School had now broken up for the holidays Charles Belton was free and he also added himself to the party, with his mother. Mrs. Belton did not particularly want to go, for she was expecting her daughter Mrs. Admiral Hornby on a visit from Scotland with her children, but when one's young invite one to do anything with them it becomes almost a point of honour to fall in with their views, however inconvenient, boring, and tiring to oneself. As far as her own wishes were concerned Mrs. Belton was always glad to see her cousin Agnes Graham, but her husband liked her to be at hand on Sundays—or shall we rather say that he enjoyed grumbling if she wasn't there. However Fate settled this all very nicely for her by making her daughter Elsa come down from Scotland two days earlier than she had intended so that Mr. Belton would have someone to grumble to and be happy.

As all Lady Graham's friends know, there is a stone-flagged terrace along the south front of Holdings, on which the long windows of the room known as the Saloon open. It is a pleasant place on warm summer days, but in the far too frequent cold wet summers it can be depressing. Lady Emily Leslie, who had spent the last years of her life with her daughter at Holdings, used to say that in wet weather the terrace was like the Ghost's Walk at Chesney Wold, but deeply as we love and revere Charles Dickens we feel that here her Ladyship was going a little too far. Be that as it may, the rain was falling with a chill determination in the face of a chill southeast wind, and Mrs. Belton was very glad to find a large wood fire in the Saloon where Lady Graham was occupied with her embroidery, for her Ladyship was an excellent needlewoman and if her daughter had inherited her gift for drawing from her grandmother it was from her mother that she had her exquisite neatness of finger.

Agnes Graham, very comfortably seated on one of the sofas that faced each other across the Persian hearthrug, greeted Mrs. Belton with her soft dispassionate scented embrace after which Charles, with an agreeable gaucherie and perhaps a faint affectionate mockery, kissed her hand.

"And don't tell me, darling Cousin Agnes, about Uncle Robert's Austrian friend who used to kiss your hand," said Charles, "because I simply cannot bear it."

"Do you mean it makes you jealous of him, or just bores you?" said Clarissa, looking up from the table where she was amusing herself with her paints.

"*Not* the way to talk, my girl," said Charles, upon which Clarissa raised her head, looked steadfastly into his eyes, and then down again at her painting. There was something in her glance that Charles could not understand and he sat puzzling over it while his mother and Agnes talked about Elsa Hornby and her children, for in Agnes lived much of her mother's insatiable interest (far more than mere curiosity) in every doing of her relations and her friends. Mrs. Belton, who had not observed this by-play, continued her account of her Hornby grandchildren.

"How lucky you are, Lucy," said Lady Graham. "There is nothing I should like more than grandchildren but none of my children seem to get married. I was married when I was twenty-one and I did hope Emmy or Clarissa would. But Emmy is so busy at Rushwater that I don't suppose she ever sees anything but bulls and in spite of Europa that is really out of the question," a remark which reminded Mrs. Belton very forcibly of David Leslie who had described his sister Agnes as a divine idiot. "Besides which," Agnes continued with one of the flashes of insight which were more common than outsiders supposed, "if she liked anyone it was that nice boy of the Grantlys' and now he has gone into some government job at Silverbridge."

"It is the Red Tape and Sealing Wax," said Clarissa, who like most of our very young never bothered to collect gossip, but somehow found facts about her friends and her friends' friends being as it were added to her. "And he is under a man called Geoffrey Harvey with a quite too dreadful sister."

"I know them," said Mrs. Belton. "At least thank goodness I don't, but they took a cottage at Marling during the war and Miss Harvey made eyes at Oliver."

"Poor sweet, he does *ask* for eyes to be made at him," said Clarissa. "Is he still in love with Jessica Dean do you know Cousin Lucy?" to which Mrs. Belton replied that she thought he was, though his mother said it was more a habit than love.

"Like the Statue and the Bust," said Clarissa, "only Jessica isn't a bust," to which Mrs. Belton made no answer, feeling, as even Clarissa's best friends occasionally did, that she sharpened her wits too often and not always quite kindly at other people's expense.

"What are you painting, Clarissa?" said Charles, looking across the table at her.

"Things," said Clarissa. "Thoughts. Silent Thoughts."

"Tennyson?" said Charles.

"Oh dear no," said Clarissa. "Just Walt Whitman," and she applied herself again to her quick graceful work, so Charles came and looked over her shoulder, telling himself firmly that it was just Clarissa and that he refused to feel snubbed. The painting in Clarissa's free untaught style, so like her grand-

mother Lady Emily Leslie's, was of a man apparently impris-
oned in a round tower, with a beam of silver light striking down
upon his face from a window high in the wall. Charles asked
what it was. If Clarissa felt any annoyance at his persistence she
gave no sign of it beyond murmuring: "*Phantastes*, my dear.
George Macdonald. Really too, too uneducated."

"Hang it, Clarissa, I'm not," said Charles. "I've been at
Oxford and in the army and I've been a schoolmaster for years
and years; three years in fact. And I read *Phantastes* in the
nursery. Of course if your picture is meant to be the hero in the
tower that melts in the moonbeams and is stone walls by
daylight, I'm with you. But it looks more like the Pit and the
Pendulum."

"Schoolboys, schoolboys," said Clarissa in a tolerantly superior voice, and then looking up at Charles gave him a smile so
like her grandmother's in its piercing sweetness that Mrs. Belton who happened to be looking at her almost gasped and
wondered for the thousandth time whether the relationship
between her Charles and Clarissa was only an understanding, as
the young people had decided to call it, or something more. She
was too shy and too proud and perhaps also too wise to ask either
of them right out what they felt, but she often wondered
whether Clarissa could become a house-mother to small boys,
or Charles were a good enough horseman to subdue this enchanting suspicious creature who would need riding with the
lightest of hands. A very mixed sentence, but our thoughts are
mostly mixed. They are all very well so long as they remain
adumbrations or images in our mind, but are the very dickens
when it comes to explaining what they are, or whether they are
really anything at all.

A rather loud noise in the hall now proclaimed the advent of
Lord Stoke who was examining the kitchen-maid Marlene, now
promoted to general utility, on the subject of kitchen waste, to
that young lady's extreme terror.

"Now what you must have," said Lord Stoke, putting his well

known hat, rather like a grey bowler with a flat top, on a chest, "is at least four dust-bins."

"Yes, Lord Stoke," said Marlene in a whisper.

"Worst of you people," said Lord Stoke, "is you won't sort your kitchen stuff. What do you think pigs need?"

"Bacon, please Lord Stoke," said Marlene in a yet hoarser whisper.

"No, no. That's what pigs ARE, not what they need," said Lord Stoke. "And even then there's a lot of 'em that isn't bacon. There's ham, chitterlings, Bath chaps, pig's face very good potted or with greens, trotters boiled and then you fry 'em in breadcrumbs, black puddings and white puddings, sausages, and that's only the beginning. Where's Cook?"

Marlene, to whom it dimly appeared that Lord Stoke might dismember Cook and boil, bake, or fry her, began to cry.

"Now don't cry, there's a good girl," said Lord Stoke. "Where is Lady Graham? I've brought her some faggots, best I ever had, off one of my own pigs and I gave the Inspector some too so *he* won't talk," said Lord Stoke, with so triumphantly devilish a laugh that Marlene, film-sodden, fled with a shriek to the kitchen.

"Well, what's the matter with *you*?" said Cook, looking up from her Sunday reading of the *News of the World*.

"It's Lord Stoke," said Marlene. "I read in your paper last Sunday, Cook, that girls mustn't listen to old gentlemen not if they're *ever* so nice and there was a girl used to meet an old gentleman and he gave her a ever so lovely wristwatch and they found her boiled in the copper and the wristwatch too."

"That's enough from you, Marlene," said Cook, justly outraged. "You go and get the tea things ready and mind you put a big cup for Lord Stoke because his Lordship likes one. Wristwatches indeed! That's the way girls go straight to hell, Marlene, and don't say I didn't tell you. I'll see to his Lordship," and Cook went into the hall where Lord Stoke was fighting a parcel that wouldn't come out of his capacious pocket.

"Extraordinary thing," said Lord Stoke, enchanted to have another member of the staff to talk to. "*Most* extraordinary thing the way things won't come out of one's pockets. Went in all right. Here we are. Faggots. You know how to cook them, eh?"

"Oh yes, my lord," said Cook. "My mother was Eliza Margett over Winter Overcotes way and she had the lightest hand with a pork pie in the whole Woolram Valley. Proper lard we got then, my lord, and proper flour too."

"Now what relation was she to Margette the builder?" said Lord Stoke, settling down for a good gossip. "He built Mr. Palmer's new barn, about 'thirty-five that was, and a poor job too."

"Mother was his sister, my lord," said Cook, flattered. "Jasper Margett, that's Sir Harry Waring's keeper, was her first cousin, though of course I ought to say Sir Cecil now, but it seems more natural-like to say Sir Harry."

"Take my tip, and if they offer you a title, take a barony," said Lord Stoke, whose ancestors had been undistinguished peers of great local patriotism for several hundred years. "Always know who you are then. Keep the same name going."

"Yes, my lord," said Cook.

"As for Viscounts," said Lord Stoke, but what his Lordship had to say about his social superiors in precedence (though in his opinion otherwise negligible) we shall never know, for Emmy coming charging in from the farm carried Lord Stoke into the Saloon. Here he was able to tell Lady Graham all about how to cook faggots, to which she listened with the deceptive look of attention so well known to her family and friends.

A chastened Marlene brought in tea. Lady Graham said they wouldn't wait for Lord Lufton. The party arranged itself round the big table and fell to, for Lady Graham's teas were famous, largely owning to the kindness of American friends who went on remembering their English friends not once, but at more or less regular intervals. General conversation was a little difficult, for Lord Stoke, having finished with faggots, asked Emmy three seats away how Rushwater Churchill was coming on and as part of his lordship's deafness was real and increasing, Emmy with her elbows on the table bellowed amicably at him.

"Hullo, Charles," said Edith, who was seated next him.

"Hullo, yourself," said Charles, "How's poetry?"

"That's just it," said Edith. "There isn't a rhyme for Charles. I've tried all through the alphabet."

"Where on earth are you girls educated?" said Charles. "You've only got to begin at A. Arles," to which Edith quite reasonably said that wasn't a word.

"Well it is," said Charles, "but no one uses it."

"Then it isn't a word," said Edith. "There is carles. But you aren't a carle, are you?"

Charles said one might be anything in poetry.

"All right," said Edith, evidently much relieved. "I'll put it into a poem for your birthday. I'm going to boarding-school next term and I expect I'll stop being a poet, so I wanted to write your poem before my sad demeese."

"Then I hope they'll teach you English," said Charles, most unchivalrously. "It's demise. Rhymes to surprise."

Edith was silent, considering Charles's point. Marlene opened the door, said in a breathless way: "Please it's Lord Lufton Lady Graham," and turned to fly, becoming rather involved with the new arrival as she did so.

"I'm awfully sorry, Lady Graham," said Lord Lufton with his awkward courtesy. "I didn't quite know what to do with my cowman, so I went round to the back of the house and found your Cook who is most kind and is giving him tea."

Lady Graham's lovely mild eyes beamed appreciation of his thoughtfulness as she asked after his mother and both his sisters by their right names, and though her Ladyship's interest was often quite deceptive we think that in this instance it was real.

"I was so very sorry about your father's death," she said. "Not that I knew him well, but people liked him. He did all the right things. And your mother is so charming. She must have married very young."

"She was nineteen, I think," said Lord Lufton, "and Father did absolutely everything for her. I do wish, if it isn't ungrateful Lady Graham, that Father needn't have died."

"Not ungrateful, Lord Lufton," said Lady Graham. "I wish my darling mother hadn't died. We can't help it. But there it is."

"I know," said Lord Lufton. "All the same one oughtn't to complain, ought one? And please don't call me Lord Lufton, I can't help thinking people mean Father. It's awful, because Father did everything so well."

"Of course I'll call you Ludovic," said Lady Graham very kindly. "I know a little what you feel like. I can't do all the heavenly loving things my mother did, but I love thinking of her and sometimes it helps me to be more tolerant and to think of other people. I am sure you will do as well as your father, dear boy."

"I do try," said Lord Lufton, his pale worried face almost good-looking for a moment. "But there's a lot to learn and then there's the Lords and I never know how to vote. I mean I always vote with our side, but sometimes I think I ought to think about it more and read it up."

Agnes asked with interest what he would read.

"Oh—I don't know exactly," said Lord Lufton uneasily. "I mean I know what I think about things, but I don't know why I think them. If only there were a book to tell me *everything*."

"But, dear Ludovic," said Lady Graham laying her hand on his arm, "there is no need to know why you think things. My darling mother thought the most extraordinary things but she never asked why. She just thought them."

Lord Lufton, though not convinced, looked distinctly comforted and began to talk to Lady Graham almost as easily as if she were his sister Justinia now doing secretary to the Dean, for of his sister Maria who bred cocker spaniels he was never quite unafraid. But before he had finished the list of improvements he

intended to make at Framley, Lord Stoke, in high good humour
after worsting Emmy in an argument about contagious abor-
tion, called to him in the loud voice of the very deaf to bring his
man along to the farm. Lord Lufton spilt some tea as he got up,
went very red in the face, began to wipe the cloth with a not very
clean handkerchief, stammered his apologies to Lady Graham
and looked as if he might cry.

"Too, too gauche, my dear," said Clarissa to Charles Belton in
a low mocking voice.

"Too, too rude and uncivilized, that's what you are, my girl,"
said Charles, partly from a habit he had acquired of speaking to
her for her good, partly a genuine protest against bad manners to
a guest in her mother's house. But far from objecting Clarissa as
usual took his remarks with perfect meekness.

Mrs. Belton had heard them and wondered again for the
ninety-ninth time whether the rather vague engagement between Clarissa and Charles really meant anything, but she put
this thought at the back of her head and talked to Agnes.

"I am really quite worried, Lucy," said Lady Graham to
Mrs. Belton "about Emmy. When she made friends with Tom
Grantly and he went to work at Rushwater we all thought there
might be something in it. Darling Emmy has never looked at a
young man before. Not," said her Ladyship with the common
sense she could so surprisingly show "that there were any young
men to look at there, but you know what I mean. And now he
has gone off to that dreadful Red Tape and Sealing Wax place
near Silverbridge. You know they wanted to take The Lodge,
but Lord Silverbridge and his wife got in first. I have never met
Mr. Harvey who is one of the heads of it, but from what Amabel
Marling tells me he is quite dreadful and unscrupulous."

"How?" said Mrs. Belton. "I mean what could you be unscrupulous about in an office. Do you mean he steals the stationery?"

"Not quite," said Agnes with an air of profound reflection.
"Of course one never really knows what one means till one has

said it, but I think I mean that he would be horrid to anyone he took a dislike to."

Mrs. Belton said she often felt like that herself.

"I know," said Agnes. "Where can I have put my scissors? Never mind. I can use the other pair. Oh, but this *is* the other pair. How can that have happened? Things are *so* extraordinary. But if you disliked a person *very* much you would try to be nice to them in case you caught some of their nastiness," and her Ladyship placidly went on with her work, evidently under the impression that she had made everything perfectly plain.

"I wouldn't," said Mrs. Belton. "But I would try to keep out of their way."

"But poor Tom can't," said Lady Graham. "You see this Mr. Harvey is above him and Tom has to work for him, so he simply can't avoid him. I wonder if Robert could do anything."

Sorry as Mrs. Belton was for Tom Grantly if he had a chief who had what is known as a down on him, she did not see how Sir Robert Graham could interfere and wondered if she ought to tell Agnes.

"I mean, Robert might run into him at the club and put in a word," said Agnes. "Unless of course they have different clubs. Do you think Mr. Harvey would belong to either of Robert's clubs?" and she named two institutions which can still use the misused word exclusive in its better sense.

Mrs. Belton thought it best to squash this idea at once and said firmly that it was improbable.

"Or if one knew anyone who would speak to him," said Lady Graham. "When my nephew Martin went to the Argentine before the war, Robert spoke to a man he knew who put Martin up for a delightful club in Rio. It was so lucky that he was twenty-one that year or he would not have been eligible. He saw seven of our Rushwater bulls there. Darling Martin," and her Ladyship relapsed into a pleasant dream of life as it used to be.

Mrs. Belton felt very sorry for young Grantly, but as she only knew him and his parents slightly and did not know any of the real facts of the case, she did not see her way to doing anything and began to read a number of *Country Life* which had an article about the Chinese rococo garden-house in Mr. Belton's grounds at Harefield, now alas in very poor condition, and so fell to thinking of all the families who were gradually sinking as THEY increased their senseless rapacity and bled every goose whether its eggs were gold or land, which led her to think of rationed eggs and so to gratitude for her own lot with hens and some ducks, and so again to a kind of pleasant lapse of consciousness in which we believe Lady Graham also participated.

Meanwhile the cow party were down at the farm. Lord Lufton had torn his cowman Pucken from the kitchen where he had made a considerable impression on Cook. Pucken had been introduced formally to Goble and both men had become perfectly speechless; the one feeling too proud and too shy to ask questions; the other determined not to divulge anything unless asked a question point-blank. In vain did Lord Stoke and Emmy put leading questions. In vain did Lord Lufton suggest to Pucken that he might tell Goble about the cow who had suddenly dried up for no reason, got into the remains of what had been Lady Lufton's Italian garden, eaten three beds of nasturtiums (planted in lieu of the old bedding out) and completely recovered. From neither Goble nor Pucken could more than: "Ar. There's some as says so," or: "I can't say I've heard tell of it though maybe there's some as has," be extracted. Lord Stoke, being deaf and seeing their mouths move from time to time, was pretty cheerful, but everyone else was in considerable gloom and Emmy ready to cry at the failure of her great plan, when who should come up but Tom Grantly.

"I say, Tom," said Emmy, pulling him aside as soon as he had greeted the others. "It's awful. Lord Lufton brought his cowman over to talk to Goble about a dairy herd he wants to try and now they won't talk. It's too awful."

"All right, Emmy, don't fuss," said Tom, though very kindly.

"We'll see what we can do. Well, Goble, how is your boy?" for Tom had frequently been to Holdings with Emmy during the last two years and was welcome in drawing-room and farm.

"Doing nicely, Mr. Tom," said Goble. "Got his wings last week. I said to him: 'Your old Dad mayn't know much about aireoplanes and all that, flying in the face of Providence right among the stars,' I said, 'but there's some stars your Dad knows better than you'll ever know them, my lad.' He says: 'What stars is that, Dad?'" and here Goble paused to mark the climax.

"I say, what stars were they, Goble?" said Emmy, rising to histrionic heights unsuspected by any of her audience.

"'There's some stars you'll never know as well as your Dad, my boy, I says,'" Goble repeated, not sorry to keep his audience in quivering suspense, "'and that's the Milky Way,' I says, and he says to me: 'Well, Dad,' he says, 'you're about right.' You should'a heard him laugh, Mr. Tom."

This interesting anecdote though it seemed rather pointless was received with sycophantic laughter by the audience, Pucken alone remaining serious.

"Can't you see it, Pucken?" said Lord Lufton.

"I seen what Mr. Goble said all right, my lord," said Pucken, "but I don't fare to laugh. My old mother she'd have boxed my ears if I'd laughed at that."

"Why?" said Emmy.

Lord Stoke then requested to have it all explained to him, which was done with hearty bellowings.

Pucken was heard to murmur something about it being rude.

"Come on, Pucken," said Tom. "What's it all about?"

"Well, sir," said Pucken, at once recognizing Tom as one of those set by heaven in authority over cowmen, "there's ladies here."

"Oh, they're not ladies," said Tom, jerking his head towards Emmy, Clarissa, and Edith. "Come on Pucken."

"Well, sir, I dessay Mr. Goble being a foreigner doesn't know what he's saying," said Pucken. "But in our parts, sir, we calls it—"

But before he could finish, Goble, who though living at least fifteen miles from Pucken was not entirely ignorant of foreign customs, suddenly burst into a loud laugh, betokening the sharing of a joke common to the real Barsetshire people, no property of the gentry however much one's friends. Goble hit Pucken on the back, Pucken poked Goble in the waistcoat and the two men, one a master the other a worthy aspirant in the craft, walked away towards the cow-sheds together.

"How *did* you do it, Tom," said Emmy in pure admiration.

Tom said he had read a bit and knocked about a bit.

"You're one of the ones people tell things to," said Emmy, without any envy in her generous nature, but rather wistfully.

A half-hearted attempt was made to find out what had made Goble laugh but Tom and Emmy, steadfast in purpose, finding Lord Lufton anxious to learn, took him round the cow-sheds at a decent distance from Goble and Pucken and answered his questions with endless patience while Lord Stoke, never averse to female society, followed them with Clarissa and Edith who was meditating a poem on a very young calf which she had seen nuzzling into a pail of milk and knocking it over.

When Tom and Emmy had given Lord Lufton what Emmy described as a good do they brought him back to the house, faint but still pursuing, handed him over to the older ladies as if he were a schoolboy out on a half-holiday, and went for a chilly walk along the river Rising, by the edge of the water-meadows.

"I say, Tom," said Emmy after a friendly silence. "What's wrong?"

Tom said Nothing; a word which never deceives anyone.

"I mean I daresay you miss being out of doors a bit," said Emmy.

Tom said oh, that was all right and he could be out of doors all the weekend if he wanted to, and kicked some small stones with calculated cruelty.

"Is that Harvey man *very* awful?" said Emmy. "I mean the Marlings say he is pretty ghastly."

Tom said oh, he was all right and one had to take things as one found them, to which Emmy made no reply.

"How's Macpherson?" said Tom, with a shabby-jaunty air of changing the subject, but there was again no answer.

"What's wrong?" said Tom in his turn and stopped short, looking down at Emmy, who was making the faces one makes if one is not crying, oh no, nor wanting to cry; not in the least.

In a kind of suppressed choke Emmy was understood to say something about being unhappy.

"Who's making you unhappy?" said Tom. "I'll shoot him at once. I've still got my army revolver though I oughtn't."

"*I'm* not unhappy," said Emmy. "But you are. It's too *awful*," and with a great effort she checked her wish to sob and banged her handkerchief against her eyes. "Tom!"

"Well?" said Tom, with a worse sinking feeling than he had ever had, even when he had to use the top of a factory chimney as an observation post and wondered if he would ever dare to come down.

"Oh Tom, why *did* you leave Rushwater?" said Emmy. "I mean I wouldn't have minded—not really minded—but this horrible job is making you unhappy. You know it is. *Please* stop having it. I'll let you show Rushwater Churchill yourself at the Royal Show next year."

There was no getting away from so devoted an offer. Tom felt his face hot with shame at Emmy's generosity.

"Look here, Emmy," he said, "I can't. I chucked Rushwater and took this on. I can't chuck it now. I've been a beast."

"You haven't," said Emmy indignantly.

"And Ungrateful," said Tom, rather enjoying himself. "And a perfect Hog. I didn't mean to tell even you, Emmy. I don't know how to stick it, but I must."

"But why?" said Emmy, the blood of the Leslies and the Pomfrets rising in her. "They can't put you in prison."

"No. I've damn well put myself in, like a fool," said Tom, "so I must stick it. I can't run away from everything. It's all right, Em. It's not a bad job, only—"

"Only what?" said Emmy after waiting for a moment.

"Oh, nothing. My imagination," said Tom. "Let's go back."

"Wait a minute," said Emmy. "It's that dreadful Mr. Harvey. I know it is. He's got his knife into you. Cousin Amabel says he was ghastly at Marling and so does everyone. I'd like to kill him."

There was a silence and then Tom, looking across the Rising, never meeting Emmy's eyes, said a fellow couldn't chuck jobs like that. He had wanted to go to the Red Tape and Sealing Wax, he said, and he had got what he wanted and serve him right and anyway the work was very interesting and Emmy must cheer up.

"I get a long weekend soon," he said, "and I'll come to Rushwater and we'll clean Wooden Spring. That's a job that ought to have been done long ago."

Emmy said it would be great fun and they went back to the house, but only Emmy knew how hard it was to pretend one wasn't wretched and anxious. The rest of the cow party had returned to the Saloon and were having South African sherry; for fourteen and sixpence a bottle is quite enough when one knows that They are pocketing most of it. Clarissa was feeding the wood fire with dry fir cones, the flames were leaping on the hearth, the sherry though slightly liverish was warming, and no one wanted to face the summer evening. Clarissa had taken Lord Lufton under her wing and was patronizing him, but his Lordship seemed grateful for even this notice and his worried face became almost tranquil. Agnes was not a matchmaker for her own children beyond trying to guide them towards the friends that she (and very luckily they too) preferred, but no mother can help wondering. She looked at Lord Lufton mellowing in Clarissa's ambience; she looked at Clarissa, her aloof, elegant daughter, entertaining Lord Lufton. Then her maternal glance moved to Emmy, the eldest of her girls, who had lived almost entirely at Rushwater for some years now with her cousins the Martin Leslies and she wondered why Emmy looked sad, for Emmy's was one of those heaven-sent dispositions that take everything in the days' work and whose hard-working days are rounded with deep and refreshing sleep. Not unnaturally she had wondered from time to time whether Emmy would fall in love with Tom Grantly, or perhaps rather whether Tom Grantly would fall in love with Emmy, but had not seen any particular signs of either. However she loved her Emmy and trusted her and one cannot manage one's independent daughters now, so she looked elsewhere and saw Charles and Edith in deep converse. No talk of falling in love there with some fifteen years between them, but a dear nice boy and a nice friend for the girls. What Clarissa was feeling about Charles, her mother very sensibly decided she would never know. The understanding, as Charles had called it, was still there: what else might be there she would not yet try to discover. Her fingers would not pull aside the petals yet unfolded.

"A nice boy that of Grantly's," said Lord Stoke to her in his useful, loud, thought-destroying voice. "It's a pity he's gone into one of those meddlesome government offices. They'll break him there all right. *He* knows a cow when he sees one," which last remark Lady Graham took in its wider and more philosophic sense. "Why can't he settle down at Rushwater, eh? Marry some nice girl with a bit of money and be useful on the place. That girl of yours, Emmy, that's the name, has a good head, Lady Graham. Like your mother. *She* knows a cow when she sees one."

"Darling Emmy," said Agnes, gazing at her eldest daughter who with her yellow hair very untidy was shouting down Charles Belton about the small pig-establishment he had started at the Priory School. "When she was small, she fell into the pond in the kitchen-garden at Rushwater and got quite wet. There was a charming Frenchman who got her out. Ivy, who is Rose's nurse now, was nursery-maid then and she ran for the perambulator rug and Nurse took Emmy to the house and dried her," overcome by which beautiful recollection of time past, her Ladyship fell into a kind of motherly trance.

"Frenchmen, eh?" said Lord Stoke. "No Frenchmen here, Lady Graham. Shouldn't care if I never saw a Frenchman again myself. People that call a turnip a navvy. Shows they haven't any idea of grammar. My people used to go to Mentone every winter and take all the servants with them. Sensible idea I call it. What's the use of taking a villa with a lot of servants that can't understand you?"

Lady Graham said that her husband had a very good soldier servant in the first war who had been in Gibraltar and learned Spanish.

"Well, good-bye," said Lord Stoke. "That young Grantly has a head on his shoulders. *He* won't be long at the Red Tape place," with which vague but comforting reassurance he went away.

It had for some time been obvious to Lady Graham and Mrs. Belton that Lord Lufton did not know how to go. Whether he wished to go and was unable through shyness, or did not wish to go because he was enjoying himself, they were not sure. But it was rapidly becoming evident that unless something was done about him he would still be there at midnight, his hands damp, his face working with nervousness.

"You wouldn't stay to supper with Charles?" said Agnes to Mrs. Belton. "Then poor Ludovic could stay too and he would simply have to go afterwards."

Mrs. Belton said she would have loved it but her husband was expecting her.

"I wish Charles could stay," she said, looking across the room to where Charles was exercising the attraction of a good-looking young man on Edith's susceptible heart, "but I can't drive and even if I could how would Charles get home?"

"Oh dear, I do wish Merry were here," said Lady Graham with a half sigh, thinking of Miss Merriman, once the invaluable secretary of old Lady Pomfret, then the invaluable secretary-companion-friend and, if we may borrow the term from the Dean of St. Patrick's, flapper to Agnes's delightful wayward and quite maddening mother Lady Emily Leslie; now again at Pomfret Towers helping and supporting the family she loved. "She always knew exactly what to do. Darling Clarissa is too clever. She sees other people as they are, but not always quite kindly as they are. And so aloof, if that is the word I mean," she added, casting one loving look at her pretty self-contained daughter entertaining Lord Lufton and Tom Grantly in one breath. "Charles," she called in her soft voice, "do come here and give me good advice."

Charles, with a flatteringly grown-up apology to Edith, came over to Lady Graham's sofa and curled his long legs up on a pouf at the ladies' feet.

"If you want a proud foe to make tracks, Or to melt a rich uncle in wax," he said conversationally, "I'm your man. What can I do for to run, for to fetch, for to carry?"

"You silly boy," said Lady Graham, which Edwardian remark so enchanted Charles that he hugged his own knees and rocked backwards and forwards till he nearly fell off the pouf. "Listen, Charles, I *know* Ludovic doesn't know how to get away."

"And I know he doesn't want to. Proceed," said Charles.

"So I thought if you all stayed to supper it wouldn't show so much," said Lady Graham, "only your mother says she must go home."

"If she must, she must," said Charles. "I'll drive her back, Cousin Agnes, and then I'll come back here."

Both ladies of course raised a confused and henlike chorus of protest, when with a loud cheerful noise John and Robert Graham came back full of their triumphs at a tennis party, and as they boasted in their young self-confidence to their three sisters Mrs. Belton thought she had seldom seen such good looks allied to such intelligence and charm in one family.

"If only James were here," said Lady Graham, "but he is on a course. I cannot think why," with which helpful comment she resigned all her cares to fate.

"Hi! John!" said Charles. "Can I borrow your car and run Mother home? It's quicker than mine. And much more expensive," he added.

A great hubub then arose of people being unselfish and trying to plan other people's lives simultaneously, under cover of which tumult Charles said quietly to his mother that he would drive her home and then come back to Holdings and it wouldn't take more than half an hour. His mother, with private reservations as to the time mentioned, said that would do perfectly and with a quick good-bye to Agnes she left the room, followed by Charles. And so intoxicating are the joys of arguing from no particular premises about nothing in particular that their departure was not noticed by the young people.

"Why don't you ring up Framley and say you're staying to supper too?" said Clarissa to Lord Lufton. "Goble will give your cowman supper. He keeps an extremely good table," at which piece of affectation Lord Lufton laughed in a sudden and artless way.

"You sound as if you didn't laugh often," said Clarissa, at which Lord Lufton looked so wretched that she tried on him a smile which she was engaged in copying from her uncle David's wife Rose Leslie and Lord Lufton's face suddenly melted to a look of such pure pleasure and admiration that Lady Graham, catching sight of him across the room, wondered why she had thought him rather awkward and uninteresting.

The sun after the most disgraceful sulks all day had changed its mind. Gradually while the tumult was going on in the Saloon the wind had dropped, the grey clouds had unhastingly moved onwards and now only showed as grey billows above the line of the downs, under the blue arch of the sky. The tennis players annexed some of the stay-at-homes for another set and carried Tom Grantly and Emmy away with them while Edith very importantly volunteered to be umpire if she could sit on the garden steps. These were obligingly brought by her brother

Robert who was also a poet but only in his mind and not, as Edith was, in occasional verse.

"Would you care to walk by the river?" said Clarissa to Lord Lufton in her society voice, which even three years of college had not altered.

"Of all things," said Lord Lufton gravely. Clarissa, turning a quick glance on him, saw that his eyes were amused and wondered what he was really like, to which end she asked him about his mother and sisters. Either Lord Lufton was not very good at describing or Clarissa was not very quick at understanding, for no particular impression was left on her mind. His mother sounded as if she were kind, his sister Maria who bred cocker spaniels sounded rather terrifying and his sister Justinia who was doing secretary work for the Dean must, she thought, be very dull, though this she did not say aloud. But always in her mind was the picture of her companion in the bull's stall. Of course Emmy wouldn't have asked him in if there had been any danger, but even so not everyone would have liked to go into Rushwater Churchill's home uninvited. Clarissa was naturally fearless, but sooner than go into that den she would have shown any number of white feathers, and all these thoughts needed so much attention that she was silent. Had she known that Lord Lufton's heart was beating a little faster beside her, she would have been extremely surprised. He had no intention of speaking to her about the state of his heart, yet ever since lunch at Rushwater he had remembered the look that met him across the lunch table. No, it had not met him. It was a thousand miles, a thousand years away from him, but it had pierced him to the quick. Now, walking by the side of this pretty and proud creature, he wondered if his memory had played him false—if he had seen something that was not really there. But such poetic musings are not of any particular help to a young peer worried by the cares of an estate and feeling unequal to a burden which he cannot avoid.

"This is where my Uncle David got engaged to Rose," said Clarissa, pausing in front of an uninteresting seat by the path. "I wish I could live with them. They have a house in London and a tiny flat in Paris, and lots of friends in America and they fly everywhere. Rose is too too ravishingly smart."

Lord Lufton, not really much interested in this story, gallantly tried to do his best by asking if she was like Cora Palliser, and Clarissa said in a lofty way that she did not know her very well.

"You ought to," said Lord Lufton, upon which Clarissa took a violent dislike to her Ladyship and determined never under any conditions to admit that she had beauty, wit or charm. "And I wish you knew Justinia, that's my younger sister. I mean she's older than me but she's younger than Maria. She is only being secretary to the Dean till she can get a better job, but she loves being at the Deanery so I don't think she will."

"Was she at a secretarial college?" said Clarissa. "I only went to Cambridge," and then heard, like an echo, how odious her voice must sound, but Lord Lufton was apparently unconscious of any spikiness and said Justinia had done a year's training and had been offered a job in the Red Tape and Sealing Wax, but she had heard that the Dean wanted someone and preferred the Close.

"And I don't blame her," said Lord Lufton. "That man Harvey seems to be quite impossible and has a name for being unfair to his people if they are ladies or gentlemen or interested in anything but getting on. I must say I'm awfully lucky to be so busy on my own job. I mean Framley and all that sort of thing and county work. Your mother does a lot, doesn't she? And your sister and those nice cousins of yours at Rushwater?"

Clarissa was about to answer when she suddenly realized how little she knew of what the Leslie family in general was doing. Alone for so much of the war, her brothers at school and panting to get into the army though only James had been old enough to begin his career as a professional soldier in an O.C.T.U. before peace broke out; living her own self-centered life at Holdings with her child's and girl's adoration of her grandmother Lady

Emily Leslie; ambitious to go to college and study engineering draughtsmanship and trying to stifle the dull pain of her grandmother's death by working harder than ever; and now, perhaps, finding that things were more or less dust and ashes. She had got a degree and wondered why she had worked so hard to get it. Mr. Adams the wealthy ironmaster had promised her a job in his drawing office, amused and indeed impressed by the ambitions of this pretty, self-possessed young lady, but she could not feel any elation. She had been liked at college but never made close friends, for her family gave her all she wanted. There had been a summer when she set her cap at Captain Belton R.N., Charles's elder brother, but his heart was with Susan Dean and he had scorned her—though if we may discount Clarissa's self-dramatizing it was not so much scorning as barely noticing her existence. It was then and once again later that Charles Belton had come to her rescue with a kind of rough chivalry, not without thought for her, and considering her youth, her charm, her silliness, had suggested that they should be as it were engaged. Clarissa had told her mother who approved and pondered it a good deal in her own heart. Charles had told his mother, who had suggested as a compromise that one might call it an understanding. On that footing it had remained and Clarissa was no nearer knowing what her true feelings were than she had been a year ago. What Charles may have been thinking we cannot say, but he had inherited a strong sense of responsibility and was not likely to lay down any burden until such time as one better qualified than himself might take it up.

It might have embarrassed even Clarissa to answer all Lord Lufton's questions, but the weather, feeling that it had given people a long enough run for their money, was now going to the dogs again with all its might. A dull wind blew, spiky rain began to lash their faces and they reached the house breathless just as a cold storm broke, driving the tennis players indoors.

"I ought to have put my coat round you," said Lord Lufton, just before they joined the rest of the party. "Are you wet?"

Clarissa smiled brilliantly, said she was quite dry and slipped into one of the family groups.

Charles was back in an alarmingly short space of time and rather to Clarissa's annoyance fell into motor shop with John Graham till supper was ready. In normal times (that is to say never again, *consulibus Illis*) Edith would have been in the schoolroom quarters by this time and having a light supper before going to bed, but there was no governess, no old nurse, and much to her elder brothers' and sisters' indignation she had been made free of the evening meal; and indeed we shall be lucky if all our children are not eating fish and chips at ten o'clock at night after a happy evening at the movies.

Lord Lufton, safely ensconced between Lady Graham and Emmy, listened with admiration to the foolish, sometimes brilliant, always amusing gabbling that went on between Charles Belton and Tom Grantly and the younger Grahams and wondered how one learnt to talk easily. Even Edith took her part with an aplomb he deeply envied. Lady Graham was deep in talk with her youngest son Robert about the cubbing season, and planning a morning or two for him before he went back to school. Lord Lufton would have liked to join them, but was too shy.

"I say," said Emmy, her kindly heart feeling that their guest needed cheering up, "what are your cow-sheds like? The Rushwater ones aren't bad, but the buildings are pretty old."

Very cautiously, for he did not wish to expose his ignorance, Lord Lufton gave Emmy an outline of the Framley farm buildings and the improvements he proposed to make, expecting to be told that everything was wrong. But to his astonishment and pleasure Emmy, after listening with real attention (a state of things he was not used to at home), gave it as her opinion that it might be worse and very handsomely suggested paying him a visit of inspection.

"Would you really?" said Lord Lufton, flattered by the expert's condescension.

"Rather," said Emmy. "I say, what about your mother? I mean
wouldn't she like to do the asking? I mean I'd love to come
anyway, but I've never been to Framley before."

Lord Lufton was at once self-convicted of a gross breach of
decency and looked anxious and miserable and mumbled something about his mother always being awfully nice to everyone.

"Of course she is," said Emmy, to whom such a contingency
as the disapproval of Lady Lufton had not occurred. "Look here
you tell her you want me to have a look at the cow-sheds and
then if she says yes, you ring me up. It's a bit far to bicycle, but I
can borrow Martin's car one day."

"Or I would come and fetch you," said Lord Lufton, wishing
to do all in his power for an honoured guest.

"But then you'd have to take me back too," said Emmy, whose
mind was extremely clear and practical.

"Oh, I could easily do that," said Lord Lufton. "I say, you
don't think I didn't mean to?"

"Well, as a matter of fact I didn't think," said Emmy. "But
anyway thanks awfully. If Lady Lufton will say when it suits her
I'd love to come. Are you going in for artificial insemination?"

Lord Lufton stood this very well.

"I don't know," he said. "You see I really know so little about
it. But I could easily learn—I mean try to learn."

"Oh, you'll learn all right," said Emmy and then her mother
claimed Lord Lufton.

The far side of the table was now getting rather noisy where
Edith, intoxicated with late hours and company, was laying
abandoned siege to Charles amid her brothers' jeers.

"Shut up, you Grahams," said Charles. "I want to hear Edith's
poem."

"It's only a short one," said Edith, at which her brother John
said Hurrah and Tom Grantly put a strong hand over his
mouth.

"*Pax!*" said John, indistinctly.

"Right, Edith," said Tom.

"It is short," said Edith.

Her brother John made as if to speak but thought better of it.

"It says," continued the poetess:

> "If I had a band of carles
> I would make them work for Charles.
> I would beat them with my belt on
> If they did not for—'"

"False rhyme! false rhyme," said her brother John.

"Leave the baby alone," said her brother Robert and a subdued battle took place across Edith, who sat rather smugly, appearing to consider herself as a kind of Queen of Beauty in whose honour a passage at arms was being conducted.

"Wicked ones! wicked ones!" said Agnes in her soft voice and not without a touch of maternal pride. "I do not know what you will think of us, Ludovic."

"I think you are so kind," he said. "Could I come again?"

"Of course, dear boy," said Agnes. "And perhaps your mother will let me come over to Framley. I don't think I have seen it since before the war. Let us go into the Saloon."

There is little more to say about that evening. Edith got decidedly above herself owing to Lord Lufton's and Charles's attentions and was quietly sent to bed. Tom Grantly said if anyone would like to see where he was working he could offer them a nasty lunch at the Red Tape Canteen but he wouldn't advise them to accept it. Lord Lufton's cowman was sent for and the party gathered on the steps to say good-bye, Lord Lufton in his old but once good car, Charles in a kind of battered small touring-car bought for fifteen pounds and lovingly kept alive by himself and Sergeant Hopkins, Tom on his bicycle. Then the Graham circle closed again as though no party had ever been.

CHAPTER 8

Among his other preoccupations Cecil had not forgotten the suggestion made previously by Charles Belton that they should devote a day to cutting the rushes on the lake at Harefield, too long neglected through the war, the peace, and the shortage of labour. A kind of mass meeting was held at the Priory School with Charles in the chair, Cecil Waring representing the navy, and most of the staff representing the army. The junior master Mr. Swan, who was to be on duty on the Saturday in question, was rather depressed, giving as a reason that he nourished a permanent dislike of his cousins who lived on the lake on account of some other swan cousins who used to flap their wings at him when he was sculling on the river at Southbridge School, hearing of which the Headmaster very kindly said he would do Saturday duty himself that day and anyway it was the last Saturday of the term. The ranks were further strengthened by the three young Perrys, sons of the doctor, and the two young Updikes, sons of the lawyer, who knew the lake inside out.

As no ladies were present we are not able to give much information about the rush-cutting except that it was an enormous success. Old Humble who had been about the place all his life enjoyed himself immensely, sometimes on the bank, sometimes in an old boat which he rowed in a kind of sea-going way with short oars and a circular motion. And wherever he went misfortune perched on the prow, or quite as often at the helm, for the boat had no particular front or back and old Humble rowed backwards and forwards according to his whim, and wherever his creaking rowlocks were heard so surely did a rush-cutter wading round the island have a boot sucked off in the mud, or a boatman come up against a hidden snag and wind himself severely with an oar, with the exception of Sergeant Hopkins who worked steadily and quietly in his own way.

However by six o'clock the growth of the last ten years had been satisfactorily dealt with and the workers, very hot and dirty and happy, had a kind of gigantic high tea, or shall we say high beer, at the upper end of the lake where the ruins of the old pumping-house stood. Just as Gus Perry, the skin disease specialist, now in partnership with his father, was demonstrating with a Spam sandwich a peculiarly revolting form of fungoid growth on the human face, a motor horn was heard and a car came down the track, strictly forbidden to motorists, that led to the main road. It slithered in the damp ground and came to a standstill.

"Cora?" said Cecil, with mingled surprise, pleasure and—we regret to say—annoyance. For however attractive and delightful a woman may be, she can and often does spoil the fun.

"The same," said Lady Cora, smiling at the group of workers. The three Perrys, both Updikes, the senior master who had just got his second pip by the skin of his teeth before peace broke out, the junior master who had been a captain and the new master, Mr. Swan, all fell in love with her at once, while old Humble, scenting quality, dragged a rotting tarpaulin from his boat and spread it over a muddy piece of road in the manner of Sir Walter Raleigh.

Lady Cora gave him a dazzling smile and asked Cecil Waring for a shilling.

"Not now," he said. "I'll give him one when you have gone."

As Lady Cora said nothing he added rather lamely: "How are you?"

"Well," said Lady Cora, "but requiring help. Shall we walk a little?"

Wondering what help she could need, Cecil adapted himself to her whim and they walked slowly along the edge of the lake.

"It's that nice boy Tom Grantly," said Lady Cora. "The one who quotes Browning at me. And don't look misunderstood for he does not aspire to my hand—nor do I if you see what I mean."

On hearing these simple words Cecil decided not to commit suicide as he had been proposing to himself one second earlier.

"I would do anything I could to help you—I mean him," he said, "but I don't quite see how at the moment."

"Nor do I," said Lady Cora. "It's that dreadful man Geoffrey Harvey who has got his knife into him. Probably because Tom was a soldier. It takes them that way, you know. Perfectly Freudian. And Tom looks so worried, poor lamb. Could you perhaps have lunch with me on Wednesday in Silverbridge and I'll collect Tom. About one, or a little before, because everything is off so soon."

Cecil Waring was not particularly interested in Tom, but somehow the thought of lunch in a Silverbridge café was very attractive.

"I should love to lunch with you," he said, "but—"

"I didn't think *you* would say that," said Lady Cora.

"Say what?" said Cecil.

"You were going to say But you must lunch with me," said Lady Cora.

"Not in the least," said Cecil, lying with a swiftness and apparent guilelessness which did great credit to the British Navy. "What I *was* going to say was that I would have to make it a little later as I have to see my lawyers in Barchester that morning. Is that all right?"

"Perfect," said Lady Cora. "Thank you so much. What a handsome house up on the hill."

"That," said Cecil, following her look, "is Harefield House. It

was a girls' school in the war and I hope to persuade my
brother-in-law to take it for the Priory School. Then I can get
going with my own plans," and Lady Cora thought, or perhaps wished to think, we cannot be sure, that though his words
were plain his meaning was not and she thought it might be
amusing—no more than amusing of course—to know the meaning that lay behind the words. So she said good-bye and got into
her car.

"It's all clear, my lady," said old Humble, who had come
hobbling up and was pretending to be a policeman dealing with
traffic on Derby Day.

"Thanks," said Lady Cora, as she swung her car round.
"You're a Wheeler, aren't you?"

"My old mother was a Wheeler, my lady," said Humble. "but
my father was a Humble and that's my name. Leastways it's the
name I've always gone by and it's a wise child that knows its own
father."

"All right, Humble," said Lady Cora. "I expect your mother
knew anyway. Sir Cecil will look after you."

And she drove up the track and vanished onto the road.

"Thanks, Humble," said Cecil, as he tipped him.

"Thank you, sir," said Humble, who by the weight and the
milled edge had recognized the coin as a half-crown. "A fine
young lady, sir. Might be a Duke's daughter."

"She is," said Cecil. "The Duke of Omnium's daughter, Lady
Cora Palliser," and when he had said it he felt slightly ashamed.
Not because it sounded snobbish, a thought which we may say
would not have come into his head, but because he had named
her for the pleasure of hearing his own voice saying the name, a
pleasure most incident to both sexes when the heart is engaged.
Was not David Copperfield sometimes moved, at home, in his
own room, to cry out: "Oh, Miss Shepherd!" in a transport of
love?

"Is the young lady coming to see the show, sir?" said old
Humble.

Cecil said he hoped so.

"Her Ladyship will have something to see, sir. That old spring in the lake she don't fare to do no good," said old Humble whose conversation was an alternate joy and irritation to all folklore enthusiasts, as he was very old and very wicked. Old enough to remember what his elders had told him going back some ninety or a hundred years, but also cunning enough to tell the gentry exactly what they wanted to know. They used to want arrow-heads on the downs, in which the young Humble had done a thriving trade, and now they wanted places to have something unpleasant connected with them, a task for which the wicked old man was peculiarly fitted. "There's a rhyme about that old spring, sir, as my granfer learned me," Mr. Humble continued, though in private life he very rightly said grandfather, usually with an unpleasant adjective preceding it.

"All right. Let's have it," said Cecil, suddenly and for no reason feeling that old Humble was not a bad old chap.

"I wouldn't say her, not before ladies, sir, nor maidens neither," said old Humble, becoming deliberately more archaic.

"All right. Five shillings then," said Cecil, who was in a mood to give hostages to fortune right and left.

"It's this-a-way, zur," said old Humble, or that was what Cecil thought he heard him say:

> "Young Job Potter's a gormed young fool
> Couldn't swim and went on the pool.
> Went on the ice and the ice went crack
> Young Job Potter went down on his back.
> Went on his back and went down in the pool
> Young Job Potter's a gormed young fool.
> Fishes they ate all his guts away
> He'd ha' been ninety-nine if he'd lived till today,'

and thank your honour very kindly," added old Humble, touching his hat as Cecil gave him the five shillings. He then folded up the piece of rotting tarpaulin and threw it into his boat.

Cecil, reflecting in a rather addled way upon life in general, said good-bye to his young helpers, collected Sergeant Hopkins, walked up to Arcot House where he had left his car, and drove back to the Priory.

He was dining, as indeed he mostly did, with his sister Leslie Winter and when, as it says in old novels, he had made a slight change in his attire, or in other words washed his hands and looked at his collar and decided it would do, he went by the garden to the School House where, as he had rather hoped, he found his sister Leslie alone, darning socks.

"I often think that little boys are centipedes," said Leslie. "At least four pairs of ordinary socks a week, not to speak of football stockings and white socks in summer for the first eleven. How did the rush-cutting go?"

Her brother said Not too badly, in an absent-minded voice.

Leslie asked if anything else had happened.

"I don't think so," said Cecil. "An old man called Humble sang me a wonderful ballad about someone called Job Potter who was drowned in the lake. Pure fake it was, but I had to tip the old impostor. Oh, and Cora Palliser came to look at us for a few minutes," he added in an off-hand way which did not deceive his sister in the least. "She wanted me to lunch with her in Silverbridge on Wednesday."

His sister in the course of her life, which had included a good deal of experience in work requiring discretion, had learnt that most people are bursting to give information and if given no encouragement will spill the beans to any extent, so she went on with her mending.

"You know Tom Grantly, the clergyman's son at Edgewood," said Cecil. "He is in the Red Tape and Sealing Wax—that bit of it that lives in Silverbridge—and apparently he has been getting across his chief—that man Geoffrey Harvey."

"Oh, *that* man," said Leslie.

"So Cora asked me to meet him at lunch to see if I could help him or give him some good advice," said Cecil. "Of course I can't. I would if I could, but I don't think anybody can. I thought I might as well accept as she had asked me."

"A quite dreadful man," said Leslie with unusual warmth. "I came across him in the war. Everyone in the department loathed him, but he always worked things his own way. He was always too important to fight."

"Come, come, be fair," said Cecil. "Some people are important."

"And equally," said his sister, "some people aren't. He wasn't. He only got a measly B.E. of sorts out of it though. I read a novel once where a man started an insurance society against getting any rank of B.E. There is that dreadful sister of his too, with the General Interference people at Gatherum. She made a dead set at poor Oliver Marling, I believe."

"I wonder exactly how awful one has to be for people to call one poor?" said Cecil meditatively, to which his sister answered that he would never have to know.

"And by the way Cora Palliser seems quite keen on the School," said Cecil.

His sister gave him a quick, loving, suspicious look; for when people say by the way it often means that they wish to say something very important to themselves, something they must say or burst, but they also burrow their heads into the sand with quite unwarranted faith in the blindness and idiocy of their audience. So Leslie said they must have her at the School again next term because the little boys all adored her.

"Do you know what that young devil Dean did?" said her husband who had joined them. "In the Latin exam they had to decline a first declension noun of their own choice, and he did Cora."

"And what did you do, darling?" said his wife.

"I took off five marks because *coram* is a preposition," said the Headmaster. "But I'm afraid he didn't mind in the least."

"Lucky child," said Leslie. "I always minded *everything*. Why do girls think school matters, Philip?"

"Because they are so silly, my love," said her husband. "What they want is good but firm husbands to knock the silliness out of them," at which his wife looked at him in a way that her brother thought too Patient Griselda for words. And then he was confused, for it was an echo of Lady Cora's manner of speech.

"Anything wrong, Cecil?" said his sister, for her thoughts often hovered round the piece of metal that was somewhere inside him and she imagined sudden and agonizing deaths. "I hope you didn't overdo it on the lake."

But her brother said it was only a thought.

On Wednesday he went to Barchester, did his business (which we shall not go into for we do not know what it was), went on to Silverbridge and arrived at Babs's Buttery, for such was the revolting name of the town's lunching-place, a little after one. Here he found Lady Cora inquiring with the sincere falseness of the practised hand after the health of Babs's old father. Babs, who was a red-faced jolly woman in her fifties wearing a flowered dress, a flowered apron, and plaited sandals with raffia flowers on them, with a fierce mop of grizzled hair that stuck out in all directions, had just finished telling Cora with perfect cheerfulness how Father had rung for her six times that night because he thought it was breakfast-time; which she appeared to think an intelligent and meritorious action on Father's part.

"That's the way to look at it," said Lady Cora when she had introduced Sir Cecil Waring. "The poorer you are the more fun your dotty old parents have. I always hope the parents will die on the same day, sweet lambs, and be buried in the same grave, because if one of them dies, the other will go gently dotty and we shall have to have nurses or companions and everyone's nerves on edge. When it's the cottagers it's different. When their fathers are dotty old men they make a bed for them in the kitchen or the sitting-room if there is one and everyone comes and goes and it's fun for the poor old thing. Then I should say: 'Come and talk to

Father, Mrs. Brown. He's quite bright today, aren't you Father?'
And Father would love it. He *adores* people."

"And what would happen if your father died first?" said Cecil.

"That we will *not* discuss," said Lady Cora. "Now. About
Tom Grantly. He ought to be here now."

"I shall be delighted to do what I can for him," said Cecil.
"But again I must ask you what *can* I do?"

"Stand by," said Lady Cora. "No, Miss Lefevre," she said to
Babs, who was making suggestions from a well-fingered menu
in smudged purple ink, "minestrone we will *not* have."

"You are wise, Lady Cora," said Miss Lefevre. "There wasn't
enough left on the plates yesterday to make a really good basis.
What soups need is a basis."

"You're telling *me*," said Lady Cora, and Cecil wondered how
this silly hackneyed phrase could sound so witty, so fitting.
"We'll have the Hamburgers and not till my other guest comes
please. I know they're only bits left over but they are minced, so
you can chew them which is more than you ever can with beef or
mutton. Yes, two vedge, please. And what about raspberry flan?"

"They are very nice deep freeze ones," said Miss Lefevre.

"They would be, in the raspberry season too," said Lady Cora.
"We've got loads of raspberries at the Castle. I can sell you all
you want at cost price. And I'll put some eggs in for your father,"
at which Miss Lefevre confounded herself in thanks and and
went off to the kitchen.

As Lady Cora had asked for a table for three, it was rather
naturally a table for four squashed into the wide bay window
with another table of the same size, commanding a good view of
the steep High Street.

"This," said Lady Cora suddenly, "has torn it."

Her escort asked what had torn what, to which her Ladyship's only reply was a very expressive look towards the street
and a grimace of disgust, which Cecil we must confess found
most attractive. To his horrified eyes there appeared Geoffrey
Harvey accompanied by a large woman with an earnest face,

dressed in what we can only describe as a very expensive style of unbecomingness.

"It's that ghastly Mixo-Lydian Ambassadress," said Lady Cora, "with the gallant, gay Geoffrey," which description of Geoffrey Harvey's tall form, dark saturine face and rather important manner made Cecil laugh. "No laughing matter, Cecil. We have had it."

We need not say that Mr. Harvey's eye, always on the lookout for his own advantage, at once seized Lady Cora and he came straight to her table.

"Lady Cora!" he exclaimed in the deep voice which he had found peculiarly fascinating to some of The Sex, and sketching a courtly bow over her hand. "Waring! my dear fellow I had the pleasure of meeting you at The Lodge when our charming Lady Silverbridge carried the prize away under my eyes, and I may say with hers."

Cecil's immediate impulse was to say If I am your dear fellow there is no need to tell me where we last met, knock Mr. Harvey down, throw a handful of gold on the table for the reckoning, and call for his horses. So he merely said Good-day.

"And may I introduce two most charming ladies to one another?" Mr. Harvey continued.

"*Czy pròvka, pròvka, pròvka*," said his companion. "Which eet is known that I have not any need for soch protocol for I am already acquaintink with Lady Cora at the Conservative Fête."

"It is a pleasure to meet your Excellency again," said Lady Cora.

"Ha! Of excellencies we will not speakink," said the Ambassadress, "for we have sympathy together when we meet at your father's castle. Is it not?"

"It is," said Lady Cora, pleased to see Mr. Harvey ruffled by this unexpected friendship.

"We shall sit with you, yes? We shall be which you coll boarders together?"

"I can't think of anything nicer," said Lady Cora, "but we are expecting a friend to lunch. Here he is, in fact," and Tom Grantly came in, full of apologies for being late, and at the same moment even fuller of horror at the sight of his chief.

"You will introducink," said the Ambassadress.

As this was evidently a diplomatic command, Lady Cora gravely introduced Tom to her Excellency, adding that his father was a distinguished clergyman.

"Eet is good, your church," said the Ambassadress, shaking hands with Tom and evidently pleased with the slight bow that he made. "Your priests are married, so as ours. Of single priests we say pouf. In Mixo-Lydia must each priest have two wives."

"The one to wash the other?" said Mr. Harvey jokingly.

"Bog! what is that stupidness you are speakink!" said the Ambassadress. "For washink, we have but twice yearly the wash. Then all the maidens comm to the river and wash the house linen, like our Princess Nskh which was washink her father's linen and was becomm in love of Odsh which is leavink her."

"It's Nausicaa and Odysseus," said Tom to Cecil in an awe-struck voice.

"My dear boy, we must not interrupt her Excellency," said Mr. Harvey. "*Affaire de protocol.*"

"Aha! which says me protocol?" said her Excellency. "I say pouf of it. I continue to tell you that our priests have two wives that when one is dead he may still have the other. God wills it so."

"And what happens if they both die?" said Tom, so fascinated by the Ambassadress that he hardly noticed the rest of the party.

"Then mosst he go back to the seminar which you say monk-house and do his examen all afresh. Bot why do we standink? Let everyone sit. To friends all is common," and pushing the other table up against Cecil's she sat down, patting the chair beside her with a look at Tom.

Tom, in spite of a want of self-confidence about his future, was no laggard in love. He looked at Lady Cora, saw amused permission in her eyes, and sat down by the Ambassadress.

"For your English food, it repugnates me," said the Ambassdress. "Which I eat is all equal to me. Give to us, Mistress Babs, which bill of fare Milady Cora has."

"I say, your Excellency," said Tom, "you can't call people mistress in England. It means someone who is living—" and then he stopped, wondering how much English she knew and understood. Partly to his relief, partly to his embarrassment, she burst into loud laughter, and saying "Roguey-poguey," poked him in the ribs.

"In Mixo-Lyida is Gradka, for which I am named, the un-married mother of our national hero Gradko which is the sonn of the maiden Gradka by her three hozbands which have *eventré* her, eventuated you would say," said her Excellency. "You would be like them?"

"If your Excellency doesn't mind," said Tom, his delight in the Ambassadress getting the upper hand of prudence.

"Then do we stroke the bargain," said the Ambassadress. "I call you Tom—weech pretty little name—and you call me Gradka. *On peut même dire* Grad," she added. "And we must drinkink."

"I'm afraid you can't here," said Lady Cora. "Too, too sick-ening, but it isn't licensed."

"In that case one can go out and get some," said Tom, and went into the kitchen, while Lady Cora and Gradka fell into conversation about the hot-water system at the Castle where her Excellency was spending a few days with Miss Harvey, and Cecil admired the little red decoration on Mr. Harvey's lapel.

"Nothing. Really nothing," said Mr. Harvey. "The French—*so* charming if you know them—absolutely *insisted*. I gave a couple of talks behind the Maginot Line. A most moving experience I can assure you."

Gradka interrupted the conversation for a moment to say "*Ces Français! On va vous en dire des nouvelles.* I tell you what they have done to my Mixo-Lydian friends in Algeria, yes?"

"No darling," said Lady Cora. "Absolutely not. And here is Tom with lovely, lovely beer. Bless you, my sweet."

The two large earthenware pitchers which Tom had borrowed from Babs, otherwise Miss Lefevre, made lunch a very pleasant affair for four of the party. Gradka gave a delightful account of her years in exile in England and how she had, while acting as cook to Sir Robert and Lady Fielding at Hallbury, worked so hard that she had passed the examination of the Society for the Propagation of English (by correspondence course) and in due time became head of the Bunting College (so called from the Fielding's old governess Miss Bunting who had helped Gradka with her studies), then a member of the Mixo-Lydian Trade Delegation, and so Ambassadress. Her conversation was supported and encouraged by Lady Cora and Cecil, who were enchanted to see Mr. Harvey for once entirely at a loss.

We do not wish to be unkind to Mr. Harvey. No: this is not quite true. We should dearly love to be unkind to him, but if *noblesse oblige*, so does middle class. We will merely say what our reader has doubtless already noticed, that Mr. Harvey was not by nature kind; that, a pillar of the Civil Service since he left Cambridge, he had stuck close to his desk and never gone to sea and if not actually Ruler of the Red Tape and Sealing Wax Department was well on the upward way and in a position which gave him every chance of gratifying his likes and dislikes. Even in the upper ranks of the Ministry he was cordially and increasingly unpopular, but he was a good, almost a brilliant official, so every now and then Whitehall allowed the wolf to accuse and then devour a lamb; or in other words to use every possible means fair or foul, and there are many which while ungentlemanly are perfectly legal, to frighten, wear down and finally get rid of any junior to whom he took a dislike. Tom Grantly had from the first earned his chief's bad opinion. The reasons were several and unreasonable, and some of them undoubtedly were that Tom was of good county family and had done quite well in the war and quite well at Oxford. But the last and unforgivable reason for his dislike was that Lady Cora had taken Tom under her wing from the moment of their meeting and paid no attention to Mr. Harvey at all. Petty, one may say. But a great many people and ideas are petty, and so goes the world. Therefore had Mr. Harvey made Tom's life increasingly difficult and Tom had felt it keenly though he kept it mostly to himself, only overflowing occasionally to his friend and ally Emmy Graham. To be spiteful makes one more spiteful and so on in geometrical progression (one hopes that to be kind and generous has the same effect, but as nasty things are usually more obvious than nice ones, we may say that arithmetical progression would be the better term), and Mr. Harvey could now hardly look at Tom without indulging in a Soliloquy in a Spanish Cloister; which comparison is reasonable, seeing how much Browning had passed between Lady Cora and Tom.

Tom had just told Gradka about what he called his one real battle when, after twenty-four hours' artillery fighting in Normandy and a rapid advance, the only breakfast his batman could find was *pâté de foie gras* and benedictine, and never had these delicacies been less welcome.

"My poor *lamb!*" said Lady Cora, while Gradka crossed herself in the Mixo-Lydian fashion, once described by the well-known novelist Mrs. Morland as upside down and irreligious.

"Ah, Tom," said Mr. Harvey, "your sufferings were indeed great. But pity us, my dear fellow, condemned to an *embusqué* life—"

"At Marling Melicent, well away from the bombing," said Cecil Waring so that Lady Cora and Gradka could just hear him and Mr. Harvey suspected the worst.

"—chained to our desks for as much as sixteen hours a day in times of stress."

It had gradually dawned upon the Ambassadress that Mr. Harvey, whose sister she already cordially disliked, was deliberately being sarcastic and rude to a lower rank who could not well answer back. Tom's unfortunate essay on the word mistress had thoroughly suited her sense of humour and to see Mr. Harvey baiting him annoyed her excessively. Strong in the sense of diplomatic privilege she flew to her friend's rescue.

"Hah! Hark me this type which chivvies and worrits a yong man," said the Ambassadress. "Let me tell you, Mr. Red Tape, this yong chap as you say is not sayink sixteen hours is too moch when he is fightink for you, and for your sister which is a woman repugnate to me. I say Pouf of you. *Czy pròvka, pròvka, pròvka.*"

There was a complete and—except in Mr. Harvey's case—pleasurable silence. Lady Cora, who was almost fearless, was the first to speak.

"But my dear Ambassadress, how too, too Dickens," she said. "Chivvies and worrits."

"Ollready is your Dickens translated into Mixo-Lydian," said Gradka, "of our most best translators. I am myself translatink Bleak House which in Mixo-Lydian is said *Hroj Czandik.*"

"How do you say chivvied and worrited?" said Lady Cora.

"Ah, eet ees free lessons you are havink," said Gradka laughing. "But I shall tell you eet is *skrobda na hjrani.*"

"I cannot, alas, read Dickens myself," said Mr. Harvey with a deprecating yet conceited smile. "It has been a delightful lunch, Waring. I must fly to my desk. My junior will doubtless not be far behind me if not otherwise engaged."

Tom Grantly, goaded by many pin-pricks and petty slights, said, quite respectfully, that he was due to clock in at two fifteen and would be punctual.

"And let me tellink you, Mr. Red Tape Secretary," said the Ambassadress, "that Red Tape is all robbish and you are a robbisher. God wills it so. Allso who does not read Charles Dickens is a Schwenk, which is a vermin that is died and becomm eaten by maggots. Ha!"

It is not easy to say a good exit after such an address from a large determined lady with diplomatic privilege, so Mr. Harvey gave a kind of collective bow to the company, putting into it respect for a landowner, admiration for Lady Cora as a fine figure of a woman, lofty scorn for Gradka with a nuance of respect for her status, and ignoring Tom. At least that was what he meant to convey, though we doubt if any of his audience had sufficient feeling for the finer shades to understand it. He then paid for the Ambassadress and himself and went away.

Lady Cora was the first to recover and asked Miss Lefevre, otherwise Babs, for her bill. Neither gentleman offered to pay it; Cecil because he remembered her words by the lake, Tom because he was too much bewildered by the recent events to think of anything else.

"I shall beink English and thus be tactful," said her Excellency. "I shall quickly goink back to Gatherum and laugh of Miss Harvey that her brother is souch outsider. I say it right, yes?"

"I'll say you do," said Lady Cora. "You have been most helpful, your Excellency. Come and have a drink any evening, but don't bring Miss Harvey."

"*Czy, pròvka, pròvka, pròvka,*" said her Excellency in heartfelt tones and departed to catch the bus to Gatherum.

"Well, we haven't done those things we ought not to have done, Cecil," said Lady Cora, half laughing, half ruefully, "but we seem to have left undone everything we meant to have done. Tom dear, have we made it worse?"

Her anxiety was very plain.

"I don't know," said Tom honestly. "Harvey was out for my blood anyway. I'm only on approval, you see. Gradka made a bit of a mess, didn't she? I must get back to the office now. Thanks most awfully for the lunch."

"One moment," said Cecil with the voice of authority. Tom stopped, straightened his shoulders and stood as if at attention. "If you will take my advice, Tom, you will leave the office before it drops you. If you will excuse me, Cora, I must get back to Barchester. Don't take things too hard. If I can be of any practical help, Tom, let me know."

He took Tom's hand in a strong, comforting grip, looked at Lady Cora, made as if to speak but did not, and left the room.

Lady Cora saw his tall figure walk across the High Street and up Market Street towards the car park. Then she turned.

"Tom," she said, and stopped.

"When I was at Rushwater I was in a better place," said Tom, looking out into the steep High Street. "But travellers must be content. As soon as I've finished work today I shall go to my father and tell him what happened and—probably—take his advice. I've been a damned fool. I'm sorry, Lady Cora."

"So am I," said Lady Cora. "I can't forgive myself."

"But I can," said Tom. "You have been so good to me."

"Good!" said Cora. "A meddling old woman. Tom—"

"I must go," said Tom, "or Harvey will have a very legitimate ground of complaint against me. Thank you for so much. Will you walk as far as the bridge with me?"

Lady Cora smiled and together they walked down the steep High Street and onto the bridge. There was a kind of embrasure built out over the central pier and Tom stopped there.

"There is one thing I want to say," he said.

"I think not," said Lady Cora, looking over the parapet at the river.

"I think yes," said Tom. "I like Cecil Waring immensely. He could have put sense into me if I could have listened. Good-bye."

"Only for the present," said Lady Cora, strangely unsure of herself. "You are a dear," and she took his hand in both of hers. "Good luck to whatever it is."

"I think I know what it is," said Tom. "Say it with Browning is the answer. He has talked for us more than once. May I hold your hand but as long as all may?"

"Or so very little longer," said Lady Cora, with a laugh and rather dim eyes.

"You see there is one other thing," said Tom, giving her hand back with great care as they stood in the embrasure, oblivious of the passers-by. "Cecil Waring is a better man than I am ever likely to be."

"Don't," said Lady Cora and on an impulse, entirely indifferent to what passers-by might think, she drew close to him and they stood looking over the water.

"I think," said Tom in a measured voice, "that This is the heart the Queen leant on. Need I go on?"

"No don't, don't," said Lady Cora.

"I won't," said Tom. "In fact, I don't think I can."

And he went away, over the bridge, to return to the Red Tape and Sealing Wax Office.

Lady Cora did not look round for several minutes. Then she walked to the far side of the bridge and up the hill to The Lodge. The front door was not locked so she went in. The drawing-room was empty. She went to the kitchen where Gloria Fletcher, hoarse with shyness, said her Ladyship was lying down and his Lordship in the garden in the summer-house, so Lady Cora went across the lawn and found her brother on the terrace over-looking the river.

"How are you and the future Duke?" said Lady Cora.

"Isabel says he is very well, but I am very bored with waiting," said Lord Silverbridge.

Lady Cora said it was better to wait for something than for nothing.

"What do you mean exactly?" said her brother.

"Only that something has happened that makes me feel as mean as a piece of ration cheese," said Lady Cora.

"Tell me if you want to," said her brother. "Not if you don't."

"Only that dear boy Tom Grantly," said Lady Cora, from the height of her year or so more than Tom. "He thinks he cares for me. He is having a poor show at his office and I think it will be worse. But he didn't think of himself at all. I am ashamed of being cared for by anyone."

"But why?" said Lord Silverbridge. "No one else would say that."

"I don't quite know," said Lady Cora, getting up and giving

herself a kind of shake as if to get rid of a burden of thoughts. "I think of Cecil. Tom thinks of me. I don't think of Tom."

"And Cecil Waring thinks of you?" said Lord Silverbridge.

Lady Cora carefully removed a little piece of moss from a crack in the balustrade and threw it into the river.

"Good old Cora," said her brother, putting an affectionate arm round her. "I like Cecil."

"So do I, so do I," said Lady Cora. "Give Isabel my love. Is the baby's name settled?"

"It was always to be Gerald," said Lord Silverbridge, thinking of their young brother Lord Gerald Palliser who was killed on D-Day, enjoying every moment up to the very last. "And if it's a girl we can't decide."

"Then it won't be a girl," said Lady Cora.

Her brother said they could go and ask Isabel, but Lady Cora left her love, walked back to the town, overtipped the old car-park attendant and drove home to Gatherum.

CHAPTER 9

It is one of the mortifications of this life that as we get older we see in ourselves those characteristics which we have least liked in our elders. One finds oneself with Aunt Agatha's cough, with Cousin Edith's way of carrying her head on one side, with Uncle George's annoying way of saying "Yerss, yerss" while being addressed, and it is a poor consolation to reflect that one's children will in their turn equally dislike such of one's own personal peculiarities as they inherit. But there are also harmless idiosyncrasies which pass from generation to generation, and in the case of a person with such gifts and charm as Lady Emily Leslie one cannot but be glad that something of her lived in her descendants.

Her daughter Agnes Graham had much of her mother's gift for making a home and spreading love about her, and had also as part of her inheritance her mother's interest in other people's lives, their families and their houses, an interest that in anyone else might have been called curiosity, but was really an all-embracing passion for humanity. To poke about in other people's houses was one of the entertainments most to her Ladyship's mind and when she had suggested to Lord Lufton that she should go over to visit his mother at Framley, it was with something as near excitement as she ever showed.

Lady Lufton was approached on the matter by her son at breakfast on the morning following his visit to Holdings.

"So shall I tell Lady Graham that Saturday would do, Mother?" said Lord Lufton.

"Yes do, darling," said his mother, who looked if possible more lost and anxious in her own home than when we saw her at The Lodge. "Whom shall I have to meet her?"

Lord Lufton said, quite truly, that he didn't think Lady Graham would want anyone else.

"Then what about Maria?" said Lady Lufton anxiously. "I am sure she could find something to do in the garden if Lady Graham wants to be alone. It is so important to be alone when one wants to. Almost as important as not to be alone if one doesn't want to," she added, thinking as she so often did of the husband who died not so long ago, who had been her support in everything.

"I didn't mean that, Mother," said Lord Lufton. "I only meant not a tea-party."

"Because," said Lady Lufton, "Mrs. Marling was coming over next week and perhaps that would be a good day. On Saturday. Or is Saturday *not* a good day? There is something about Saturdays that makes them very good or very bad."

Her sad stormy eyes and sensitive mouth expressed a despair which afflicted her son, and at the same time gently irritated him; a not uncommon effect of parents. So he said Saturday would do splendidly and he would ring up Lady Graham.

"And perhaps Justinia will be here for the weekend as the Dean is away," said Lady Lufton. "Do you think I should ask Mr. Macfadyen, Ludovic?"

It was Lord Lufton's private opinion that to ask the manager of Amalgamated Vedge was quite unnecessary, but knowing from experience that to dissuade his mother from one plan would only mean that she would at once improvise another yet more unsuitable, he said it would be a very good plan to ask Mr. Macfadyen.

"Or perhaps shouldn't I?" said his mother. "Perhaps Lady

Graham wouldn't like him. He doesn't talk very much. Is she interested in gardens, Ludovic?"

"There's a nice garden at Holdings," said Lord Lufton, "but it doesn't exactly look loved. Not like your garden, Mother, on the south side. When we were little and looked out of the nursery window into it, we thought it was Fairyland."

Lady Lufton smiled, for this little garden, against the house and walled on two other sides, was the joy of her heart and to work in it was her remedy for most troubles and sorrows.

"It is nice for Maria to have that room, but I do wish it was still a nursery. Your father said it had always been the nursery since the Luftons bought Framley for a dower house. But why should a dower house have a nursery? Perhaps because of grandchildren," said Lady Lufton, looking pleadingly at her only son.

"I can't do anything about it, Mother. I'm not even married," said Lord Lufton, half irritated, half amused.

His mother looked at him wistfully and spoke of something else, and Lord Lufton blamed himself for feeling irritated, though we think he was hardly to blame. He had been deeply fond of his father and missed him both as a father and as a friend. Being a conscientious creature he had felt more responsible for his mother than most young men and was very fond of her, but sometimes it was almost more than he could bear to be the centre of her life and he would willingly have exchanged with a fifth child where eight were kept. Could he but have expressed his feelings he would have used the words of the great man Mr. Guppy and excused the waywardness of a parent ever mindful of a son's happiness by saying that though highly exasperating to the feelings she was actuated by maternal dictates.

"Never mind, darling," he said. "Maria can marry someone delightful and bring him home here and I'll live in Mr. Macfadyen's new glass-house. It has heating all the year round. Or Justinia can marry one of the Dean's nice young clergymen."

"I always hope she will," said Lady Lufton, who was a gentle but staunch supporter of the church, "because she would probably have a large family."

"Who would have a large family?" said the Honourable Maria Lufton, violently entering the room. "Look at Seraph. Come along then, Seraph. It took me an hour to get those burrs out of her ears," and in trotted a languishing cocker spaniel like a fair edition of Elizabeth Barrett Browning, who laid a yearning head on Lord Lufton's knee.

Lord Lufton, who in spite of his worried face was not without a sense of humour, said that if anyone was going to have a large family it would appear to be Seraph, who on hearing this rolled her eyes like a Negress and whined.

"All this talk of large families was because Lady Graham is coming to tea with us on Saturday," said Lord Lufton. "Will you be here, Maria?"

His elder sister Maria was a tall handsome woman, her short curly hair touched with grey, the athlete's figure and long hands and feet. While her brother looked anxious she had an air of undamaged confidence in herself and the world. She said she would show Lady Graham the new kennels she had made out of the old loose-boxes, and who else was coming.

"Mrs. Marling and perhaps her son," said Lady Lufton, on hearing which Maria Lufton said that young Marling was a pain in the neck.

"Darling!" said her mother.

"Well, he is, Mother," said Maria. "Down Seraph! No toasties for doggies that jump up at breakfast. Look, Ludovic, isn't she divine? All right, you shall have some toasties then, poor old lady. He writes books or something and goes mooning about after Jessica Dean, and his trousers always look as if they'd been pressed."

"But why not, darling?" said her mother. "Your father put his trousers in the press every night."

"But Oliver Marling's young!" said Maria rather slightingly.

"Well, so am I," said Lord Lufton. "And I press mine with an

iron and a damp cloth when I want to make a good effect. The
army does teach you a thing or two. But be nice to him, Maria,
won't you?"

"Oh well, I suppose I'll have to at home," said Maria. "Anyone else? It sounds like a real party."

Lady Lufton said she hoped Lady Graham would bring some
of her daughters.

"I know Emmy Graham," said Maria. "Down, Seraph! She
helps to run the farm at Rushwater. She's a jolly good sort.
What's her sister like? Is she coming too?"

Luckily the form of Maria's question made it possible for
Lord Lufton to answer the second half by saying that he hoped
she was coming and ignore the first. We say luckily because
Lord Lufton would have found it difficult to say what Clarissa
was like. Pretty, yes. Elegant features, a proud carriage of her
head, dark eyes that would pierce one and hold one. He did not
know if he loved Clarissa or not, but she had cast a spell over him
and he was for the time being in her thrall. Whether the spell
would be binding, who could say. He could not help seeing
Clarissa's defects, her egoism, her capabilities for unkindness
and was even a little in awe of her imperious ways.

Saturday arrived, as it usually does, and as it was just as cold,
damp and disagreeable a day as the others of that summer we
will not say anything about it.

The first to come were Mrs. Marling with her younger son
Oliver in the rackety old family car, thankful to leave the outdoor
air for Lady Lufton's warm sitting-room with a large fire. This
room was on the first floor looking out over the garden and a
very pleasant sunny room if there was any sun, while the large
drawing-room downstairs with its draught-inviting French windows on the lawn were kept aired and clean but rarely used.
Upstairs Lady Lufton wrote her letters and did her county work.
Here, not altogether to Lady Lufton's pleasure, did Maria bring
her dogs to enjoy the summer fire. And here, tradition said, had

a former Dowager Lady Lufton held a momentous interview
with Lucy Roberts, the parson's sister who married her son and
won her true affection.

A messenger was dispatched to collect Lord Lufton and his
sister Maria from their various avocations and Lady Lufton
talked committees to Mrs. Marling while Oliver looked at the
books and out of the window and admired the George Rich-
mond drawing of Lord Lufton's great-grandmother, with her
oval face and beautiful eyes and the high light upon the tip of her
nose which we take to have been a sign of virtue in that
delightful artist's sitters to whom powder would appear to have
been unknown.

"You are looking at my predecessor?" said Lady Lufton from
her seat near the fire. "She must have been extremely charming
and we think Justinia is like her—my younger daughter."

Oliver asked if Justinia, a charming and uncommon name,
was a family heritage. Perhaps that pretty Lady Lufton, he
said, giving a last look at the drawing, but his hostess said it was
that Lady Lufton's sister-in-law, who had married Sir George
Meredith out of another county, and then Lord Lufton came in,
anxious and apologetic for his delay.

"The fact is," he said, "we are short-handed at the moment
and I was helping Pucken, my cowman that is."

Mrs. Marling said that no one with any land or an animal
could call his time his own now and returned to her talk with
Lady Lufton while the two men had some skirmishing conversation, but did not find very much in common. It seems to be a
result of any war that the noncombatants mostly age sooner than
the combatants, which is hard on people like Oliver who had
been turned down on his eyes in particular and his physical
condition in general almost without an examination, and though
the difference in age between the two men cannot have been
much more than ten years it might almost have been a generation. Oliver even had an absurd impression that Lord Lufton
would call him Sir at any moment, which was all the more

unreasonable in that Lord Lufton was a peer if an impoverished one and Oliver merely a younger son who had a job in London and came home for the weekends. However an end was put to this uncomfortable situation by the discovery that they had both been, at different times, at the same prep school, and remembered a master called Blackstone who had the most fascinating tufts of hair in his ears. It would have been just like things if Blackstone had turned out to be doing time for misappropriating stock, thus cutting short the beginnings of friendship as in the case of Peter Gray and Somers and their friend Robinson, but luckily he had taken orders and was now a Rural Dean in Loamshire. So on this basis they began to talk afresh and got on very well, and when Lord Lufton had confided to Oliver that he had written an article on *Cows in Poetry* which the *Spectator* had refused and Oliver had told Lord Lufton that he was having some notes on the Caroline poet Bohun published privately by the Barchester *Chronicle*, each gentleman was able to talk about himself and think how intelligent his new friend was. Oliver said in a lofty way that he would give the proceeds of his book to charity. Lord Lufton appeared to be much struck by the idea and said wistfully that even if the *Spectator* had published his article he didn't suppose they would pay more than three guineas. Oliver said he didn't know if it would be three or five and Lord Lufton said if he ever did get any money for it he would give his mother an electric pad to use in bed because they had no central heating and she felt the cold so much, which simple statement made Oliver feel that he had been snobbish and affected about his own work.

Then Lady Graham came in with Clarissa and in Lady Graham's benign radiance everyone felt a little more as he or she would wish to be. Clarissa attached herself in a grown-up way to Lady Lufton, and was heard by her cousin Oliver to say how delightful the sitting-room was with a voice and manner that would have become a dowager Duchess. Lady Lufton with her usual simplicity took the remark kindly and asked if she would like to see the rest of the house.

"It's nothing very special," she said. "The house is not really very old, but it is just as uncomfortable as if it were, only we are all used to it. When Ludovic marries, the girls and I shall probably live in what used to be the parsonage. Do you know my daughters?"

Clarissa, her grown-up airs subdued by Lady Lufton's kind easy manner, said she had seen Justinia at the Deanery but didn't know Maria.

"You would like each other very much," said Lady Lufton, on no grounds at all. "She can do everything with dogs and she loves riding, but of course we can't afford to keep horses. Do you ride?" and Clarissa for the first time in her life was ashamed because she couldn't.

"At least I don't really like it," she said. "Mother never did either. They put their heads down and you have nothing to hold onto. I should like a horse with a golden barley-sugar rod through its neck like the ones on Packer's roundabout."

"Then I know what you *would* like," said Lady Lufton, eager to please, for her son had let fall a few words about Clarissa which had set her matchmaking. Not that she knew anything about that art, but she had heard that mothers sometimes looked for suitable wives for their sons and did not wish to be backward in doing her duty for her own. "There is an old pony-carriage in the coach-house. I can't think why it is there, but I found it when I came to Framley and my husband said it had always been there. You would love it. I will tell Ludovic to take you round."

"Has it a parasol-whip?" said Clarissa, suddenly alert.

"How clever of you," said Lady Lufton. "I found one among a lot of old boxes when we let part of the house to Mr. Macfadyen. You shall see it. Ludovic!" she called to her son. "Could you find the parasol-whip?"

Lord Lufton said it was in the press in the back kitchen

passage and Oliver admired his patience, or rather the complete want of artificial patience in his voice, for we all know the false heartiness we put on when we have a smile on our lips and great annoyance in our hearts on account of our mothers' behaviour. So willy-nilly the whole party went downstairs from the warm sitting-room to the cold stone-floored back passage where Lord Lufton opened a large pitch-pine cupboard and took out from swathes of tissue paper an authentic parasol-whip of faded splitting dove-grey silk with a fringe and a tortoiseshell end to its long handle.

"You must carry it," said Lady Lufton to Clarissa. The pretty proud creature took it in her hand and her cousin Amabel Marling thought it suited her as to the manner born; but she also wondered where on earth Agnes Graham's clever, difficult girl would finish if she could posture so unconsciously at her young age. Lady Lufton led the way, with Clarissa (as her cousin Oliver afterwards poetically said) prancing like a proud popinjay beside her, across the kitchen yard, through an archway and into the stable yard.

"Most of it is let to Mr. Macfadyen of Amalgamated Vedge," said Lord Lufton to Mrs. Marling, "but we kept the old coach-house as a kind of store-room and Maria has the two loose-boxes for her dogs," as was indeed apparent or rather audible, from the yelps and whines and scuffles behind the partition. "And here is the pony-carriage."

And it was indeed. A real pony-carriage, rather like a small Victoria, a comfortable seat facing the ponies, an uncomfortable seat with its back to them, its basketwork body low between its four wheels, its elegantly curved shafts up-ended.

Lady Graham said her father used to drive a two-wheeled dog-cart and once the groom fell off the back seat but wasn't hurt.

"May I get in?" said Clarissa. And hardly waiting for an answer she opened the low door and set her foot on the step.

"One moment," said Lord Lufton. "I had better see if it is clean," and he took a cloth off a nail and dusted the seat.

Clarissa with a brilliant smile of thanks got in, settled herself, put up the parasol-whip and sat back peacocking to her heart's content.

The yelps and whines and scuffles behind the partition had now reached a climax to greet Maria Lufton, who came striding across the stable yard, greeted the company with a kind of salute and went into the loose-box.

"She is *so* good with dogs," said her mother. "Now we will go in and have tea."

Clarissa dismounted unwillingly from her pony-chaise, folded the parasol and gave it to Lord Lufton. Maria's voice from the loose-box said Would someone come and help her with Framley Challenger. Lady Lufton turned to Oliver who was just behind and said: "Oh, would you go in. I expect Challenger is trying to fight his grandmother again," and so passed on with that complete confidence in any man to do any job which most men find so annoying. Oliver did not know much about dogs. He had always done his duty by them but no more and felt certain that the Lufton kennels would scratch his shoes or bite his trousers. One of the disadvantages of being a man is that sometimes you are called upon to prove your manhood and this was undoubtedly one of those distressing occasions. With considerable dislike for Lufton's elder sister in his heart he opened the loose-box and went in. Here Maria, seated on an empty corn-bin, was holding a cocker spaniel on her knees and examining one of its ears while all its relations yelped hysterically.

> "'Hush ye, hush ye, dinna fret ye
> And the Black Douglas willna get ye,'"

said Maria as Oliver appeared.

"If Oliver Marling is English for the Black Douglas," said Oliver courteously, "I am your man. Can I help?"

"Oh, it's you, Oliver," said Maria. "It's Framley Challenger. He's got something wrong with his ear, probably canker. Just hold him while I have a good look," and to the fastidious Oliver's annoyance a large golden cocker, whose hair he knew would come off all over his clothes, was thrust into his arms.

"Sit on the corn-bin," said Maria kindly. "I can see him better that way."

So Oliver sat on the corn-bin holding his loathed burden, while Maria examined the ear amid continued shrieks from the other dogs who knew Oliver was a Sweeny Todd in disguise and undoubtedly intended to turn their respective grandfather, father, uncle, cousin, and nephew into substitute sausage.

"Canker all right," said Maria, with evident satisfaction. "Look."

Oliver shut his eyes and bent his head over the patient.

"Podgens!" shouted Maria, making Oliver jump and the cockers yelp even louder.

An elderly man came out of another building and walked slowly across the yard, from whose slightly bandy legs Oliver guessed him to be a superannuated stableman.

"Look here, Podgens. What did I say?" said Maria. "This is Mr. Marling. He says it's canker."

"I don't," said Oliver feebly and unheard.

"That's over Northbridge way, Marling is," said the old man, as if accusing Oliver of a nameless crime.

"Poor old fellow," said Maria. "Look here, Podgens, I'm busy just now. You do his ear and I'll come and do it again before he goes to bed. Down then, poor old fellow," with which words she lifted the cocker very gently, laid him in the straw and saying to Oliver "Come on!" unceremoniously bundled the other dogs out who fawned round Podgens as their friend and saviour against dog-torturers.

As he and Maria Lufton walked away, Oliver weakly said that Podgens must be an old Barsetshire name, to which Maria replied that Podgenses had always been the Framley grocers, combining that office with sexton, while a Mrs. Podgens by custom immemorial cleaned the church.

"They used to be pew-openers but none of the pews have doors to open now," said Maria. "Are you High?"

Oliver nearly said About six-foot two, but suddenly grasping her meaning said he was sorry but he wasn't.

"I shouldn't have thought much of you if you were," said Maria. "Come and look at the garden. The rest of them are somewhere about. What's Marling like?"

Heaven at this point was good enough to make Oliver realize that what his conductress probably meant was to inquire about the livestock, so he said they had cows and a couple of farm horses and some pigs and poultry and then, searching for some way of regaining her favour, he bethought him of Turk.

The old friends of the Marlings will remember Turk if we say that he was the property of Oliver's young sister Lucy, now Mrs. Samuel Adams. She had not taken him with her when she married because she thought his attachment was rather to the place where he belonged than to any member of the family and she was probably right. He was a large shaggy dog of no particular parentage with a very large face which he was apt to push at strangers, much to their discomfiture, and always slept upstairs in or near Lucy's bedroom, to the considerable annoyance of Oliver who slept very badly and woke at every whine or scuffle. "We have a dog called Turk," he said. "He really belongs to my sister, but she's married now."

"What breed?" said Maria, taking such manly strides that Oliver had to stretch his long legs to keep up with her.

"I'm awfully sorry but I don't know," said Oliver. "Some kind of a mixture I think. He's more like a Pyrenean sheep dog than anything else, but he's not one. And," he added, as Maria's face showed an increasingly poor opinion of such a dog, "I'm afraid he's got rheumatism because he howls if you touch his hind leg in wet weather and moans in his sleep. He's fourteen years old and probably more and he has bitten the vet."

"Good for him," said Maria. "I'd better come over and see him. I know the vet if it's Leadbitter. He's all right on horses, but I wouldn't trust a dog with him for Cruft's Gold Cup. There they are, just going in. Shall we look at the garden or would you rather have tea? Macfadyen's got the best part of the garden anyway. Tea, I think."

By this time Oliver was so bewildered that he thankfully accepted the suggestion of tea and followed his hostess indoors and up to the sitting-room where the fire was cheering the summer afternoon.

Clarissa was the temporary heroine of the party since her impersonation of a lady of quality in the pony-chaise and Lord Lufton though slightly disquieted by her chattering brilliance admired her more than ever. Yet all the while he missed something; the look which had captured him unresisting across the lunch table at Rushwater. It was the same Clarissa, but she was hiding her flame from one who was ready to worship her. Lord Lufton was not impatient. He had known sorrow and anxiety and responsibility when very young and these trials, borne on the whole with patience and a very real desire to do his duty and help his mother, had made him thoughtful for his age. In Clarissa's look he had seen an intimation of some happiness beyond what he had known. But what is a look? The tilt of an eyebrow, the elegance of a nose, the mouth that looks as if it would drop diamonds and pearls; all are wished upon us without our choice, just as are squints or sticking-out ears.

However Lord Lufton did not allow his preoccupation with the Clarissa of his thoughts to interfere with his duties as a host, and his mother was glad to see him talking as a respectful equal to the elder ladies and wished a little that her firstborn, her tall handsome Maria, would do the same. But the tall handsome Maria was happily laying down the law about the less pleasant diseases of elderly dogs to Oliver and arranging a day, with little or no reference to his wishes, for visiting Marling and giving her professional views on Turk, till she was interrupted by the distant clanging of the old-fashioned doorbell. Lady Lufton wondered aloud who it could be.

"I expect it's Charles Belton," said Lord Lufton to his mother. "You know I told you I met him at Lady Graham's and we were in the same bit of France together after D-Day and he's a very good chap. He's a schoolmaster now," and in came Charles, whom Lord Lufton greeted warmly and took up to his mother. Lady Lufton was always glad to see her son's friends and if she could by any twist of her imagination think that they might become suitors for either of her daughters she liked them all the more. Oliver Marling was obviously no use in that way, being too old for Justinia and not doggy enough for Maria, and now here was exactly the kind of son-in-law she had been thinking of. Perhaps not old enough for Maria but very nice for Justinia, and she lamented inside herself that Justinia was at the Deanery this weekend.

It is, we think, much to Charles's credit that mothers always liked him at sight and continued to like him on further acquaintance. There were connections between the womenfolk of Belton and Graham which were enough to make Charles a kind of favoured cousin with Agnes, and as Mrs. Marling was also connected with her it put Charles into the family circle at once. And we may say that whenever the Leslies or the Grahams with their various interrelationships met any of their other relations blood became so much thicker than water that they drew into a compact family group, deaf and blind to the outside world. A member would break away by marriage, but sooner or later the outsider would be drawn into the circle, with the notable exception of Sir Robert Graham, K.C.B., who had the deepest love, admiration, and respect for his wife and had refused with unflagging firmness ever to bother about her many relatives, so much so that Mrs. Belton had once said that if she hadn't been to the wedding she would never have believed in Robert's existence. So now was Charles on the verge of being absorbed by Mrs. Marling and Lady Graham, but he had a kind and we may be allowed to say chivalrous nature and Lady Lufton with her sad face and her kind ways had made an immediate conquest of him. By this Clarissa was not best pleased, for her appetite for admiration had been whetted by her peacockings in the pony-chaise and she longed for more. Presently Lord Lufton hospitably brought up the sherry and some soft drinks and offered them to the company. Charles took some orange drink.

"How too, too schoolmaster, my dear," said Clarissa with real or artificial scorn, looking round for approval. But approval was there none. The grown-ups had not heard. Charles's face had reddened, slowly and angrily. Lord Lufton looked aghast. Charles did not say a word. He finished his orange drink, put the glass down carefully on the tray so that it should not mark the furniture and said good-bye to the three elder ladies who luckily had not overheard the brief dialogue.

"Are you going, Charles?" said Clarissa. "Why?"

"Because I am going back where I belong. To School," said Charles. "Thanks awfully for the drink, Lufton. Come and see the Priory School some day," and he slipped swiftly away.

Clarissa was gradually being overcome by a feeling of guilt which was going to be her companion for some time. The weight was not yet heavy but it would be constant and her heart already had its premonitions. She turned to Lord Lufton and in his eyes, to her intense mortification, found no reply.

"How could you?" he said half to himself and then Lady Graham took her daughter away.

"What a very pretty creature Clarissa is," said Lady Lufton. "She reminds me of Lady Emily Leslie. The same beautiful eyes. Don't you think so, Ludovic?"

Lord Lufton said she was very pretty indeed. His conscience then smote him and he said she had lovely hands. And was very amusing, he added. His mother looked pleased, so he was also pleased by her pleasure, but inside himself he was wondering what had happened to the Clarissa he knew. He was still ready to worship the owner of the eyes that had pierced him to the heart, but could not forget the words spoken so insolently to someone who could not answer back, though Charles's answer had, he must admit, been an effective one. Altogether it was very uncomfortable, nor was his discomfort lessened by knowing that his beloved mother would probably make tactless and probing inquiries when the guests had gone. The Marlings were in no hurry to go, or rather Mrs. Marling was in no hurry to go. She did not often have an afternoon of complete relaxation but today her husband had gone to Edgewood for the afternoon to see Miss Amabel Adams of whom he was almost embarrassingly proud, her son Oliver was at leisure, and she could have a pleasant talk with Lady Lufton and really get down to the question of the Women's Institutes at Winter Overcotes and Winter Underclose and whether they should amalgamate. In pursuing this fascinating subject Lady Lufton lost her habitual air of troubled surprise at being alive and became quite violent on the subject of Lady Bond at Staple Park who really had no business at all to interfere, being a foreigner from Skeynes, several stations further down the line.

Meanwhile Maria and Lord Lufton had taken Oliver to see Mr. Macfadyen's glass-houses. Lord Lufton did wonder if Oliver really wanted to see about half an acre of regimented glass, but Maria had no such scruples. Mr. Macfadyen himself had gone to Eastbourne for the weekend to attend the Conference of Amalgamated Glass-Growers and Cloche Addicts, but his second in command, Mr. Hoggett, was delighted to show a defenceless foreigner (for as such he looked upon Oliver) every inch of hot-house, warm-house and potting-shed. However here Mr. Hoggett met his match, for Oliver was far from ignorant about growing flowers and fruit under glass and was able to talk to Mr. Hoggett as gardner to gardner; all of which raised him considerably in Maria's opinion. As for kind Lord Lufton, he continued to be distressed and puzzled by Clarissa and was glad to walk behind the others and reflect on human nature.

"Of course it stands to reason, sir," said Mr. Hoggett, "that

Southerners couldn't know rightly about tomatoes. Now Hogglestock, that's the place for tomatoes, sir."

"Then I daresay you know my brother-in-law, Mr. Adams,"
said Oliver, which was a good thing to say in that Mr. Hoggett's
sister turned out to be the Miss Hoggett who was Mr. Adams's
housekeeper, but a highly bad thing in that Mr. Hoggett talked
more than ever, till even Maria began to notice it. Or rather, to
her credit, she noticed that Oliver was beginning to look grey
and tired, and dismissed Mr. Hoggett with a tactful determination that Oliver much admired.

"How *do* you do it?" he asked. "I mean get rid of Hoggett?" to
which Maria replied with a good-humoured laugh that people
were much the same as dogs and if you could handle dogs you
could handle people.

"Mother," said Maria, "is like a St. Bernard."

"You do surprise me," said Oliver, speaking with no less than
the truth, for the comparison seemed to him so peculiar that you
could not call it a comparison at all.

"Well, look at her," said Maria. "It's her eyes. I mean the sad
look. It's since Father died. It was hard luck on Ludovic too,
really worse than it was for her. He's got a kind of idea you can
help people, but if you know people you'll know that you jolly
well can't. They've got to help themselves. When he marries,
Mother and Justy and I go to the old Parsonage. It's a bit of a
squash but at least you can keep it warm. But the stables aren't
up to much."

Oliver asked if she rode.

"Oh Lord! no," said Maria. "Haven't time. If I had time and
a horse I might. But the garden and the dogs take all my time
and I run the young Conservatives. No; the stalls at the Parsonage wouldn't do for my dogs and there isn't a proper paddock
now. You write books, don't you?"

Oliver said he had written a short account of a seventeenth-
century clergyman called Bohun who wrote poetry, though
having a sensitive nature he did not mention the word erotic.

"Oh *that* man," said Maria. "The one that's got a thing about him in Latin in the cathedral? How on earth do you do it?"

Encouraged by her interest Oliver said he had done it in his spare time.

"Well, what do you do in your un-spare time then?" said Maria and by this time they were back at the house and standing in the porch. A sound of voices approached from within.

Oliver said he worked in London but did not mention the nature of the work; nor will we, for we have never had the faintest idea what it was, nor troubled to inquire. What goes on in London is no concern of Barsetshire. But whatever it was we are certain that Oliver did it well or he would have been sacked long ago. Something, we have always imagined, to do with business, only the kind of business where you don't have to add or subtract, and where you have or share a secretary. However Maria appeared to be quite contented with this explanation and then the voices resolved themselves into Mrs. Marling and her hostess, who asked them to come again soon.

"And I'm coming over to Marling if I may," said Maria to Mrs. Marling, "to have a look at your dog. That Leadbitter's no good with dogs. Horses yes! I'd let him fire a horse's leg as soon as anyone, but when it comes to worming dogs he might as well be Mr. Attlee," which perhaps unmerited comparison made Oliver laugh suddenly.

"That's right," said Maria, looking at him approvingly. "It does you good to laugh. I expect you don't laugh half enough. Ludovic says I haven't any sense of humour, but I laugh much more than he does."

At this point Mrs. Marling, seeing a chance of getting a word in edgeways, said she would be delighted to see Maria at Marling and hoped she would ring up and suggest a day. And if she was going to be kind enough to look at Turk, the sooner the better and she hoped Maria would come to tea.

"If it's in the week I shan't be there," said Oliver, in we fear rather a spoilt child voice.

"That won't matter a bit," said Maria. "I always make friends with dogs at once."

"Then you will come again when Oliver is down, I hope," said Mrs. Marling. "He will be at home for a fortnight after next week," and Oliver felt he was being treated like a schoolboy and could have turned his back and walked home with pleasure except that it was too far. Besides he had to drive his mother home, which he did in silence to show that he was offended, but as his mother was a little tired by the afternoon's outing and had to consider the affairs of the Skeynes Women's Institute carefully, she did not particularly notice it; for Oliver's moods were a rather boring matter of course.

At dinner Mr. Marling, who had immense county curiosity, wanted to hear all about Framley, which he remembered as a boy in the time of the present Lord Lufton's grandfather when the hounds used to meet there, and described the top-hatted long-habited ladies and the hunt breakfast.

"This young Lufton's father was an only child," said Mr. Marling, turning the pages of county history with an antiquarian's love, "and his grandmother was a bit of an heiress—can't remember her name—good-looking woman from the shires, and when this young man's father married she settled a good bit of her own money on his daughters. This Maria you've been talking about, she must have come in for something."

Mrs. Marling said there was another daughter who was doing secretary work for the Dean.

"Then they both came in for something," said Mr. Marling, as triumphantly as if everyone had maintained the contrary and he had proved himself correct. "I'd like to see her when she comes. Well, Amabel, you haven't asked after Miss Adams."

Mrs. Marling, who had held back her desire to know about her youngest granddaughter while her husband talked about the Luftons, felt the injustice. But she was used to domestic injustice from her husband and loved him none the less for being himself; which is perhaps the best compliment any wife can pay a husband.

"She's a fine young woman," said her besotted grandfather. "She was asleep all the time and I only saw the top of her head. She'll have a fine head of hair soon. Like my aunt. She could sit on her hair when she was young. My sister and I used to come into her dressing-room and ask her to do it. Well, poor Aunt Lucy," and he sighed without much real emotion at the memory of his Aunt Lucy who had married a brother of the late Duke of Omnium and then drowned with him in the *Titanic*.

CHAPTER 10

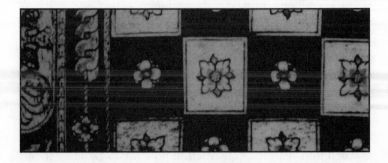

As we already know Tom Grantly had come to the decision, partly on his own initative and partly from what Cecil Waring had said, that embarrassing as it would be, mortifying as it would be, his wisest course would be to tell his people exactly what was happening. It cost him unhappy painful hours of thought to decide this, but as chill dawn appeared in the east he told himself that to have to confess to them that he was wrong was what he must do, and little as he liked it we must do him the justice to say that he was thinking almost as much of their unhappiness as of his own. If the first words on that Sunday were I will arise and go to my Father, he could not be blamed for taking them as an omen, with the rider that at least the Prodigal Son had had a run for his money, whereas he had found husks almost from the start; the largest and most indigestible husk being Mr. Geoffrey Harvey. We are glad to say that Mr. Grantly steadfastly refused to shorten or otherwise mangle the first prayer and Tom, trying for once to follow the well-known words with his mind as if they were new, felt heartened to join in the general confession; if we are to tell the truth with a mental reservation that though there was no health in him there was far less in Mr. Geoffrey Harvey. Prayer is not learnt in a day, nor in many days, and the old Adam is strong in us.

As we know, Tom's sister Eleanor had married that successful young lawyer Colin Keith, brother of Mrs. Noel Merton, and was living in London. His younger brother Henry was still doing his military training and his younger sister Grace had now left Barchester High School and was vastly improved as, so her ill-wishers said, anyone who got away from the Head Mistress, Miss Pettinger, was bound to be. What she was to do next had yet to be decided. Grace wanted to stay at home on the reasonable grounds that home was the nicest place she knew. Her mother said she would be lonely, to which Grace replied that school was much lonelier and in the end a compromise was reached by which she consented to go daily to Barchester and learn typing and shorthand, and whatever other arts civilization requires. Her reports were good, she did as she was told, but she nourished in her heart a constant desire for home. Her own home would be best, but if her heartless parents chose to drive her out of it she said she would much prefer to be a cook or a children's nurse to sitting in an office.

"Why not go into an office and marry the boss?" said her brother Henry, but Grace said that the secretaries who married their bosses were not the ones who knew shorthand, adducing several well-known names to prove her point. Finally her parents had to do what they might just as well have done at first and let her have her own way.

"But there is one thing you must understand, Grace," said her father when he had capitulated. "You couldn't think of living at home if it weren't that I am fairly well off, thanks to my people. But most of that will have been taken from me, soaking the rich as one of His Majesty's ministers chose to call it, before long. And then what will happen?"

Grace, no whit perturbed, said in that case she would get married, as it was cheaper for two than for one and when her father attempted to argue that it might be more expensive she kissed him very affectionately and said she would marry with pleasure, only he must be very tall and handsome and brave and clever. Or if not, Mr. Churchill, she said, at which point her father gave it up in despair and told his wife they really must talk it over. Mrs. Grantly said, very sensibly as we think, that Grace would in any case do exactly as she wished, and there was no way in which they could stop or control her.

"She has grown so handsome since she left Miss Pettinger," said Mrs. Grantly, rather unjustly we think. For though Miss Pettinger no doubt deserved the name of Beast Pettinger, which was her unofficial title in the Barchester High School, it cannot be said that she had actively interfered with Grace's progress from a slightly more civilized Miss Hoyden to a girl whose looks were well up to the family standard on both sides, whose heart though not quite free yet from its prickly coat was warm and kind, whose manners were vastly improved since she had so artlessly impeded the courtship of her sister and Colin Keith two years ago. The change from the schoolgirl, at once too bashful and too bold, is an interesting social phenomenon; and as she pays little or no attention to the advice of her elders (given in fear and without much hope), we can only conclude that it is in the course of Nature. And if it was Nature who had made such a good piece of work out of the lump that Grace was, it is a miracle that is happening every day.

"She is so like the picture of my ancestress who married the Archdeacon's son," said Mr. Grantly. "Much more than any of the Dean's girls, though the blood is the same. And we were always told how extremely capable she was, in spite of a very poor background and no worldly experience. Grace would take the Queen Elizabeth to sea tomorrow without the slightest hesitation, I believe, and make a good job of it. I wish I could think the same of Tom," he added, his face suddenly worried and sad.

"You will," said his wife, on absolutely no grounds at all except wishing with all her heart. "We *must* remember the war."

"We do. I do," said Mr. Grantly. "All of us do. But it doesn't help much. We are grieved and anxious, but that doesn't exactly help Tom. One does so dislike to think evil of anyone—"

"I don't," said his wife stoutly. "I *like* thinking evil of people who are evil. And what's more I *shall*. And if you mean that man Harvey, I mean him too."

So Grace had worked at her typing and shorthand and attended classes and lectures on civic and county matters and become much nicer at home, and when she went to tea with her cousins at the Deanery, Mrs. Crawley said how very like she was to Mrs. Henry Grantly who had been Grace Crawley, and found an old daguerreotype of that lady in her early married days which might certainly have been Grace if her hair and her clothes and the shape of her face had been different. However likenesses are independent creatures and no number of portraits or photographs can affect them and it is probable that Grace was like her great-grandmother. But what is more important is that she was like herself and her parents found her a very agreeable companion. And if we could all feel that we had been agreeable companions to our parents during our awkward age, we should be very glad.

Tom had decided to speak to his father after church, but people came in for a talk and a glass of sherry before lunch; and then there was a children's service and then there was tea; and then Mr. Grantly had to finish some letters in a hurry for the post and then there was evening service; and Tom spent a very uncomfortable day trying to summon up the courage to say the simple words, "Can you spare time to talk about my job, Father? I'm in rather a muddle," for which words his father would willingly have tossed everyone and everything seventeen times as high as the moon, and even rung up the Dean to ask if someone from Barchester could take his place for the evening service. But the words stuck in Tom's throat and he told his sister Grace he would like to cut it.

"No you wouldn't," said Grace. "You'd be too frightened. You're a soldier so you ought to know that," which words of his young sister struck Tom as sensible. "What's the matter, Tom?" she added, upon which poor Tom, battered and worried by the last year, poured out to his young sister all that had happened. How he had felt that he was not doing enough at Rushwater and had left it for the Red Tape and Sealing Wax Department and how Geoffrey Harvey had always had a down on him and his life was wretched. "I know I oughtn't to mind," he said. "I mean war was much worse—only it wasn't really, because there was always a chance of something else. You might be killed, or nicely wounded, or get moved on."

"Well you can't get killed or wounded at the Red Tape," said Grace, "but why can't you move on?"

"No chance," said Tom. "Harvey'll see to that. There's only one person that can down him and that's the Mixo-Lydian Ambassadress," and almost forgetting his own troubles, he gave Grace so lively a description of the lunch with Lady Cora that they both laughed till they couldn't laugh any more.

"How I'd *love* to meet her," said Grace. "But look here, Tom. Why don't you leave the Red Tape people? You're not permanent, are you?"

"No chance," said Tom. "I'm only on approval and it lies mostly with Harvey. I mean if it came to a showdown it would be his word against mine; and it *would* be against it.."

"Well then, why don't you resign, you idiot?" said Grace, at which simple sisterly words a great light broke upon Tom. But being of a self-distrusting nature he at once found more cause for anxiety and said to Grace: "But what on earth would Father say? I've not done much since I came down from Oxford except be a nuisance," at which foolishly self-deprecatory (which is rather the same often as self-indulgent) words his sister Grace fell on him horse and foot saying that that was, as far as she could see, what parents were there for. For one to be a nuisance to them she meant, and Father had just gone into the study because she had heard the door.

"Go in and tell Father everything," she said. "Poor old Tom," and she rubbed her head very affectionately against his shoulder and he gave her a very affectionate hug with one arm.

"It's half past seven," said Grace, as the clock struck from the church tower. "I'll keep everyone out till you've done."

"I know you will," said Tom gratefully and went away to the study, wondering as he went, for our fancy refuses to be bound as the poet Shelley well knew, what methods his sister would adopt; whether she would lie before the door like a faithful Indian servant during the Mutiny, or hold the door like Kate Barlass only there weren't any staples on the study door, or hang from the clapper of the bell like Curfew Shall Not Ring To-night. And at this point he laughed to himself, which gave him just enough courage to open the door, shut it behind him, say "Oh, Father," and be stricken dumb.

Mr. Grantly, and we do not attempt to deny it, had been hoping, expecting, fearing this interview ever since Saturday afternoon when Tom came home, but whether he ought to encourage Tom to come up to the scratch or leave it to him to do as best seemed fit to him, he could not decide. It is most difficult for parents to know how to treat the grown-up children whom they recognize as personages in their own right and yet must partly think of as needing the help and defence of our older generation. One does not like to take the first step in case it should be misinterpreted and one's last case be worse than one's first. On the other hand one is longing to help and yet on the other hand (for if there is three-handed bridge why not three hands in other cases) one wonders if any help one can offer will be of the slightest use. That it will not be accepted one takes as a matter of course.

"Well, Tom?" said his father, in whose voice Tom, super-sensitive at the moment to overtones and undertones, at once detected curiosity (intolerable), boredom (reasonable), entire want of interest and several other sentiments, and he would have gone away again if he hadn't shut the door so firmly. Besides Grace wouldn't be pleased. So he stood just far enough from his father to make conversation difficult, picked up a paper-knife and dropped it. It fell on the table with a bang, scratching the mahogany.

"Oh, I say, I'm sorry, Father," said Tom. "I'll come another time." He then picked up the paper-knife again and dropped it again, this time on the floor. He knelt down to look for it and found, as Richard Tebben had found many years earlier, that if one is on the floor with one's head under a table it is somehow much easier to talk to one's father.

His father's voice was heard saying that this was as good a time as any other.

"It's about the Red Table and Sealing Wax," said Tom, still well hidden from his father who was on the far side of his writing-table. "I'm afraid I've been a ghastly fool. Here's the paper-knife. I had a sort of idea that it was better work than Rushwater. I mean I thought it seemed rather waste to have been to Oxford and then farm and I thought the Red Tape would be something rather important, a sort of career, I mean," and by this time, considerably emboldened as one so often is by the sound of one's own voice, he got up and dusted his knees and continued, though looking at a point to the right of his father's head and about a foot above it, "but it isn't. I have honestly tried my best, Father, and I didn't want to bother you, but it's no good. Harvey doesn't like me. I mean there's no reason why he should, but he dislikes me in a horrid way. I wouldn't mind a fellow who just loathed you and that's that, but he will hate me *at* people, I mean people I like. I can't explain. I'm most awfully sorry, Father, and I wish I were dead," after which clear and concise apologia he wished he could burst into tears or, even better, fall down dead at once.

There was a silence that must have lasted at least three seconds, though during that time Tom had failed in everything he undertook, broken his parents' hearts, and made his sisters and his younger brother ashamed of him. What was going on during those three seconds in his father's mind and heart never occurred to him, as indeed why should it.

"I was afraid this was coming," said Mr. Grantly, which made

Tom think of bursting open the French window, running all the
way to the main line and throwing himself before the Sunday
evening up-express. "I wish it had come sooner. It would have
spared you a great deal of unhappiness," and even in his misery
Tom felt how decent it was of his father not to add And your
mother and myself as well. "Where was this Mr. Harvey, by the
way?" which question Tom guessed to refer to Mr. Harvey's
college and said Lazarus.

"Oh, *Lazarus*," said Mr. Grantly, implying without a word or
a sign that of all colleges he ever saw, None were so wicked, vain
and silly, So lost to shame and Sabbath law as that one. "The
Master invites certain people of importance to preach lay ser-
mons on Sunday evening, I understand."

"Yes, Father," said Tom, snatching at this straw. "He had that
woman called Mothersill that's in the Cabinet—"

"A woman in a college chapel!" his father ejaculated.

"—and he had the first Lord of the Treasury and he quoted
poetry and got it all wrong and a man from Paul's stood up and
said: 'Always verify your references, sir.'"

The worst was over. At the allusion to his old college we
cannot exactly say that Mr. Grantly's face softened, for it had
expressed little beyond worried compassion, but it lightened and
he could not help a smile of exultation.

"The sword of the Lord and of Gideon," he remarked. "And
now you have told me all about it, Tom, I ask you to think very
seriously if an official life is your life. But I imagine you have
thought. I know I have," he added, half to himself, and Tom
suddenly began to realize that while he had been so worried
about himself his parents might in their turn have been worried
about him.

"I'd give anything to get back to Rushwater, Father," he said.
"I was a damned fool to leave it," and then he felt that the day,
the place and his father's cloth were extremely unsuitable sur-
roundings to damn people in, even oneself.

"In which I fully and absolutely agree with you," said his

father to Tom's great surprise, and somehow they were laughing and he felt Christian when he had run along the walled highway called Salvation and his burden fell from his back. "You have been a long time finding it out, Tom," and as that was his only reproach we think Tom escaped lightly. "When can you leave?"

Tom said that as he wasn't permanent he thought there wouldn't be much difficulty, unless of course Geoffrey Harvey chose to be difficult.

"I don't think he will," said Mr. Grantly. "These Lazarus men have no stamina. And after that: what?"

But at this moment the supper-bell rang and since Edna and Doris, the delightful unmarried mothers who ran the house, always took their children of shame to the pictures on Sunday night, it was desirable to hurry. As they left the room Mr. Grantly, as if by accident, laid his hand on Tom's arm for a moment and Tom touched his father's hand with his own free hand and both men hastily talked about other matters in rather unnatural voices, by which Mrs. Grantly knew as soon as they came into the room that all was well and her inside, which had been feeling tight and quivering and hollow for the last weeks, suddenly became normal. As for Grace, that young lady contented herself by kicking her brother under the table. Tom, looking at her carelessly, suddenly thought what a very good-looking girl she was, better-looking even than her elder sister Mrs. Colin Keith, and more able to deal with life, as indeed the younger children of a family so often are and we do not attempt to explain it. Tom's affairs were not discussed again that night and harmony reigned.

After taking advice from one or two older men at the office he wrote a letter resigning his temporary post, gave it to Mr. Harvey's secretary and quietly went on with his work with such a sense of all for freedom and the world well lost that he almost wished he were not leaving. But there was still something very serious, very important to be done. He must summon all his courage and go to Rushwater, see Martin Leslie, ask if they would have him back, and break the news to Emmy. And somehow this did not seem the easiest part.

Our reader will not be surprised to hear that Maria Lufton, rightly considering that Oliver as a bachelor younger son had no particular status in his parents' house, rang up Mrs. Marling and asked if she might come over on Saturday and look at Turk. Mrs. Marling had not any self-abasing love for dogs but felt it part of her duty as the Squire's wife to be responsible for all animals belonging to the family, and Turk's melancholy state had been an anxiety. Her daughter Lucy Adams, bringing Miss Amabel Rose Adams to visit her grandparents, had looked at Turk, who expressed no particular enthusiasm for her. When she felt his leg he pretended he was grateful, but all he really wanted was to keep quiet and doze on his blankets upstairs, or wherever a warm sunny spot in the house invited him.

"Poor old Turk," said Lucy Adams to her mother. "He must be fourteen or fifteen. It was the year they found the badger in Pooker's Piece. Leadbitter's no good, I saw Maria Lufton in Barchester yesterday and she told me she was coming today, so I thought I had better come too. She can run rings round anyone in Barsetshire about dogs. Amabel knows Sam now. She has a special kind of squeak for him, haven't you, my sweet?" but as Miss Adams was fast asleep on the sofa in a bed of cushion she could not answer. Oliver, who had got down from London the night before, came in with a small parcel.

"A present from London for my favourite niece," he said. "I mayn't be a father, but I have more nephews and nieces than anyone else in the family," which statement his sister queried, but was reduced to silence when it was proved that Oliver's elder brother and his two sisters, being parents of the nephews and nieces, could not have as many as Oliver with no encumbrances of his own. Lucy opened the parcel on her daughter's behalf and found a necklace of small pink coral beads.

"How heavenly," she said. "She can cut her teeth on them," at which Oliver made a strong protest, and it was decided not to put the necklace on until she woke up.

During lunch Oliver thought that his dear father was more than usually ponderous and when after lunch Mr. Marling announced that he had something to say to them all, Oliver said aside to Lucy that he supposed Papa had married the cook and cut them all out, to which his sister Lucy very sensibly said that as their mother was alive he couldn't.

Mr. Marling, who dearly loved a fuss if he was the centre of it, then made a long and rambling speech to the effect that he was getting on and wouldn't be long for this world, which caused his daughter to say under her breath, as rebelliously as Lucy Marling used to do, that he would be the whole afternoon unless he got on a bit. After a good many aimless reminiscences of his early life and his family, including his old uncle Fitzherbert Marling who used to be carried to bed by two footmen, he said he was a poor man now. He then paused.

"So we all are, Father," said Oliver, finding it all rather a bore.

"That's what I'm sayin'," said his father. "I'm a poor man now and most of us are poor men. But you can't take your money when you go," and he sat looking out of the window at his garden and his lands beyond.

"All this'll go when I go," he said, not addressing anyone in particular. "I've pulled along somehow until now and your husband has been a good friend, Lucy," and he put his hand on his younger daughter's, "and you're provided for, my dear, so long as there's any security left. So's your mother. Bill won't be able to live here when I die, but he's all right. So is Lettice; her girls will have their father's money and her boys will have Barclay's," for Lettice Marling had lost her first husband in the war and married again, very happily. "But there's Oliver here."

"Don't worry about me, Father," said Oliver, terrified of something which might become emotional. "I'm not doing badly at the office."

"That's nothing to do with it, boy," said Mr. Marling, falling into an old way of speech. "You may have ten thousand a year"—"I haven't," said Oliver indignantly under his breath—"or you may have five hundred. But you've not got a home."

"But he has Marling, Will," said his wife.

"Marling's no inheritance, my dear," said Mr. Marling. "He lives here and he's welcome here as long as I'm alive. But when I'm dead where will he be?"

No one answered. From time to time everyone had thought of this and Oliver not least, but so long as his old home was his home he could not imagine his life elsewhere.

"Well, I'll tell you what I've done," said Mr. Marling. "I've made over The Cedars to Oliver. It was to have been my aunt Lucy's, the one that married Algy Palliser, but that came to nothing."

"She was drowned in the *Titanic*," said Mrs. Marling softly.

"So it's Oliver's," said Mr. Marling. "I talked to Bill about it last year and he agreed. It's a small house and there's good stabling. Keep your books in a bookstall, eh, my boy?" said Mr. Marling, quite above himself with his own generosity and his brilliant joke about books and bookstalls. "I don't suppose I'll live long enough for you to get out of death duties, but you'll have somewhere to live when I'm dead."

Oliver was suddenly smitten with a kind of self-contemptuous remorse which he did not like at all. For all these years he had lived with and on his parents and kept his earnings, quite good ones now, for his own use. Now here was his father, an old man, thinking how he could help a child from whom he had never got a great deal of pleasure.

"I can't thank you enough, Father," he said and then stopped, embarrassed for words.

"I know you can't, my boy," said Mr. Marling, without any rancour, but suddenly showing Oliver that his father was far more observant and also far more tolerant than he had ever suspected. Oliver was overcome by one of life's small tragedies which is that we can hardly ever realize our elders till it is too late. Here was his father whom, for a long time now, he had been in the habit of considering, when he considered him at all, as a kind of character in a play or book. The old-fashioned gentleman farmer who lies on his land and by his land, rides to hounds, sits on the Bench, reads the lessons in church, and in his highest state of development disinherits his elder son and turns at least one daughter out of doors. In many respects Mr. Marling had fallen short of this ideal figure. Far from disinheriting Oliver's elder brother Bill he had done all he could for him, working ceaselessly to keep the place going and free from debt. Neither on her first nor her second marriage had he disinherited his elder daughter Lettice. As for Lucy, Mr. Adams had refused to take money with her and had made a very handsome settlement himself, though Mr. Marling had cunningly got round this by settling what was to be Lucy's portion upon her children. All perhaps useless now when money is merely made or inherited to be taken away and squandered on unconsidered megalomaniac schemes. And now, with things getting darker and more difficult every day, he had thought of the son who had been, as Oliver could not help knowing, a disappointment to him.

All these things had gone through his mind with incredible swiftness even while his father spoke, and he was casting about for a way in which he might show his father some measure of what he felt, when a kind of scuffle was heard outside the door, which was then opened by Mrs. Pardon, the gardener's wife, who announced Miss Lufton and fled.

Maria Lufton came in and Oliver, though he blamed himself, noticed that his father's eye brightened at this handsome new arrival who probably seemed to him a mere girl.

"I hope I'm not too early," said Maria, coming to Mrs. Marling's end of the table.

"Not a bit," said Mrs. Marling. "We have been talking too much. Do sit down," for Oliver had brought a chair and placed it by his mother. "I expect you have met my husband. And

Oliver you know. And this is my younger daughter, Lucy Adams."

"I hope you won't mind," said Maria Lufton to Lucy Adams, "but I believe it's your dog that I've come to see. Isn't he Turk?"

"Poor old Turk," said Lucy. "He's old and I think he is rheumaticky. I left him here when I married because he's really a place-dog, not a person-dog. He's pleased to see me when I come but he would fret away from Marling."

"Too human," said Maria Lufton. "Dogs oughtn't to go on like that. What I say is, dogs should be dogs," and then, as if Lucy were a nice child and had had enough of her attention, she devoted herself to Mrs. Marling and gave her various messages from Lady Lufton about the Women's Institutes.

"I've got a suggestion, Amabel," said Mr. Marling from the other side of the table. "Why don't we all go down and look at The Cedars? I daresay Miss Lufton would like to see it. It's empty at the moment and I want to do some repairs to the roof. It's a house that I'm making over to this boy of mine," he added to Maria. "It's only a few minutes' walk to the village. And then you can see the dog when we come back. It's very kind of you, young lady."

Accordingly they all went down the drive and so into the little village, past the shop, to where the ground rose gently again. Here had stood for the past two hundred years or so the dwelling house known as The Cedars, though of the trees only one gaunt giant was left.

"It was the bad winter early in the war that finished them," said Mr. Marling to Maria. "The snow lay on the branches and they snapped. Now what do you think of the house?"

The Cedars was a small two-storeyed house with a bow front from basement to roof on each side of the front door, of warm old brick. A low wing at one side masked the outbuildings.

"I haven't been in The Cedars since old Mrs. Foster died," said Oliver. "Shall we look?" and accordingly the whole party went over the little house of which we shall only say that it was elegant, well lighted, and the paint and floors in good condition.

"Now can we see the outside?" said Maria Lufton, who had been champing at the bit while the Marlings inspected the rooms. "I saw a very good yard out of the back windows," so led by Mr. Marling, whose courtesy to his guests grew more eighteenth-century at every step, they went through the little kitchen wing and so into a yard which was a vision of the beautiful combined with the practical, paved with red bricks which sloped gently to a drain in the middle, the kitchen on the south side and the house on the east. On the west side was some modest stabling and to the north was a fair-sized paddock with the church tower rising beyond. A large clock over the stable door bearing the date 1751 chimed three o'clock with such a Tennysonian mellow lin-lan-lone that Mrs. Marling felt unaccountable prickings behind her eyes.

"I had the old clock done up," said Mr. Marling, not even trying to hide his gratification at the perfection of this gift. "Pocock from Barchester did it. He says it is the best stable clock in West Barsetshire."

"Father," said Oliver and then he had to stop. Partly from real emotion, partly from a keen sense of how incredibly perfect was the whole scene, obviously drawn by Randolph Caldecott to a story by Washington Irving, or Mrs. Ewing, redolent of all we should like that period vaguely known as the 18th Century to be; though whether we mean William and Mary or forty years of George the Third, we should not like to say.

"All right, my boy," said Mr. Marling, much gratified by his own generosity and his younger son's being stricken dumb with pleasure. "When I'm in the churchyard you'll be able to write your books and things here. He's an author, you know," he added to Maria Lufton. "Wrote a book about a clerical Johnnie that wrote some naughty poems," with which dashing words he became so increasingly Olde Englishe Squire that Oliver fully expected him to kiss the Honourable Maria Lufton and be slapped for his pains.

"Look here, Mr. Marling, I mean Oliver, because Mr. Marling is too confusing," said Maria, whose meaning was clearer than her words, "are you going to live here?"

If Oliver had spoken the truth, he would have said "Not till Father is dead," but he could not think of suitable form for this statement.

"Not he," said Mr. Marling with a laugh which struck his son as little less than fiendish. "He'll live with his old parents as long as they'll have him. Free board and lodging, eh, Oliver?"

"Yes, Father," said Oliver and was just going to make some well-meant and ill-put-together remarks about not wanting to leave Marling Hall if his father could find a good tenant for The Cedars when Lucy said: "Oliver! Frances Harvey!"

If Oliver had been a better runner he would have taken to his heels. During the winter that Frances Harvey and her brother Geoffrey had spent in Marling as refugees in the cottage of the widowed Mrs. Smith, he had almost been fascinated by that masterful woman. Then their paths had separated, but last summer, at the Conservative Fête at Gatherum Castle, he had met her again and she had been gracious and distinctly oncoming to him and had said: "We shall meet again—Oliver," in a way which had made him extremely uncomfortable, betokening as it appeared to him the female spider's determined wooing of the male. This disagreeable and sinister incident had passed from his mind, but here was Frances again, unexpected, unwanted, and he wished he could hide under the copper in the old laundry.

Miss Harvey was now walking across the stable yard with a firm step and Oliver, fascinated as a rabbit by a snake, had to admit that she walked well and certainly (which was generous of him) did not look her age, though if he had really given his mind to it he did not know what her age was.

"I was in this direction and thought I would see if you were in," said Miss Harvey, addressing Mrs. Marling, "and they told me at the Hall that I might find you down here. How delightful to see Marling again."

Mrs. Marling, who had never cared for Miss Harvey or her brother when they were refugees in the village, said civilly how nice it was to see Miss Harvey.

"You remember Miss Harvey, Will," she said. "She and her brother took the Red House from Joyce Smith in the winter of '41."

"Joyce Smith?" said Mr. Marling. "Dreadful woman. Always bein' a widow."

"Only once, Father," said his daughter Lucy.

"You know what I mean," said Mr. Marling. "Once a widow always a widow. Don't see her nowadays!"

"Of course you don't," said Lucy Adams, as loudly as Lucy Marling would have said it, but more tolerantly. "You know perfectly well she sold the Red House and went to Torquay."

"Alas! there goes my dream cottage," said Miss Harvey. "The Ministry of General Interference is fascinating work, but no inheritance, and I had hoped to make a real home here. What a delightful winter it was when my brother and I were near you. I suppose you don't know of a house to let in Marling, do you, Oliver? About the size of this. What a gem it is."

We shall not attempt to describe Oliver's feelings, for we have never been in the position of a bachelor, no longer young, who has escaped more by luck than skill a predatory female whom he did not wish to marry and meets her again after nearly ten years not in the least faint and still pursuing.

Mr. Marling, whose want of tact sometimes astounded even his family, said the house was Oliver's so Miss Harvey had better ask him, and then made matters worse by laughing in what his exasperated son considered a perfectly senile way at his own pleasantry; but civility, not to speak of gratitude, prevents you from killing your father however great the provocation. Oliver looked round for someone to help him, somewhere to hide.

"There is always the chance that you will be looking for a

tenant then—Oliver," said Miss Harvey, with exactly the same inflection, Oliver realized to his horror, that she had put into her voice the year before at the Conservative Fête. A voice of invitation, with just that touch of auld lang syne which he could well have dispensed with. Oliver was not at all conceited or blind about his own personal attractions, thinking indeed quite poorly of himself as a ladies' man; also his hopeless attachments to Jessica Dean, that enchanting minx now a happy mother, had made him indifferent to the fair sex in general. But the remembrance of the evening when Francis would have caused him, quite against his will, to propose marriage to her still haunted him; and had not his empty glass fallen from the too narrow sham marble mantelpiece onto the hearth and shattered the intimate moment, she might have been Mrs. Oliver Marling, a thought too horrible to contemplate. Now, he strongly felt, fate was at him again.

For a moment Miss Harvey's attention was distracted by Mr. Marling who with senile lechery (so his son considered, though unfairly we think) said it was a nice little house and would suit a charming woman down to the ground. In that brief moment Maria took a dislike to Miss Harvey so violent as to be unreasonable, except that to dislike her was the sign of a liberal education.

"If you're letting your house, I'm taking it," said Maria Lufton to Oliver in a low but distinct voice. "Ludovic's bound to get married and I'm not going to live at the Parsonage. It's not good enough for the dogs," and as Oliver stared at her as one bereft of his senses she repeated: "I'm taking it. First refusal anyway. Tell her."

With a sensation of being in a particular but pleasant dream from which he was bound to wake to disappointment of some sort, Oliver gasped, recovered his breath and said: "Oh how very unfortunate, Frances. Miss Lufton has the first refusal."

Miss Harvey behaved very well, but Oliver saw on her still

handsome face the angry sulky look it had worn on the evening when the glass fell off the mantelpiece.

"How terribly disappointing," she said. "The Duchess will let me have a cottage, I know, but there is something rather special about Marling. That happy winter Geoffrey and I spent here! Now I must fly. I am going on to the Nortons, my cousins you know," and she said a kind of general good-bye with a last look from her fine eyes at Oliver and the words, "Well, good-bye— Oliver," dropping to a kind of mute secret understanding on the last word which made him feel as if he had been saved from the Pit and the Pendulum and was all the worse for it.

"Handsome woman," said Mr. Marling, when the noise of her car had died away, "a bit long in the tooth though. Oliver was sweet on her the winter she and her brother were in Joyce Smith's house. Never liked that feller Carver," which irrelevant remark puzzled his family till Oliver reminded them that his father had formerly insisted on calling Mr. Harvey Carver against all reason.

"Thank you more than I can say," said Oliver to Maria Lufton. "It was a wonderful piece of camouflage."

"But I meant it," said Maria, and without giving him time to speak she added: "And now we'd better see the dog. Mrs. Adams, it's your dog Turk that's out of sorts, isn't it?"

"Poor old Turk," said Lucy in a perfunctory way, for we fear that her house, her husband, and her adored Amabel Rose had left her very little room to consider her old friend. "Oliver says he's rheumatic. You're awfully keen on dogs, aren't you? Come on," and she led Maria at a good round pace back towards Marling Hall. Oliver would willingly have accompanied them, but decency and filial piety commanded him to stay with his father who had shown such astounding generosity. So the two young women walked up the hill, talking of really interesting matters such as dogs (diseases of) and vegetables (growing of, for commercial purposes), on which subjects both were practical and well informed. But even as Maria Lufton had to admit that

Lucy Adams had a mastery of cows and vegetables that she, Maria Lufton would never attain, so did Mrs. Samuel Adams have to admit that the Honourable Maria Lufton had forgotten more about dogs than she, Lucy Adams, had ever known, and they got on very well. When they reached the house Lucy took her guest upstairs to where, in a rather nasty piece of blanket, in a round basket, the dog Turk was curled up and gently whining to himself.

"Poor old Turk," said Lucy. "He's about fifteen years old. Hullo, Turk!" but even the voice of his old mistress did not rouse Turk's interest.

Maria knelt beside the basket and felt Turk with firm capable hands. Turk, recognizing an expert, did not complain, only giving a little whine occasionally when Maria touched a tender spot.

"I don't think there's much you can do," said Maria standing up and dusting her hands one against the other.

"That's what the vet said," said Lucy and the two women stood silent, looking at Turk as he moved uneasily in his basket.

"If he were mine, I'd get the vet to give him a whiff," said Maria, her voice full of compassion.

"So'd I if he were yours," said Lucy. "But you see I've known him all my life. I say, are you really going to take The Cedars?"

"I hope so," said Maria Lufton. "I've got a bit of capital and if you don't spend it They take it. Ludovic's bound to marry some time and The Cedars would make splendid kennels. About that dog. Keep him warm and give him a drop of brandy in warm milk."

"I would if I lived here," said Lucy. "Perhaps Oliver would. Oliver!" she called as her brother's tall form came into view at the door. "I'll tell you what, Miss Lufton says brandy in warm milk is about all we can do. Could you see about it?"

"Of course," said Oliver, forgetting the many nights when Turk, by howling and whining and scratching at the door, had disturbed his sleep, never very sound at the best of times. "Do you want it now?"

Maria said it might be as well.

"Oh dear," said Lucy, a catch in her voice. "is he going to die?" to which Maria made no reply, looking down on Turk with the kindly unmoved attention of the Good Physician who sees a power beyond human control. Presently Oliver came back with warm milk and some brandy in a saucer. Lucy knelt down and offered it to Turk who sniffed it, tasted it, and laid his head on the cushion.

"Do you mind if I hold him?" said Maria and as no one answered she knelt on the floor and gently took Turk in her arms, trying to tempt him with the milk.

"Oh, *please*, Turk," said Lucy. "Oh, do come back, Turk," but Turk did not want warm milk, or brandy, or anything else in this world. Maria laid him again in his basket and set herself to comfort the survivors.

England, our beloved country, battered and bullied by Them, still has one source of real comfort in every affliction. They have rationed it; They have caused it to be made of dust and bits of black straw; They allow government offices to glut themselves on it while the working housewife with a husband and children hardly knows how to last till the end of the week; but as long as a spoonful of tea is to be had, England will keep her heart. Hardly had Turk's limp body been covered by Oliver with a large clean duster when Mrs. Pardon rang a king of muffin bell violently in the downstairs passage to show that tea was ready. When they got downstairs Mr. Adams was there, greatly admiring his daughter whom he had not seen since that morning.

"Anything wrong, girlie?" he said.

"It's Turk," said Lucy. "He's been having rheumatism and we went to see him and Miss Lufton said brandy and warm milk and when Oliver got it he died. *Poor* Turk," and she unashamedly laid her head against her husband's coat. "Oh, this is my husband, Miss Lufton."

"Pleased to meet you," said Mr. Adams. "I've heard of you from Macfadyen. Amalgamated Vedge. He tells me you're breeding dogs in a big way."

"Quality, not quantity," said Maria, shaking his hand with a grip that surprised him. "But I mean to do more."

"Tell me, Miss Lufton," said Mr. Marling, "did you mean what you said about The Cedars?"

"Well, when I said I'd like to take it, I really didn't think much about what I was saying," said Maria candidly. "I wanted to take that Harvey woman down a peg. But if my trustees agree it's just what I want. Small house, stables and paddock. I can shut up the two other bedrooms and the third sitting-room, or get a friend to share or something. What length of lease could I have?" she asked Oliver, who had to confess that he had only heard about his father's gift that day and would have to go into the details.

"I won't stay for tea," she said to Mrs. Marling. "It's a family affair about Turk. You won't want an outsider," and though all the Marlings had liked her and such of them as had heard her words to Miss Harvey admired her presence of mind, there was a general feeling that she was doing the right thing. Mrs. Marling asked her to come again soon and Mr. Marling was so outspoken in his admiration of her brilliant cutting-in operation with Miss Harvey that he got as far as putting a fatherly arm round her and showed every symptom of what is called stealing a kiss. Oliver and Lucy exchanged glances of resignation over their father's profligate conduct and couldn't help laughing when Maria disengaged herself neatly and kissed Lucy in a very sympathetic way.

"You were *awfully* good about poor Turk," said Lucy. "I say, do come and look at Amabel. She is having a tiny bit of bread and butter."

Maria Lufton, gathering that Lucy was showing her what she had of greatest value as a token of gratitude, looked dispassionately upon Miss Amabel Adams who was waving a nasty piece of buttery bread in one fat fist and occasionally making a dab at her mouth with it, though rarely achieving any contact.

"Funny little person," said Maria without much interest, but Lucy forgave her because of her kindness to Turk and her courage towards Miss Harvey. "I can't think why people ever have babies," to which Lucy responded, quite reasonably, that dogs had puppies, and they parted each with considerable respect for the other. Then Oliver took her to her car. "I'll come down to the bottom of the drive and open the gate for you," he said and got into the car, nearly falling over a couple of cocker spaniels.

"I ought to have warned you," said Maria Lufton, pitching her dogs neck and crop into the back seat. "I never bring them into the house when I don't know people well," which unusual consideration in a dog-lover struck Oliver as evidence of a very kind and thoughtful nature.

In a couple of minutes they were at the bottom of the hill and Maria stopped.

"I haven't really thanked you for saving my life," said Oliver. "I don't wish to appear conceited but I think Frances Harvey tried to marry me when she and her brother were here in the war and I know she would have done something equally embarrassing today if you hadn't stopped her. Forgive me, but do you really want The Cedars?"

"I didn't till this afternoon," said Maria Lufton. "But then I did. It's the perfect house for just two people and the dogs and I'm sure I can find someone to share with me. Are you likely to want it for yourself?"

"I really don't know," said Oliver. "It's my people, you see. Now Lucy is married I think they do like to have me there even if it's only weekends. When Father dies Marling goes to my elder brother and as he doesn't want to live there and anyway couldn't afford it I suppose it will be a private asylum or an orphanage. One really doesn't know *what* one wants."

Maria looked at him almost as she had looked at Turk; with real sympathy but no sentiment.

"What you want is someone to make up your mind for you," she said, not unkindly. "Look here. Let's have another look at The Cedars and then I'll know what to say to my trustees. If I'd known that Harvey woman was coming I'd have looked at everything more carefully."

Oliver, though feeling rather as people must feel when they have arranged to shoot Niagara in a barrel and the last hoop has been hammered into place, saw the point of her suggestion and they drove on to The Cedars. Here they went over the house again, which did not take long for it was very compact with three rooms on the ground floor and three bedrooms and a bathroom on the upper floor and then Maria Lufton wanted to see the garden, which lay on the side away from the stables. It was small but well laid out with a lawn, flowerbeds, and a small kitchen-garden beyond an evergreen hedge. On the far side of the lawn the great cedar spread its boughs.

"I'm glad that's not too near the house," said Maria, indicating the cedar. "Can't bear trees up against the windows. You ought to have it properly looked at. I know a man at Kew. I'll get him to come down some time."

Oliver said he had always thought that the large branch which seemed to be dead in places was rather unsightly, and they went round the house into the yard where Maria re-examined the old stables and told Oliver what alterations she would like to make, asking his opinion of them.

"I'd tell you if I knew," said Oliver, "but I really don't. You see I'm not doggy and I'm not really much good at country things except flowers. Lucy was the real son of the house."

Maria considered this and Oliver felt she was beginning to despise him for a mere Cockney who could never be of Barsetshire.

"I'm awfully sorry," said Maria Lufton suddenly, as if she had determined to dive into a freezing lake on a winter morning, "but I'd forgotten."

"Forgotten what?" said Oliver.

"Oh, you know," said Maria. "Books."

"What books?" said Oliver, really at a loss.

"Well," said Maria, her handsome face averted from him and speaking apparently to someone in the paddock, "I mean you know all about them. And you've written a book, haven't you? I mean a real book, not a novel. I can't think how you do it. It must be marvellous to write something. Of *course* you wouldn't know about heating for the kennels. I've been awfully stupid, but you see dogs are about the only thing I can do. And the garden and the Young Conservatives," she added.

Never, we think, had Oliver's rather dilettante and quite self-centered opinion of himself received such a shock as when Maria spoke these artless words. Jessica Dean had laughed his work away as of no value in her life (or indeed, had she been pressed, anyone else's life). Isabel Dale, now Lady Silverbridge and future Duchess of Omnium, had typed the opuscule (as Oliver with shame remembered he had agreed pretentiously to call it) for him while she was doing secretary for his mother. Frances Harvey—and here his shame was so great that he felt his face burning—had discussed it seriously with him and indeed had used it as a way to gain his esteem and possibly his heart. And now Maria Lufton was apologizing for her own ignorance and looking at him as a scholar, an authority on literature.

How Jessica would laugh at this was his unspoken thought, followed by the reflection, also unspoken, that it would serve him right. Never before in his rather self-centred life had he felt so small.

Maria Lufton, seeing his sallow face darken, humbly attributed it to the divine rage of the Artist when misunderstood by ordinary people, and remained silent, almost respectful, a little afraid of one who had fed on honey-dew.

"Look here," said Oliver, speaking with a desperate earnestness that Jessica would at once have recognized as the real thing. "You mustn't, please, talk like that. I've produced one little book and I was silly and vain enough to have it printed at my own expense. All I can say for myself is that I am fairly good at my job in London, but as a literary genius I am nowhere. Absolutely nowhere. If I knew half as much about writing as you do about your job, I would be a very successful writer. But I don't and I'm not."

Maria looked at him with an air bewildered, yet trusting, which somehow touched him deeply.

"But you would want a literary tenant, wouldn't you?" she said, almost pleading.

"I would NOT," said Oliver, with an energy that would have surprised even Jessica Dean who knew him so well and had borne with him so kindly. "I would want someone exactly like you who knew her job and knew what she wanted. And I can't tell you how glad I shall be if you do come here. It will be such fun to have you at The Cedars. And even if my father hopped the twig the day the lease was signed I would want you just the same. Besides you have saved my life from that ghastly Frances Harvey."

It is improbable that the Honourable Maria Lufton in all her dog-loving, hard-working,, conscientious life had ever been praised by a man more or less her own age. Her father had adored her, but the young men of her generation, where were they? The war had taken its toll, elder sons had married or gone to try their fortunes elsewhere, younger sons had married even more and were doing their best with hard-working wives and delightful, exhausting young children, but this had all passed Maria Lufton by, and her heart swelled with gratitude to Oliver.

"If that's all, I'll set the dogs on her if she comes here," said the future tenant of The Cedars. "I say, I must be getting home."

So Oliver saw her into her car with her two dogs and walked back to Marling. Lucy had laid Turk on his own rug in what used to be her bedroom and after supper Oliver dug his grave in the corner where other family dogs had been buried and then there was nothing to mark that Turk had been except a low mound with sods replaced on it. Later a small stone or a board with Turk's name and age would mark his resting-place. Then he said good-night to his parents, and so to bed. His elder brother and sister had long since left Marling. Then Lucy had married. Now Turk too was lost. Marling Hall was thinning fast; a melancholy thought. But The Cedars would have a mistress and bring fresh interest. Maria had spoken of the possibility of sharing it with a friend. There rose in Oliver a feeling of such violent dislike to that unspecified friend that he was ashamed of himself. But shame or no shame the thought of anyone sharing The Cedars pained him greatly.

CHAPTER II

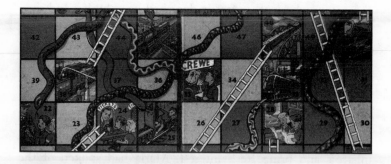

When Tom Grantly had written his letter of resignation and sent it to the right quarter he was prepared for an extremely unpleasant interval at the office, for if anyone knew how to make himself thoroughly disagreeable by innuendo, by sarcasm and even by personalities, that man was Geoffrey Harvey. Nor, though Tom having a decent mind had not thought of such a thing, would he have been above telling his sister all about it, and though the brother and sister disagreed over most things in a very outspoken way, they would have enjoyed baiting a younger man who was still a servant on approval of the Red Tape and Sealing Wax Department. One foretaste of this Tom did have when a day or two later he rashly let slip something about going to Rushwater at the weekend and Mr. Harvey had said that a man who was so keen on cultivating the county could never be any use to the Department. But Tom, in spite of crackling red Catherine wheels of rage in a black infinity inside his head, had managed to say nothing and now by the greatest of good luck Geoffrey Harvey had gone on a fortnight's leave and the office was at peace. His resignation was formally accepted by the people concerned who took little interest in him except as another of those returned soldiers who couldn't stand up to the job, and his service would come to an end within a measurable period.

But Rushwater must be faced and, after another very heart-

ening talk with his sister Grace, Tom rang up Martin and asked
if he could come over and talk to him. Martin's voice, un-
changed, friendly as ever, said why not come for the weekend.
There would be people on Sunday, he said, but if Tom would
come on Saturday for supper and stay till Sunday night, or
Monday morning if possible, Emmy wanted to tell him about
an offer for Rushwater Churchill.

How to get through the time till Saturday supper was the
difficulty, but his old army training came to his aid and he
managed to keep so calm and do his work so well that the typist
in his section told another typist over elevenses that Mr. Grantly
really didn't seem to know what he wanted. But when Fortune's
wheel begins to turn she sometimes throws up a lucky number
by mistake and it occurred to that incompetent goddess to
inspire Mrs. Philip Winter to have a tennis party on Saturday
afternoon, for all the little boys had gone home and though it
was restful without them, she and her husband rather missed
their high chattering voices. The end of the summer term is
sometimes harder for Headmasters and for their wives than
parents realize, for devilish as all those pleasing anxious beings
are, the rooms are sadly empty without their dirty hands and
knees, their chirpings and twitterings, their perpetual excuses
for sins of omission and commission.

A good many people had been rash enough to go abroad that
summer on the pittance allowed by THEM. For those who had
friends and relations on whom they could sponge, it was not so
bad, for they could offer (though strictly speaking this was
illegal) to give equal hospitality in return, though well they knew
that English rations, trains, restrictions, and general oppression
would make their kind friends' and relations' stay a disappointment to all concerned. For those who had no links abroad there
was the mortifying experience of having to count one's francs
like gold and be despised by hotelkeepers and natives for being
mean. In Switzerland, owing to the exchange, the value of the
franc was easier to understand, but as one got so very few francs

the understanding was not much use. In France, owing to the exchange, there were so many francs, millions and billions it seemed, that any financial understanding was impossible and as the Dean had said amusingly, A thousand francs in Cripps's sight, Are like a sixpence gone, which was perhaps more witty than accurate. We are pleased to be able to state that among those who had a delightful holiday were Bishop and Mrs. Joram, who spent a month in France with a Count whom Dr. Joram had met when holiday-making in Madagascar, and they ate and drank and sat in the sun without stopping, which did them a great deal of good, as did the compliments which their host and his country neighbours paid to Mrs. Joram's lovely eyes and appealing middle-aged charm. Owing to all this abroading there were fewer tennis players than usual, but as Leslie Winter said it was all for the best as they wouldn't have to ask their neighbours the Tebbens who had gone to Sweden to visit their son and his wife, where the amount of food (and drink) eaten (and drunk) worried Mrs. Tebbens's frugal mind a good deal; though not her husband who carped at not only the diem but everything else that was offered to him.

But the friends with whom we are most concerned were in England, with no intention of leaving it. Tom Grantly and his sister Grace were among the tennis players, as were Lord Lufton and his sister Maria, Charles Belton and a sprinkling of young Grahams. Lady Cora said she was only low average county family but willing to oblige.

Clarissa Graham had never been much of a hand at tennis, as her younger brothers were only too apt to remind her, and though she looked charming in white and had brought her racquet she was in no hurry to play. It would be much more amusing to talk to Lord Lufton and Cecil Waring and even Philip Winter, or even Charles if the others failed. Of course Charles was a dear, but one knew him so well. In the others she saw more promise of amusement. And then her eye fell on a young man unknown to her, so she asked Leslie Winter who he was.

"Oh, that's our new master, Mr. Swan," said Leslie. "He was at Southbridge under Philip and then in the war. I'll get him for you," and she brought the underling across and introduced him.

"My cousins the Leslies were at Southbridge," said Clarissa, "at least Minimus still is, but the others are doing army."

"I've heard about them from Philip," said Mr. Swan. "One of them climbed the School Chapel roof and up that ghastly iron spire, didn't he?"

Clarissa said that would be Minor who had climbed everything in the county except the obelisk at Pomfret Towers. And hadn't one of them been rude to a dreadful mistress in the Prep School?

"I don't know," said Swan. "You see I was in the army one way and another for quite ages till I got out and came here. We'll ask Philip."

"I do find it a little shocking," said Clarissa in her most priggish manner, "when masters and boys Christian name each other. Don't you?" which question was, we fear, meant to bring Swan to confusion.

"As they all do now, I don't find it shocking or unshocking," said Swan. "I say, Philip!"

"Well?" said his Headmaster.

"Miss Graham wants to know which of her cousins was rude to a female mistress at Southbridge," said Swan.

"Oh, I know what she means," said Philip after a moment of puzzled thought. "It was Miss Banks—after your time—who taught Latin in the Prep School and said Uraynus."

"Oh, Lord! What would Mr. Lorimer have said?" said Swan. "What exactly happened to him, sir?" he continued, dropping back to the old manner of address. "We only knew he died—in the hols one summer."

"Heart," said Philip. "He got Hacker through his scholarship exam and died of heart. He knew he would sooner or later."

"Of course!" said Swan. "I remember now. It was the summer Tony Morland and Hacker and I stayed with the Keiths' old Nurse in her cottage, when Lydia Keith cleaned the pond out with Geraldine Birkett and you—" and he stopped suddenly.

"Yes, I was engaged to that lovely moron Rose Birkett," said Philip, "who thank God threw me over," and the two men fell into talk of Southbridge School before the war and how Hacker was a Professor of Latin in a famous university and Tony Morland had absolutely hundreds of children, at any rate two; and in the middle of this delightful talk Clarissa was entirely neglected, so she walked away with her pretty head held high, thinking poorly of schoolmasters, and nearly banged into Lord Lufton, who apologized very politely.

"Mrs. Winter wants me to play now," he said. "Are you in this set?"

Clarissa said she didn't know and accompanied him to the tennis court where Charles Belton was knocking up balls with Maria Lufton and Grace Grantly. With another apology Lord Lufton left Clarissa and went on the court.

"You two are too tall," said Charles to the Luftons. "Will you play with me, Maria, and Grace with your brother? Sixpence on the set" but Maria said she never bet because she always lost.

It was certainly a very handsome four though several of the spectators thought that one had to be an Honourable to get away with being so tall and Charles wondered if he could ask his partner to stand back to back with him and see which was the taller. Their opponents were less evenly matched in height, but Grace Grantly, owing to a natural aptitude, the games mistress at Barchester High School, and coaching from kind but unsympathetic brothers, played a very good game.

"How very handsome Grace Grantly is," said Leslie Winter to Lady Cora, who entirely agreed and said she had good bones.

"So have I," she said, with her customary aloofness about herself. "But mine take after the American Duchess, rather like birds' bones. Grace's are more English. I suppose you haven't a little boy left for me? I did enjoy them so much."

Leslie said they had all gone home and the Priory felt so lonely that they were having the tennis party to keep themselves going and then the games were so close and so well played that conversation dropped. Charles Belton and Maria Lufton were playing very well, Maria's height and long arms giving her considerable advantage. Lord Lufton was also tall and could reach the balls with ease, and Grace though not very tall played not only very well for her years but well up to county tournament standard, and all the spectators stopped talking to watch the set which finished in a spectacular rally between Lord Lufton and Charles with some hard hitting. Finally Charles hit the ball with a swift low stroke and it spattered along the court so fast and low that Lord Lufton missed it on the rise and the set was lost.

Maria Lufton and Charles Belton congratulated one another and Grace with Lord Lufton joined the spectators, while Lady Cora with Tom came on the lawn. The games were hard fought. The audience talked and looked, and then looked less and talked more. Lord Lufton paid Grace Grantly a compliment on her playing and asked her if she had ever been to Framley. Grace said she had never been there but knew all about it because her father had some old letters that a young Lady Lufton had written to his grandmother, or was it great-grandmother. She thought that the Lady Lufton of those days had been kind to that Mrs. Grantly when her father was the parson at Hogglestock.

"Mother would love to hear about those letters," said Lord Lufton. "She is much more family-minded than her children. Could you come to tea one day and tell her about them? Hers are in an awful mess. She got them all mixed up with the Women's Institute papers when she was tidying her writing-table after we let most of the house to Amalgamated Vedge and I don't think she will ever get them straight."

"I'd love to," said Grace. "I've done a secretarial course and I do know a bit about old letters. I can read crossed ones, but not double crossed. Father has millions and Mother has nearly as many. Families are rather a trouble."

Lord Lufton said they were.

"I always thought it would be rather fun to be a real secretary," said Grace. "Like Isabel Dale when she secretaried for Lord Silverbridge and then she married him."

"I hadn't got as far as offering matrimony—not that I'm much of a catch," said Lord Lufton, at which Grace said not to be silly and of course she hadn't meant that at all; only that she would love to help his mother with her old letters, so long as his sisters wouldn't mind.

"Oh dear, no," said Lord Lufton. "Maria only cares for dogs and Justinia is a career girl, so if you secretary for Mother that will be quite fair."

Grace looked searchingly at him and said she had never learnt logic but she was sure what he said didn't make sense somehow, though how exactly she couldn't make out. Lord Lufton said probably the Fallacy of the Undistributed Middle, at which Grace laughed and he thought what a pretty laugh it was and he would like to hear it again. Then Lord Lufton noticed that Clarissa was rather out of things and tried to include her in the conversation, but her bad mood was on her and she was almost rude to Grace. Grace was in some ways better equipped for the battle of life than Clarissa and though we yield to none in our loathing of Miss Pettinger we must admit that in the world over which (apart from her hate-worthiness) she so successfully reigned, her pupils did learn to face life and even to discriminate between good and less good, which last, much to Mrs. Grantly's relief, had finally caused Grace to stop wanting to go to the Barchester Odeon with Jennifer Gorman, with whom she now exchanged threepenny Woolworth Christmas cards once a year and to whom she had secretly decided not to send one next Christmas. Grace, after pretending not to notice Clarissa's rudeness and trying to find common ground with her, was defeated and talked to Lord Lufton about typewriters and how their teeth always wanted brushing and what a check to one's thought it was when a word, ignoring the little bell, ran on over the paper onto the roller.

"I suppose it's like anything you get used to; you don't hear it," said Lord Lufton. "Like the guns in Normandy. If one got a bit of sleep you had to be blown up before you heard a noise," and then the game became so fast and exciting that they stopped talking till Lady Cora lobbed a ball over the net in a very nasty way. It fell dead and though Maria Lufton and Charles both rushed for it, it died under their eyes and they nearly knocked each other down.

"Well done, Tom," said Lady Cora.

"But it was your ball that did them in," said Tom.

"But I was your partner," said Lady Cora "So it was ours."

Not so very long ago Tom's heart would have leapt to these encouraging words, but he had told himself with a wisdom bought of a good deal of unhappiness that what Lady Cora had said on the bridge she had meant, and his world had altered since then. Though his future was still very uncertain he felt more sure of himself and could parry her threats without flinching. No bones were broken and he enjoyed her company. Then over the grass, self-consciousness oozing from every pore, came Marigold, whose writhings as she approached so many gentlemen and one a real Lord, would have called down the severe criticism of Mr. Geoff Coxon.

"Ow. Mrs. Allen said to say tea, Mrs. Winter," said Marigold, whose sight was no longer impeded by the flabby golden lock. But she had done far worse and had acquired in Barchester the latest windswept cut by whose means she looked as if a spiteful rival had taken vengeance on her with the nail-scissors, and in the kitchen Nannie Allen had said darkly that once you cut it that way it never grew again.

Leslie thanked her, but Marigold lingered.

"That's all, Marigold. Tell Mrs. Allen we're just coming," said Leslie Winter.

"Please, Mrs. Winter, it's the Lord," said Marigold. "Didn't we ought to have the silver teapot? It says in the book on Etikwet—" but Leslie said the china one would do nicely and was Sir Cecil anywhere about.

"Please, he's dragging the ponds with Sergeant Hopkins," said Marigold. "Do you think it's a corpse, Mrs. Winter?"

"Not a bit," said Leslie. "Tell Nannie and Selina we're coming in," and she began to round up her guests for tea.

The tennis itself had been quite good enough, the weather not colder than usual, but Leslie felt the afternoon had been rather flat and attributed it partly to Clarissa who was not helping and partly to her brother for not being there. Then she blamed herself for being fussy and took the party in to tea. The players were replaying their games with a good deal of laughter and Mr. Swan was making very good running with Grace Grantly, while Lord Lufton, who must have been about Swan's age, looked on them benignly, thinking how amusing they both were, and again thinking what a pity it was that Clarissa hadn't a better temper, for her pert condescension to Charles Belton in his mother's house had remained as an ugly memory, and while he admitted her good looks and charm he had but a poor opinion of her manners and even poorer of the kind of disposition that could underlie such manners. And Clarissa, conscious that she was in some kind of disgrace, probably knowing why and therefore all the more resenting it, felt herself getting less and less agreeable. We all know the feeling. And once that fatal moment has begun how very difficult it is to stop it, for whatever we do we do wrong and then blame ourselves and then start doing wrong again.

"Oh Lord Lufton," said Grace Grantly's voice, breaking across his thought. "I know your sister Justinia. I only just thought of it. She secretaries for the Dean, doesn't she?"

Lord Lufton said she did. "She spends the week there and comes to Framley for the weekends as a rule."

"I thought that must be it," said Grace. "The Crawleys are cousins, about a million times removed, of Father's. It's all too complicated, because we all have large families. The Crawleys have eight and Octavia says she's going to have eight too. You know, her husband's the clergyman here with one arm because he was in North Africa. She's got four now. What do you do? I mean not being a Lord, but just ordinary."

"I'm afraid it's all pretty ordinary," said Lord Lufton, amused by his new friend. "I try to farm and do county work and I sit in the House of Lords sometimes," upon which Grace, who had a practical mind, asked if he had bought his Lord's robes or hired them, to which Lord Lufton replied with equal seriousness that luckily his father's robes had been put away very carefully with mothballs. And what was more, he added, his mother's robes as a Baron's wife were also put away and so far the moths had not touched them.

"Would you like to see them when you come to Framley?" said Lord Lufton. "Mother would show them to you, I know."

Grace, awestruck, said she would love it and already in her fertile mind was the germ of a hope that she might be allowed to try on a peeress's robes and see what she looked like. Grace was then claimed by Swan as an equal and Lord Lufton reflected upon Clarissa with the parasol in the pony-cart and how well she had looked the part and how wantonly unkind she had been to Charles Belton, quite unprovoked. If Grace Grantly put on his mother's robes and coronet he was certain that she would not be unkind by mistake or on purpose to anyone and that his mother would enjoy it. And being a good son his mind wandered to his mother's affectionate tolerance of all that her children did; of Justinia becoming a secretary, of Maria preferring dogs as friends, of himself probably very boring about the farm and the cows and his county duties and doing nothing about marrying and producing an heir to acres which, though far fewer than they were, would not be barren if he could prevent it. Arising from these thoughts, though he may not have been conscious of the connection, was a small shadow. He had read that a woman in love will sometimes, being a woman, be disagreeable in public to a man whom she secretly cares for. If this were true, Clarissa might really be very fond of Charles Belton and choose this peculiar way of showing it. It was no business of his, but he did not wish to think ill of that pretty girl and he wondered if he had been too severe, too cold. We could tell him that poor Clarissa deserved all she got and more, but his kind heart was exercised in the matter.

About halfway through tea Cecil Waring came in with apologies.

"I was dragging the Dipping Ponds with Hopkins," he said to his sister Leslie, squeezing a chair in beside her. "Old Jasper says there used to be fish till a pike came and ate them. How the pike came, do not ask me."

"One always wonders how fish *do* come into ponds unless somebody puts them there," said Maria Lufton.

Several people then instanced ponds, or even better concrete pools, in which fish had appeared by a kind of miraculous birth, but as no one was quite sure of the facts or details the conversation died down round the table.

"But we did get two nasty big ruffians, jack by the look of them," said Cecil. "And as for saucepans and kettles with holes in them and two broken cane chairs and a sackful of bottles and old china and some false teeth, it was like the old Army and Navy Stores catalogue that Aunt Harriet used to have. You remember, Leslie."

"But why false teeth?" said Maria Lufton, who had a practical mind. "It's not reasonable."

"That's what Hopkins and I thought," said Cecil. "You don't go chucking false teeth into ponds for fun."

Swan suggested that it was in the nature of a sacrifice to the new so-called Health Service by someone who wanted a free new set, to which Philip replied that surely they would keep the old ones in case of emergency, but Maria Lufton said the lower orders were notoriously extravagant, which truth put an end to the theorizing.

"And a silver button," said Cecil. "Jasper knew something about it, but he wouldn't tell me."

"But I know," said his sister Leslie. "It was Lydia Merton's. She gave it to Jasper to shoot his old granny with. She was a witch," Leslie added for Maria's benefit as a stranger to the Priory, "and used to change into a black hare. Oh, but he shot her with an ordinary bullet and gave the button back to Lydia. Then how did it get into the pond?"

"Please, Miss Leslie," said Selina, who had brought in freshly made tea for second cups, "Mrs. Merton she didn't like the button after Jasper had it and she gave it to me. So Hopkins he said to me What's that my girl and I told him Jasper had had it and he lost his temper ever so," said Selina proudly, her pretty silver curls almost writhing with emotion, "and he threw it in the Dipping Pond."

"I say, what an awfully good detective story," said Mr. Swan.

"But it doesn't get you anywhere," said Lord Lufton.

"Things mostly don't," said Tom, from the depths of his experience, and then there was more talk of tennis, but the sky looked so grey and the trees were so waving that they decided to be cowards and stay indoors.

"I don't want to be a secret drinker," said Cecil Waring, getting his sister to himself for a moment, "but may I take some brandy? It was pretty cold in the pond and waders may keep the water out but they seem to keep the cold in."

"You do look pretty awful," said Leslie, but being a well-trained sister she did not bother him and took him into the dining-room where he had a stiff drink and said he was sure that would do the trick. Meanwhile Philip had routed out the cards for a game called Pit which our older readers may remember before the Germans began the beginning of the end. It is very simple and consists almost entirely in shouting, and whoever shouts loudest may, or may not, get all the cards required. In fact it is not unlike Happy Families except that bad manners and yelling are encouraged.

It amused Leslie, as a Headmaster's wife, to watch the gradual disintegration of manners among well-bred people, most of whom were nearer thirty than twenty except for Clarissa and Grace. We need hardly say that most of the players were red in the face and hoarse within ten minutes and each man present, every one of whom had seen war in its sternest aspects, said that he had never enjoyed himself so much since North Africa, or Crete, or Italy, or D-Day, or the North Sea according to his experience. Lady Cora said it was as good as the night the City was on fire. Another game was begun. Leslie looked at her brother and didn't like what she saw. He left the game, hardly noticed among the shouts and snatching, and she followed him to the dining-room.

"Worse?" she said, giving him some more brandy.

"Foul," said Cecil. "Somebody else will be the Bart if this goes on. By the way, is there another heir?" and he drank the brandy and sat down.

"I thought there was something wrong," said Lady Cora who had quietly left the table and followed them. "What is it?"

"Hell," said Cecil who was white and green with pain. "Can you get onto Ford, Leslie?"

His sister went away and he concentrated on not feeling ill, with such success that Lady Cora decided on swift practical measures.

"Barchester General for you at once, Cecil," she said. "Well, Leslie?"

"Ford's not in," said Leslie Winter. "But he's at the Barchester General. I'll ask Philip to take Cecil in at once."

Cecil, speaking out of a nightmare of pain, was understood to say that he would be damned if he would go into hospital.

"And you'll be dead if you don't," said Lady Cora coldly. "I'll

take him, Leslie. My car's here and I didn't drive Generals in the
war for nothing. You come too, only hurry. I'll take him out
right away."

Leslie hurried, panic-stricken, to tell Philip what was happening and then ran out of the house and got into the car beside
Cecil. Lady Cora, alone in the front seat, drove as she had driven
during the war, and by a special providence did not see any of the
county constabulary, many of whom were her friends and would
not have liked to pull her ladyship up for furious driving. By the
greatest good luck Dr. Ford was talking to Matron on the steps
of the Barchester General Hospital as they drove up and after a
word from Lady Cora took command. A couple of orderlies
come out and Cecil Waring was on a stretcher and being carried
down a long corridor before he knew what had happened.

"Anything wrong with your brother before this attack?" said
Dr. Ford to Leslie Winter, but it was Lady Cora who said: "He
told us he had a bit of shrapnel inside him."

"Splendid," said Dr. Ford. "Matron will look after you," and
vanished.

It was not Leslie Winter's fault that her work in peace and
then in war had lain outside Barsetshire. Since her marriage she
had reaffirmed her roots and become again a native, almost
indistinguishable from the landscape. But those years before the
war and during the war had left a gap and though Matron knew
her and liked her, there was not the bond of work and suspense
and cups of tea shared. Whether Leslie or Lady Cora was the
more sick, terrified, and shaken inside we do not know, but at
least Lady Cora could discuss with Matron the High Old Time
they had in the plastic surgery ward when Corporal Hoggett,
who had been given coloured plasticine by a kind lady who said
it was psychotherapy, did counterfeit on his own face such a
hideous presentment of facial disfigurement that pretty little
V.A.D. Coxon from Northbridge went quite white and had to
be given a *sal volatile* by that nice young doctor dear me I shall be
forgetting my own name next and came out of the dispensary

with her face quite a study; while Leslie could only move with dreadful slowness or nauseating swiftness from knowing all would be well to standing by her brother's grave and having to decide what to do with his clothes—for these trifles are very large.

So the time passed, or did not pass, as neither lady knew whether the hours were going backwards or forwards, for everything had become stationary; horribly still and dead with people coming in and out of Matron's room who moved like marionettes and uttered sounds without sense. Once Dr. Ford looked in, remarked, "Hastings is at it. Don't worry," and disappeared.

"That's the best surgeon in the West," said Lady Cora in a very natural voice that no one would have recognized. Leslie looked at her and smiled a wintry smile and Matron, who had just popped out to have a word with Dr. Ford, told Nurse Poulter to put a bromide in a cup of tea for Lady Cora and one for poor Mrs. Winter such a devoted sister. But though Leslie's sufferings were probably even worse than Lady Cora's, being rooted in nursery days, we regret to say that the interest of the staff was with the unmarried lady and Nurse Poulter nearly put both bromides into Lady Cora's cup from sheer sympathy.

We have every confidence in our readers and we hope they have enough confidence in us not to have been unduly alarmed by Sir Cecil Waring's sudden illness, adumbrated by us in earlier chapters. Never would we willingly kill anyone. Older people come to the term of their natural life and their deaths are chronicled. There is grief; then time passes and our minds, in earth's diurnal course, move to other things. The ripples on the water die away. Clarissa may pick the sweetbriar on her grandmother's grave, but we think her sorrow is by now not so much for Lady Emily's absence as for her own pretty, bewildered self, caught in a world not of her making and kicking against the pricks. Miss Merriman may think of her own Countess, the Lady Pomfret of the years before the most recent war (for the last war, double-edged word, we dare not say), but less and less, for her life now belongs to another generation of Pomfret. But these and others had reached the allotted span of life and, we believe, fell unshuddering into the breast that gave the rose.

To Leslie and to Lady Cora it seemed that their vigil had lasted for rather longer than eternity. It was the chill Summer Time dusk when Dr. Ford came in and said it was a nice little bit of metal and Hastings had nipped it out like two o'clock and there was no need to worry.

Lady Cora looked at him.

"Now, Lady Cora, don't come the Castle over me," said Dr. Ford good-humouredly. "I've been at doctoring too long to try to deceive people like you—or Mrs. Winter," he added, for he had helped Leslie a good deal after she had broken down in health during the war. "Hastings got that bit of metal out beautifully. And there will NOT be a septic condition and there will NOT be complications," he added firmly. "Now you two young women go home and tomorrow one of you can come and see him. Not both," and waving aside their rather incoherent thanks he turned to go.

"National Health?" he said, turning with his hand on the door.

"Good God, no!" said Leslie, roused from her apathy of fear and relief.

"Just as well," said Dr. Ford, most unpatriotically and unprofessionally. "You'd have had to wait till old Bevan had got his new uppers. There are two poor women in High Rising who have been waiting for more than two years to get their children's tonsils done. Well, the children will probably be mentally defective for life by the time the National Health gets round to them—and it's not a bad plan," said Dr. Ford thoughtfully. "If it weren't too late I'd go mentally defective and lead a happy, carefree life. Now go home and go to bed, both of you. I'll drop you at the Priory, Mrs. Winter."

"You'd better go and see Cecil tomorrow," said Leslie to Lady Cora. "You saved his life. I couldn't have driven so fast."

"I don't know really if he wants to see me," said Lady Cora, looking into some distance visible only to herself. "You go. And if he would like me to come, you can tell me. Come on. Philip will think they have put you in cold storage for the dissecting-room," and after thanking Matron Lady Cora drove back to Gatherum. Her parents had gone to bed. There was no one to talk to, nor did she much want to talk to anyone. Once before, perhaps not only once, she had staked her happiness and lost. Could one, after teaching oneself to be content with nothing, aspire to something with the chance of finding oneself back in the mud hovel? She did not know. And all that night she did not know. But anyone else would have told her.

CHAPTER 12

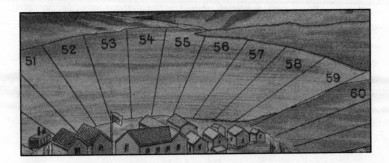

Philip Winter was as we know on excellent terms with his brother-in-law, but when Leslie told him what had happened his first thought was of extreme annoyance with Cecil for troubling the beloved Leslie. Then he pulled himself together, told Leslie to try not to worry and went back to the guests.

With great clamour they told him how Lord Lufton with Grace had cornered pretty well everything that could be cornered. Grace was bright red in the face from her exertions and looking extremely handsome, while Lord Lufton had enjoyed himself more than he had thought possible, being young among the young instead of a worried landowner with a sad worried mother; which description of his life is ours, not his, for we do not think it occurred to him that there was still a good deal of fun and silliness to be found among his contemporaries.

For Clarissa everything had gone wrong. She had not shone. She had not been asked to play tennis and though her common sense told her it was the wet and the cold that had stopped the playing and also that she was not in the class of the good amateurs, she chose to feel offended and her pretty face was sullen. Everyone seemed to like talking to someone else and even Eric Swan, on whom she had cast a mildly interested eye, cared far more for schoolboy talk. As for Pit, it was a stupid horrible game. Oh, if only Gran had been there, how lovely to have talked to her and let the others make a silly, babyish noise if they liked. As for Charles, if he liked to shout OATS or BARLEY at the top of his voice for hours and hours, let him. Also let him get off with Maria Lufton, who must be about a hundred, if he wished. If she had had a car, or even a bicycle, she would have gone away, but Charles in his rackety little car had promised to take her back to Holdings and there was no other way. So she sulked determinedly and was justly rewarded, poor silly Clarissa, by no one noticing the sulks. Possibly Charles did; but Charles was not to be hurried.

The Headmaster of a preparatory school needs patience. Philip, in his early years, had possessed very little of that quality and his flaming red hair appeared to be an outward sign of the inner man. Then responsibility, his Territorial training, the war, his rise to the rank of Colonel, and also his love for Leslie had done their work and only very seldom did he lose control, but even the smallest and the most impudent of his pupils knew better than to misbehave when the Headmaster grew polite. With Cecil's danger and Leslie's anguish fresh upon him Philip's voice was unusually mild as he beckoned Eric Swan out of the hurly-burly and told him what had happened.

"See what you can do," said Philip. "There's so much noise I can't talk. We were going to ask some of them to stay to supper, but you'll have to get rid of them."

"Right, sir," said Swan. "I'll carry on," and Philip, blessing the British Army, went to talk with Nannie Allen, for among the humble, he felt, would be comfort. Not that Nannie, he thought to himself with an amusement that could not be suppressed, could truthfully be described as humble, for if ever there was a masterful, overbearing old lady, presuming on her age and her many ex-nurslings, Nannie was the one. But under it all was true humility, Philip thought; and then his mind was too tired to think, as one's mind sometimes is after a shock, so he followed his instinct and went along the passage to the cheerful kitchen where the light was nearly always on and a kettle on the range;

for Selina had an electric cooker and a gas cooker (for little boys must be fed whoever strikes, whatever shortages there are) and also a coal range which had been described by the senior assistant master as the fire that is not quenched.

"What's wrong now?" said Nannie Allen who was alone, reading the Barchester *Evening Chronicle*.

Philip said Nothing. Only—

"Now, that's not being Open," said Nannie, fixing Philip with the eye that had made even David Leslie cower. "Tell the truth and shame the devil Father used to say. Tell Nannie what's wrong. It's not Miss Leslie?" she said with alarm in her eyes.

"No. She's all right. It's Cecil," said Philip. "He felt queer after tea and Leslie and Lady Cora took him to Barchester."

"Now don't you commence to worry, sir," said Nannie. "If Miss Leslie's all right you've no reason to worry," which reasoning, though fallacious to the last degree, soothed Philip a good deal. "What ever's happened to Master Cecil I daresay it's his own fault, but he never was one to listen to good advice. Three times he's been to ask me for something for stomach trouble, so I gave him some milk of magnesia. It can't do no harm and the bottle's a pretty blue," said Nannie, who appeared to have a superstitious belief in the manner in which drugs were presented.

"If the silly fool had gone to the doctor we shouldn't be in this mess," said Philip, quite unable to contain himself and in the same moment ashamed of what he had said.

"Now, Master Philip," said Nannie looking at him over her steel-rimmed spectacles, "that's not the way to talk. You tell Nannie nicely," and the successful Headmaster of the Priory School felt convicted of Rudeness to Nannie; an unforgivable nursery crime. "Haven't they rung up from the Hospital?"

"Not yet," said Philip. "Good Lord! how did you know?"

"Nannie always knows everything," said that lady, a remark which was as near truth as anything in this mortal vale and had been proved true by generations of little boys, much to their discomfiture. "And if Hopkins did happen to see poor Mr. Cecil looking like his own ghost and her ladyship and Miss Leslie putting him in the car, it stands to reason the Hospital is where they were going. It'll be all right, Master Philip. Don't you commence to worry. Time enough to worry, when worry worries you, my father used to say."

"But it *is* worrying me," said Philip querulously, yet at the same time comforted; quite unreasonably, but we are not creatures of reason.

"Hopkins will tell us," said Nannie. "I sent him up to Master Cecil's house to telephone, so as that Marigold wouldn't hear. The ears that girl has you'd think she'd been growing them ever since she was born," which seemed to Philip, even in his anxiety, an unfair description of a natural process. "And I'll make you a nice cup of tea," said Nannie, getting up slowly from her chair and going to the range where a large kettle was gently simmering and from time to time spitting a drop of water with a sizzling sound upon the polished top. "I've told that Marigold a hundred times if I've told her once NOT to fill the kettle so full," said Nannie. "It's you as'll have to clean the rust marks off, my girl, I've said. But you might as well talk to a screech-owl. It's just on the boil, sir."

Whenever Philip went into the kitchen, his by right of tenancy but inalienably the property of Nannie Allen and Selina and Sergeant Hopkins, even as the Sussex valley belonged to Old Hobden, he felt that he was in a better world, a new and richer life, and had even carried this fancy so far as to maintain that like Antæus he drew fresh strength from his mother earth as exemplified in the true Barsetshire people, unaffected save in externals by Saxon, Dane, Norman, wireless, or the newspapers: and we think he was right. He sat down and waited more or less patiently while Nannie Allen made the tea, trying to forget everything except the present moment.

"There sir," said Nannie Allen, setting a large cup beside him. "I've put the milk in and you're not one for sugar," after which perfectly true words Philip felt that even if he were a sugar fiend he would not dare to ask for it.

"It's a shame, that's what I say," said Nannie, stirring her own tea busily. "A gentleman like Master Cecil! Now if it had been some of that government as they call themselves there'd be some sense. Well, Hopkins?"

"Having got onto the Barchester General after two wrong numbers," the Sergeant began, apparently under the impression that he was giving his testimony at a court martial—

"Why didn't you get through to Palmyra Phipps at the exchange?" said his mother-in-law. "She'd have put you through."

"I did, Ma," said Hopkins and taking a breath he began again. "Having got onto the Barchester General after the blighters had given me two wrong numbers and I had contacted Miss Phipps at the exchange who went off the deep end about it the way it was a real pleasure to hear," said Sergeant Hopkins, in a monotonous delivery, "I contacted the porter—he used to be a Corporal in the Barsetshires, sir," he threw in to Philip—"who informed me that Sir Cecil had been successfully operated on and they got out a nice bit of shrapnel those bleeding Eyeties had plugged in him. *All* right, Ma, bleeding I said, and if you knew the Eyeties the way I do you'd say it was what our Sergeant-Major used to call Fair Comment."

We are now obliged to report that Nannie Allen's thanks to her son-in-law and her comment on the good news were included in the indignant words: "Why couldn't they have done it sooner? Keeping me in the dark like that!"

"If they'd known you was there, Ma, I dessay they would," said Hopkins, at which his mother-in-law, after a few seconds of terrifying silence, said complacently she dessaid they would, at which moment Eric Swan and Selina Hopkins irrupted from opposite ends of the kitchen and began to speak at once.

"That's enough," said Nannie Allen sharply. "Let the young gentleman talk, Selina."

"I'm awfully sorry, Mrs. Hopkins," said Swan, overcome by

one or two tears that rolled like crystal down Selina's cheeks. "It's all right, sir. Dr. Ford has just rung up. Hastings was in the hospital and operated almost at once. He told Dr. Ford that Sir Cecil was all right and if anyone said he was quite comfortable they'd make Ananias look like a beginner, but we could take it from him that he was in no danger and could have one visitor tomorrow. I've cleared everyone off, sir, and Belton's taking Miss Graham home, and Dr. Ford is bringing Mrs. Winter back."

"Thanks, Swan," said Philip. "Thank God."

"And may I add," said Swan, "that I would like to apologize now, sir, for having looked at you through my spectacles at Southbridge. The year you were engaged to Rose Birkett, sir," which impertinence made Philip forget all the past anxiety and laugh till Nannie Allen said the best cure for the hiccups was to drink out of the wrong side of a glass. Swan said a glass hadn't got a wrong side because it was round and Euclid had defined a circle as a thing that hadn't got any straight sides and Philip began to laugh again.

"Oh, it was ever so dreadful, sir," said Selina, seizing her opportunity. "I was having a cup of tea with Mrs. Pollett and I said I'd give her a hand in the bar if she was short and then Palmyra Phipps that's at the exchange rang up and said wasn't it dreadful poor Sir Cecil in the hospital and poor Lady Cora as white as a sheet and Miss Leslie crying her eyes out. It made me and Mrs. Pollett cry ever so. So I came back in where I was needed."

"And where's Marigold?" said Nannie Allen sharply. "She ought to be in by now," and even as she spoke the errant Marigold came in, stopped short appalled by the sight of so many gentry, and made as if to fly.

"Come here, Marigold," said Nannie. "Where have you been?"

In a voice so hushed that none of her friends would have recognized it, Marigold mumbled something about Mrs. Coxon.

"That's Geoff Coxon's mother," said Nannie, with such awful aloofness that most of her audience felt there were milestones on the Dover Road.

"Yes, Mrs. Allen," said Marigold. "And Mrs. Coxon gave me a brooch."

"What did she want to do that for?" said Nannie Allen. "First time I've ever heard of Ruth Coxon giving something for nothing."

"Please, Mrs. Allen, Mrs. Coxon said if she was losing a son she was gaining a daughter," said Marigold, which rendering of a well-known saying obviously meant nothing to her at all. "It's a lovely brooch. Would you like to see it, Mrs. Allen?" and she unpinned the gift and handed it to Nannie. It was an oblong piece of some base metal with the word MIZPAH in Gothic lettering intertwined with what might have been ivy leaves. "Please what's Mizaph, Mrs. Allen?"

"If you read your Bible, Marigold," said Nannie Allen, in a voice which caused all her hearers to be self-convicted of not reading their Bibles, "you'd know it means The Lord watch between me and thee when we are absent one from another, and the good Lord knows you need watching, Marigold. You can ask Geoff up to tea on Sunday and tell Mrs. Coxon I'll come to tea with her on Wednesday," which royal command struck admiration and terror into the hearts of the hearers. Philip took advantage of the stir caused by what he concluded to be Marigold's formal betrothal to Geoff Coxon, son of Mr. Coxon who owned the garridge, to withdraw his troops in the person of Swan to the school quarters, where they quietly ate the cold Sunday supper while awaiting the return of the Headmaster's wife.

According to previous arrangement Charles Belton had driven Clarissa back to Holdings. Lady Graham had gone over to Pomfret Towers and was not yet back. Charles said he would wait a little. The river path and the terrace were no place in such horrid weather so they lighted the wood fire in the Saloon and talked about nothing in particular. But Clarissa's thoughts were not in the Saloon and she answered at random, not at all like herself. Charles had put up with a good deal from Clarissa since he had taken on the job of being as it were her guardian. Only once, at Framley, had he allowed his temper to rise. Lord Lufton had seen the provocation, had approved Charles's retreat, and had thought the less of Clarissa ever since. The look that had gone to his heart remained an extraordinary memory, a glimpse of some lost world of romance; but never again, on his midnight pallet lying, would he sigh for Miss Clarissa Graham. His thoughts were for a girl who would like to go over old letters with his mother and who had shown consideration for his sisters' feelings. Not that they had any, or so Lord Lufton considered in a brotherly way, but Grace had said and done exactly the right thing, and he must ask his mother to let her see the peer's robes. And the peeress's. Grace and his mother were much of a height.

"Well?" said Charles presently.

"Well what?" said Clarissa. Not pertly, not even pettishly, but with a voice of sadness, of depression, which touched Charles's tender heart. But he was not disposed to be very tender at the moment. Duty must come first.

"*You* know what," said Charles. "Look here, Clarissa. I said I'd keep an eye on you and I've done my best for the last year. But this sort of thing can't go on."

"What sort of thing?" said Clarissa, who possessed to the full her sex's peculiar passion for self-abasement and was eager to be scolded.

"I'm not going to tell you," said Charles. "It would only obscure the issue, only you don't know what that means. If you like to snub me in public, I'm old enough to look after myself. But if you can't go to a tennis party without being rude to guests, and what's worse condescending to them, we simply can't have an understanding."

"They might have asked me to play," said Clarissa in a rather whining voice.

"If your game was better and it hadn't rained, all sorts of things might have happened," said Charles. "Disallowed."

"Of course if you like to talk to Maria Lufton—" said Clarissa.

"Of course I do," said Charles. "A handsome, sensible woman with no nonsense about her and understands dogs."

Clarissa was understood to say, indistinctly, that she hated the Honourable Maria Lufton, adding that Eric Swan was very stupid.

"I don't agree with you," said Charles. "And better stupid than rude, anyway."

"And better rude than unkind and horrid like you," said Clarissa and burst into a veritable schoolgirl boohoo of tears, imploring her grandmother to come back. Charles had no experience of a clever, rather conceited, sensitive young woman who suddenly finds that the world is taking no notice of her at all, but he had seen delayed war shock in other men and had himself set his feet on the fringes of that dreadful world before he found work and happiness at the Priory School. One might try shock treatment and throw a bucket of cold water over Clarissa, but he would have to face Cook and Marlene to get the bucket and he very much doubted if his Cousin Agnes would like to find a sofa in the Saloon soaked to the springs. Reasoning and scolding he had tried. Hope and faith he had tried. Perhaps there was another way.

"Clarissa," he said. "Do you remember the Palace Garden party last year?"

A damp snuffling voice from the sofa said yes.

"And do you remember when you told me about wishing your grandmother were alive? And what old Kipling said about that sort of thing?"

A snuffled voice made a noise which might have been assent, or might not.

"Then I shall say it again," said Charles.

"'The dead they cannot rise, and you'd better dry your eyes,
And you'd best take me for your new love.'"

There was a silence during which Charles's heart bumped rather uncomfortably, broken by a very small voice, impeded by tears, saying: "But would you still like me for your love?"

Of course there was only one answer and while the answer was still going on in a manner most satisfactory to both parties, Lady Graham came back. So quietly had she come in that the young lovers did not hear her. She was not surprised. To her it had always seemed that the understanding between Charles and Clarissa was a delicate prelude to something more lasting. Lady Graham with her generous loving nature had more reserves in her than anyone except perhaps her husband and her mother knew, and Miss Merriman; though exactly what that lady thought of people will never be known. Clarissa had always been Agnes's anxiety. Almost too precocious, too devoted to Lady Emily to the exclusion of others, certainly too self-willed; and though not selfish, centred most deeply in herself. Her mother had to confess herself for the first time in her life completely baffled, which had increased her anxiety for her second daughter. Of late things had not improved. For all her vagueness Agnes Graham had sound instincts. She had not heard what Clarissa said to Charles at Framley, but she had seen Charles's face and Lord Lufton's face and had been most concerned. The Foster blood was not an easy inheritance, as had been visible in her grandfather Lord Pomfret and his odious heir Major Foster. Luckily the Major had died and dear Gilly had inherited the Towers, with an angelic disposition. But the strain was there and was appearing in some of Gilly's children and poor Clarissa had it. In the right hands all that was difficult in Clarissa could be turned to favour and to prettiness. Charles had kept his trust: Clarissa had behaved very badly, had suffered from her own bad behavior, and had been ready to hurt anyone in her misery: even Charles.

Some slight movement made Charles look up. Clarissa's head was comfortably on his shoulder, his arm round her. With an impertinent smile he stretched his other hand to Lady Graham who drew near and took it. Charles raised her hand to his lips and looking up at her he said: "Mother-in-law." A coal crashed down in the fire and a flame sprang up. Clarissa lifted her head and said: "Oh Mother darling, it's CHARLES," and everyone was dissolved in tears and laughing and congratulations.

"But mind you," said Charles, when he at length began to tear himself away, "this is not beer and skittles. I've got board and lodging and a decent salary at the Priory and my people give me a bit which is jolly decent of them and I think Freddy and Elsa and I come in for a bit of something from an aunt. But school-mastering is no inheritance."

"You might—" Clarissa began.

"No, I might *not* find a job in Shell or I.C.I. or something with initials," said Charles. "Do you know the first thing they ask you? They want to know if you are interested in what dividends the firm makes. Nothing to do with your salary; just the firm. If you say yes, they look at your speaking countenance and know you are lying. If you say no, they say All right, you're no good here. You'll have to be a school-master's wife, my silly bird, and darn my socks."

Lady Graham said that Clarissa was a beautiful darner and needlewoman, thus apparently settling the whole matter to her own satisfaction.

Charles asked a little nervously, and it was the first time he had felt any doubts, whether he ought to see Sir Robert Graham.

"I don't think so," said Lady Graham reflecting. "You see he is always in town in the week and at the weekends he doesn't like to see people, which is so awkward. He is away till next week, but I shall write and tell him tomorrow. I am sure he will be pleased. Of course I would have liked Clarissa to marry a Duke, or even a Marquess," Lady Graham continued, a little wistfully, "but I can't think of any hereabouts. Silverbridge is married and as for the Marquess of Hartletop the heir is only a few years old. But I know darling Mamma would have been so pleased, and your mother being a Thorne makes it so comfortable. You know Aunt Edith Pomfret, the one Edith was called after, was a Thorne, so it is all in the family. Did I ever tell you, dear Charles, how I got engaged to Robert?"

"You did, mother-in-law," said Charles, adding with surprising firmness and slight impudence, "and it has been the talk of the county ever since," upon which Agnes laughed charmingly and said Charles was so like her brother David. And as she cared for her brother David Leslie almost as much as she had loved Lady Emily, this may be considered a real tribute to Charles.

Of course Charles stayed to supper and equally of course Marlene, her wit sharpened by the films, guessed at once what had happened and told Cook, getting well snubbed for her pains. Then Charles had to go.

"Dear Charles," said Lady Graham, gently pulling him down to her soft, scented embrace. "Nothing could be happier and I know darling Mamma would have been so pleased and meddled quite dreadfully. There is only one thing—" and she paused.

"Tell me," said Charles, who was in a mood to drink up eisel and eat a crocodile. "Sixpence will not part us," which allusion was, we fear, lost upon her Ladyship, never much of a reader.

To his surprise and discomfiture Lady Graham's eyes were brimming with tears.

"I know it is foolish," said Lady Graham, "but one can't help that sort of feeling. It is only Emmy."

"But what about Emmy?" said Charles.

"I did hope she would be married first," said Lady Graham, with great simplicity. "My aunt Agnes, darling Mamma's elder sister, was engaged to a Detrimental with a wonderful moustache and he was killed on the northwest frontier, in the same little battle where darling Mamma's nephew, Mellings, was killed, and Aunt Agnes never married, but Mother did."

Charles said to his mother afterwards when trying to describe this scene that he knew there was a fault in Agnes's logic somewhere but he wasn't clever enough to put his finger on it; but at this present moment he had no time to think of logic and very rashly said he didn't suppose he and Clarissa would be married just yet and he simply must go home. So with many good wishes and fond embraces he left Holdings and went back to Harefield where he was spending most of the summer holidays.

When he had, about a year earlier, arrived at what his mother called an understanding with Clarissa, he had found his mother in bed and broken the news to her in her room, leaving the door ajar when he left her in a most annoying way. This evening, when there was far more momentous news to impart, he found her

in the drawing-room with his father, his elder brother Captain Freddy Belton, R.N., and his elder brother's wife, formerly Miss Susan Dean.

If he had cherished a hope of making a mild sensation by his news he was the most deceived, for Philip Winter had rung up when his wife got back, meaning to speak to Charles, but in default of Charles had told Mrs. Belton about Cecil Waring's rush to hospital, the luck of catching the best surgeon in Barsetshire, the success of the operation, and that Cecil was only to have one visitor tomorrow and as that visitor was to be Lady Cora, there was no doubt at all what the result would be; all of which Charles's family related to him in strophe and antistrophe.

"Stout fellow," said Charles. "But I'm even stouter. Yes, Mother," he said, as she looked at him, "it's Clarissa. We are really engaged and she is heaven. She sent you her love," which was a heaven-inspired lie on Charles's part, for the proud fastidious Clarissa had been as deeply moved and bewildered as any other girl and had not given a thought to her future mother-in-law.

Mr. Belton said Who was engaged and he didn't know why people couldn't speak up, thus forcing his younger son to explain to him in a deliberately patient voice, that he. was. engaged. to. Clarissa. Graham. His people took it very well. His brother and his sister-in-law, after affectionate congratulations, looked at each other in a way which showed their opinion of all love-matches but their own. His father then melted and wished Charles luck and lamented that he could not give him the handsome wedding portion he would have had if he had been born before 1914, while Charles heard himself saying that one couldn't expect everything and it was jolly decent of his father, who then remembered some champagne that his son-in-law Admiral Hornby had given him and they drank everyone's health.

"No chance of getting married just yet I suppose," said Charles. "But I could wait for ever and so could Clarissa," which sentiment was received by his family in the spirit in which it was uttered. When the Freddy Beltons had gone back to Dowlah Cottage and his father was happily occupied in counting the remaining bottles of champagne and putting them in another place in no way differing from the place where they were before, Charles went up to his mother's room to say good-night, as he had done before.

"You will love her, Mother, won't you?" he said, at which words any prickly feelings that Mrs. Belton may have had about the girl who had given so much trouble were melted by the love she felt for the girl who was to be her younger son's wife and there was such rejoicing between them that even when Charles shut the door so hard that it came open again she could find nothing in her heart for him but love and a prayer that he was now in a safe haven.

"And as for you, my love," said Philip Winter to his wife when

Dr. Ford had deposited Leslie at the Priory School, "bed." But though they went upstairs there was so much to hear and to discuss that it was almost midnight before bed became a fact.

"Of course," said Leslie, in the effortless superiority of a happily married woman, "Cora was splendid, but if it had been her husband it would have been much worse. I mean she is terribly in love with Cecil though she thinks she isn't. It sticks out of her all over, like a porcupine. She would have sat by his bed all night till she fainted if Dr. Ford had let her see him."

"And when do they propose to get married?" said Philip, yawning.

"But they haven't even *begun* to think," said Leslie. "They'll be like Thomas à Becket's mother and say nothing but 'Cecil, Cecil' and 'Cora, Cora,'" which made Philip laugh.

"You and I hadn't much else to say, *mutatis mutandis*, when you so forwardly came and proposed to me at Winter Overcotes station, my love," he said, "and then I didn't see you for more than two years. These happy young people can get married whenever they like, I imagine. How will you like having a Duke's daughter for your sister-in-law?"

"If it's Cora I shall like it of all things," said Leslie. "You know, Philip, I always thought I'd be jealous of Cecil's wife, but if he isn't nice to her, I shall be *entirely* on her side," to which Philip remarked that *varium et mutabile semper* was as true today as it was nearly two thousand years ago and his wife told him not to be a prig.

There was one person who would have rejoiced above all others that Clarissa had at last found her love. Had Lady Emily still been alive she would have lavished all her affection on the young couple. She would have taken possession of Charles body and soul; she would have made a thousand preposterous plans for their wedding, their honeymoon, their future life; plans which her daughter Agnes would silently have countered. She and Clarissa would have had long talks together to which

Charles would sometimes have been admitted. We do not think that Clarissa, whose worship of her grandmother had been so intense for so young a creature, had given one thought to Lady Emily since she had laid her proud silly head on Charles's comfortable shoulder, and so full was she of her new found joy, so full of wonder that she could have had this jewel for the asking and had neglected it, that she went to bed early, wrapped in dreams of life and love to come.

But her mother sat alone in the Saloon and presently rang up Pomfret Towers. Miss Merriman's voice was heard.

"Dear Merry," said Agnes, "will you tell Sally and Gillie that Clarissa is really engaged to Charles Belton. There isn't much money but he is a dear boy. She will be a schoolmaster's wife, which seems most unusual, but I suppose all engagements are unusual. How are they all?"

The voice of Miss Merriman said that Lord and Lady Pomfret and all the children were well and then there was a pause.

"If only Mamma were here, Merry," said Agnes Graham. "She loved Clarissa so much. How happy she would have been."

"She would," said Miss Merriman, her usual calm voice slightly troubled.

"You are the only person I can say that to now, Merry," said Lady Graham, "except perhaps darling Martin. He is so like her and so like his father that it nearly breaks one's heart. We may go over to Rushwater tomorrow. I would like to tell darling Martin myself."

"Please give them all my love, Lady Graham," said Miss Merriman's voice. "And thank you for ringing up. I will go and tell them now. Good-bye."

Admirable, competent, understanding Merry (thought Agnes), whom none of us have ever known or ever will know. And she wondered, as she had occasionally wondered before, whether Gillie Pomfret had once moved Miss Merriman's heart when he was young Mr. Foster. But no one would ever know. She heard such of her young family as were at home coming back. Edith had been in bed for a long time. She went quietly upstairs. A night of memories and of sighs. But no one would have known it next day.

CHAPTER 13

Owing to Eric Swan's skilful staff work the other guests had gone off unsuspecting and by the time Cecil Waring was in the clutches of Mr. Hastings, Tom Grantly on his bicycle was already nearing Rushwater. How often had he bicycled down the river valley and along by the little Rushmere Brook, tributary to the Rising, through the village, into the park where the road crossed the brook, and so up the back drive to the stable yard.

He put his bicycle in the shed where it used to live and went by the kitchen passages, dark and beetle-haunted, and so into the house itself. There was no one about, but on the terrace, sheltered from the wind and getting what sun there was, he found Sylvia Leslie with Miss Eleanor Leslie and her younger brother who was still chiefly called baby. Tom was feeling more and more like the Prodigal Son and did not like it, as indeed we daresay the Prodigal Son himself did not like it either. For to have to eat fatted calf when you are thoroughly ashamed of yourself and only want to slink in and not be noticed must be a severe trail; not to speak of one's Good Brother. However at least there was no good brother at Rushwater. Nurse came and removed the children and Tom sat with Sylvia, picking up the threads of Rushwater. As usual the tides of life were flowing so strongly that the present became the past and the future, and he felt as if he had only been away a day instead of a year; which is what people always feel if the Queen of Elfland has taken them

away. In Tom's case the Queen of Elfland had been his own self
who, still restless from the wars and so turning from the way,
had found himself with Mr. Geoffrey Harvey in the village of
Morality and like to come to a bad end with Mr. Legality and
Mr. Civility who for all his simpering looks was but a hypocrite.
And, to carry the parable a little further, if his father had stood
for Evangelist, who better to do so?

Of course no real thoughts even as little formulated as these
were in Tom's head, but as he sat with Sylvia on the terrace
where he had so often sat and heard her talk about her babies
and now and then about the fields or the cattle, the lost content
returned to him. Tomorrow some sort of decision would have to
be made. This evening should be entire peace. But in the
comparative backwater of the Red Tape Department and his
own home, Tom had forgotten a little what a quiet evening in
the country was like. Sylvia said she was sorry but she must go
and see if the honey was straining properly. Old Herdman came
slowly along the terrace to find Martin who was not there and
greeted Tom as if a year had not passed. Martin, limping as
usual, came from the woods above, where he had been working,
shook Tom's hand warmly and said they must have a good talk
and he would never get all this tar off his hands if he didn't
hurry. The welkin was then rent by a shriek which disclosed
itself as Deanna, the village girl who helped in the kitchen,
chasing or being chased (for Daphne pursues Apollo as much as
Apollo ever pursued Daphne) by one of the men about the
stable, to which was added Cook's voice calling Deanna. Piercing yells from a window above showed that the nursery was
viewing bed with disfavour. Emmy in breeches strode round the
corner, stopped short, wrung Tom's hand painfully, said she
would see him at dinner only she might be a bit late as the fools
had left one of the chicken runs open and almost in one breath
strode away. Mr. Bostock, the Vicar, came up on his bicycle and
asked Tom if he knew where the vestry key was as it wasn't
there, apparently not realizing that for twelve months or so Tom

had been away. A very old man, known as "the boy," who had
done nothing on weekly wages for many years, shuffled up to
him, said he hadn't won nothing in them gormed pools all this
year and had the gentleman seen Herdman anywhere. Then, as
Anne Fielding now Anne Dale had experienced on her first visit
to Rushwater, the gnats began to dance and bite, and bite and
dance. To tuck one's trousers into one's socks, turn one's collar
up and sit on one's hands was of little avail. By this time Tom
had had enough of the great peace of the country and went up to
his old room which was waiting for him with the same stain in
the faded paper of large roses with sprawling foliage, the same
very low step that one fell up or down as the case might be, the
upper sash of the window still crooked because no one had
mended the old sash cord. And it was all so nostalgic and
homelike that he felt the Red Tape and Sealing Wax Department was merely a bad dream. But though he would be leaving
it, that did not settle his life. Something else he must do and it
would probably depend on Martin. If Martin didn't want him,
and why should he when Tom had left Rushwater of his own
free will, there was Canada, also Australia, also South Africa,
also a lot of other places that one never knew where they were (a
looseness of construction to match Tom's looseness of thinking); and then it came to him as these things sometimes do that
the noise he hadn't heard was Emmy beating the large gong and
that he would be late. Full of shame he ran downstairs. No one
had waited for him but everyone was glad to see him.

To be back in Rushwater talk was like a hot bath after hunting
and Tom wallowed gratefully in it. Polite questions were asked
about what he had been doing, but no one really wanted to hear
about the Red Tape and Geoffrey Harvey, or a tennis party at
the Priory, and Tom began to wonder if such things had really
happened. Also Mr. Bostock, who was dining with them, told
Sylvia that he had been privileged to meet Mrs. Joram, formerly
Mrs. Brandon, who had lately married the ex-Bishop of Mngangaland, now a Canon in residence in the Close, and had found

her very charming. But as no one knew her, even politeness did not get the conversation much further till Mr. Bostock mentioned that Mr. Needham from Lampton was going to preach for him on Harvest Sunday with only one arm, which led to some confusion till Mr. Bostock said that Needham had lost an arm in North Africa, a land, he said, which he had not himself been privileged to see though he believed that there were some very interesting Roman remains, which were not so generally known as the better-known remains in, say, Rome.

"How nice," said Sylvia. "Martin, we must ask Mr. Needham to lunch."

"And his wife," said Tom. "She's the Dean's daughter. I say, I'm sorry. I didn't mean to butt in."

"But you didn't," said Sylvia. "That's the kind of thing one ought to know. The sort of thing you don't know unless you know it," which remark was really very intelligent. "And you can talk to Mr. Needham about his arm, Martin, and tell him about your leg. It was better this winter, Tom, but the summer work hasn't been too good for it and poor old Macpherson can't do much now," and Tom, almost before he knew what he was saying, asked abut the Five Acre.

"The best grazing we've ever had, this year," said Martin. "It's partly owing to Lucy Marling, Adams I mean. Her husband controls a lot of fertilizers and he gave me some very good tips. You remember the red heifer, Tom?"

"The one with a crumpled horn?" Tom asked.

"That's the one," said Martin. "She won a first in the milking class at the Wumpton Pifford show."

"Oh, good!" said Tom. "I say, Martin, do you remember how I called it Westhampton Pollingford and how Macpherson laughed? I must go up and see him."

And so they talked their way through dinner and then Martin took Tom away to the estate office, which was in one of the out-buildings with windows which commanded the stable yard on one side and the kitchen-garden on the other, with a sideways view of the cart road to the farm. It was plainly furnished with two large tables, a filing cupboard, some shelves, a library of technical books, a few guns, and three or four solid chairs with leather seats which had come down in the world. A large map of the estate hung on one wall and on the wall opposite were photographs of all the Rushwater champion bulls down to the present hero, Rushwater Churchill, who was probably going to the Argentine.

"Now," said Martin. "Tell me all about it.."

A most difficult thing to do, for in telling any story at length one is bound to be unfair to someone, and if one is an averagely nice person it is probably to oneself that one will be unfair. If Martin had believed all Tom said, that unfortunate young man would have stood self-convicted of incompetence, want of perseverance, idleness, conceit, besides taking money from the government under false pretences. But Martin had not been an officer and at one time regimental adjutant without learning something of human nature, and gradually he extracted the whole story. To do Tom justice he was at first unwilling to talk about himself, having at the moment so low an opinion of Mr. Thomas Grantly that he felt he was likely to do him more harm than good. But under Martin's kind, wise handling he emptied his worries on the table and felt all the better for it, and then ashamed of his relief.

"H'm," said Martin. Then there was a long silence, and Tom wished he had never come.

"Nothing else?" said Martin.

"Well, I did think I loved someone very much," said Tom, "and they didn't seem to mind and they were awfully decent and told me they really loved someone else—so I felt an awful fool and it made everything worse."

"I suppose I may take it that They is a woman," said Martin.

Tom said oh, of course, and felt like someone who has been hiding under a bed with his boots sticking out.

"She quoted Browning," said Tom, emboldened by Martin's

not unfriendly silence. "She was really quite wonderful and made me feel a perfect fool," which, Martin felt, covered some aspects of love very competently. "But that's all over because there was a much better fellow, with a title and pots of money. I hadn't anything to give her."

"You know," said Martin gently and, as it seemed to Tom, irrelevantly, "I am extraordinarily lucky. I saw Sylvia and that was that. I never had to wait or wonder. But most of us don't strike lucky the first time. And sometimes the one person in the world is so near that you don't see her, like my uncle David Leslie who had known Rose all his life and didn't know he loved her till he was nearer forty than thirty. Look here, Tom, Macpherson is still nominally my agent, but I've got him to do less and less and he has been good about it. I did think you might take over the job in time. I know enough about it now not to need a professional. All the best men round here are county men with a background who love the land and get on well with people. Wickham's one of them, over at Northbridge. I don't see why you shouldn't be another. They say the farmer's boot is the best muck and yours certainly was. One doesn't come of a farming family for nothing. Will you come back to us, Tom? On approval?"

"Any way you like," said Tom.

"Good," said Martin. "We can talk about details tomorrow. Would you like to go up and see Macpherson now? You'll find him older. He won't give up, which makes it a bit hard on my blasted leg," said Martin with a rueful smile, "but Emmy has done wonders. Grandpapa would be prouder of her than of any of us if he were alive. When do you leave your job?"

Tom gave him the date and was going to say he could come the very next day, when Martin said it was always better not to hurry and it wouldn't be a bad idea if Tom put in some book work and what accountancy he could and came to them in the New Year.

Two things were at once clear to Tom. The first that Martin didn't really want him, the second that the New Year would

never come. Then he told himself not to be a fool and looked out
of the window and said thank you.

Martin went back to the house and found his golden Sylvia
darning socks, sewing on buttons, snipping, stitching, cutting,
and contriving; in fact the Sisyphus task of every housewife
every week.

"I think it will do," said Martin, letting himself down into a
chair. "He's a good lad. We haven't all the luck to drop into the
work we love and find the woman we love all in one breath after
a war. I did," and he looked at her with love. "I've sent him up to
call on Macpherson. He'll be pleased to have a visitor."

Sylvia said she had been up that afternoon and he was not in
pain but didn't want to talk much, and she thought Emmy had
gone there not long ago.

"You go every day," said Martin, thinking for the millionth
time how perfect a wife Sylvia was in all her ways.

"Of course," said Sylvia. "Poor old Macpherson," and then
they talked or didn't talk in perfect contentment.

Tom walked up to the old agent's house in the hard unsympathetic light of a nasty Summer Time. The door was never
locked, but for civility's sake Tom flapped the knocker, prepared
to allow a decent interval to elapse. Before the interval had time
to appear the door was opened by Emmy Graham.

"Oh, Hullo," said Emmy. "Come in. Martin did say something about you coming but I forgot. Here's Tom, Mr. Macpherson," and she stood aside for Tom to enter the sitting-room and
shut the door behind him. The old agent was sitting in an
armchair looking over his lawn to the Rushwater Brook and
away to the distant hills, over the land that he had tended
so long.

"Well, Tom," said Mr. Macpherson. "I suppose you and
Martin have settled everything."

"Martin was awfully kind," said Tom. "He said I could come

back. He said he thought I ought to learn something about
bookkeeping and things and come here after Christmas," for
though these last were not Martin's exact words, to say after
Christmas made it all feel nearer than if one said the New Year.

"I will not say," said Mr. Macpherson cautiously, "but that it
will be a help to me to have you here. I shan't last long, and I
should like to see Rushwater in good hands. Will you serve
Rushwater with hand and heart, Tom; in sun and rain; in
sickness and in health, without thought of yourself?"

"I will, sir," said Tom, with a feeling that he was at his own
wedding to someone he didn't know.

"Fifty years I have served this house—her house," said the old
agent. "In the eyes of the Lord it is but a moment, the twinkling
of an eye, but it has been a long road. And a weary road since she
died, though Martin is a good wean, as her grandson should be.
When I am gone, Tom, they will lay me in Rushwater churchyard and I charge you to plant some of the sweetbriar from her
grave upon my grave. You and Emmy shall do it. Little Clarissa
loved her and is so like her sometimes that it pierces me to the
heart. But Clarissa will not be here. Emmy will do it. And
you, lad."

"Yes, sir," said Tom, for he could think of nothing else to say.
Mr. Macpherson said no more and Tom was not sure whether
he was asleep or not, so he tiptoed out of the room and went to
find Emmy who was sitting in the kitchen in an attitude of
dejection that smote Tom to the heart.

"What is it?" he said. "You aren't crying, Emmy? It's all right,
old girl."

"It may be," said Emmy, "but I can't bear it."

"Don't worry," said Tom, very kindly.

"I wouldn't if I didn't live here," said Emmy, which words
smote Tom to the heart, "but he can't do any of the things he
used to do and he can't escape. And he thinks of Gran all
the time."

"I didn't know," said Tom.

"He loved her for fifty years," said Emmy. "When Mother was a baby and Uncle John and Martin's father were little boys and Uncle David wasn't born. And it went on all the time. *Poor* Mr. Macpherson."

"Well, please don't cry, Emmy," said Tom. "I can't bear it. I feel such a beast leaving you all and then making a hash of everything and then Martin being so kind. And Macpherson too. I shall cry myself in a minute."

"Oh, poor Tom," said Emmy, forgetting her own grief. "Please don't cry. I'll do anything for you not to cry. Oh please, *please*, Tom. We'd better go home."

She stood up, looking so desolate, so unlike the ruler of field and cow-shed, that Tom saw nothing for it but to take her in his arms and comfort her; a sensation which he found uncommonly pleasant.

"Listen, Emmy," he said, "we shall disturb Macpherson. Could we go away quietly by the back door?"

"Yes," said Emmy, looking up to him with frank adoration. "And I'll tell his housekeeper we've gone. Oh, Tom, how *kind* you are," and she went across the little garden to a cottage and knocked on the door.

"It's all right," she said, when she came back, "I've told her we are going. She says he often sits up very late and we needn't worry. But, Tom, he must be so unhappy."

"No reason why *you* should be unhappy," said Tom. "I want to tell you something, Emmy."

"About Macpherson?" said Emmy.

"No. About myself," said Tom. "When I was in the Red Tape—not but what I still am now, but I mean when I thought I was going to be there for the rest of my life, I met Lady Cora Palliser."

"She's awfully nice, isn't she?" said Emmy.

"Very nice and very beautiful," said Tom. "And she was very kind to me when I was miserable there."

Emmy said she would like to give Lady Cora a pigling out of

the next litter, which practical form of gratitude made Tom laugh. "I'd give a pigling to anyone who was kind to you," she said, "because you really have had a horrid time and I *am* so glad it's over. Is she *very* beautiful?"

Even while she was speaking Tom suddenly saw himself as he was, or as he might appear to others. Undoubtedly he had loved Lady Cora with deep devotion: and equally undoubtedly Lady Cora had accepted his devotion up to a certain point and then, with great kindness, had explained to him that his love meant nothing to her at all, that broadly speaking there was Another, and that to put it bluntly there was nothing doing. In fact, he thought, with rising indignation, she had Amused herself with him. Of course her being a Duke's daughter made a difference and she had every right to thrill him for a moment ecstatic, Till Cecil Waring's bosom she bent on, Fit for love's naval dalmatic. He did not yet know that Cecil Waring was in hospital and feeling as wretched as people do who are said to be quite comfortable; he did not know that Leslie Winter with real unselfishness had told Lady Cora that she could be the one visitor, knowing well what the result would be. But it did not much matter, for even if she had trifled with his affections, those affections were now very far from her orbit. The very nicest, best, truest, most loving girl in the world, the girl with whom he had worked early and late on every task pleasant and unpleasant, the straightforward, the utterly reliable Emmy Graham had laid her head on his shoulder and he would have liked it to have stayed there for ever only it would be so uncomfortable.

"Yes," he said, answering her question. "She is exactly what a Duke's daughter ought to be like. Tall, dark, handsome, well dressed, lovely legs, lovely hands, dances beautifully and isn't afraid of anything. But I'm not thinking about her at all now."

"Oh. Who are you thinking about then?" said Emmy; but it may be noted that she did not offer to move from Tom's side.

"You, of course," said Tom. "Look here, Emmy. I simply can't *bear* you to be unhappy. Macpherson will be quite well after a night's rest. Or even if he weren't, you couldn't be very unhappy if I comforted you, could you, Emmy?"

"Of course not," said Emmy. "Are we engaged?"

"Bless your heart, my girl, I don't know what we are," said Tom. "But I'm going to marry you whether we're engaged or not. And we had better go before we wake Macpherson. He'll probably want to be best man. Come along, darling. The back way."

Emmy paused on the threshold of the door.

"No one ever called me darling before," she said. "I mean mother and Gran and people did, but—"

"Just as well," said Tom. "If any man had ventured to call you darling I would run him through with a skewer and eat his heart for breakfast," and so they passed quietly into the nasty cold twilight and walked back to Rushwater. In the village they met Mr. Bostock.

"Hullo, Mr. Bostock," said Emmy. "Have you found the vestry key?"

"My fault. My extremely stupid fault!" said Mr. Bostock. "I had put it in a particularly safe place and my housekeeper was dusting and put it somewhere else. I must hasten on my way."

"Ought we to have told him?" said Emmy.

"Certainly not," said Tom. "My father's been a clergyman much longer than he has and my people must know first. Besides father's a Rural Dean now."

"Then shall we tell Sylvia and Martin?" said Emmy, when they were near the house. "It's so private. And so precious," she added softly; and we may say this was as far as we know the first time Miss Emmy Graham had been moved to such romantic words; words so alien to all she had been.

But of course when they came into the sitting-room, with the proud yet deprecating expression of a cat who has brought her kitten from its comfortable bed in the kitchen to show it to the quality, Martin, who was alone, took off his spectacles and put them in their case, the better to see what had happened.

"I couldn't help it," said Emmy.

We need not say what heartfelt pleasure her cousin Martin felt and expressed. There was a discussion about ringing Lady Graham up, but it was late now, and they decided to leave it till next morning. Tom's parents, it was generally considered, were of tougher metal, Emmy even going so far as to say that she thought clergymen never went to bed properly. Like doctors she said, with a bell by their bed. Tom assured her that his father slept very well and was furious if anyone woke him, but it was worth risking. But it was not Mr. Grantly who answered the telephone.

"Hullo," said Tom. "It's Tom Grantly speaking. Is Father in?"

A loud crackling and booming burst out of the telephone.

"It's Doris or Edna," said Tom. "I suppose my people are out. There's a telephone extension in the kitchen and they have the wireless on all the time. Is it Edna? Look here, Edna, where are Father and Mother? Oh, dining with Mrs. Adams. Is Grace there too? Oh, bother. All right, Edna. I say, Edna I'm engaged. I'll tell you and Doris all about it tomorrow when I come home. Good-bye. It's a nuisance," he said as he hung the receiver up. "They're at the Adamses."

"If I were in your place," said Martin, "which I'm not, I should ring up the Adamses at once. That girl of yours is bound to try to get in first with the news."

The advice seemed good. For the next quarter of an hour the air was thick with rings and counter-rings and engaged, till at last the calm voice of Miss Palmyra Phipps at the exchange was heard.

"Good evening," it said. "Exchange speaking. Oh, is that you, Mr. Tom? Those girls of yours at the Vicarage rang up the Old Bank House, because I was listening, and everyone seemed to be quite delighted and I'm sure I congratulate you and wish you and the young lady all the best. It's Miss Emmy Graham isn't it? Were you wanting to get on to Holdings, Mr. Tom, because I know for a fact that her Ladyship has gone to bed, because Cook rang me up and said Miss Clarissa had got engaged to Mr. Charles Belton and her Ladyship had gone to bed and didn't want any calls unless it was Sir Robert from London. But I'll put you through if you like, Mr. Tom," which information Tom rapidly relayed to the company.

"That's all right. We'll tell Mother tomorrow," said Emmy placidly. "I'll tell Palmyra. Hullo, Palmyra," she said. "It's Emmy Graham. I say, do you know what time Clarissa got engaged? Before supper? Oh, what a shame. I didn't get engaged till after supper. Oh, and please don't let anyone else tell Mother. I'll ring her up first thing tomorrow if you'll tell Norma Pollett. Thanks awfully."

"And who is Norma Pollett?" said Martin.

"Oh, she's the other girl at the exchange," said Emmy. "Her people live down the Worsted line. I just told Palmyra so that she could tell Norma when she comes on duty."

"And so the old woman got home that night," said Martin. "Bed now. How was Macpherson?"

"He was talking about where he wanted to be buried," said Tom.

"How like him," said Martin. "And enjoying it, I presume."

"I think so," said Tom. "He wants some of the sweetbriar from Lady Emily's grave planting on his grave. It was rather sad, and Emmy was so unhappy that I had to comfort her and so we got engaged."

"It's late now. We'll settle everything tomorrow," said Martin, and drove the young couple upstairs.

"I don't suppose," he said to his wife Sylvia in their bedroom, "that you will be surprised to hear that Emmy is engaged to Tom. It's not a bad thing. He's a very good boy and he will settle down. His father is well off as people go now and I don't think the lawyers will have much trouble. Emmy will have a bit too. Gran's sister Agnes left her money to my aunt Agnes's girls, at twenty-five or on their marriage. What a good girl Emmy is. And what a good cousin you have been to her, darling."

"Well, she is your cousin," said Sylvia, as if that explained everything. As indeed to her it did.

Early next morning the elderly woman who looked after Mr. Macpherson came up to Rushwater and sent in word that she would like to see Mr. Martin, who came hurriedly downstairs and took her into the great drawing-room, all unused and dust-sheeted, where no one would interrupt them. When she went in at seven o'clock to make Mr. Macpherson's breakfast she had found him asleep, as she thought, in his chair by the sitting-room window. She had run up Dr. Ford, waited till he came, and then walked down to Rushwater to break the news.

"I can manage nicely, sir," she said, being a village woman to whom life and death were familiar, "and I'll get Mrs. Brown over from Rushwater Parva to help. We'll see to it all nicely, sir. The dear gentleman had the Bible on his knees, sir, so I took the liberty of bringing it along. I thought you might like it. There's a photo in it where he was reading last night."

Martin thanked her and went upstairs to tell Sylvia. Both of them were grieved, but they could not be surprised, for the end had been but too apparent of late. He laid Mr. Macpherson's Bible on a table and opened it where the photograph lay; an old *carte de visite* photograph (and when have any been better?) of Lady Emily in the year of her marriage with a slim waist and a little bustle and a hat crowned with ostrich feathers.

"They knew how to photograph then," said Martin. "Look at her," and indeed her young form and face with its fine proud features and falcon eyes looked at him as if she were alive, but in silence.

"The fifty-first psalm," said Martin. "Not a bad choice, though I can hardly imagine Macpherson with a broken spirit. But we don't know. God bless him."

"I think he would like the book and the photograph with

him," said Sylvia and Martin thought, as he had thought every day since his marriage, how perfect his quiet golden Sylvia was in every way.

There was a gentle sadness over the house, but not great unhappiness, for Mr. Macpherson had longed for his latter end and peace that passes mortal understanding.

"If he finds Gran he will be happy for ever," said Emmy, who had cried a little, but soon returned to her quiet happiness. "*How* Gran will fuss when he comes," at which they could not help laughing, so true it was. Martin rang up Mr. Bostock and asked for the bell to be tolled. Eighty-odd years, longer than the allotted span of life and all spent in service.

By the kind offices of Miss Norma Pollett Emmy was able to speak to her mother and tell her the news of love and of death. Lady Graham was as overjoyed in her daughter's happiness as a mother can be and then Clarissa and Emmy had an incoherent and agreeable conversation about how heavenly everything was. It was arranged that Lady Graham and Clarissa should come over to Rushwater to mourn and to rejoice and then Martin took the telephone for the business of Mr. Macpherson's burial.

The church was fuller than usual this morning. Mr. Macpherson had been so long at Rushwater that he was looked upon by the cottagers and the workers as one of themselves. Many had tales of his kindness, while others with the peculiar pride that human nature takes in its shortcomings, told their admiring friends how Mr. Macpherson had laid it on with the rough side of his tongue like anything when that bull got loose, or how Mr. Macpherson had told Arthur Brown off properly when he let the pig drown itself in the pond. When Martin and Sylvia came out a good many villagers stopped to say an embarrassed word of sympathy.

As they nearly always did after church the Squire and his wife went to see the grave where Mr. Leslie and Lady Emily Leslie were buried, the sweetbriar fragrant in the air. Tom and Emmy followed them; so happy in their new happiness that they could not grieve very much. Martin picked a piece of sweetbriar to lay in Mr. Macpherson's Bible, and they lingered till the churchyard was clear.

As they were walking back to the house Dr. Ford overtook them in his shameful little car and came up to the house, ostensibly to speak to Mr. Macpherson.

"A quick painless death, Mrs. Leslie," he said to Sylvia, "as far as we can know about something we have never experienced. His heart stopped beating and I don't suppose he knew it. I must get back to the Barchester General. I've got a distinguished patient there, Commander Sir Cecil Waring R.N."

Martin asked what had happened.

"Those naval surgeons!" said Dr. Ford, with the fine contempt of the old country G.P. for such of his brethren as are attached to His Majesty's Forces. "He had a piece of shrapnel roaming about inside him and no one bothered about it. Well, to make a long story short, he was dragging the Dipping Pond at the Priory yesterday afternoon, suddenly collapsed, and was rushed off to the Barchester General. Luckily Hastings was there, and I'd sooner trust Hastings than any of your London men," said Dr. Ford with fine local pride, "and I was there, for what that's worth, and he had Waring on the table and cut him open and got the bit of metal out and sewed him up again and he'll be as fit as a fiddle by Christmas."

No one knew Cecil Waring very well, but the country houses must stick together and Rushwater, like Beliers Priory, was a comparative parvenu, though Rushwater had a far more beautiful setting.

"But that's not all," said Dr. Ford. "Lady Cora Palliser was at the Priory too, and if she hadn't driven Sir Cecil into Barchester at her own speed, Hastings would have sharpened his knives for nothing. I know one or two of the policemen on the road and they told me when they saw her Ladyship streaking along at a good sixty they reckoned it wasn't their job. That girl has the best nerves and the best hands I know."

"Let me see. Waring's sister married the Headmaster of the

Priory School, didn't she?" said Martin. "I ran across her in the war when she was in some kind of hush-hush work."

"She's a very fine woman is Mrs. Philip Winter," said Dr. Ford, who though discreet when discretion was necessary, was known as one of the biggest gossips in the county. "Hastings said Sir Cecil could have one visitor today and one only. Mrs. Winter knew that her brother was fond of Lady Cora and she had a pretty fair guess that Lady Cora felt the same only more so. So she gave her turn to her Ladyship. As a matter of fact," said Dr. Ford, who could no longer restrain himself, "they got engaged at eleven-thirty this morning. Nurse Poulter told Matron and Matron told me, and when I was in Matron's room Lady Cora was ringing up her brother, Silverbridge you know, to tell him."

"Then that's three," said Emmy determinedly. "Sir Cecil and Lady Cora. Clarissa and Charles Belton. And I got engaged to Tom last night, after we had been to see Mr. Macpherson."

Dr. Ford wished Emmy joy very sincerely, and said he was sure nothing would have given Mr. Macpherson more pleasure. "I must tell Mrs. Morland about all this," he said. "Three engagements in twenty-four hours. She could do something good in one of her books with that," for Dr. Ford was one of the large number of people who believe that anything which strikes them as interesting will be of immense value to an author whose subjects are entirely different. "Well, I must be off. If I can do anything else for you, Mrs. Leslie, let me know," and with hearty handshakes to Tom and Emmy he went away in his well-known, rattling old car.

Emmy, complaining that this Sunday felt more Sundayish than ever, got back into her farm clothes directly after lunch and went round the cow-sheds with Tom, while Martin occupied himself with the necessary notices for local papers and the formal announcement for *The Times*. About half past three Lady Graham arrived with Clarissa and there was a happy orgy of hugs and kisses and congratulations. By an extraordinary

chance Charles Belton also found it convenient to be at Rushwater that afternoon and all the young people went up to the
Temple, that peculiar monument on the hill behind the house,
a combination of Italian villa and crocketed obelisk, full of dust
and stuffiness.

Lady Graham and Martin drove up to the agent's cottage
where his housekeeper was giving ceremonial tea to one or two
friends. Agnes, whose memory for faces was far better than her
friends suspected, at once recognized the housekeeper and said
all the right things and gave very true thanks to her.

"Would your Ladyship like to see him?" said the housekeeper.

So with Martin she went into the room where Mr. Macpherson's mortal body was lying, very quiet and removed from
worldly things, on a low bed covered with a white Paisley shawl,
a Scotch heritage from his mother and rare even in the days
when these shawls were made. Martin lifted the shawl to show
her the Bible under his crossed hands.

"There was a photograph of Gran in it," said Martin. "The
one that was taken just after she was married. He must have had
it all these years. I never saw it."

"Darling Mamma," said Agnes, smiling with tearful eyes.
"How she teased him and bullied him. And how they understood each other. I have brought him a last gift from her," and
she took from her bag a handkerchief of finest Indian lawn,
embroidered in Paris with Lady Emily's initials, cobweb frail, to
be drawn easily through a wedding ring, and laid it over his face.

"You know, Aunt Agnes," said Martin as they walked down
the hill to Rushwater, "that this house is to be Emmy's. It was
Macpherson's thought. He spoke to me about it on the day of
Gran's funeral. I have arranged for her to have it for her life. It
has been the agent's house for years, and if she is going to marry
Tom they might as well marry soon. He has resigned from the
Red Tape and Sealing Wax Department and I advised him to
work hard at estate accounts this autumn and I hope he will

come to us for good at the New Year. He is a born farmer. The war made him restless. I know it. I should probably have been selling cars on commission if I hadn't had dear Rushwater and my blessed Sylvia to keep me steady. What do you think about it?"

"How generous you are, dear Martin," said his Aunt Agnes. "Like dear Papa. He was so generous. And so just too. So are you. Bless you, my dear. You are so like your own father. How he would have loved you. The Flowers of the Forest, as darling Mamma used to say."

"I wish I remembered him well," said Martin, "but I really only remember now what people told me about him."

"And there is one other thing that makes me very happy," said Lady Graham. They were looking across the Rushwater valley now to the hills in the west, a peaceful land of river, pasture, corn, and grassy sheep-runs on the hills. The voices of the two young couples coming down from the Temple echoed through the rides among the beeches. Youth was once more at Rushwater, and Martin's and Emmy's babies would be free of village, field, and downs as their elders had been.

"What is the other thing, Aunt Agnes?" said Martin.

"Darling Mamma's older sister Agnes was engaged to a man who was killed in India," said Lady Graham. "She was older than Mamma and she never married. She left some money to my girls. I always worried a little about Emmy, because she was the eldest girl and it made me a little superstitious. But now she will be married quite soon. Before Clarissa, who will love to be a bridesmaid. It is all so happy. How darling Mamma would have loved it all."

"And how darling Gran would have meddled," said Martin.

And then they met the young people at the bottom of the hill and went back to Rushwater.

CHAPTER 14

Up till the present time the county had not felt any very great interest in Cecil Waring. His uncle and aunt though devoted to their public duties had never taken much part in the social life of the county. This was, we think, because Lady Waring's life had in part finished when her only son was killed, so long ago, and though she had done her duty and more than her duty in that station of life to which it had pleased God to call her, much of the real love and tenderness in her nature had been buried below her grief, and we believe that only her feeling of responsibility for her husband had supported her. When he died there was no further need for her to live. What affection she had to spare was given to her niece Leslie Waring, now Mrs. Philip Winter, and might under other conditions have been equally shared with her nephew Cecil Waring. It was not that she resented his being the heir in place of her son, for she was a true soldier's wife and mother, trained to the chances of war, and if her son was killed then the next man of the family must take up the duties that would have been his. But a sailor begins his remote appointed task very young, and Cecil had never known the villages, the fields, the woods of Lambton Priory as his cousin George the soldier had known them, and his visits to his uncle and aunt at long and uncertain intervals had not produced any very great affection. There was strong family feeling, strong sense of duty on both sides, but the warmth was lacking. And

then when Cecil inherited the title and the property there was
no hostess for the Priory and the county felt it was hardly
wanted. His sister Leslie would have done all she could but her
life as working wife of the Headmaster of a thriving preparatory
school was a very busy one, leaving her little time for social
intercourse other than what was necessary for the needs of the
school.

If Dr. Ford had not made the whole of West Barsetshire
aware of the engagement it would doubtless have permeated
through other channels, but for a time, owing to the suddenness
of the whole thing and Cecil Waring's temporary invalidism, a
social halt was called, as it were. Lady Cora's car was seen daily
outside the Barchester General and then when Cecil could be
moved to the Priory her Ladyship visited him almost every day,
to the intense joy of Sister Heath, one of the two pals that Sister
Chiffinch shared the flat with, who was luckily disengaged at
the time.

"Well, Lady Cora," said Sister Heath, when about ten days
after the operation her Ladyship appeared at the Priory as usual,
"we have a nice surprise today. We have shaved ourselves. We
are just a wee bit tired, for you know it *is* an exertion though as
I tell Sir Cecil nothing to what we ladies go through with our
hair and really when I think of the time it takes to put my perm
to bed—that is just my joke of course but you know one must
get the perm nicely in place before you put the net over it at
shut-eye time—shaving is simply a flea-bite. I did suggest that
that nice Sergeant Hopkins might do it, but Sir Cecil was just
the wee-est bit peeved at the idea. So today I said, Well Sir
Cecil, if Lady Cora does come to see you today and far stranger
things have come to pass, wouldn't it be a nice surprise for her to
find you with a nice smooth face. Not that I *meant* anything of
course," said Sister Heath with an archness tempered by her
proper feeling for a Duke's daughter, "but I always think gentlemen must feel so much comfier without those bristles on their
faces, not that Sir Cecil shaves black the way some gentlemen

do, but still shaving does make a difference. So I thought I'd tell you."

Lady Cora, whose war experience had given her valuable lessons in speaking foreign languages, said if she had seen Sir Cecil suddenly, without his whiskers, she might have felt quite upset and how kind it was of Sister Heath to warn her. She then went to see her affianced who had a temporary bedroom downstairs looking over the garden.

"*Darling*," said Lady Cora, in a voice that had probably not been heard since Arnhem.

"You too," said Cecil, taking her hand and laying it against his cheek. "Angel! I hope you didn't drive too fast."

"Only up to the limit," said Lady Cora. "Did it tire you frightfully to shave?"

Cecil lay back, shut his eyes and said Yes.

"Impostor!" said Lady Cora. "Look here, darling—"

"I do love the way you say that," said Cecil, still with his eyes shut.

"It's just my voice," said Lady Cora off-handedly. "I can do anything with my voice. You should have heard me sing *Keep the Homes Fires Burning* at the Conservative Do at Gatherum last year. Everyone was in tears. Listen, darling."

Cecil said he could listen quite well with his eyes shut.

"No you can't," said Lady Cora. "It's like not being able to smoke when you are blind. Now listen. Dr. Ford and Matron at the Barchester General and everyone else are taking my name in vain all over the place. Of course the proper thing would be for you to call on my people and explain that your intentions are honourable, but as you can't, they are coming to see you."

"Oh Lord!" said Cecil, opening his eyes and sitting up again.

"Not with any bad intentions," said Lady Cora. "I think it is really because they want to see the Priory School. And of course they want to see you too. You see you can't marry without lawyers, nor can I, so the sooner we get them onto the job the better. I adore your Mr. Winthrop and I am sure he will make a

heavenly settlement for me. Only we shall have to let him and
father's lawyers pretend we can't be married without them. So
they are coming over this afternoon."

At this moment Sister Heath came in with Cecil's lunch.

"Look here, Sister," said Cecil. "My fiancée says her people
are coming to see me this afternoon. I'm not strong enough,
am I?"

"Now, Sir Cecil, we must just think of Nelson," said Sister
Heath. "If the stitches were still in I might have a word to say,"
said Sister, pursing up her mouth very wisely into what the
French coarsely but truly call a *cul-de-poule*, "but now our
stitches are out and we are going on nicely, I think a little
company would do us good. And when you've eaten that nice
lunch, Sir Cecil, I'll make everything nice and tidy," and the
good creature rustled away.

"Need I?" said Cecil. "I mean I frightfully want to meet your
people, but I'd rather just have you," to which Lady Cora replied
that Sister Heath had been an angel right through and the least
they could do for her was to let her entertain a real Duke and
Duchess, as she could then talk about it for the rest of her life. In
fact, she said, it was their absolute duty to have her parents over.

"Yes, you are right," said Cecil. "You always are."

"Not always," said Lady Cora. "But it's a bit like the Royal
Navy. There are things we must do, and that's that. What would
Nelson have said? Barsetshire expects that Cecil and Cora this
day will do their duty," and to Cecil's surprise and rather to his
alarm her lovely dark eyes suddenly brimmed with tears.

"What is it, my *darling*?" he said. "Here, take my handkerchief."

"It's nothing," said Lady Cora, taking the handkerchief. "It's
only Nelson. Whenever I think of him I cry. Because he is
England, I suppose."

"Good girl," said her affianced.

"And I always cry if His Majesty speaks on the wireless," said
Lady Cora, who had recovered from Nelson and now showed

symptoms of crying again. "It's because He is so GOOD, I think. When you remember the sort of people He has to meet and be polite to, it is more than I can *bear*. Sorry." But to Cecil her behaviour seemed in the highest degree reasonable and patriotic.

"Listen, my lamb," said Lady Cora. "Did my ears deceive me, or did I hear you speak of me to Sister as your fiancée."

"I know," said Cecil, with an air of proud guilt. "Darling, I just could not help it. It was really false pride, because I have learnt etiquette beautifully while I was in bed. If you can suggest an alternative I'll use it. Intended is rather nice. One really couldn't say Betrothed."

"I know. It's too difficult," said Lady Cora. "The best plan is to say Wife as soon as possible."

"And then," said Cecil, "you go and hold everything up with lawyers. There's no pleasing you."

"Just go on being alive," said Lady Cora.

We do not know whether Sister Heath had communicated with Dr. Ford, but shortly before the Duke and Duchess were expected he turned up in his rattling little car at the Priory to see his patient, whom he found shaved and dressed in the sitting-room with Lady Cora at his side.

"I always tell my patients to kill themselves in their own way," said Dr. Ford when he had found Cecil's pulse calm and had looked at Sister Heath's temperature chart. "They'd do it just the same even if I didn't give them permission. I shan't come and see you again. Don't be more of a fool than you can help. None of this boat business at Harefield. I heard all about it from Mrs. Winter. Punting canvas boats and cutting rushes with two ounces of scrap metal in you. It's the Luck of the Navy that you haven't a perforated inside. And you're not a young man, Waring."

"All right, Ford, I've been a fool," said Cecil. "But Cora will take me in hand now. Her people are coming over to see me this afternoon."

"They won't hurt you," said Dr. Ford. "Not more than half an hour, Lady Cora. And what's the news of Lady Silverbridge?"

"She looks rather like the Plum Pudding Flea," said Lady Cora. "Otherwise remarkably well. I hope I'll manage it as well as she does."

"Really, Cora!" said her future husband, but Dr. Ford laughed and said she needn't worry. Then he went away and Sister made such a to-do about tidying Cecil's room that his affianced took refuge in the garden. It was not in particularly good condition, but one was used to that and Lady Cora almost mechanically began to weed the rosebeds, just as she was used to weed after supper at Gatherum. Gradually she was conscious through the back of her head of a Presence hovering near her. She looked round and saw a tall dark man in outrageously picturesque coat, breeches, and leggings, leaning on the gate with a gun in his hand. Then she remembered that Cecil had told her he had a half-gypsy keeper called Jasper Margett. This was undoubtedly he, so she looked up and said Good-afternoon.

"Good-afternoon, Duke's daughter," said the man.

Enchanted by this irruption of Cold Comfort Farm and the Frog Prince, Lady Cora with great presence of mind replied: "Good-afternoon again, Jasper. How is your grandmother?"

Now it was common knowledge in those parts that Jasper Margett's grandmother was a white witch who usually went abroad at night in the shape of a black hare till her undutiful grandson shot her, some years ago, as she was cleaning her whiskers on Copshot Bank. Lady Cora had not conversed with Nannie Allen and Selina Hopkins for nothing and her reply caused Jasper, probably for the first time in his life, to feel at a loss and be unable to answer.

"Sir Cecil is getting on very well and I am going to marry him," Lady Cora continued, "and my father and mother the Duke and Duchess of Omnium are coming to see him this afternoon and if you want to be really obliging do bring up a few young rabbits. My father's old keeper won't let him shoot them. He wires them all himself and sells them in the Barchester Black Market," which interesting statement did great credit to her Ladyship's powers of invention.

"Wires them, does he?" said Jasper. "I'll lay a silver fourpence that old keeper he doesn't know how to wire. Lets the young fools from Barchester come out with their ferrets more likely. Old Jasper doesn't need no ferrets. He calls the rabbits and they come to his hands."

"Just as you like," said Lady Cora, entirely unmoved. "Put what you can spare in the Duke's car. I will let you know when we need some more," and standing up she faced Jasper, who gave her one of his quick, sidelong glances. He turned his head, muttering something about the Dark Eye, and slouched away, melting into the landscape. Lady Cora went indoors where she found Cecil ready for his visitors and told him about her interview with Jasper, thus greatly increasing his admiration for her. Then Sister Heath, crackling with starch in a way that almost drowned conversation, brought Cora's father and mother into the room and rather ostentatiously retired to the far end of the room with her crochet to allow host and visitors to make the best of each other.

"It is very good of you to come, Duchess," said Cecil. "I must ask you to forgive me if I don't get up, but Dr. Ford is all against it."

"Quite right. Quite right," said the Duke. "I can't say that I believe much in doctors myself, but if you have one you might as well do what he says. A nasty operation you've had, so Cora tells me. A bit of shell? Dear, dear. I remember when I was a boy one of my father's keepers got a handful of shot in the fleshy part of his calf and my brothers and I used to run away from our governess to look at him. But that was a long time ago and I daresay things are different now. Penicillin and all that. Wonderful things they invent, but I must say no one seems to be much the better for them. What was that film we saw, my dear," he continued, turning to the Duchess, "where the villain supplies hospitals with bad penicillin on the Black Market so that everyone goes mad and they run up and down the drains somewhere abroad?"

Sister Heath, who alone had kept her head, largely owing to her silent determination to see everything when a real Duke and Duchess were concerned, said it must be *The Third Man* that the Duke meant and there was something about the zither that made her absolutely shiver all up and down her spine, it seemed so old-world and the same tune all the time only sometimes it sounded different. The Duchess said she did so agree and it was just like Bayreuth where you *had* to know the tunes, only you never quite knew which was which, and somehow this led to the discovery that Sister Heath had once nursed the Honourable Mrs. George Rivers who, or rather whose husband, was connected with the Pomfrets, and the two ladies had a most delightful time running down in the kindest way that really insufferable female novelist.

"It wasn't so much her books, your Grace," said Sister Heath, "for as I always said to the probationers no one can *force* you to read a book you don't want to read, as a *something*," with which the Duchess fervently agreed.

"Well, you and Cora have arranged it all, so she tells me," said the Duke to Cecil. "She is a good girl and has a head on her shoulders. We always hoped she would marry, but there was someone in the war, I think. She doesn't talk about it. You know we lost our younger son. On D-Day it was. Well, well: you were at sea and know what it's like. I was in France from 1915 to 1917. Now, about settlements."

"One moment, if I may interrupt," said Cecil. "I really ought to ask if you and the Duchess have any objection to our marrying."

"I don't think so," said the Duke after a pause during which he appeared to be searching industriously for any possible impediment. "No, I'm sure we haven't. She always does exactly what she likes. She'll have a little bit of money—not much now, but something. I'll tell you what I have been thinking, Waring. You get your lawyers onto it and I'll get mine and let them fight it out, then everything will be quite pleasant."

As Cecil had been much of the same way of thinking himself this point appeared to be settled and both gentlemen felt they had been very businesslike.

"Cora tells me you were getting up some sort of regatta at Harefield," said the Duke. "You must be careful you know, my boy. Can't run risks now. I used to yacht a bit myself, but we had to give that up before the last war. Too expensive, you know. You didn't ever hear of the *Planty Pal* did you?" said his Grace with an air half proud, half apologetic.

Of course Cecil had heard of this famous yacht and had watched her at Cowes before the war with hopeless and unenvious admiration.

"What happened to her?" he asked.

"Sunk, my boy," said the Duke. "She did some good work first. You wouldn't have known her in her war rig. I have her captain over to Gatherum once a year. You must come and meet him," and then Cecil felt that he had been entirely accepted and also felt very tired, which Sister Heath observing said we still had to be careful and perhaps the Duke and Duchess would like to go over to the School now for tea and then see Sir Cecil again before they left.

"Of course we mustn't tire your invalid," said the Duchess, getting up. "Tea would be delightful," and Lady Cora took her parents away, pausing at the door to look back. Cecil had shut his eyes and was so quiet that her heart suddenly hit her with great violence.

"Are you all right, darling?" she said.

"Come here and I'll tell you," said Cecil.

"Have they killed you?" said Lady Cora, kneeling by his side.

"Not yet and not likely to," said Cecil, looking at her with quiet affection. "It would take wild horses to kill me so long as you want me," upon which the competent, practical, worldly, self-reliant Lady Cora Palliser laid her dark head on his shoulder while Cecil for the thousandth time wondered if such happiness was a dream.

"Now," said Lady Cora, gently extricating herself and rising with one swift graceful movement, "I must take Father and Mother to the School. And then I shall show them the Priory and I shall say Good-bye and go home with them. Don't worry. Don't think about business. Mr. Winthrop will deal with that and if he doesn't hurry I shall stick pins into him."

With real kindness Sister Heath had arranged to give Cecil his tea herself, foregoing the delights of the ducal tea-party at the School, and it was perhaps as well for she was able to get on with the sweetly pretty blue bedjacket she was crocheting for her married sister's youngest girl who was expecting her second, while Cecil could lie back in his chair and think of Lady Cora.

Meanwhile Lady Cora led her father and mother by the garden way to the School House where Philip and Leslie were waiting for them. The only other guest was the assistant master Eric Swan who had stayed on to help Philip with some work.

"I do wish," said Leslie, "that we could have shown you the School when the boys are here. It all feels so empty now."

"I know," said the Duke sympathetically. "When you are used to having people about it is quite different when they aren't there. I remember once when I had mumps at my prep school and had to stay on in the Sanatorium for a week after the others had gone home, and how dreadfully lonely it was. If it hadn't been for the boot and knife boy I would have cried. But he brought me all the lowest comic papers and ginger beer in those proper bottles. One doesn't see them now."

"I know the ones you mean," said Eric Swan. "There was a ball and you needed a special wooden thing to press it down with—"

"And if you forgot the wooden thing nothing else would work," said the Duke. "And when you drank out of the bottle—"

"I know," said Swan. "Your tongue got caught by centrifugal force or suction or something—"

"—and when I was little I screamed myself nearly black in the face," said the Duke, "because I thought I'd have to spend the rest of my life with it hanging onto me," and he looked at Swan approvingly and asked him where he was at school. Swan said Southbridge.

"You might do worse," said the Duke. "My boys were at Eton of course and I shall put my grandchildren down for it. But if we can't afford it—"

"We won't talk about that," said the Duchess. "Do tell me, Mrs. Winter, how do you manage about servants? We have a few people from the village and they are really very good to us."

Leslie said she had one or two old friends from the village and her aunt's former maid with her husband who was very useful, which appeared to impress the Duchess a good deal, so Leslie suggested that when they had seen the School they should return to the Priory by the kitchen, a suggestion which the Duchess deeply approved. An excursion was then made to the nurseries where Master Noel Merton and Miss Harriet Merton were, the elder drawing a picture with a pencil that was red at one end and blue at the other, the younger banging a doll's head very hard on a tin tray, and as they were both perfectly happy and very well there was really nothing to stay for. The Duke said he did not wish to appear ungrateful but perhaps they ought to be getting back to Sir Cecil.

"By the way, Winter," he said, drawing his host aside, "my wife and I have been thinking of ways to help my son— Silverbridge you know—and his wife. Of course she was a bit of an heiress, but all the same life is hard on these young people. I had an idea of putting their eldest boy down for a good prep school and doing something about investing a lump sum in his name to start his education. I suppose you haven't any vacancies?"

Philip, surprised but not displeased, asked how old the little boy was.

"I don't really know," said the Duke, looking rather shame-faced.

"It must be very easy to forget when you have several grand-children," said Philip, vaguely.

"As a matter of fact I haven't got any—not yet," said the Duke. "But Silverbridge's wife is expecting a baby. My dear," he called to his wife, "when is it that Isabel expects the baby? No, I don't mean the exact date. Well, Mr. Winter, this autumn some time."

"You don't know if it is to be a girl or a boy?" said Philip, unable to resist his own amusement, while his wife made what the young Grantlys called "a No-face" at him.

"Well, bless my soul, I suppose I don't," said the Duke. "But couldn't we make some sort of arrangement that if it's a boy we could do something? I would let you know as soon as I know myself, if that would be any help. Isabel is the most delightful daughter-in-law and I am sure she will do what is best. Do I send a cheque on account or anything? Things do change so."

Though Philip wanted to laugh he said gravely that if the Duke would be kind enough to let him know, perhaps before Christmas, if it was a boy, he would be delighted to do what he could and they could discuss money later, with which the Duke appeared to be perfectly satisfied.

"You must not mind my ways," he said, putting his hand kindly on Philip's arm. "I'm not very quick at all these changes and I find it best to ask whenever I don't know."

Philip, feeling rather ashamed of himself before his guest's simplicity, thanked the Duke and they followed Leslie down the kitchen passage. As usual, the nearer they got to the kitchen the more cheerful did everyone feel and when Leslie pushed open the kitchen door (which was hardly ever quite shut) and stood aside for her guests to come in, they were enraptured by the large scrubbed kitchen table, the scrubbed dressers, the good fire, the shining saucepans and the lavish and unnecessary use of electric light at about half-past five on a summer afternoon. An elderly woman with grey hair drawn tightly back from her face and steel-rimmed spectacles was sitting near the fire in a Windsor chair with a cat on her lap and at the table a very pretty middle-aged woman with wildly curling hair was doing some mending.

"Good-afternoon, Nannie. I have brought the Duke and Duchess to see the kitchen," said Leslie. "This is our old nurse, Duchess, Mrs. Allen, and her daughter Mrs. Hopkins who cooks for the whole school."

The Duchess of course did and said exactly the right things. Selina blushed and bridled and her lovely eyes became moist at the view of the higher aristocracy. Nannie Allen sketched the motion of getting up (though obviously without the faintest intention of doing so) and said: "You'll excuse my getting up, your Grace. It's my leg. I was temporary once at Gatherum when Lord Gerald's nurse was on holiday. There was a Frawlein and she *was* a tartar, your Grace."

"Good Lord!" said the Duke, sitting down on a kitchen chair. "That must have been Fräulein Hagestolz. She used to bang Jeff's fingers with a ruler when he played his scales wrong and we had to get rid of her. And do you remember Hettie, the nursery maid?"

"A nice-looking girl, your Grace," said Nannie Allen, "and had the footmen after her all the time."

"Once too often," said the Duke, warming to these *échos du temps passé*. "The boys never knew why she was sent away. Pity it wasn't now. Girls can get away with anything," which last words were overheard by Marigold, who of course chose that moment to come in, all prepared for the further conquest of Mr. Geoff Coxon her more or less affianced, and caused her to wriggle and to take hastily from her dirty pink plastic bag a dirty pink comb with several teeth missing and run it through her shining yellow locks, though the shine was less from careful brushing than from a preparation called Slinkykreem, much patronized by the leaders of fashion in her circle.

"Now then, Marigold, put that stuff away and behave properly. It's the Duchess of Omnium. Her Grace has come over to see Sir Cecil," said Nannie Allen sharply.

Marigold said "Ow" and looked round wildly for help. The door was half open, but Sergeant Hopkins was standing by it and escape was impossible.

"And what is your name?" said the Duchess.

Marigold looked madly about her, opened her mouth, shut it again and turned pink in a way that Poudre Blushema (also made by the proprietors of Slinkykreem) could not have imitated.

"Please, miss, it's Marigold," she said in a hoarse whisper.

Nannie Allen drew in her breath with a hissing sound which boded no good to Marigold. The Duchess, who appeared to find everything quite normal, said that Lady Gwendoline Elphin's second girl was Marigold but she was always called Boodle. Nannie Allen said sharply under her breath to Marigold to go and get herself tidy at once and the unfortunate Marigold dropped her pink plastic bag which disgorged its horrible contents on the kitchen floor. She picked most of them up and fled away along the corridor. Meanwhile the Duke had been exchanging experiences of the 1914 war with Sergeant Hopkins who had never got further than a training camp in the West Riding, but as the Sergeant did not speak at all no harm was done, and then the Duchess shook hands with Nannie Allen and Selina, invited them to come and have tea with the bailiff's wife at Gatherum, and so departed.

"Excuse me, my Lady," said Nannie Allen as Lady Cora was going, "but how is Sir Cecil? Don't you let him put the wedding off, my Lady. When is it to be? It doesn't do to let them think too much about it, my Lady."

"How right you are, Nannie," said Lady Cora, who had managed to win Nannie Allen's heart and become an adopted ex-charge almost at once. "But I'll tell you before I tell anyone except my own people and I'll see that you get over."

"Thank you, I'm sure, my Lady," said Nannie. "Young Coxon at the garage has a nice car. That Marigold is going with him and he's a nice steady boy. Which is more than she is," said Nannie with dispassionate disapproval.

Lady Cora said she would see that Young Coxon brought Nannie and her daughter over and so in a cloud of popularity went away with her parents.

Cecil was very happy to see her but rather tired, so she told Sister Heath she would take her parents home at once.

"You aren't worried, are you?" she said, her dark eyes rather fearful, but Sister Heath said there was nothing to worry about and Sir Cecil would be all the better for the visit and so they went away, Lady Cora driving her parents and the old stableman who had brought them over following with the Duke's little car. At the bottom of the drive Jasper was waiting by the gate. Lady Cora pulled up and looked out of the window.

"I put them old rabbits in the boot," said Jasper. "Nice and young they are, my Lady. Plenty of onions and they'd be fit for His Majesty. Three brace there are. There's some as would be glad to buy them at a good price."

"I'm paying you market price," said Lady Cora. "And that's pure profit for you. And when I am mistress here I shall expect at least half the game you shoot or snare to come to the Priory," and she looked steadily at Jasper whose sidelong glance avoided hers. The car drove away, followed by the other car. Jasper shut the gate and walked towards his cottage in Golden Valley. His grandmother the witch had an old rhyme which ran:

"When the Dark Eye comes to stay
Then the Romany must obey."

Jasper had forgotten it for a good many years, but of late it had been in his mind. If his old granny were still about in the woods, there might have been ways of finding out what she really meant. He had shot her himself and there was no one to unriddle her words. But he had now a pretty shrewd idea what the meaning might be.

CHAPTER 15

At a kind of Sports Sub-Committee at Harefield, run largely by Gus Perry the young doctor who was a skin specialist and the young Updike who was his father the lawyer's partner, it was finally decided that the idea of a race for punted collapsible boats should be abandoned. Charles Belton who had been co-opted as a junior member was disappointed, for it had been largely his idea, but he had a very nice disposition, and took it in good part. At least, he said, cheering up, the rushes had been cut and that was something and now the worst of the job was done they might have a rush-cutting once a year with lots of beer.

"If anyone had known that Cecil Waring was going about with a lot of loose metal inside him," said Gus Perry, "they could have told him not to be a lunatic. I wish I'd been there when they had to operate."

"Cecil hadn't got dermatitis, you fool," said young Updike.

"Well then, I wish Jim had been here," said Gus, for the Perrys were a very loyal family. "He'd have nicked it out in a jiffy."

"But Hastings is pretty good, isn't he?" said Charles Belton.

"Oh, very good," said Gus. "A lot of these provincial men are excellent. But Jim is absolutely tip-top," to which young Updike retorted that he remembered Jim opening a boil on his, young Updike's, leg with a penknife when they were both small and how he had blood poisoning.

"But that's what surgeons are like!" he added. "That's why they have to invent penicillin and things. It's all a ramp," whereupon Gus Perry fell upon young Updike till their host had to intervene, for this scene took place in Dowlah Cottage where Captain Freddy Belton, R.N., who was honorary chairman of the committee, allowed their meetings to be held. The Great Day, on which the annual meeting of the Barsetshire Archæological Society and the Harefield Lake Regatta were to be combined was not far off and as it had suddenly occurred to the Committee that they had done little or nothing about the aquatic events, as the radio-soaked village would call them, they felt that they had better get down to it.

The real difficulty of getting down to anything to do with the lake was that it was most unsuitable for sports, being mostly muddy and shallow. Also there were hardly any boats and those mostly a kind of primitive punt formerly used for shooting duck by Mr. Belton's grandfather who suffered from gout, sitting on a kitchen chair. Perhaps Cecil Waring would allow his two collapsible dinghies to be used, though it seemed a bit thick when he couldn't compete himself and perhaps the Mertons might lend theirs if anyone could fetch it. But it all seemed rather flat now.

"Well, how is it all going on?" said Admiral Hornby, brother-in-law of Freddy and Charles Belton, joining himself unofficially to their meeting, for he and his wife, formerly Elsa Belton, and their children were staying with her parents at Arcot House. "I've got a good mind to enter for this dinghy-punting myself, if I'm not too heavy."

An uproar of talk succeeded his remark, beginning with young Updike's statement that the heavier you were the faster you would go only he didn't know why, continuing with Gus Perry who (a) questioned the premises and (b) denied the conclusions, and complicated by Freddy Belton who said punting a dinghy was rather like being towed on a raft by a speedboat and if you went much faster you would find yourself right out of the water: which all led to a final and regretful decision that the dinghy-punting races had better be cancelled until such time as Cecil Waring should be well again, and another round of beer.

"I must say," said Admiral Hornby ungratefully, "that it is very pleasant when there aren't any women about. There are no nicer, better-looking, more intelligent women than my wife, Freddy, and yours, but it is almost like Paradise when they aren't here."

Gus Perry said like Adam before Eve was created, though speaking as a doctor—

"No you don't," said Admiral Hornby. "I understand you are a skin specialist, *not* a skeleton-expert or whatever you call people who know about ribs. By the way, Gus, my old coxswain who does general utility up at Aberdeathly had some filthy West African disease when he was on the Mngangaland station and every two or three years he comes out in red and purple blotches down the calf of his right leg and it suppurates. If you could ever get north I'd give you some good rough shooting. We're on the slopes of Ben Gaunt, just above Loch Gloom and about ten miles by boat from Inverdreary where the train stops twice a week. Or you can get off the express at Auchsteer and I'll send a boat down the loch to meet you."

"Oh, I say, that's most *awfully* good for you," said Gus, his eyes gleaming at the double prospect of a Scotch holiday and a new and revolting form of skin disease. "I was thinking of Paris, but that would be ever so much better. I say, it *is* a shame Cecil Waring can't race." But Admiral Hornby had not yet heard of Cecil's operation so the story was told in strophe and antistrophe by the committee. Admiral Hornby said he must look him up.

"I went over to see him last week," said Freddy Belton to his brother-in-law. "You know he is marrying the Duke's daughter. The Admiralty aren't going to want him for much active service I think after his operation and he has an idea of turning that dreadful Priory into some sort of home for the orphans of naval ratings. I don't know how one manages these things, but I shouldn't have thought the Priory much good for that sort of thing. Too many big rooms and not enough little ones. And you know what happens if you try to divide these big rooms; you get a kind of oubliette twenty feet high and eight feet square. It's like that at Gatherum now."

Admiral Hornby said it all sounded a bit complicated. The Priory School was just what Waring wanted and Philip Winter wanted a bigger building for his prep school and couldn't find one, so they were both at a standstill.

"Look here, Chris," said Freddy Belton. "You know Harefield House."

"The Hosiers' Girls' School is still there, isn't it?" said Admiral Hornby.

"That's just it," said Freddy Belton. "But they are going to get ahead with their new school—you know, on that bit of land they bought from Father over on the Southbridge Road. Well, when they move, in a couple of years or so, Father will have the house on his hands again. Now do you put two and two together?"

"General Post," said Admiral Hornby.

"Just so," said Freddy Belton. "The Hosiers go to the new school; the Winters move the Priory School to Harefield; Waring and his wife take over the Priory School for their whatever it is. I think a little staff work for you and me, Chris."

"Well, chiefly for you," said Admiral Hornby, "as the place will be yours some day. But it sounds all right. Go ahead and tell me if I can help. By the way when I was in London last week—" and the two men fell into a delightful naval talk about subjects of which we know nothing and what Rear-Admiral Sir Crossjay Patterne had said about the naval program.

Then the younger men, with the consideration that the young most touchingly show from time to time to their elders, said they were going up to the Nabob to have a quick one before closing time. It was obvious to their host that they felt they had drunk quite enough of his beer and he liked them for it, though as a matter of fact he was well off at the moment, having managed to get a whole barrel, never ask us how. So Freddy Belton said he would walk up to Arcot House with his brother-in-law and fetch his wife.

Here they found Mr. and Mrs. Belton with Mrs. Freddy, all very friendly and happy and slightly exhausted by the high spirits of Miss Catriona Hornby (called after her father's old flame Lady Ellangowan) and her younger brother, whose high spirits had lasted till nine o'clock when they had turned into tears and almost immediate sleep. Their mother was still upstairs.

"They look so divine, Christopher," said his mother-in-law. "They fell asleep quite suddenly in that heavenly way babies do, in whatever attitude they were in at the moment, all upside down and inside out."

"Catriona was *exactly* like the Quangle-Wangle with his head in his slipper after he had hurt his foot," said Mrs. Freddy.

"Let us now praise famous children," said Mr. Belton, suddenly looking up from *The Times* in which he had apparently been immersed, which made his wife and daughter-in-law laugh.

"Well, I must take Susan home," said Freddy Belton. "By the way, Father, have you got any plans about Harefield House?"

Mr. Belton put his *Times* down and looked suddenly older.

"None," he said, "except that the Hosiers' Girls go out in a year or two. It was a great piece of luck to have them and I can't complain—"

"—but you do, Fred," said his wife gently.

"That's right, my dear, I do," said Mr. Belton, so that everyone present felt frightful remorse; and then Mrs. Admiral Hornby formerly Elsa Belton joined them, slightly shattered by her offspring's bedtime behaviour, but as handsome as ever and with a kinder, a softer manner.

"I must say I am rather interested in its future myself," said

Freddy Belton. "Father, I believe we might be able to foist it off on another school. Would it amuse you at all to hear my idea?"

"Extraordinary words you young people do use," said Mr. Belton. "Amuse? Don't know that it would amuse me. If I don't let it again it won't be amusing at all."

Freddy Belton, knowing his father, kept a discreet silence and winked at his brother-in-law.

"Oh, well, I suppose I might as well hear," said Mr. Belton ungratefully.

"Tomorrow would do quite well, sir," said his son. "It was only that Philip Winter, Charles's boss, is thinking of larger quarters. But not if it bothers you."

"It's not letting it that bothers me," said Mr. Belton crossly. "It's *not* letting it. What does Winter propose? I'm an old man. I shan't be here much longer."

"Don't be silly, Father," said Elsa Hornby, who had always treated her father as an equal, which he rather seemed to like. "You know you will. Look at your grandfather."

"I don't want to," said Mr. Belton. "If his money in Consols had been entailed as well as the land, we'd be in a much better state. You can break an entail, but you can't get back money that's spent. It's all a worry now. All a worry. Well, what was it you were saying?"

"Not if it depresses you, Father," said Freddy, winking again at the rest of the company.

Mr. Belton said ungraciously that he might as well hear what Winter wanted.

"I can't answer for him," said Freddy, "but I believe with the least encouragement he would make you an offer. How schools do it, I don't know. He hasn't any money to speak of. His wife has some. And of course her uncle and aunt made very easy terms for them. And anyway he has made that school into a roaring success. Nice little chaps and Mrs. Winter tells me that the Duke wants to put the baby down for it, if it's a boy. But it's only an idea, Father."

There was a silence while Freddy wondered if he had gone too far.

"Give us good advice, Elsa," said her husband. "Shall we or shall we not make Philip Winter take an interest in Harefield?"

Some of us may remember the handsome, capable, rather spoilt Elsa Hornby whose only reaction to the Hosiers' Girls' School, which was to make all the difference to her father's financial position, was to burst into tears and say she hated them. Then she had married Captain Hornby, R.N., and had been taken away to be a Scotch landowner's wife and had improved so much that we would hardly have known her. She was more handsome than ever, but had lost her prickly coat and become quite kind and friendly to most people; even, after a severe inner struggle, to Lady Ellangowan, who had refused Christopher Hornby some years earlier. This is not an uncommon attitude, though why we should dislike and despise a woman who has made it possible for one's adored husband to propose to one it is difficult to say—or perhaps rather shamefully easy. But Elsa had vastly improved, was great friends with Catriona Ellangowan, and had called her little girl after her. She had always had a good deal of influence over her father who adored her, and it was apparent that she was prepared to use it. After some flattering and cajoling Mr. Belton went so far as to say that he would sleep on it. The Hornbys looked at each other. Freddy Belton said Good-night and took his wife home.

"You didn't say much, darling," he said, as they walked the short distance between Arcot House and Plassey House.

"I didn't need to," said Susan Belton. "I wasn't a Head Librarian in the war for nothing. When I think of the scene between the Hogglestock St. John and Red Cross Librarian and the Barchester General Hospital Librarian about a bookcase twelve by six, and how those two men nearly had tears and hysterics and I had to use my important voice, this evening is like twice two."

"Angel! How *could* you give that up for *me*?" said her husband.

"I didn't," said his wife. "It was for you and the children. *Darling.*"

The Barsetshire Archæological was not only a Society or Institution of excellent birth and good breeding, including most of the foremost people in the county whether they cared about archæology or not, but had under present circumstances an even greater use as a meeting-place for many people otherwise cut off from one another. From East and West Barsetshire, from the down country, from the woodland, from the pastures and water-meadows, from Barchester Cathedral and Close, from Hogglestock and Mr. Adams's roaring works, from little towns, from villages, from mansions, people would turn up if the weather were anything like possible.

The only disadvantage of Harefield, as the secretary of the Archæological admitted, was that there was no archæology there, unless the Garden House, that lovely but decaying piece of rococoterie built by Mr. Belton's ancestor the Nabob, could be counted. On the other hand it had the advantage of a real lake with some grassland round it where people could walk and between it and the road a sloping meadow which could be used as a car park. Tea was the chief difficulty (as we may say also that it was the chief attraction) for a marquee adds enormously to the expense, when Admiral Hornby had the excellent idea of using Harefield House itself. After the inevitable objections Mr. Belton agreed, provided the Hosiers' Girls' Governing Body were agreeable. They were agreeable and Messrs. Scatcherd and Tozer the well-known Barsetshire caterers named a figure which after a little *pro forma* argument was accepted by both parties. It now only remained for the weather to be fine, though this was improbable. Hopes were entertained that the Dowager Lady Norton might be enjoying a Mediterranean cruise and incidentally preventing a good many of her fellow passengers from enjoying it. Lord and Lady Pomfret had promised to come. The Hogglestock Brass Band, which melodious body had been ris-

ing to fame steadily and had been third in the Brass Band
Competition, was to play by kind permission of Samuel Adams,
J.P., and of the conductor Mr. Giles Hoggett, nephew of Miss
Hoggett who was Mrs. Adams's housekeeper.

There had been some discussion at Marling Hall as to who
would go to the Archæological, for with Lucy away Mr. Marling
went about much less. He did not complain. He had once or
twice felt rather ill while driving himself and with extraordinary
good sense and thoughtfulness had decided never to drive alone.
So Ed Pollett the local half-wit, who had a genius for cars
unsurpassed in West Barsetshire, now always drove the Squire,
which he did as willingly as he did everything else, having that
almost angelic disposition not infrequently bestowed by heaven
upon those it has afflicted, as had his wife Millie and all their
eight or nine children—for no one ever quite knew how many
there were and they were all beautiful and dirty and happy.

On hearing that her husband was going to the Archæological
Mrs. Marling said she would come too and asked Oliver what
his plans were. Oliver said in a rather remote and *affairé* way that
he didn't quite know, but not to trouble about him, as he would
probably come on later, for his sister Lucy after her marriage had
given him the hard-working little car she had used for all her
local activities and her market gardening.

It was on the Saturday before the meeting that this conversation took place. Oliver had planned to visit The Cedars during
the afternoon, as he often did now, there to meet the builder and
Maria Lufton. For the Honourable Maria Lufton, having seen
the house and what was even more important the stabling that
she wanted, had not let the grass grow under her feet. Hardly
was the ink dry on the paper that conveyed The Cedars from
Mr. Marling to Oliver, when the Lufton solicitors were in touch
with the Marling solicitors and Maria was already planning
alterations in the stables. As for the house, so long as there were
a few beds and chairs and tables she appeared entirely uninter-

ested, so that Oliver, not altogether to his displeasure, hoped
under the pretext of helping her to get everything as he liked it
and as his taste was good and intelligent we think The Cedars
was on the whole grateful. Maria was grateful too, having the
wits to recognize Oliver's taste and knowledge, and so Oliver
found himself being looked up to indoors (though outdoors
Maria went entirely her own way), an experience almost unknown to him, except from some of his London friends who
were apt to treat him as an unpaid decorator who could fetch
and carry.

On this afternoon he was down at The Cedars by half past
two and had a very happy hour with Mr. Crump from over
Allington way who knew exactly how much altering old houses
would stand, being specially bitter against people who wanted to
throw two rooms into one and put a steel girder across to
strengthen the floor above.

"For it stands to reason, sir," said Mr. Crump, "that if there's
a parti-wall it's taking the weight from above. You go and take
down that parti-wall, there's nothing to support the ceiling.
And then if you say to yourself, Ah, that old floor above she'll
give way she will, and you put a girder in, well, sir, that girder she
does take the weight, but there's a outward thrust, if you take my
meaning. And sure as eggs is eggs you'll get a lateral thrust as we
call it, sir, a kind of pushing sideways as you might say, and next
thing you'll find cracks in the walls. *And*," said Mr. Crump
seriously, "plug those cracks and plaster those cracks as you will,
they come again. You may plaster them and you may put a little
strip of paper across, high up where no one's likely to see it, and
within a year, or two years, or maybe ten years or even longer,
that little piece of paper will begin to tear. And when it begins to
tear, the crack she's opening again."

> "'And when your something begins to crack
>   It's like a something in, or is it on, your back . . .'"

said Oliver aloud to himself, with nursery memories of that terrifying nursery rhyme *A man of words and not of deeds.*

"Just as you say, sir," said Mr. Crump, who knew how to humour the gentry. "Now about those rooms upstairs, sir. You said the lady that's taking the house wants to throw two bedrooms into one. Well, we can do it of course sir, but I wouldn't advise it myself. Three bedrooms *with* a bathroom, is a gentleman's house. Two bedrooms isn't. And whichever rooms the lady wants to throw together it'll upset the layout, if you see what I mean."

Oliver, with a growing conviction of his own incompetence in all matters concerning the structure of a house (though he would have fought to the death about a carpet or a curtain), weakly said he was sure Mr. Crump was right, but he must see what the lady thought. At any rate, said Mr. Crump, he would carry on with the work that was needed in the kitchens and he could see the lady later about the bedrooms, at which moment Maria Lufton drove up and emerged with cockers rampant about her as if she were a female Actæon.

"How nice to see you," said Oliver, who had gone downstairs to meet her. "The builder is here—Crump from over Allington way. He understands old Barsetshire houses better than anyone and he is in the kitchen now, testing the taps and the drains. What would you like to do? You said something about wanting two bedrooms thrown into one. Crump isn't very sure about it. Shall we have a look?"

So they went up the wide, shallow-stepped stair to the first floor, which was also the top floor, and looked at the bedrooms.

"It's difficult to decide," said Maria. "I'd like one big room for myself, but then it only leaves one spare, and if I share with someone it means no spares."

"Have you found anyone to share with?" said Oliver, rather resenting the thought of his house having someone he didn't know living in it. Maria Lufton was a different matter.

"Not specially," said Maria. "There's a woman I'd thought of vaguely who is keen on cockers—but hers aren't golden and we might have a mix-up. I shall see. *What* a pretty fireplace."

And indeed it was a very elegant fireplace with a quite sufficiently near-Adam mantelpiece in the centre of which was a carved monogram; not very usual in that style.

"L.M.L.," said Maria, tracing the letters with her finger.

"Probably Lucius and Lucinda Marling," said Oliver.

"But they are *my* initials," said Maria.

Oliver asked what about the other L.

"Oh, that's me," said Maria. "I'm Lucy Maria Lufton really. I think the Lucy was after a great-grandmother or something of the sort, the one that was a parson's daughter" (though we know that Lucy Robarts was the parson's sister; so is history made), "but Mother didn't like Lucy and there are a lot about. There's your sister and Mrs. Belton and I can't think who else but I know there are several more. So when I was about three or four I turned into Maria. I think she was a great-grandmother or something. Anyway it stuck to me. How funny to find it here. It looks as if the house were meant to be mine, doesn't it?"

"And you won't share it?" said Oliver, somehow drawn to her by the coincidence of the initials, disliking even more the possible doggy female friend.

"I don't know," said Maria. "I'm not awfully keen. Still, I'm alone, and when your father dies I shan't know the people at the Hall."

"When Papa dies, *I* may want to live here," said Oliver, who hardly knew whither his words were leading him. "You see that's why he gave it to me, so that I could stay near Marling. And that's why I can't give a long lease. I don't want to seem unkind, but you do understand, don't you?"

"Well," said Maria, looking out of the window towards the cedar, "it's going to be three years anyway, isn't it? Of course I'd rather have seven, fourteen, twenty-one, but one can't have everything."

It was now or never.

"I think one might," said Oliver, who knew quite fatally that he had gone mad.

"How?" said Maria, in a not very well simulated tone of abstract interest.

"Haven't you any female intuition?" said Oliver. "I offer you my house and my hand. Only you'll have to pay rent till we are married."

Maria Lufton was a courageous woman and no fool.

"Wait a minute," she said. "This is so sudden, but it's more sudden for you than it is for me. I've noticed you were working up to it lately. Are you SURE?" and she faced him, almost his equal in height, very handsome.

"Sure?" said Oliver. "As sure as one can be. Of course I can't offer you an untouched heart," and as he said these very silly words he felt very beautiful and romantic.

"Good God, my lad," said Maria Lufton, "if it's Jessica Dean you mean, the whole county knows you've been mooning about after her for the last four years or so. That's nothing. It's taken you a bit longer than most to get over calf-love, that's all. No one else? Not the kitchen maid?"

"Shut up and don't be so coarse," said Oliver, half outraged, half flattered.

"That's better," said Maria. "I never suspected you of a sordid intrigue—what a heavenly expression that is. Well; have you accepted me?"

"But I thought it was you that had to accept *me*," said Oliver rather peevishly.

"I have," said Maria. "I always meant to and of course those initials finished it. Darling Oliver, you may be a bit thin on the top, but you *do* want looking after. Angel!" and before Oliver knew where he was, he was holding the Honourable Maria Lufton in his arms kissing her in a way he had never kissed anyone in his whole life.

"That's all right then," said his future wife. "I don't see why we shouldn't get married quite soon. It would save all that trouble about leases. Say as soon as the builders have finished."

"And what about the bedrooms?" said Oliver.

"Oh, we'll leave them now," said Maria. "One for us, a dressing-room for you and a spare room for Jessica. And when we have a family we'll do something about those rooms over the kitchen wing," which comprehensive survey of past present and future took Oliver's breath away.

"And now," said his betrothed with her usual calm, "I think it would be only civil to go and tell your people. Your father will *love* kissing me."

"Old devil!" said Oliver, but quite kindly, and they went downstairs where Maria told Mr. Crump she had decided to keep the bedrooms as they were and asked him to carry on with the kitchen quarters, and forcing their way through the cockers they got into the car.

"A turtle pair, by Gurk!" said Mr. Crump, slapping his thigh, which exclamation was peculiar to that part of the country and generally taken to be a local corruption of Gundric whose ditch or Fossway was still to be traced running almost due north and south. But Oliver and Maria, quite unconscious that the word ENGAGED was written on their speaking countenances, pursued their way to Marling Hall, where they found Mr. and Mrs. Marling at tea.

"Well, Miss Maria," said Mr. Marling, who was in very good humour after a visit from Miss Amabel Rose Adams, "how's your house gettin' on? Oliver's got a handsome tenant."

"If you don't object, Mr. Marling, we are going to do without any of the landlord and tenant business," said Maria.

"Do without—the boy's a fool!" said Mr. Marling. "Here, Oliver, what the dickens are you up to?"

"I'm sorry, Papa, but we got engaged," said Oliver.

There was a moment's silence and then Mrs. Marling, very

near tears, came over to Maria and took her into her arms and both ladies embraced violently and sniffed and blew their noses and became incoherent.

"And isn't there a kiss for an old feller like me?" said Mr. Marling, who was enjoying it all hugely.

"Of course there is, Papa," said Maria, "and if I weren't so tall I'd sit on your knee," which made Mr. Marling laugh in his best English Squire way and make witty remarks about cutting Oliver out.

"You easily could," said Maria. "You're much better-looking than Oliver" (which was indeed true) "but he is exactly what I want. I do hope you don't mind?"

"Mind?" said Mr. Marling. "I was married and had all my family when I was half his age," said Mr. Marling, a little untruthfully. "No, my girl, I'm as glad as I can be. You know that boy of yours has always been a worry. Not very good health when he was younger and runnin' after that little baggage Jessica Dean and writin' his books. But there's an end of all that now. We must tell Lucy," for his beloved younger daughter was always, though he loved his other children, first in his mind.

After that everything was gas and gaiters till at last Maria had to go back to Lufton and before dinner Lady Lufton rang up, also almost crying with joy, and never had the kitchen at Marling Hall been so popular as that evening, with nearly every woman in the village having cups of tea and saying how she had had a something as told her there would be a wedding. Then later, when his parents had gone to bed, Oliver went quietly downstairs and rang up Jessica Dean. Her invaluable housekeeper-guardian answered.

"Oh, Miss M.," said Oliver, for so was this treasure known to all Jessica's friends, "It's Oliver Marling. Is Jessica back from the theatre yet?"

Miss M. said she was back and having some supper in bed and she would put Mr. Marling through.

"Well, my sweet?" said Jessica's lovely voice.

"Oh, Jessica," said Oliver, suddenly wondering how to break to her, in a gentlemanly way, that his lifelong allegiance was shattered by a Woman's Eyes (or smile, or touch, or anything else).

"How utterly sweet of you to ring up, my poppet," said Jessica. "It's too, too marvellous and Aubrey and I are thrilled and it is Heaven and we shall come to the wedding even if it means cancelling a matinee."

"But I didn't know—I mean it's only just happened—I mean I wanted to tell you first," said Oliver.

"Too late as usual, my sweet," said Jessica. "Maria rang me up before I went to the theatre."

"Maria?" said Oliver. "But she hardly knows you."

"Oh God! Need he be such a nitwit?" said Jessica's voice, evidently to her husband, for Aubrey Clover's voice then said: "Fine, my boy. Couldn't be better. You must bring her to see us. Say which night and I'll tell them to give you the stagebox with gold-edged program, just like Royalty, and then you must both have supper with us. Jessica always said you were a bit of wet flannel, but I knew you had it in you. May I be godfather? That's a part I've never done and I'd *adore* it. Good-night. Jessica wants you."

Willingly would Oliver have slammed the receiver down, as people do in books, but he was of a careful nature. Still one could replace the receiver, to use the language of the G.P.O. But before he could replace it—and perhaps he did not hurry to replace it—the lovely voice of Jessica Dean came to him again from her bed in London.

"Happy times, darling," she said. "You have been an angel and I've loved every minute. And always the gentleman. Don't be too gentlemanly with Maria, my pet. Good-night. Good-bye."

Oliver went up to bed full of fatigue and happiness and a faint unhappiness. The past misery with Jessica had been very clear to him. Now he would be Benedick, the married man. Then a great thankfulness for his Maria filled him and overflowed till he fell asleep. No longer would Turk disturb his rest. But Turk was forgotten.

CHAPTER 16

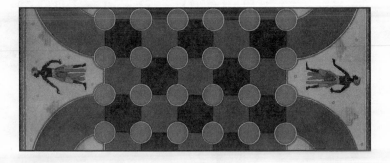

W hat with four county engagements almost in the same
week and the possibility of an heir to the Silverbridges,
society felt that there was practically nothing left remarkable
beneath the visiting moon. But there was always the hope of
seeing one or two of one's friends or relations falling into the
lake, and considering Them and everything else the Barsetshire
Archæological had a gratifying large attendance. The hero of
the day was of course Cecil Waring, who had been driven over in
his 1949 Ocelot by his affianced at a speed and with an apparent
carelessness which, so he complained, had made his stitches
come unsewn, to which Lady Cora had replied heartlessly that
as they had been taken out last week she was not interested.

"I'm glad to see you, Waring," said Mr. Belton coming up to
the car. "My congratulations to you and Lady Cora," and several
other friends who had not seen Cecil since his operation joined
them. Lady Cora smiled at him and was going away to talk to
Bishop and Mrs. Joram when something pulled at her hand.
Looking down she saw a little boy with a gap in his front teeth.

"I say, Lady Cora," said the little boy.

"Bless my soul," said Lady Cora, summoning all her social
powers to remember who the toothless child might be.

"You came to see us at the Priory, in bed," said the little boy.

"So I did," said Lady Cora, beginning to see light, "and you
made a song about me. You're not Pickering; you're Dean."

"Sucks!" said Dean contemptuously to another little boy. "Pick said you wouldn't know me. Pick is a fool; Bottom of the school," at which words a short, violent, but harmless battle took place. "I say, Lady Cora, have you found your brother?"

"What brother?" said Lady Cora.

"The one you said had gone away," said Dean.

"Not yet," said Lady Cora, remembering how the little boys had asked her about Gerry and how she had tried to answer them. It was difficult to answer some questions and one's answers were too likely to come home to roost.

"Where did you lose him?" said Dean, with the maddening persistence of little boys, still clinging to her hand. She said in France.

"Then I suppose he was killed," said Dean cheerfully.

Lady Cora said Yes. There was no more to say.

"I say, was he *really* killed?" said Dean, jiggling up and down with interest.

"Yes," said Lady Cora, giving up the unequal contest.

"Rotten luck," said Dean sympathetically. "Please, Lady Cora, you said you expected you'd go to him. Are *you* going to be killed?"

"Oh, bless the boy, too many questions," said Lady Cora, half laughing, half remembering that such things were, and then Dean loosed her hand and threw himself upon a group of newcomers, shrieking: "Aunt Jessica! Aunt Jessica! come and see Lady Cora."

Enchanting as Jessica Dean had often appeared to Lady Cora on the stage, she looked just as enchanting in broad daylight, and in both ladies could be observed the not uncommon phenomenon of two women outstanding for looks, carriage, grace, and charm, each admiring the other, and so much did they find to talk about that the little boys lost interest and went away to the lake, where, on a shallow part, staked and roped off by Mr. Belton's orders, Old Humble was taking children for excursions at threepence a time in his old flat-bottomed boat with short oars, while he told his young passengers the story of young Job Potter who had been drowned because he would go on the ice when he was told not to, and Addison (from the Priory School) had already spent four-and-ninepence of the five shillings his doting parents had given him.

"Now, my boy," said Mr. Belton, who had hardly seen Cecil since he was a boy and used to come over from his uncle's house to play with Freddy Belton, "you must be careful. Come and sit outside the boat-house. I've got a few seats there and you'll be out of the wind. Nasty business that of yours. I remember getting a stray pellet in my arm when I was out with the guns over at Pomfret Towers, years ago. There was a doctor with us. I've forgotten his name now and he got it out on the spot with a penknife. Didn't bother about clean knives in those days. And old Lord Pomfret—not the one you knew, his father—laughed quite fiendishly. But he gave us the best champagne I've ever tasted at lunch. A footman and a hamper to every four guns. I was only ten or eleven then."

So Cecil made appropriate comments and began to wonder if Dr. Ford hadn't been right when he told him to take things easy and not be surprised if he felt a bit under the mark. But it was no use reflecting upon Dr. Ford's advice, for a number of county people, mostly old friends of his uncle and aunt, without as yet the time or the energy to call upon a house with no mistress and a master whose life had kept him at sea, came almost to pay their respects. It is on the whole difficult not to like a sailor and Cecil had, for perhaps the first time in his life, the intoxicating feeling of being liked and wanted. With Lady Cora he could cheerfully have lived on a desert island, but he began to realize that it would be far more fun to live with her at the Priory. Sir Edmund Pridham, doyen of the county in age and service; Lord Pomfret, tired, conscientious, hard-working, with his wife; the Dean; Everard Carter the Headmaster of Southbridge School and his delightful wife who was Mrs. Noel Merton's sister; Captain Gresham, R.N., and Mrs. Gresham from Hallbury; Mr. Dean the wealthy engineer from Winter Overcotes, apologizing for his wife on the grounds that she had gone to sleep after lunch and he didn't like to disturb her; the great cow-magnates from Staple Park and Worsted, Lord Bond and Mr. Palmer; Mr. and Mrs. Middleton from Laverings with their nephew Denis Stonor the wildly successful composer of light operas over from America; these and others came to introduce themselves, to welcome him to the county. Some of this perhaps was due to the Omnium connection, for a Duke is still someone, we are glad to say; but we believe that most of them came to welcome a newcomer whose roots were fast in Barsetshire.

"I don't suppose you'll know me," said a middle-aged woman with a pleasant tired face and hair which needed perpetual pushing and tidying beneath her unfashionable hat, "I'm Mrs. Morland. I had the pleasure of talking to the men at the Priory when it was a hospital in the war and I admired your aunt excessively. This is George Knox who writes biographies, which must really be much easier than writing novels, because you needn't *invent* anything. It's all *there*, if you read old books and papers and things, and all you have to do is to get it tidy. But as for writing novels—"

"You write those Madame Koska books, don't you?" said Cecil. "We all adored them in the war. Even the ratings fell over themselves to get any new ones."

"As a matter of fact they are all *exactly* the same," said Mrs. Morland, pushing a strand of hair determinedly behind one ear. "That's why people like them. Now George's books are all different which is to me quite extraordinary."

"Our dear Laura, if I may so call her in public," said George Knox, "exaggerates, or rather, for I am a devotee of the *mot juste*, speaks erroneously. It is she who relates facts. Her female detective works in fact; each of her delightful—and if ephemeral, who are we to complain?" said George Knox, looking about ferociously for nonexistent complainers, "—her delightful, I repeat—"

"You repeat repeat far too often, George," said Mrs. Morland in a rather didactic way.

"—I repeat, her *delightful*," said George Knox, glaring round him for imaginary contradictors, "I say her delightful *romans policiers* though that is not the term one would use—words fail me—Laura! What *am* I talking about? Nay—I have it. Laura has to get her *facts* correct, or where would be the plot, the *Entwicklung*—ah! memories of Goethe and Schiller, lost bards of the Stepfatherland—the dénouement, though not altogether in the French sense. I, even I, poor hack, poor quill-driver, must fill with romance, with perception, with atmosphere, the dry bones of History. I fail doubtless to make myself clear—"

"You do, George, and you are tiring Sir Cecil," said Mrs. Morland and led the celebrated biographer away.

But Lady Cora had not really taken her eye off Cecil and now she came up and asked if he would like to go home.

"Please," said Cecil.

Telling herself firmly that to look upon a Commander who was also a Baronet as a little boy was sheer sentiment, Lady Cora's heart nevertheless was moved by his dependence more than she could have thought possible, and before he could alter his mind she had apologized to Mrs. Belton, got him into the car and taken him away.

"There's no one like you, darling," said Cecil as his love sped far too fast along the lanes towards the Priory.

"Idiot!" said Lady Cora.

It is perhaps fair to say that a number of people visited the Garden House and the ruins of the pump-house, so that a mild archæological flavour was imparted, but as in all English out-of-door entertainments, the one aim and object of everyone present was tea. This, as we already know, was to be at Harefield House, at present empty for the Summer Holidays, and thither by four o'clock nearly everyone present had gone. It was nearly ten years since the Beltons had left their old home, and now they would probably have disliked leaving the comfort of Arcot House, but even so we think their hearts beat a little faster every time they returned as guests to Harefield House. Now there was further reason for a troubled heart for as we know the plans for the Hosiers' Girls' Foundation School's new buildings were approved and within the next two years the move would probably be made. Then what would they do? Mr. Belton had let Harefield House before They had fully embarked on Their policy of destroying estates, small and large, and if possible having open-cut coal works in the gardens and turning the mansions into more government offices. Soon the smaller country houses too would go. And soon, if They had Their way, universal darkness bury all.

"Not much hope for us, Mrs. Morland," said Mr. Belton, as he escorted his distinguished guest across the park and up the hill to the Nabob's Palladian mansion, its East and West Pavilions connected by a screen-corridor with the main building. "I can only hope that the next lot will take Their houses and savings."

"And so on till everyone is dead," said Mrs. Morland sympathetically. "*I* know who I hate most."

"So do I," said Mr. Belton. "Hating doesn't kill people though."

"But writing their names on a piece of paper and putting it in a drawer sometimes works," said Mrs. Morland.

"I sometimes feel sorry for the P.M.," said Mr. Belton, who had a generous spirit. "Fancy having to meet that lot every day."

"I am *not* sorry for him," said Mrs. Morland. "Not since I heard what he said," which vague but ominous statement caused Mr. Belton to feel quite flummoxed: as indeed Mrs. Morland's hearers often were.

"It was the opening of something to do with William Morris," said Mrs. Morland. "And why I went I cannot think except that George Knox took me."

"And where did the P.M. come in?" said Mr. Belton faint, but still in a gentlemanly way pursuing.

"He thinks he was converted by Morris or something of the sort, though I think he can hardly have been born then," said Mrs. Morland with great dignity. "Perhaps one ought to know that. I didn't. And after he had made a very long speech through a loudspeaker, which always makes it impossible to hear anything, not to speak of the way he mumbled, he Misquoted."

"What?" said Mr. Belton.

"Misquoted," said Mrs. Morland.

"I mean *what*?" said Mr. Belton.

"Oh, sorry," said Mrs. Morland. "Well, I believe William Morris was a very good poet, though I must say I have read hardly any of him except his early ones, but there is one line that is quite well known and he said it, through the loudspeaker, and did it wrong."

"What was it?" said Mr. Belton, bored but courteous.

"He said: 'The idle singer of an idle day,'" said Mrs. Morland in her most impressive voice.

"Don't know much about poetry myself," said Mr. Belton. "It all sounds a bit like the Labour lot though."

"Yes, but it was *wrong*," said Mrs. Morland, giving her hat a determined shove forwards. "It ought to be 'The idle singer of an *empty* day.'"

"As yes, empty," said Mr. Belton, more bored than ever.

"So quite a lot people said 'empty' in a loud voice; and so did I," said Mrs. Morland.

"Charlotte Corday," said Mr. Belton, at which unexpected piece of wit Mrs. Morland had the giggles.

They had now got to the house and Mr. Belton stood aside to let Mrs. Morland enter the home of his ancestors. The Hosiers had kept it in excellent repair and, Mr. Belton had to admit, in better repair than he could have afforded, but his heart still ached a little. There was already a considerable and rather greedy crowd, among whom Mr. Belton saw the Vicar, Mr.

Oriel, and Mrs. Sidney Carton who had formerly been the Headmistress of the School. Mrs. Morland, for the moment alone, saw Oliver Marling with a tall handsome woman whom she did not know.

"Oh, Mrs. Morland," said Oliver. "I did enjoy your last Madame Koska book so much."

"At least it can't have done you any harm," said Mrs. Morland. "I always say that," she added with some pride.

"And I do want you to know Miss Lufton," said Oliver. "She is doing me the honour of marrying me and we are going to live at The Cedars on Father's ground," at which news the kind creature was delighted and congratulated them till her hair began to come down.

"Maria!" said Oliver suddenly, in a voice of anguish.

"What is the matter?" said his love.

"Look!" said Oliver. And there coming in their direction were Frances Harvey and her brother Geoffrey.

We shall not say that Maria Lufton rolled her sleeves up and spat on her hands, for she did not. But our readers will gather our meaning.

"Oliver!" said Frances Harvey in the voice which had once almost thrilled Oliver, almost lured him to destruction.

"Oh, Frances, how nice to see you," said Oliver. "Maria, this is Frances Harvey."

"And how are you getting on with The Cedars?" said Frances Harvey. "A charming house, but rather poky I thought."

"So did I, till I found it wasn't," said Maria calmly.

"You know Tom Grantly, don't you?" said Oliver to Maria, as Tom came up.

"I ought to if I don't," said Maria Lufton. "I believe your great-aunt or whatever she was, Lady Hartletop, nearly married my great-grandfather. If she had I'd have been Griselda Maria instead of Lucy Maria," and she and Tom fell into families at once.

"It was really distressing to me to get rid of young Grantly," said Geoffrey Harvey to Mrs. Morland. "But these young men haven't the stamina. They aren't tough enough."

Mrs. Morland, quite innocently, said she supposed the war had done more harm to them than anyone would ever realize.

"I have four boys myself so I ought to know," she said, a little sadly.

"One fears," said Mr. Harvey, in a quiet ogreish way, "that some of them will find it very hard going. They lost so much time in the war and expect the older men, like myself shall I say, to carry them. But we are having a real purge, Mrs. Morland. You could write a book about it," and he smiled.

If he had not smiled Mrs. Morland might have borne it, but her motherly heart was very soft for the men who had been on active service; who had seen and heard and felt what we shall never know, who were not armed against the Punic faith of their superiors.

"I only write books about *nice* people," she said. "Heroines and villains. Not mean, petty jealousy," and she turned her back.

Maria laughed. As a matter of fact she was laughing at something Tom had said, but Mr. Harvey chose to take it as directed against himself.

"Well, Tom, how goes it?" he said, with what Maria considered odious familiarity. "I'm sure you've found something."

"Yes, indeed," said Tom, who was so happy in his new prospects and his long-lost, new-found Emmy that he would have forgiven the whole government. "I'm doing accountancy and then I'm going to be agent at Rushwater. Oh and I'm engaged to Emmy Graham. It is all the most wonderful luck."

"You deserved it all, Tom," said Mrs. Samuel Adams, who had just joined them. "You worked like a Trojan for me when I was market gardening. Hullo, Maria. I say, I'll tell you what, everyone. Maria's engaged to Oliver. It's quite perfect. And they're going to live at The Cedars and breed dogs and I'll let Amabel Rose come and play with them."

There was nothing to do but to congratulate, which both the Harveys did, and to do them justice they did it quite nicely.

"Hah! which pleasure, which joy!" said the voice of the Mixo-Lydian Ambassadress. "Mrs. Morland, you will recollectink me. Gradka. When I was beink with Lady Fielding; yes, no?"

"But of *course!*" said Mrs. Morland. "And what a lovely lunch you cooked. I have never forgotten it."

"God wills it so," said the Ambassadress. "And I am readink your books. Hah! which frill!"

"Thrill, I think," said Mrs. Morland.

"So, I thank you, thrill," said Gradka. "I shall havink them translated for Mixo-Lydia, so will they possessink themselves of English manners. Not manners such as som people are havink," she said with a glance at the Harveys, "bot manners such as Mr. Marlink and Prodshkina Maria."

It was obvious to everyone that they were on a volcano which might at any moment blow up. No one knew quite what to do. Oliver vaguely wondered whether Frances Harvey would advance on Maria with a bottle of vitriol in her hand and if so what was the best thing to do. But at this moment there appeared a small, dark, wiry-haired woman in a leopard-skin coat followed by a man huddled in a sheepskin coat and wearing a beret from beneath which his dark miserable eyes roamed in a terrified way round the room.

"*Tiens! C'est l'ambassadrice, Gogo,*" said the woman. "*Abordons-la. Nous pourrions bien arranger un petit job pour toi à l'ambassade, hein? Dites-donc, madame, vous ne reconnaissez pas des compatriotes.*"

Gradka said something in what everyone supposed to be Mixo-Lydian, to which the woman replied in the same language.

"Ah!" shrieked the Ambassadress. "*Czy pròvka, pròvka, pròvka!*"

"I know what that means," said Mrs. Morland proudly. "It means never, never again."

"Hov I not givink this person a job at the Embassy ollready?" said the Ambassadress. "Is he not bootink for spikulation?"

"Her Excellency," said Frances Harvey with great presence of mind and in a loud whisper, "wishes to say that he was dismissed for dishonesty."

"*Czy, pròvka, pròvka, pròvka,*" said the miserable Gogo.

"*Espèce de chameau,* wheech is peeg-woman," said Madame Brownscu to the world in general. "*Viens Gogo. Nous allons rater l'autobus,*" and to everyone's relief the couple went back to the Cotswolds. If hate could have killed anyone it was obvious that several of the company would already be dead. With one accord Oliver and his Maria said good-bye and oozed through the crowd, followed by Mrs. Morland and Tom Grantly.

"And you, Mr. Harvey," said the Mixo-Lydian Ambassadress, only too ready to attack anybody and anything, "when I hear how you are treatink this young man Tom, I say Pouf of you. Ollso of your sister. Now I shall speakink with the Fieldings which are gentlemen people," and she was received with great friendliness by her former employers Sir Robert Fielding, the Chancellor of the Diocese, and his wife.

"What a fool you are, Geoffrey," said Frances Harvey to her brother.

"You aren't particularly clever yourself," said Geoffrey Harvey. "I thought you were going to marry Oliver Marling."

"If I had meant to marry him, I should have married him long ago," said Frances Harvey with great dignity, to which we regret to say her brother answered: "Sez you."

During the term the Philip Winters rarely went out together, so this was a delightful occasion for meeting old friends and in general renewing county ties. Presently they found themselves near the Aubrey Clovers, to whom Jessica's nephew, young Dean, had attached himself. With them was also Denis Stonor, the well-known composer of light but heart-rending musical plays, over from America to talk business with Aubrey.

"Sir," said Dean.

"Well?" said his Headmaster.

"Oh sir," said Dean, "Mr. Stonor came from America in an aeroplane and he had things to eat and drink all the time. I wish I could go in an aeroplane."

"Too true," said Denis, his melancholy monkey-face more melancholy than ever. "A charming and natty air-hostess—blast her—woke me up whenever I mercifully lost consciousness and offered me Coca-Cola. And when you think that owing to the precession of the equinoxes, or gravity, or something, you practically get to England at the same time as you left America, it is too much."

Jessica said not to mind, because going back it would be one step forward and two steps back all the way. Relativity or something, she added, and gratified her hearers by Mrs. Carvel's famous wink.

"It doesn't make things any better," said Denis, "because I had a very beautiful idea about a lyric and it has gone, like the Lost Chord. I had it in my sleep and if that nylon-legged devil had left me alone it would have turned into something."

"I never thought much of that Lost Chord gent," said Aubrey Clover in an abstracted way. "That's the worst of the amateur. A little musical training and all chords would have been an open book to him. What was your lyric, Denis?"

"I told you I'd *forgotten* it," said Denis peevishly, to which Aubrey replied that Denis only thought he had forgotten it, and shock treatments often brought things back.

"Ah!" said Denis's uncle, Mr. Middleton from Laverings, who had joined them with his wife while this foolish conversation was going on. "Ah," he repeated, in case anyone else should speak, "that thought between sleeping and waking—"

"It flies forgotten, sir, does it not?" said Aubrey Clover, now an admiring disciple of the Great Man.

"As a dream," Denis was continuing, when he saw Mrs. Middleton looking at him. Many years ago, long before the war, a rather selfish young musician in poor health had adored his aunt by marriage, Catherine Middleton, for a few summer weeks. America, the war, had parted them. Now Denis was famous in America and well-known in England, while Catherine Middleton had remained in her own quiet domestic life, cherishing the husband about whom she had no illusions, growing older. Denis had almost forgotten his young heartbreak. If no other woman had touched his heart it was not because he remembered Mrs. Middleton; rather, we think, because he only remembered music, to which everything in his life was a food. But as she looked at him he suddenly remembered the summer afternoon when they had parted, speechless except for the common words of farewell, and for a moment he felt the pang. And then, cursing himself for his dullness, he realized that Mrs. Middleton was not looking at him in memory of that day, but calling upon him by the memory of that day not to laugh at her husband, whose overpowering egoism must be protected by her till she died.

"I'm sorry, Catherine," said Denis, meeting her eyes. "Aubrey!"

"Don't shout, darling. Here he is," said Jessica. "Say it nicely, whatever it is."

"Have you got a Tennyson?" said Denis, as if this were a normal thing to carry about with one.

Aubrey at once became the poor scholar who has no books of his own and must read, standing, in booksellers' shops; assuming a face and attitude to express the same.

"I've got one," said Leslie Winter, who had been enjoying the professionals at work though she did not quite understand what was going on, "but it's at the school. What do you want?"

"*Maud*," said Denis impatiently. "Something about hearing people walking about on top of you when you are dead. I thought I had it, but I haven't. Damn!"

"I expect Philip will know," said Leslie. "He reads aloud to me a lot. Philip! Mr. Stonor wants a piece of poetry, preferably by Tennyson, about hearing people when they are dead."

> "'My heart would hear her and beat,
>   Were it earth in an earthy bed;
> My dust would hear her and beat,
>   Had I lain for a century dead'—

is that it?" said Philip.

"Thank God!" said Denis. "I don't suppose there's any copyright in it is there? Good! I'll wring the heart of every music fan in America with that. And I'll wring my own heart too," he added, not without some complacence.

"Always showing off, darling," said Jessica. "Come along, both of you. I see Mother going to sleep in a corner and we really must take her home," and with an enchanting gesture of farewell she took her gifted husband and his gifted friend away, while Philip and Leslie also moved on.

"Genius! that wayward spirit!" said Mr. Middleton. "Who would have thought, Catherine, when my nephew Denis came to Laverings looking like an owl in daylight that has fallen into a bucket of water, who, I say, would have thought that he would be—words fail me—"

"They never really do," said his wife kindly. "Shall we go home now, Jack?"

"Your word, my dear Catherine, is law," said Mr. Middleton, "as always. You are tired. I have been a brute to keep you here. The Archæological is not what it was."

"Not tired," said Mrs. Middleton. "Only remembering that such things were. You are quite right though, Jack. The Archæological is rather dull."

Meanwhile the Winters in their friendly progress had met a great many county friends. The crowd in the tea-room grew thicker and thicker and presently they were wedged up against a window with no immediate prospect of escape. A slight surge in the crowd almost flattened them against the window seat.

"Philip!" said Leslie suddenly. "Do you see what I see? Over there, just by the Archdeacon?"

"I do," said Philip. And even as he spoke a kind of ninth wave came surging towards them, on the crest of which so to speak was a woman, built on ample lines, in a sage-green dress and a wine-coloured straw hat well off the face, with dark auburn hair set in hard waves.

"Well, well, WELL," said the apparition. "Wonders will never cease though I say it that shouldn't, but fancy seeing you here. It really seems as if it was Meant, because this very morning I said to Bobbums—you remember my husband, Mrs. Winter, just the same as ever but the old forehead a bit further back, dear old pet—I said to him only this morning at breakfast, because we are having a little motor tour through this part of the country and staying in Barchester at the White Hart which always makes me think of cherries if you see what I mean, so as I was saying I said to Bobbums, Why not go and see the Barsetshire Archæological Meeting because, believe it or not, show me a flint arrow though how they shot flints is more than little me can grasp, show me a flint arrow, I said, and I go all Stone Age and Prehistoric. So remembering those happy Old Times when Bobbums was at the Hush-Hush place near Lambton though of course it isn't Hush-Hush now but I always say you can't be too careful because if we get another war you never know, I said, Let's have a stab at the Archæological. You never know, I said, and lo! and behold! you don't, for who would have thought to see Colonel and Mrs. Winter here. Bobbums will be absolutely beside himself when he hears I've seen you. He has gone to look at a ruin somewhere in the grounds, but take it from me, Mrs. Winter, he needn't have gone further than this room. Talk of ruins! What with the tax on cosmetics and the tax on clothes and the way anything nice is Export Only till I feel quite like Joan of Arc and could kill Everybody, it's a wonder we're all alive though we look perfect WRECKS. Now I *know* you want to know all about the children and the boys are doing splendidly at Harberton Grammar School down in Dorset and all het up to do their military service though as I said to Bobbums it gets worse and worse because fighting Germans or even Russians is one thing, I said, but fighting China is quite another and all Communists which is quite senseless besides being so un-Christian, I mean the Communists, said she coming over all religious, but Clarissa, my girl that is, is just loving being a boarder at the Barchester High School and her front teeth are getting much straighter, such a tragedy, for her first teeth were like pearls, *real* pearls I mean not those cultured ones, but the second teeth came through till really I thought she must have rabbits' blood in her, only in fun of course, but the Barchester dentist has done *wonders* and she passed her School Certificate a year too soon. And here's Bobbums!" and she pulled from the crowd a thin, sensitive-looking man with a harassed expression, who appeared gently pleased to see the Winters.

"Now, you and Colonel Winter, or is it Mr. Winter now, you never know and some ex-officers though I won't say ex-gentlemen as you can't be ex what you never were, prefer to keep the title and others to drop it, must have a good old chin-wag, Bobbums," said Mrs. Spender, "while I pump Mrs. Winter about all our Barsetshire friends. And how is the dear old pet of a General?"

Having with an effort recognized her Uncle Sir Harry Waring under this disguise, Leslie said he was dead. Shocked but undaunted Mrs. Spender asked after Lady Waring, who was also dead.

"Well, if that isn't like little me," said Mrs. Spender. "I don't know if I'm psychic or something, but I no sooner ask after someone that I haven't seen for some time but believe it or not they are DEAD. Well, as I always say, when people are dead there's nothing you can do about it and one hopes they are having a good time if you see what I mean, for down here what with the government and the World Situation and the National Health Service you really might as well be in heaven, for as I always say there's a chance for everyone somewhere, though of course exactly where said she, coming over all religious, it is not given to us to know, but I always say FAITH is the great thing, because if you have FAITH practically nothing matters because you can't do anything about it if it does. You know, I think a lot though you'd hardly think it of little me, but when I see dear old Bobbums getting on with his job and the children all doing well at school and that wonderful film at the Barchester Odeon, it's quite an old one but the old friends are often the best friends, about the airman who recites poetry to the radar girl while he is being burnt in his aeroplane in Technicolor and then they go to heaven with all those wonderful historical characters arguing about him, well, it really makes you THINK, though why heaven isn't in Technicolor never ask me, for we Are Not Told what it is really like and there is Mrs. Villars, so you will forgive me if I take Bobbums to see her or he will never forgive me after the kind way they had him billeted on them during the war and a sherry party in the middle of an air raid," with which final words she grasped her husband's arm and propelled him through the crowd towards her next victim.

"Lord!" said Leslie to her husband. "Let's get out before she catches us again."

Philip entirely agreed and they sidled and squeezed till they got into the hall and could breathe again. Presently a pleasant-faced middle-aged man came near them, looked at Philip, appeared uncertain, and then evidently determined to do or die.

"Winter, I think," he said.

"Weaver!" said Philip. "How very nice to see you. I don't think you have met my wife. Sir Hosea Weaver, Leslie, who was at the Dower House with me on that Hush-hush job."

Leslie expressed her pleasure and said how sorry she was that Philip had not brought Sir Hosea to the Warings.

"You must come and see us," she said. "We have a prep school at the Priory now."

"Then," said Sir Hosea, "we have something in common. The Hosiers' Company, of which I have the honour to be Past Master, are governors of the girls' school here. In a year or two we hope to move to our new buildings on Mr. Belton's land."

"And what happens to this house?" said Philip.

"I know Mr. Belton wants to let it again," said Sir Hosea. "You don't want a school, do you?"

"As a matter of fact, it's exactly what I do want," said Philip. "I don't like to trouble you, Weaver, but if you could say a word about it—"

"My dear fellow, with pleasure," said Sir Hosea. "Your husband was a Colonel," he added to Leslie, "and I never got any further than an elderly Second Lieutenant. Mr. and Mrs. Belton are dining with me here this evening before I go back to town and Mr. and Mrs. Carton—she was our Headmistress you know—and I had the pleasure of presenting her with the Freedom of the Hosiers' Company before she retired. Won't you both join us?"

Philip looked at Leslie and they accepted his invitation.

"You will excuse me, I must speak to the Cartons," said Sir Hosea and then the Winters, making their way through the crowd, found themselves jammed against Bishop Joram and his attractive wife, formerly Mrs. Brandon, who was looking younger and prettier than ever.

"I do hope," said Mrs. Joram, "that you will dine with us before next term begins. I will make a very nice party for you."

"I believe we ought to have asked you first," said Leslie, "but somehow in a school time goes on like anything."

"Do ask the Palace to meet us," said Philip, laughing. "You know, Joram, now you have a wife you will have to invite them sooner or later."

"I suppose we shall," said Bishop Joram. "I had never thought of that," and he looked pale. "Never mind. With Lavinia I can face *anything*," he added, and then the crowd parted them.

COLOPHON

This book is being reissued as part of Moyer Bell's Angela Thirkell Series. Readers may join the Thirkell Circle for free to receive notices of new titles in the series as well as a newsletter, bookmark, and poster. Simply send in the enclosed card or write to the address below.

The text of this book was set in Caslon, a typeface designed by William Caslon I (1692-1766). This face designed in 1725 has gone through many incarnations. It was the mainstay of British printers for over one hundred years and remains very popular today. The version used here is Adobe Caslon. The display faces are Adobe Caslon Outline, Calligraphic 421, and Adobe Caslon.

Composed by Alabama Book Composition, Deatsville, Alabama.

The Duke's Daughter was printed by RR Donnelley, Bloomsburg, Pennsylvania on acid-free paper.

Moyer Bell
Kymbolde Way
Wakefield, RI 02879